Author of
Love's Pirate
and
Destiny's Pawn

Now...

blazes with the passions of love
in a nation torn by Civil War.

Other Avon Books by
Mary Daheim

DESTINY'S PAWN
LOVE'S PIRATE

MARY DAHEIM

AVON
PUBLISHERS OF BARD, CAMELOT, DISCUS AND FLARE BOOKS

Author's Note

While Tryon Palace in New Bern, North Carolina, was almost completely leveled by the time of the Civil War, the building was reconstructed and restored in the mid–twentieth century. Since its historical importance is so much a part of New Bern, I have taken the liberty of using the palace as part of the background for this story.

PRIDE'S CAPTIVE is an original publication of Avon Books. This work has never before appeared in book form. This work is a novel. Any similarity to actual persons or events is purely coincidental.

AVON BOOKS
A division of
The Hearst Corporation
1790 Broadway
New York, New York 10019

Copyright © 1986 by Mary Daheim
Published by arrangement with the author
Library of Congress Catalog Card Number: 85-91179
ISBN: 0-380-89849-7

First Avon Printing, March 1986

AVON TRADEMARK REG. U. S. PAT. OFF. AND IN
OTHER COUNTRIES, MARCA REGISTRADA, HECHO EN
U. S. A.

Printed in the U. S. A.

K–R 10 9 8 7 6 5 4 3 2 1

PART ONE
NEW ENGLAND
1861–1862

Chapter 1

THE MORNING BREEZE had long since spent itself among the towering fir, spruce, and pine trees. Out on the pond, a drake and his mate dove beneath the still waters for their noon meal. The July sun stood high in a flawless sky, casting only the shortest of shadows on the uneven grass which led from the shake-and-shingle cabin to the pond.

Serena shaded the blank page of her journal with her hand. As an aspiring writer, she felt she ought to try describing the structure and its setting. Perhaps in a style similar to Thoreau's. But that would be imitative; she must do it as Serena Farrar, not as a copy of that rather strange man from Concord, Massachusetts. After all, if Serena intended to prove herself as a writer, she must first *be* herself.

It might be more appropriate, Serena thought, running a hand through her rich brown hair and scratching a mosquito bite next to her ear, if she described her father's motives for building the rustic, even mean, little cabin in the Maine woods. "The hunting lodge," Marcus Farrar had called his hideaway in describing it to his family before they left Brunswick. His wife, son, daughter, and niece had speculated quietly about what they would find at the end of the forty-mile trip by wagon and horseback: a Bavarian chalet, an Italian villa, even an English manor house. After all, Marcus Farrar was known throughout Maine for his extravagances and eccentricities.

When his family had gaped in astonishment at the rude structure nestled among the evergreens, Marcus's booming laughter had rung out on the summer air. Compared to the three-story brick house in Brunswick with its rows of shuttered windows, wide-mouthed chimneys, and handsomely carved front door, "the hunting lodge" looked like the work of a niggardly woodsman rather than of the scion of a wealthy shipbuilding family.

But no one would argue that it wasn't typical of Marcus Farrar. Expansive on the one hand, he also delighted in the absurd, and his so-called hunting lodge was just one of the many flights of fancy his family had endured over the years. There were five small rooms, a stone fireplace which didn't draw, windows which blew open at night with a startling clatter—and the well was located a quarter-mile away.

Of course his family had decided to humor him; they usually did.

2

Marcus had a knack for making the grandiose mundane, and sometimes the mediocre magnificent.

Serena batted a half-dozen mosquitoes away and closed her journal. Across the pond, an elegant young buck paused among the blueberry bushes before turning back into the underbush. She smiled to herself, then glanced at her cousin, Abigail, who appeared to be asleep in the hammock a few feet away. No, Serena decided, putting the journal away in her wicker hamper, there was no urgent message or literary value in a descriptive passage of either the cabin or her father's rationale for building it. When she began writing for Cousin Josiah's *Springfield Republican*, there would be far greater opportunities to explore topics of a more serious nature. Not that Josiah Holland had yet responded to her letter asking for employment, but she had only written the week before they left Brunswick, and it was possible that their mail would not be forwarded to the cabin. That distressed Serena, but there was nothing she could do, especially since she had not told her parents or her brother, Matt, of her plans. Lydia Farrar would never approve of her daughter's unconventional ambition, and Matt would find his sister's idea comic. Marcus, however, might be amused, even encouraging.

Only Abigail, who was moving about rather cautiously in the hammock, knew of Serena's dream. "I believe I would have preferred the customary trip to the shore," Abigail remarked, trying to rearrange her petite figure in the sagging hammock which was strung between two birch trees. "I find this somewhat isolated. Except for the insects, of course."

Serena shook grass from the skirts of her cotton dress and laughed. "After Paris, I'd expect you to be discontent."

The golden glints in Abigail's auburn hair seemed to shimmer in the noonday sun as she fought a losing battle with the hammock and sat up, looking toward the pond rather than at Serena. "I think there's a deer over there. Did you see it?"

"Yes, he seemed to want a drink, but saw us and thought better of it." Serena kicked off her shoes and stretched her slim legs. "If I didn't think that pond was harboring half the mosquito population of New England, I'd consider a swim."

"I'll abstain." Abigail's green eyes slowly closed. She took a deep breath, steadying herself with both feet planted in the dirt.

"At least it's peaceful," Serena said somewhat tentatively, as if apologizing for her father's eccentricities. But Abigail, who had lived with the Farrars since her parents were drowned off Halifax eight years earlier, was quite accustomed to Marcus Farrar's whimsies.

"Oh, my, yes, it's quite peaceful." But even as Abigail spoke, the

summer air was rent by an ear-shattering blast, the rope at one end
of the hammock snapped, and Abigail tumbled onto the ground.

"Abby!" Serena scurried to her feet, half-crawling, half-stumbling
the short distance to her cousin. She grasped the other girl's wrist,
giving it a frantic little shake. "Abby, are you all right? Have you
been shot?"

Abigail's eyes flipped open. "I know there's supposed to be a war
on, but this is absurd. No, I'm not shot. But the hammock is. Keep
down, they may shoot again."

But the only sound they heard was the voice of Lydia Farrar, raised
but still under control even in times of crisis. "Serena! Abigail! What
was that? Where are you?"

Serena moved just enough so that she could see around the trunk
of the birch tree. Her mother was standing on the cabin porch, hands
pressed against her calico skirts, a diminutive but formidable presence
even from afar.

"Stay there, Mama," Serena called out. From the corner of her
eye, she saw movement at the edge of the pond. But it wasn't the
buck this time. It was a man, tall and dark-haired, with a brace of
pigeons over his shoulder and a shotgun in his hands. He was striding
rapidly around the pond, heading in their direction. Serena and Abigail
both stood up, while Lydia Farrar descended from the porch with all
the dignity of a queen going forth to meet her subjects. She reached
the stranger first, while Serena and Abigail hurried with as much
ladylike decorum as possible to view the confrontation.

"You, sir, are a trespasser and an assailant. I shall see that you
are prosecuted to the full limit of the law." Lydia was at least a full
foot shorter than the dark-haired man, but she was attired in the
invisible battle armor of self-righteousness. At one time or another,
Lydia's calm, cool air of the outraged matron had made everyone
give way before her, from the vicar of St. Paul's in Brunswick to
Marcus Farrar himself.

Serena waited for the stranger to cringe, cower, and capitulate.
But either he didn't recognize his opponent's invincibility or he chose
to ignore it. "I've been hunting here for six summers now, and if you
ask me, this is a peculiar place to homestead. Especially," he added,
with a deferential nod of his head belied by the hint of mockery in
his voice, "for a fine lady wearing sapphire eardrops with her
crinolines."

Lydia's hands jerked at her side, as if she wanted to touch the
jewels and make them disappear, but thought better of it. "That, sir,
is hardly any business of yours. You have violated our property and
come within inches of harming my daughter and my niece. I shall
press for restitution as well as punishment."

As always, Serena had to admire her mother's aplomb. And her perspicacity in deducing what had happened. But somehow her mother usually seemed to know what was going on despite her offsprings' best efforts to delude her. Serena looked surreptitiously at the stranger, who was attired in black riding breeches and a white linen shirt. He had wary sea-blue eyes and features with a certain ragged edge to them, as if they'd been hewn rather than molded by his Maker. The strong chin had a slight cleft and the dark hair seemed to crinkle. He was probably not yet thirty, though he had the air of a man whose experience was greater than his years.

The man set down his shotgun and the brace of pigeons. He looked speculatively from mother to daughter to niece before he spoke again. "I'm Brant Parnell from New Bedford. I've been tracking a fine buck for almost an hour. Unfortunately, under the noonday sun, it appeared to me that your hammock looked a great deal like the backside of a deer."

Serena glanced at the hammock which now dragged onto the ground. It was tan, though Abigail, as always, was wearing blue. But Abigail had just sat up, so that the hammock would have hidden her. It was quite possible that the color, the texture, and the movement had suggested some sort of animal. Serena frowned, wondering why she was mentally defending the man who called himself Brant Parnell.

"You may save your excuses for the local authorities in Livermore Falls," Lydia asserted primly. "Until my husband and my son return, please march to the woodshed and remain there."

"Oh, hogwash!" Brant exclaimed in exasperation. It was clear he would have preferred a much stronger epithet. "This is ridiculous. Now see here," he said, gesturing with big, sinewy hands while trying to keep his temper in check, "if it makes you feel any better, I'll wait until your husband gets back and let him decide how I ought to make amends. But I'll be damned—pardon my rough expression, ladies— if I'll go sit in that ugly woodshed. The cabin is hideous enough."

Serena had to put a hand over her mouth to stifle her laughter as she watched the sudden constriction of her mother's face. Lydia Farrar was momentarily caught off-guard, finding herself in complete agreement about the cabin's appearance but unable to say so to a stranger.

Lydia lifted her chin and gazed directly up at Brant. "Perhaps the cabin would be more secure, lest you have any notion of running away."

Brant bent down to retrieve his pigeons, feathers fluttering on the grass. "You could always hold these hostage," he commented, pausing as he reached for the shotgun. "Shall I surrender my weapon?"

All three women eyed the shotgun with distaste. Serena looked up, noting with surprise that Brant was watching her. Momentarily taken aback, she licked her lips anxiously and, with what she hoped was an air of nonchalance, moved to pick up the shotgun. It was surprisingly heavy and she staggered slightly. Brant touched the barrel, tilting it skyward. "Keep that up. It's still loaded." His back was turned to Lydia Farrar and he grinned at Serena. "Unless you want to use it on me, of course."

Again, Serena found it an effort to keep from laughing. Yet as her mother would say, the man *was* "bold as brass tacks," and perhaps, from the wary look of his eyes, not as straightforward as he seemed. But she was unable to reply, as Lydia was already leading the way to the much-maligned cabin.

Inside, it was cool and smelled of pine. The two servants they had brought with them from Brunswick, Mandy and her slow-witted daughter, Dorcas, had gone to the well to fetch water.

Now ensconced inside her own domain, no matter how rude the walls or shoddy the furnishings, Lydia Farrar assumed the role of hostess. The faintest of smiles touched her fine features, which resembled Abigail's more than Serena's. But then Abigail had taken after her aunt in many ways, mostly those which Serena felt lacking in herself.

"Tea?" Lydia motioned for Brant to seat himself on a faded mohair sofa Marcus had purchased secondhand.

Brant started to sit down, but put up a big hand. "I never take tea with strangers," he declared with a note of mock reproach. "I've introduced myself, but I don't know who I've had the pleasure of shooting at."

Only a flicker of her eyelids betrayed Lydia's annoyance with Brant's impertinence. "I am Lydia Farrar of Brunswick," she said in the same formal tones she would have used to introduce herself to a visiting professor at Bowdoin College. "And this is my daughter, Serena, and our niece, Miss Abigail Beaulieu."

Brant nodded in the most cordial manner possible. Serena thought his eyes rested longer on Abigail than on herself, but she was used to that. While Abigail was not handsome like Serena's married sister, Cecelia, nor as pretty as Lydia Farrar remained despite her years, her elegant vivacity and finely made features seemed to hold a special attraction for the opposite sex. Though only a year older than Serena, at twenty Abigail seemed more like a woman and less like a girl. The stay in France, Serena thought, but wasn't much reassured and wondered when, if ever, she would take on the same self-confidence and poise.

"Farrar," echoed Brant, seating himself on the sofa and stretching out his long, black-booted legs. "You are married to Marcus Farrar?"

Lydia nodded gravely, beckoning for Serena to help with the te kettle and cups. "The same. He and our son, Matthew, should be back shortly."

"He's a well-known man about New England," Brant said in an easy conversational tone as Abigail went to the cupboard to get napkins and a tin of Mandy's cookies which had been baked in the Brunswick house's more efficient oven. "I'm told he's considering the conversion of at least one of his cotton mills into making uniforms for the Union soldiers."

Serena saw her mother frown into the woodbox next to the big cast-iron stove. "You seem to know a great deal about my husband's business ventures, sir," Lydia said with forced lightness. "I had thought Mr. Farrar more discreet in the early stages of a new enterprise."

"Oh, I'm sure he is," Brant replied airily. "But in my trade—or former trade—I have to keep my ears open. I just made my last voyage as a whaling captain. Since they discovered oil in Pennsylvania, the bottom has fallen out of the whaling business. As you know, I'm sure."

"Yes." Lydia handed Serena some kindling. "It's a shame, in its way. It must hit New Bedford very hard." She paused, obviously still puzzled as to how, whaling captain or not, Brant Parnell could know of an embryonic plan which Marcus Farrar had confided to only his family and a handful of his closest associates.

Apparently, Brant decided he had piqued Lydia's curiosity long enough. "I heard about your husband's proposal from Judge Stanhope. I'm staying with him in Livermore Falls. The judge is my sister-in-law Peggy's uncle."

Lydia's eyes snapped. Serena watched her mother with fascination, knowing that she was thinking that Marcus Farrar kept the judge well-supplied with illegally imported whiskey. Marcus might publicly advocate prohibition, but privately he was an ardent connoisseur of the finest liquors.

The silence was growing to awkward proportions. Lydia was still rummaging in the woodbox, ostensibly chasing a spider. Abigail was seated on one of the rickety kitchen chairs, fingertips pressed together, seemingly absorbed in studying the silver leaf-shaped ring on her left hand. Brant still sat on the sofa with legs outstretched, his hands clasped behind his head. He seemed quite at home, almost as if he were the genial host and they his uneasy guests.

Serena banged the heavy lid back into place on the stove's firebox and turned to her mother. "We'll never get this going in time to make tea, Mama. Perhaps Captain Parnell would prefer a bit of whiskey."

Over her shoulder, Lydia gave Serena a look which would have withered anyone who had not grown up with it. Serena did flinch inwardly, but held her ground, closing the draft on the stove before looking in Brant's direction.

"It does sound more convenient," Brant allowed. "Unless," he added, his face suddenly too bland, "you have fresh buttermilk."

"Not today," Lydia answered primly.

"Getting milk has been difficult," Abigail said. "Mr. Birnley's cow down the road is not particularly generous."

Brant nodded solemnly as Serena went to the liquor cabinet. After Brant was gone, her mother would reproach her for letting him know that Marcus Farrar kept whiskey on hand and for providing a clue to how his host in Livermore Falls acquired his own fine Scottish imports. But the little moment of triumph over her mother sufficed: With unusual swagger, Serena got out a dusty tumbler and a bottle.

Brant had just accepted the drink when the sound of masculine voices and the tramp of feet on the porch floated through the screen door. "More luck than we had," Serena heard her father complain. "Nice pigeons, too. I wonder whose."

Marcus Farrar opened the screen door with a flurry of sound and motion. He was precisely six feet tall, one month short of fifty, square of build and strong of face. Gray mingled with his auburn hair and short-cropped beard. His enormous energy was so tangible that it seemed to transform the room.

"Ah, ladies—company, eh? Good, good, time to get acquainted with our new neighbors." He strode forward to hold out a big square hand to Brant. "Marcus Farrar, sir, glad to have a guest. This is my son, Matthew."

Matt came forward to shake Brant's hand. At almost twenty-five, Matt was an inch taller than his father, clean-shaven and much more subdued. But his coloring and build stamped him clearly as Marcus Farrar's son. He smiled broadly as Brant introduced himself and then asked if the pigeons were his. Brant assured him they were.

"Plump," Marcus commented, looking mildly surprised as he noted the whiskey tumbler next to the sofa. "We've been hunting, too, though not for pigeons." He turned to Serena. "Rena, I think your brother and I could use a bit of that," he said, jabbing at the whiskey bottle which stood next to Abigail on the kitchen table. "Are we celebrating something?"

"Not at all," Lydia asserted. "We have a problem which I trust you'll rectify at once."

The tone which usually brooked no interference even from Marcu Farrar did not evoke the customary response. "Indeed, Mrs. Farr and so I shall. It seems to be a day for problems, though, which why this whiskey is most welcome. Thank you, Rena. Where your shoes?"

Serena had completely forgotten she'd taken them off while re-clining among the birch trees. Self-consciously, she looked at her stockinged feet and flushed slightly. No doubt her mother would reprimand her for entertaining Captain Parnell while only partially clad, and never mind that he was a trespasser with alleged homicidal intentions.

"Too warm for shoes, maybe," Marcus went on, settling into a rocking chair close to the sofa. "Well, we're rusticating and recreating, so it's permissible. Yes, sir, fine pigeons. We were after deer ourselves and I'll be hornswoggled if we could find one. Thought we had, though, didn't we, Matt?"

Matt's gray eyes crinkled around the edges. "We did for a fact," he chuckled.

"And a neat piece of shooting, Matt," his father said, joining in the laughter. He rocked in the chair so hard that some of the whiskey spilled over the edges of the tumbler. "Poor old Birnley," Marcus finally managed to say, "I thought he'd have a fit when he saw how Matt had shot his cow clean through the head!"

Lydia's dark eyes narrowed and Serena could have sworn she heard her mother gasp. Abigail's hands dropped quietly into her lap while the corners of her little mouth pulled down in a concerted effort to look solemn. Brant grinned at Marcus and Matt who were once again convulsed. Serena was smiling, in spite of herself; Brant looked at her and winked. Hastily, she turned back to the liquor cabinet, making sure the doors were securely shut.

"All right," Marcus said at last, wiping at his beard with his hand and steadying himself in the chair. "That's our problem and we'll have to get Birnley another cow tomorrow. Maybe two, then we'll have plenty of milk."

Lydia came to stand in front of her husband. "We had an incident that could have been far more serious than shooting Mr. Birnley's cow," she declared in austere tones. "Captain Parnell almost shot Abigail."

Marcus's granite-colored eyes were momentarily wide. "The captain mistook Abby for a cow? Is she hurt? Or insulted?"

Serena noticed how Abigail's shoulders shook slightly while her hand touched her mouth to hide a smile. But Lydia was giving no ground. "It was trespassing, Mr. Farrar, and of a most dangerous sort. If you could somehow not make light of the situation, you might demand restitution from Captain Parnell and have this ghastly property posted at once."

"Yes," agreed Marcus, scratching his head, "I should have posted it right off. We'll get some signs, along with the cows. You'll see to that, Matt?" He saw his son nod. "Now—restitution? I'm a mite confused there, what's he to restore?"

One of the few flaws Serena had ever observed in her mother's character was an inability to always think her demands through to their logical conclusion. Her lack of immediate response and the rapid blinking of her eyes betrayed her. Lydia forced herself to look even more ramrod straight than she already was and spoke with great solemnity: "There is, in truth, no way to make restitution for the terrible fright which Abigail—and Serena, as well—received this afternoon. But I would expect there are fines and such for trespassing and endangering the lives of others."

"Well, I hope nobody around here finds out about them," Marcus replied with a glance at Matt, who began to laugh all over again. "We'd be in a fine mess, wouldn't we, son?" His own laughter burst out once more, and within seconds, Brant, Serena, and Abigail were laughing as well. Lydia Farrar, apparently conceding defeat, wore a thin, fixed smile. A quarter of an hour later, Brant was on his way, pigeons over his shoulders, shotgun crooked in his arm, and with an invitation to dine at the Farrar cabin the following Saturday night.

Ordinarily, Serena saved bedtime for writing in her journal. Her parents had given her the leather-bound volume that spring for her nineteenth birthday. It had been the same day Fort Sumter was fired on and the nation suddenly found itself irrevocably torn apart. Her first entry on that April night had been lengthy, fulminating about the outrages of slavery, the intransigence of the Southern states, the depravity of a people who held other human beings in bondage for the sake of profit.

In an entry almost a week later, Serena had calmed down somewhat, concerned for those members of her family who had taken up residence in the South, and confused that with sound, moral people such as her Uncle Luke living in the Confederacy, the South should have ever decided to secede in the first place.

But Uncle Luke was a Yankee who had married a Southern gentlewoman, sharing in her inheritance of a tobacco plantation in New Bern, North Carolina. Even her father's brother could not be expected to stem the tide of public opinion which raged throughout the entire South. Perhaps least of all her father's brother, for Luke was as unlike Marcus as two men could possibly be.

Serena's own sister, Cecelia, had been in New Bern less than two years. Married at eighteen to Fitch Moncrief, Uncle Luke's plantation manager, Cecelia had ventured south in a festive aura. Her letters had been effusive, heaping praise on her Southern hosts for their gracious hospitality. Cecelia now had an infant son, but with the encroaching

Southern blockade, letters rarely reached New England. Serena considered writing to tell Cecelia about the afternoon's adventure with Captain Brant Parnell and her mother, but her sister would probably never get the letter. Besides, Cecelia's sense of humor was limited. She only laughed, or so it seemed, when an attractive male was around to compliment her white teeth, her beautiful mouth, or the sparkle in her black eyes. Drama, rather than humor, enhanced Cecelia's dark, statuesque beauty.

So, by lamplight in their tiny bedroom, Serena began to write in her journal instead. Abigail was propped up among the pillows, squinting at one of Walter Scott's epics. Outside, the wind rustled through the evergreens and over the waters of the pond.

"I can't read any more tonight," Abigail said, closing her book. "The light is so poor."

"It is. But it's easier to write by than read by," Serena replied, trying to fix the nib of her pen, which seemed far too scratchy. "You ought to set down your account of France. It's something you'll want to keep for your grandchildren."

Abigail shrugged, the long, gold-tipped auburn hair spread out over the pillows. "I think not. I don't have the urge to put everything on paper as you do."

Serena muttered angrily as the nib broke off completely. "Still," Serena persisted, searching through her stationery cabinet for another pen tip, "you really ought to preserve your trip for posterity. When you're sixty, that year will seem so far away."

"Perhaps." Abigail's lack of concern annoyed Serena, as it usually did. While Serena admired her cousin in a great many ways, there were occasions when Abigail's unruffled exterior seemed more like indifference than inner calm. Yet Serena and Abigail had always been close, much closer than Serena had been to Cecelia.

"You owe it to yourself." Serena would not let up, determined, if not to gain agreement, to at least unsettle Abigail's complacency.

But Abigail merely yawned. "Someday, maybe." She paused in pulling the covers up to her neck. "Rena, you aren't envious of my trip abroad, are you?"

Serena was in the act of replacing her pen nib. "Why, no. I knew your parents had promised you that trip and that Papa would see that you got it."

It was true: Although Abigail had seldom mentioned the journey to France as part of the future her parents had planned for her, when the subject finally came up the previous summer, Marcus had Abigail's passage booked within two weeks. She had only returned to Maine in late June, with a trunk full of modish French fashions and the air of a woman grown to maturity. While Serena might someday enjoy

such a trip herself, it was not visiting Paris and seeing the French
chateau country that evoked her envy, but the self-assurance Abigail
had acquired.

The newspaper job in Springfield would provide Serena with a
similar opportunity for growth. Sharing ideas with other writers, discussing the burning issues of the day, meeting important personages
would expand Serena's horizons every bit as much as Parisian coteries
and French salons.

At the moment, however, Serena's creative well seemed to have
gone dry. Tapping the pen against her cheek, she uttered an exas-
perated sigh. "I must be tired, I can't seem to write this evening."

"Good," Abigail murmured. "Blow out the lamp so I can get to
sleep."

Serena made a face, but closed her journal and put her writing
materials away. Five minutes later, the lamp had been extinguished
on the tiny table between the narrow beds.

No, she told herself, there was no need to envy Abigail—not even
the piquant features or the ready wit. Once Serena had secured her
newspaper position, she wouldn't even wish for Cecelia's handsome
splendor. After all, appearance wasn't as important as substance; had
she been born a beauty, Serena might never have felt the need to
develop her writing talents. Uncle Luke, bless him, had told her as
a child that she had her own unusual charms. He'd likened her to the
fox. "Not sly," she recalled him saying, as if it were only the previous
day, "but your curious little nose, that rich, thick hair like fox fur,
those slanted eyes and brows that seem to see everything . . . and the
way you lick your lips when you're pleased or excited." His words
had made her happy—until Matt overheard him call Serena his "little
fox" and started chanting "Foxy-Loxy got the chicken poxy!" He'd
spoiled it for her, as big brothers often did, but as she grew older,
knowing that the fox had a distinctive aura of its own, she clung to
the image her uncle had given her. Perhaps she, too, would one day
acquire her own unique allure.

Serena moved about, trying to find a comfortable place on the
lumpy mattress. "I don't know about you, but I don't think I slept
well last night. There were mosquitoes in the room, too."

"Hmmm," said Abigail, burying her face in the pillow.

Serena stared into the darkness, listening to the wind and remem-
bering other summers with nostalgia, when she had heard instead the
ceaseless slap of wave on wave at the shore. She closed her eyes and
tried to picture the soothing sea, even tried to hear the sound of the
tide. But all she thought of was ships with blooming sails and soaring
masts. Were they the ships her grandfather had built at Yarmouth?
she wondered dreamily. No, it was one ship now, with a tall, dark

figure standing in the forecastle. Not her grandfather, or her father, but another man . . . She nestled further into the bed and let sleep carry her away like a piece of driftwood on the outgoing tide. The man was Brant Parnell and the figurehead which jutted boldly from his ship looked amazingly like Serena.

Chapter 2

SERENA AND MATT rode into Livermore Falls the next morning with orders to have signs made up for posting the Farrar property and to make inquiries concerning anyone who had cows for sale. Lydia seemed assuaged, apparently by Brant Parnell's offer to pay for the signs. Marcus had at first refused Brant's offer, but knew Lydia must exact some recompense to save face in the family.

Serena was riding astride a little black mare, using a weathered English saddle which had belonged to her Uncle Luke. Her rich brown hair was pulled back and tied with a dark blue ribbon, and she wore a pair of Matt's riding breeches which one of the servants had shrunk in the laundry. Lydia did not permit her daughter to wear trousers while riding in the city, but at the shore, and now in the woods, she allowed the digression from propriety because it seemed sensible.

It was not as warm as yesterday, but Serena's cotton shirt had started to cling to her back by the time they had covered the first three miles into Livermore Falls. "Do you realize," Serena called to Matt, "that we'll need at least fifty signs to adequately cover all the land Papa owns around here?"

Matt squinted at the late morning sun which shone in brilliant shafts through the tamaracks. "Papa never does things by halves. He wants the trees for pulp. Just in case he can't get the government contract for uniforms, he's hedging his bets." He grinned at Serena, the wide infectious grin so like their father's. "Now that he can't get cotton from down South," Matt went on amiably, "he's looking for other options."

Serena guided her mare around an aspen branch which had apparently been blown down by the strong winds earlier in the week. "It's hard to realize there's a war going on. Except," she added dryly, "for all the shooting we had yesterday."

"True enough." Her brother was matter-of-fact. While he might resemble his father closely in appearance, his easygoing personality was more like Uncle Luke's. Serena often wished she had gotten to know her uncle better; she would have liked very much to learn his secret in not envying the obvious, tangible talents of his older brother.

"Penny for your thoughts," Matt called over his shoulder as an oriole darted in front of them and reached the sanctuary of a wild

14

rosebush. The rough dirt road was lined with pink and white blooming clover, and from a nearby tree, squirrels quarreled with one another.

"I was thinking about Uncle Luke," Serena answered after a pause. "I wonder how he feels with North Carolina and the other Southern states fighting against the Union."

Matt laughed, a brief, low rumble. "If he can ever get a letter to us he'll say he's sorry, but no hard feelings, after all—and go back to reinventing the wheel." It was Matt's turn to pause and this time he let his horse slow down enough so that he and Serena were riding side by side. "I saw Uncle Luke's nephew by marriage the other day in Topsham. Didn't he ask to call on you last winter?"

"Clarence Prendergast?" Serena plucked at the fabric of her shirt, pulling it away from her damp skin. "Someone said he was going to. I don't think he ever did." Serena dismissed Clarence with a flick of the reins. The beardless, sober-faced Prendergast scion might be a mathematical wizard at Bowdoin College but he was hardly the sort one would want for a suitor. Besides, she could imagine Abigail's eyebrows raised in disdain if Clarence ever came to call.

"I don't know," Matt said, his wide brow furrowing slightly. "You're nigh onto twenty, Serena. You don't want to set your sights too high."

Serena turned abruptly in the saddle, momentarily startling her little mare. "What does that mean? That I won't have much of an opportunity to find the sort of husband I want? Assuming, of course, that I want a husband in the first place!"

"Now, hold on, Serena," Matt said, forcing a laugh. "I just meant that—well, Cecelia is married and Cousin Abby was almost engaged once and you haven't—well, you really haven't had a suitor. It's not that I think Clarence Prendergast is such a grand catch, it's just that ...maybe if you..." Matt frowned, the furrows etched deep. "I mean, if you let someone, even Clarence, start squiring you, then maybe there would be other fellows who would come along." Matt nodded his dark head just once, as if confirming the soundness of his advice.

But Serena was scarcely appeased. The mare was still sidestepping nervously and Serena tried soothing her with a gentle hand. "I'm not even remotely concerned about getting married. At least not for a long time." She halted, aware that she needed soothing more than her mount. "I honestly cannot understand why every young woman I know is so obsessed with marrying at the earliest possible age. Not that there is anything wrong with wanting to be married and having a family," she continued, her words picking up speed to match the whirling thoughts which suddenly seemed to be rushing out of her brain. "I think that's the ultimate ideal for most women, but the world is full of splendid things, places to see, and so much to learn. Look at Abby, going to Paris for a whole year. Look at Clarence's own sisters, they spent six months in Italy. I don't see any point in hurtling straight from girlhood into matrimony."

Matt listened to this rather lengthy and heated speech with a bemused expression. "Well, now. And what do you want to do instead?"

Serena's lips clamped shut as her brown eyes scanned the curving road up ahead. Then she spoke in quiet, measured tones. "I intend to work for a newspaper. For Cousin Josiah's newspaper. In Springfield."

Matt paused to wave at a woodsman who was carrying a crosscut saw over his shoulder and walking from the opposite direction. "A newspaper?" He sounded not so much incredulous as amused. "You—a writer?"

"Why not?" Serena flicked the reins and the mare moved from a walk to a canter. "I've always liked to write," she asserted.

Matt roared with laughter and urged his own mount to keep up the pace. "Oh, Rena! What will you write about, autumn leaves in Chicopee? Tea parties in Holyoke?"

Serena slowed her horse and held her head high. "There's more to writing for newspapers than tea parties and skittering leaves—though I don't see anything wrong with that, either. Women *do* write about other things—look at Mrs. Stowe who lives all but half a mile from our house in Brunswick. She's downright famous, and doing something worthwhile besides."

"She got a lot of people stirred up about something that may or may not be any of their business," Matt countered, having some trouble controlling his horse, who seemed to want to continue the canter. "I don't believe in slavery myself, but for all I know, *Uncle Tom's Cabin* is just a lot of melodramatic drivel. Look at the trouble it's caused. If President Lincoln doesn't squelch those rebels quick, we could have a lot of people getting killed."

"But for a noble cause. What right does one man have to force another to work for him just because he's a different color?" Serena's voice was heating up and so was her temper. She had not slept well the previous night, and while she couldn't recall her dreams, she knew they had disturbed her. "To think Uncle Luke tolerates such a society! This is supposed to be a free country—well, it's not, at least not in the South!"

"That's a whole different world, and not the same country anymore." Matt sounded reasonable, and it was that very attitude which riled Serena even further. "They feel that each state ought to make up its own mind about such things. That's freedom too, isn't it? Don't tell me you think that by going to work for Cousin Josiah, you're going to help free the slaves! You'd be lucky if you got to free the teacakes of Holyoke!"

Serena gave her brother a blistering look, dug her heels into the sides of her mare, and galloped off down the road. From behind her, she could just make out his call: "Rena! Wait up! I was teasing!" Matt's teasing only made it worse. He didn't take her seriously; all he could conjure up for her future was life with Clarence Prendergast. Or someone like him. Surely the world had something better to offer Serena Farrar than that vapid, tedious prospect.

And surely Serena had something to offer the world. Her desire to work on the newspaper was no whim. It would set her free. Smothered within the bosom of her own family, Serena felt as if her own bondage were as onerous as any Southern slave's. Ten minutes later, she was at the edge of Livermore Falls, the cluster of roofs peering out above the treetops.

Slowing her lathered mare to a trot, Serena wiped her damp forehead on her shirt sleeve. The ribbon from her hair had come undone and had been lost along the road. She and the horse both breathed heavily and for one brief moment Serena closed her eyes and felt slightly faint from anger and distress.

It was in that instant that a cat and a squirrel chased across the road directly in front of her, making the mare shy and sending Serena crashing into the dirt. Pain and shock numbed her, turning the bright summer day black, setting her head a-spin, and stifling her breath. It seemed as if she lay in misery for a very long time, but afterward she realized it had only been a few seconds. Someone was speaking to her, touching her arm, trying to push the heavy brown hair out of her face.

"Miss Farrar? Are you all right?"

Dazed and shaken, Serena could have sworn she'd heard that voice before. But she didn't know anyone in Livermore Falls. Yet whoever it was had called her by name. It was too confusing and she wasn't sure she had the strength to open her eyes. But at last she looked up into the blinding daylight to see Brant Parnell bending over her. He appeared concerned, yet there was a hint of amusement in the blue eyes.

"I don't think this part of the country agrees with you," he said, cautiously moving her right arm and then her left. "Where do you hurt most?"

"All over," Serena moaned and concentrated on focusing her eyes. "My horse—where is she?"

"Halfway to Farmington." Brant ran a big hand through her hair and felt her skull. "No bumps. Can you stand?"

Serena wasn't sure. But she suddenly recalled the disturbing dream she'd had of Brant Parnell and herself as the figurehead on his ship. Flushing at the recollection, she made a heroic effort to get on her feet.

Brant held her firmly by the arm. "If you're sure you can walk, that's Judge Stanhope's house over there." He pointed to a neat, white clapboard two-story house surrounded by a garden of asters, black-eyed Susans and trailing arbutus. Two stone chimneys flanked the house like bookends, and a brass knocker on the front door gleamed in the late morning sun.

Serena paused; a half-dozen onlookers had already gathered, watching with curious, good-natured stares. Matt would be along shortly, but she didn't want to see him—not just now. Her mare would soon tire and no doubt some kind soul would try to find the animal's rightful owner. It was hot standing in the middle of the dirt road, she ached from head to toe, she was filthy, and going any further than Judge Stanhope's house seemed impossible. "Thank you," she finally said in a small voice.

Brant kept hold of her arm as they walked the fifty feet to the Stanhope garden gate. The next fifty feet seemed twice as far to Serena, but once she was inside, the hallway was blissfully cool. Brant steered her into the adjoining parlor which was furnished in oppressive dark oak. The drapes were drawn to keep out the late morning sun and the room was gloomy by comparison with the bright summer day outside.

Collapsing gratefully on a faded brown velvet settee, Serena breathed deeply and tried flexing her neck muscles. Brant was opening a break-front adorned with heavy leaded cut-glass panes. He brought out two snifters and a brandy decanter.

"The cureall for distress," he said, proffering one of the snifters and easing his tall body onto a straight-backed chair next to the settee. "Cheers."

The brandy no doubt had come from her father, Serena thought as she took an experimental sip and almost choked. She'd tasted brandy once before and had hated it. But somehow it seemed sensible to at least try to drink some of the fiery amber liquid. Certainly it couldn't make her head ache any more and it might help.

"Is your family always so accident-prone?" Brant asked with a slightly raised eyebrow.

Serena had taken a second sip and discovered that the brandy didn't taste as terrible as she'd feared. She could focus better now, and noted that Brant was dressed almost exactly as he had been the previous day, in a white open-necked shirt and black riding breeches. The shirt was open halfway down his chest and he was very tan. The fine lines around his eyes had that look of the sea she recognized from the captains and mates and sailors she'd known all her life in Brunswick. He's actually handsome, in an unusual, rugged sort of way, Serena thought, even if he did almost shoot Abigail.

"Don't drink that too fast," Brant cautioned. "I don't believe you heard my question."

"What?" Serena clutched the snifter with both hands and forced herself to concentrate on Brant's words.

He laughed and shook his head. "Never mind. When you finish that—assuming you *should* finish it—I think you'd better go wash up. There are facilities down the hall on your right just before you get to the kitchen."

For the first time, it occurred to Serena that the house seemed empty. It also occurred to her that she had never been alone—completely alone—with a man before. She took another sip of brandy and noted that the liquid seemed to roll from side to side in the snifter. Was she still shaking from the shock, she wondered—or was it the presence of this tall, dark man with his sardonic eyes and wry expression? And why, after being so angry and then in such shock and pain, did she suddenly feel quite happy?

"Thank you. I know I'm filthy." She glanced at the dirt-stained riding breeches which were torn at the calf of her left leg, and at her hands which were scraped but not badly damaged. She knew she must look absolutely frightful and suddenly became self-conscious. "Perhaps I'd better wash right now," she said, handing the snifter to Brant and trying to stand up.

But her legs were wobbly; she teetered, and if Brant had not put both snifters down quickly and caught her in his arms, she would have fallen flat on her face.

"Wait awhile," he admonished. "You took one hell of a tumble."

"I guess I did." Serena breathed deeply, her cheek pressed against Brant's bare chest. She certainly felt trembly and her heart was beating very fast. He smells like the forest, she thought vaguely, of pine and cedar and larch . . .

"Here, sit down again," Brant urged, propping her up on the settee. "Just relax. Or would you like me to call the doctor?"

"No!" Serena replied a bit too hastily. "I mean, I'll be fine, you're right, I just need to rest." She let him hand back the brandy snifter and tried to cross one leg over the other, but failed. The snifter was nearly empty. Serena gazed vaguely at the remaining liquor and thought it looked like one of Mandy's weaker brews of tea. But it certainly didn't taste like tea and it had a much more pleasant effect. In fact, she hardly hurt anymore. She almost felt like humming. What was that tune? "I never will marry, I'll be no man's wife . . ." It was running through her head in the purest lyric soprano, very unlike her own off-key mezzo voice.

Suddenly she sat upright, jarring herself with the resurgence of pain throughout her body. "When do you go back to Massachusetts?"

Brant's eyebrows raised slightly in surprise. "Another couple of weeks. No hurry this year since I'm not going whaling in the South Pacific."

"I want to go to Massachusetts with you," Serena said, and hoped she looked serious and dignified.

"Oh?" He was trying hard to remain as solemn as Serena. "You have family there? A young man?" Amused, he leaned toward her. "Or are you seducing me?"

Serena shook her head so hard that it throbbed. "No, no, no! I want to go to Springfield."

Brant put both booted feet on the floor. "Springfield? But I'm going to New Bedford. They aren't that close. You can't seduce me if we're a hundred miles apart."

"That's so. Except this is not an amorous proposal." Serena licked her lips, wondering why such shocking speech didn't offend her. She sighed and rubbed at her scalp, wishing that her mind were functioning more clearly. She wished her head didn't ache. She wished Brant Parnell wasn't so damnably attractive. She wished she could rid herself of the desire to fall into his arms again and feel her cheek against his bare chest. "I—my family—has a cousin, Josiah Holland, who is editor of the Springfield newspaper. I've always wanted to be a writer and I've—I've been considering going to work for him."

"I see." Brant's craggy features turned thoughtful. But while he appeared to be thinking over her plans with great care, the hint of amusement was still in his eyes. "What does your family think about this?"

"I've only discussed it with my cousin," Serena said, dismissing Matt's derisive reaction from her mind. Never mind that she hadn't heard from Cousin Josiah. The letter inviting her to Springfield was probably sitting on the silver tray in the front hallway of the house in Brunswick.

Brant had gotten up to pour himself another brandy. Serena noted that he did not offer her any more. He considers me just a stupid, silly girl, she thought angrily, jabbering about writing for newspapers and distant cousins and wild ideas of running off to Springfield. He may even think I'm unbalanced, she decided, and bit her lip to keep from crying.

"I've never been one to think that a woman ought to stay home and embroider pillowcases or bake biscuits or whatever if she didn't want to. Although I'm not married, my brother, Kirk, is, and he took his wife on one of his voyages. She saw some of the world and is a better person for it. Not to mention," he added with his wry smile, "it saved her wearing out the widow's walk on their house in New Bedford. But Kirk quit the sea. He's a newspaperman himself now." Brant was standing behind the straight-backed chair, one big hand resting on the heavy oak. "Now that I think of it, they have women working there," he said, giving her a conspiratorial grin, "so maybe your idea isn't as harebrained as it sounds."

"Harebrained!" Serena's reaction momentarily sobered her. "Certainly it's not harebrained! Why should I just sit around and wait for . . . for Clarence Prendergast?"

"Who?" The heavy dark brows drew together. "You're right. I wouldn't wait for Clarence, either." He gave his head a little shake. "Do you think you can stand up now?"

But Serena was having visions of Clarence's callow countenance bobbing in front of her eyes. Never had a suitor, can't set your sights too high, Abigail off to France, Cecelia with her Southern husband and infant son . . . and here was this craggy, rugged, worldly-wise sea captain looming over her, blue eyes riveted on her suddenly eager face.

"Perhaps if you help me," Serena murmured, and lowered her lashes.

"What?" Brant frowned. "Perhaps if I scalp you? Frankly, I think you look better with hair."

"I said *help*," Serena repeated and was astounded to hear her voice squeak. Surely if she had been Abigail, Brant would have offered his hand, his arm, even his heart and soul by now. "I'm still not sure I can walk."

"Oh." Brant appeared faintly puzzled but Serena didn't notice. "Here, give me your hand."

Serena did, feeling the strength of his big frame, and he pulled her up from the settee. Her hand seemed to disappear in his. She stared at the place where her pale wrist appeared to stop and saw how brown his skin was by contrast. It was very nice having him hold on to her, a great comfort, even more than that, it seemed to stir something deep inside which mingled cozily with the brandy. Serena moved a step closer and looked up at him, her chin almost touching his chest. "I'm somewhat improved." She gave him a tentative smile which she hoped was both charming and coquettish.

"Good. The basin is down the hall," he said, pointing with his free hand. "Think you can manage it?"

Serena tried to focus her eyes. Somehow her scheme didn't seem to be working. Snatches of whispered conversations between Cecelia and Abigail skittered through her mind; how delightfully exciting they said it had been when in moments of feigned or genuine weakness, certain young gentlemen had bestowed upon them the most exciting of stolen kisses. Why, Serena wondered, was this not such a moment for her? Then she too could—reluctantly, of course—relay the delicious tidbit.

But Brant was merely looking perplexed. Concerned, perhaps, but hardly as if he had any romantic inclinations. Did he find her so utterly unattractive that he couldn't possibly countenance kissing her? Was the slightly scandalous reputation of all sea captains a myth? Was Brant Parnell an honorable man?

"You, sir, are an honorable man," Serena declared and slowly but determinedly withdrew her hand from Brant's. She gave him an uncertain little smile and trooped none too steadily toward the washroom at the end of the hall. As she closed the door behind her, the knob slipped from her grasp and the door slammed loudly. Serena jumped, shook her head, and looked straight into the oak-framed mirror atop the marble bureau.

"Oh, dear!" The brown eyes stared at her image, at the smudge on her upturned nose, the scratch on her left cheek, the unruly hair which looked more like an oriole's nest than a fox's fur. Her disheveled appearance sobered her considerably and the splashes of cold water which she applied to her face completed the job. Untangling her hair with a tortoiseshell brush, she wondered what had happened to the ribbon—out in the dusty road, no doubt. Serena adjusted her shirt and trousers, sighed ruefully at her improved but still waiflike appearance, and emerged into the hall feeling not only foolish but embarrassed. How on earth could she ever have thought Brant Parnell would find her kissable? The idea suddenly seemed pathetic.

Brant's blue eyes were still wary as he stood by the parlor window, where he had now opened the drapes. "I'd go to bed, if I were you," he said, moving toward the piano with its silken embroidered shawl and a dozen or more tintypes of what appeared to be Judge Stanhope's family. "I think you may have hurt your head."

I probably have, Serena thought bitterly, or else I wouldn't succumb to such silly fancies about Brant kissing me. She moved to the other end of the piano and picked up an ornately framed picture of Judge Stanhope. "He looks quite dignified," she remarked in cool tones, "for a sot."

Brant started in surprise, but quickly regained control. "He does at that," he replied amicably. "But at least he's an ingratiating sot."

Serena licked her lips, wishing she could retract her unkind words. "I'm sorry, that was most rude."

"Oh, no, the judge has worked hard to earn his reputation. As my pa used to say, a man's reputation is only as good as the women he's known and the whiskey he's drunk. The women may lie, but the whiskey don't."

Serena tried not to look puzzled. Either her brain was still muddled or Brant's father had possessed peculiar logic. Before she could comment, she glimpsed Matt walking toward the house. Brant had seen him too, but when the knock sounded, he didn't move immediately into the hallway.

"Miss Farrar," he said in a hurried tone, "it's been a pleasure. I can't promise to help you get to Springfield, though."

Serena's slanted eyebrows lifted in dismay as Brant moved closer, his voice lowered. "I don't find your ambition unusual or laughable. But it's occurred to me you could consider a more exciting future."

"I could?" Serena echoed as Matt knocked a second time. "Doing what?"

Brant pulled a droll face as he turned toward the hallway. "I don't have time to explain. But I intend to make you my wife."

Chapter 3

IT HAD BEEN an intriguing dream. Or perhaps a very bad joke. Despite Brant's insistence that he wanted to marry her, Serena could not take him at his word. In the three days since Brant had informed her of his intentions, she had gone through a series of reactions: dismay, anger, shock, disbelief, anxiety, even fear.

It had been relatively easy to conceal her emotions from the rest of the family. When Serena returned from Livermore Falls with Matt, Lydia Farrar seemed more distressed by Serena's finding refuge with Brant Parnell in the Stanhope house than by her daughter's dangerous tumble. "I don't know much about Captain Parnell," Lydia had sniffed, "but—with the possible exception of your father, I find the Stanhopes and their acquaintances of dubious character."

At least Lydia's fuming disdain had prevented her from questioning Serena too closely about what had actually happened on the Stanhope premises. Serena was put to bed almost immediately, bowing to her mother's insistence that sleep was the best cure for her aches and pains. The second day, Serena was up though still quite stiff and sore. She went about her activities in a detached, mechanical manner, trying to put Brant as far away from her thoughts as she could manage. On Saturday—the day he was to join the family for supper—Serena passed the hours alone by the pond, reading a book whose words seldom sank into her agitated mind. Only an hour before Brant was due to arrive, Serena hailed Abigail, who had been out bird-watching with Matt. Though the temptation to unburden herself was tremendous, Serena held her tongue. She couldn't believe Brant Parnell was serious about his intentions.

Mandy had worked against great odds to prepare the supper of pan-fried trout and baked beans in the temperamental cast-iron stove. With her daughter Dorcas's help, Mandy somehow managed to produce potato rolls, though she'd despaired of them until they emerged plump and golden from the oven.

On the surface, supper had been a most congenial meal, with Marcus Farrar playing the expansive host, Lydia assuming a gracious if restrained manner, Brant at ease with his anecdotes about life at sea, Matt regarding their guest with amused admiration, and Abigail astute as well as charming. Only Serena remained apprehensive.

24

Yet Brant had ridden out from Livermore Falls with the air of a man who knows he can easily overcome any obstacles which stand between him and his goal. Not that he behaved like a would-be suitor. He treated Serena with courtesy, though she felt his sense of irony hover at the edges of their conversational exchanges.

After supper was over, however, he and Marcus went for a long walk. Upon their return, Serena noted that her father looked smug and Brant seemed bemused. A few minutes later, Brant bade them good-night, adding that he hoped to see them soon, perhaps the following month in Brunswick.

Serena received that casual comment with a sense of dread. Surely Brant's parting remark signified that he had been given permission to court her. As Serena stood in the shadows of the cabin's porch, listening to the frogs in the pond and the distant cry of the owl, she contemplated going into Livermore Falls the next morning to send a telegram to Cousin Josiah.

The screen door opened behind her; she knew it was her father. "The night air here is most salubrious," he asserted, taking a deep, satisfied breath. "Not tangy like the sea, but fragrant with nature's heady evergreen perfume."

"Which you intend to chop down," Serena said with uncustomary asperity. She felt her father wince, but his expression didn't change. "What is this cabin really, a bunkhouse for the logging crew?"

Marcus Farrar wasn't used to overt criticism from his younger daughter. Indeed, he wasn't used to criticism from anyone, except his wife. His granite-colored eyes seemed more hurt than angry as he took Serena by the arm to guide her out toward the pond. "Most assuredly not. This monument to rustic pleasure is strictly for our family's enjoyment."

"In that case, it would probably serve a better purpose as a bunkhouse," Serena declared. "It's well enough for you and Matt to spend your days hunting and fishing, but Mama and Abigail and I are like to perish of tedium."

The thin slip of the old moon was riding just over the treetops. A trout jumped in the pond, sending silver-tipped ripples out over the water. Marcus was staring straight ahead, as if he were absorbed in the natural wonders of the night. "Ah, Serena," he said at last, in his most benevolent tone, "there's so much beauty here, such deep mystery. You must let your imagination run free. Unfetter your curiosity and enjoy!"

Serena was about to comment that swarms of mosquitoes, lumpy mattresses, and an inconvenient water supply were not conducive to her own creative mental processes. But her father resumed speaking, this time looking directly at her with a twinkle in his eyes. "I'd like to think that someday you'll consider this a treasured memory. Tell me, Rena, wouldn't this quaint abode take on an unparalleled splendor if, twenty years from now, you could look back and say, 'I first met my beloved husband there, out by the sparkling waters of Plunkett's Pond'?"

"It might, but I haven't." Serena thrust out her lower lip in a familiar gesture of defiance which always seemed to encompass not just willfulness, but disgust and contempt.

"Now, now." Marcus waggled a finger at her but he was smiling. "You've just not had much time to think about your future, at least not as a married woman. Nor would your mother and I ever attempt to influence your choice of a husband. But inasmuch as Captain Parnell has been gallant enough to seek permission to call on you, I see no reason for not granting his request."

"Yes, you can——the reason is right before your eyes. It's *me!*" Serena was shouting; her father put his finger to his lips and frowned.

"You're getting unnecessarily worked up over this, my dear." Marcus was making every effort to be reasonable, persuasive. Over the years, he had found that such an approach usually guaranteed better results in business negotiations than did threats or anger. "Naturally, if you find Captain Parnell incompatible or flawed in character, you have every right to turn down his proposal. But at nineteen, it's not too soon for you to have a suitor." Marcus paused, his eyes narrowed ever so slightly. "I might say, it's past time. At least some would think so."

The remark stung Serena, but she remembered to keep her voice low. "It's not a matter of finding the captain unacceptable——it's the fact that I don't wish to marry, at least not for some time. I have applied for a position with Cousin Josiah's newspaper in Springfield." Serena lifted her head, one hand clutching at her gingham skirts. "For the near future, I prefer a career to domesticity."

Marcus's wide mouth twitched in his beard. He prided himself on being able to predict how and why an opponent would react to his propositions so that his plan of counterattack would be laid in advance. But this time his adversary had struck from an unexpected direction, using ammunition for which he had no immediate defense. Even more amazing, the surprise attack emanated from the child he had always considered the most pliable.

"Yes, Josiah Holland, otherwise known as 'Timothy Titcomb.'" Marcus glanced to his left as a small nocturnal animal skittered along the edge of the pond. A gopher, perhaps. "His *nom de plume* for his books, correct?"

Serena knew that her father was stalling for time. "Yes. His works are very popular, particularly with people my age." She had gained the advantage; her temper was now in check.

"Well." Marcus smiled again, and patted her arm. "A most unusual, but worthy pursuit. And I congratulate you, Rena—it's a wise young woman who keeps more than one string to her bow."

Serena made a noise that was half-laugh, half-snort. "Maybe. My sister used to think it was a wise young woman who kept more than one beau to her string."

Marcus chuckled richly. "Cecelia is quite a different sort than you are, my dear. But meanwhile, there's no harm done if the captain comes a-callling, is there?"

"No harm, but probably not much good. My mind's quite made up." Serena nodded her head once, feeling as if she'd snatched at least a partial victory, but aware that her father was not yet ready to concede defeat.

"I can't go back on my word," Marcus said as they began to stroll toward the cabin, "so we'll have to let him call on you a few times."

"Of course." Serena took a deep breath, silently agreeing that the night air was indeed soft and rich. Pleased with her own forcefulness in standing up to her father, she took his arm and wondered if he were mellowing with age or if she had taken a long—and possibly overdue—stride toward becoming a woman.

Serena went right to sleep, lulled by the wind in the pine trees and flushed by her success at deflating her father's misguided matrimonial plans. It didn't seem fair when Abigail's moans and groans awoke her a short time later.

More angered than alarmed, Serena struggled from the bed, calling out to her cousin in a low voice: "Are you ill? Abby, what's wrong?" Serena gave Abigail's shoulder a short little shake.

The green-tinged eyes opened wide and blinked. "What? Serena?" She clutched at the bedsheets with taut fingers.

"Are you dreaming?" Serena held Abigail's shoulder with a firm hand.

It seemed to take Abigail some time to discern what was real and what was not. "Dreaming?" she said vaguely. "Why, so I was! A dreadful dream!" Faintly sheepish, though relieved, Abigail fell back against the pillow. "I suppose it was the apple dumplings."

Serena muttered a double curse on Mandy's apple dumplings and Abigail's touchy digestion. Her cousin already appeared to be slipping back into sleep, but Serena felt wide awake. Still annoyed, she bumped into the bed, hit her shin, and had to bite her lips to keep from swearing out loud. Abigail, however, was breathing in deep, regular rhythm, a faint smile on her face.

Straightening her bed covers, Serena jumped as a hissing noise sounded behind her. It came from the window. Cautiously, Serena tiptoed across the little room just as the moon slipped from behind a cloud to outline Brant Parnell's crinkly hair.

"Good Lord!" she whispered, clasping her hand over the deep V of her nightgown, "what are you doing here?"

Brant grimaced, his hands on the sill. As Serena peered more closely, she noticed that there was a bruise on his cheek and a gash over one eye. "I had a little set-to with the Birnley boys. All four of them." He gave Serena an uncertain, crooked grin. "It's my turn to seek succor. Could I borrow a glass of whiskey?"

Serena hesitated only a moment. "Of course. Come round to the front. But do be quiet. Everyone else is sleeping." Glancing at Abigail to make sure her cousin hadn't been disturbed by Brant's arrival, Serena grabbed her robe and fastened it securely in place. She didn't bother to search for her slippers, but moved softly on bare feet to the cabin's front room. Shafts of moonlight filtered through the uncurtained windows, somehow lending dignity to the ramshackle furnishings.

Brant had just reached the door as Serena lifted the latch. "Wait here," Serena cautioned. "I think it'd be better if I brought the whiskey outside." She fetched glass and bottle, poured out a hefty drink, and carried it to Brant, who was sitting on the top step. He was in his shirt sleeves and there was a tear in his trousers that ran the length of his left thigh.

"Thanks," said Brant gratefully as Serena handed him the glass. After he had taken a big swallow while Serena eased herself next to him on the step, he eyed her over the glass rim with amusement. "Well. We seem to be establishing a pattern. I lost my horse, too."

"What happened?" Serena looked sideways at Brant, afraid that if she actually turned her body toward him on the narrow steps, their knees would touch.

He lifted a shoulder and winced. A ruffed grouse flew out from the edge of the pond, its wings beating like thunder in the still summer night. "The Birnley boys were coming back from town, raucous as hell. Being just naturally polite, I wished them the best of the evening. They took exception to that, insisting it was morning. That seemed fine with me, since I was outnumbered, but I guess they felt I was too skeptical. The rout was on." Brant drained his glass and set it down behind him on the porch.

"They were . . . drunk?"

"Drunk as sailors in a Singapore saloon." Brant fingered the gash above his eye. The blood had congealed, but the bruise on his cheek was swelling. "They sent my horse flying off to God-knows-where. It was closer to walk back here than to go on into Livermore Falls."

Tentatively, he stretched out his legs, which reached to the ground at
the bottom of the steps. "I should borrow a horse, I guess." He sounded
a bit dubious and winced again as he flexed his left leg.

"Can you ride?" asked Serena, concern etched on her face.

"If I can walk, I can ride." He gave Serena a valiant grin. "I may
even live, given time and proper care." As he leaned toward her, his
head almost rested against hers. "Don't tell me you're worried?"

Serena sat up very straight. "I'm a bit anxious about your welfare,
of course," she responded in low, prim tones. But she was worried,
even upset. The idea of Brant enduring such savages angered and
distressed her. "You've taken what appears to be a severe beating
from those odious Birnleys."

"They don't look so pretty, either. Though I'll admit I thought I
was done for when three of them held me down while the fourth one
jumped up and down on my stomach."

Serena clapped her hand over her mouth to stifle a cry. "They
could have killed you," she gasped, her big eyes wide. "Was it . . .
painful?"

Brant shook his head. "Horrible. Especially the nails in his boots."

It took a moment for the truth to dawn on Serena. When it did,
she couldn't refrain from clutching at Brant's arms and shaking him.
"You fraud! Did you even *see* the Birnley brothers?"

Brant gave Serena an ingenuous look. "Does old Birnley have any
sons? Farmers usually do, but he could be a bachelor for all I know."

Aware that she was still clutching Brant's shirt sleeves, Serena
abruptly dropped her hands. She didn't know whether to laugh or be
angry. "What really happened?" she demanded. "Did you fall off your
horse, too?"

The sea-blue eyes didn't look the least apologetic. Brant placed a
casual hand on Serena's knee and shook his head. "Nothing quite so
mundane. I stopped about a mile or so down the road to investigate
a couple of good riffles in a trout stream." He made a wry face. "But
it was too dark. I fell down an old well."

Serena choked back her laughter, momentarily forgetting the light
yet familiar touch of Brant's hand through the thin cotton nightclothes.
"But that's almost worse than the phantom Birnley brothers! How did
you get out?"

"Oh," replied Brant airily, "it wasn't that deep. Once I got through
cussing, I climbed out pretty fast."

"And your horse?" Serena had finally controlled her laughter.

Brant gestured toward the road. "Over there. I thought I'd make
a more pitiful impression on foot. And I did need a drink."

"I should imagine." Serena still smiled, but she was trying to draw back unobtrusively from the hand on her knee. The moon was hiding again; the stars winked above the clouds.

Brant's hand was firm. "Maidenly modesty can be tantalizing, but after we're married I'd prefer you more wanton."

"Wanton! Married!" gasped Serena, jerking away and banging her elbow on the stair railing. "Don't be so damned sure of yourself, Brant Parnell!"

Brant shrugged. "There aren't many sure bets in life, but I usually feel safe putting my money on me." He stood up, not troubling to conceal how stiff he had become while sitting so still on the steps. "I'd better head back to Livermore Falls. It must be close to midnight." He bent down just far enough to ruffle Serena's hair with his hand. "Good night, Serena. I'll see you in Brunswick."

Though he moved with a slower pace, he started to whistle, apparently thought better of it, and was silent as he made his way toward the road.

Too late, several devastating retorts worked their way to the tip of Serena's tongue. Annoyed at her slow-wittedness, Serena consoled herself with the reminder that Brant Parnell didn't know how Marcus Farrar had failed to work his will on his daughter. Let Brant have his little triumph, Serena thought. He would leave the table empty-handed.

Serena wanted to be alone, out among the brilliant dahlias and bold marigolds which flanked the laurel hedge surrounding the house on Pleasant Street. It had rained just before supper and the grass was damp beneath her feet. She walked past the stable, beyond the small vegetable garden Mandy and Dorcas tended, through the rose arbor with its cluster of pink blooms, and back along the side of the house toward the gravel drive.

A much-weathered stone cherub which Grandpa Matthew had purchased on his first trip to France stood in a corner of the garden. It was only four feet tall, with three missing fingers, a chipped nose, and vacant eyes. Serena had always loved the cherub and wished she had known the grandfather who had brought him so far across the seas to stand like a faintly decrepit guardian angel in the Farrar garden.

She had called him that ever since she could remember. Whenever she was upset or worried, she would stand by the cherub and tell him her troubles. It had been some time since she had done so, however; she had grown to believe that maturity should put an end to such fantasies. But tonight Serena needed the companionship of her snub-nosed guardian angel.

The family had been back in Brunswick for almost two weeks. Long enough, in fact, for Abigail to set out for Boston to visit some of her Beaulieu relations. She had been accompanied by Matt, who had been dispatched there on behalf of the Farrar enterprises. Slowly but surely, Marcus was involving his only son in the family business.

So, in Abigail's absence, the cherub would have to serve as the recipient of Serena's confidences. It was strange, she thought, picking a purple aster and twirling it between her fingers, how swiftly certainties could dissolve into doubt. She couldn't understand why her enthusiasm for the future had been dashed.

The letter from Cousin Josiah had not been waiting for her when the family returned from the cabin. But it had arrived two days later, fulsome in its anticipation of Serena joining the *Springfield Republican*'s staff on the first day of September. Cousin Josiah was honored, the letter stated, that a member of the influential and prosperous Farrar family would consider journalism as a career. By chance, an opening had arisen on the newspaper with the immediate departure of a certain Miss Sackerson who was going to New Hampshire to care for an aged and infirm mother. Cousin Josiah would be delighted to have Lydia Holland Farrar's daughter live with the family since he often felt the ties of kinship had grown neglected with the passing years.

Serena had proudly shown the letter to her parents. Lydia pursed her lips and nodded. "Cousin Josiah is most respectable, even if his profession is sometimes suspect. I don't suppose the exercise will do you much harm."

Serena had been too elated to dispute her mother's reference to her career in the same vein as she would talk about someone's temporary mental aberration. She had even been too happy to notice that her father said virtually nothing at all. But when the second letter arrived that afternoon, Marcus Farrar's lack of voluble protest took on a different meaning. This time Cousin Josiah was considerably more subdued as he explained how the status of his staff had suddenly changed and that there would be no opening until after the first of the year. "I trust the delay will not seriously inconvenience you," he wrote with broad, open strokes. "I shan't bore you with tiresome details, but suffice to say that the fortunes of war can reach out to touch even the most obscure corners of our nation and alter the most precise of plans."

Cousin Josiah's explanation was also obscure, sufficiently so for Serena to wonder if her father had not exerted his renowned influence. To heighten her suspicion, Lydia Farrar had announced at supper that Brant Parnell was in Brunswick and would come to tea the following afternoon. The sudden shift in her future did not seem to emanate from the battlefields at Bull Run and Manassas Junction, but from the handsome granite three-story house on Pleasant Street in Brunswick.

Not that all was lost, she told herself, putting the aster up against the cherub's stone face, as if he could enjoy the fragrance. The ploy seemed to be a test, allowing Marcus to find out how determined his daughter really was about a newspaper career—and how strongly opposed she was to the idea of marrying Brant Parnell.

"I can be patient, too," Serena whispered at the statue's vacant eyes. "It's only four months. Even Papa couldn't marry me off that fast—it would cause talk and upset Mama."

She stared at the cherub, as if expecting him to nod in agreement. Indeed, there had been occasions when, as a child, she could have sworn that his chiseled curls had actually seemed to bob their assent. But now it was her own resolve that gave her comfort, and, laying the aster at the base of the statue as if making an offering, Serena smiled at her guardian angel and walked purposefully back toward the house.

Abigail and Matt returned to Brunswick on the noon train the following day. Matt closeted himself at once with Marcus in the study and Abigail went upstairs with Serena to unpack. The week-long visit with the Beaulieu relatives had proved about four days too many, Abigail asserted, but allowed that her father's people set a grand table.

"You don't seem to be bulging about the seams, at least," Serena laughed as she helped lay out her cousin's somewhat wrinkled petticoats. "I remember last year after you visited them before you went to France how you were positively paunchy!"

"Tante Honore supervises an excellent kitchen," Abigail replied crisply. "I did manage to purloin some of her recipes, but I suppose Mandy will scoff at preparing French cuisine."

"Dear Mandy," Serena said with affection. "She scoffs at many things. She has luncheon ready for both you and Matt, but I imagine he'll be with Papa for a bit. Did everything go well for him in Boston?"

Abigail closely inspected the blue-veiled hat she'd worn on the trip home. "I don't know. I rarely discuss business, if I can help it." Her thin, fine lips softened into a smile. "I'm sorry, I sound testy. Trains sometimes give me a headache. And you might as well know the latest scandal in Boston—someone shot Pembrose Stanhope last night."

"Judge Stanhope's odious son?" Serena's brown eyes widened. "How terrible," she exclaimed and burst into laughter. "Is he dead?"

"Unfortunately, no. Merely wounded. The suspects, being too numerous to mention, will probably not be sorted out for weeks." Abigail set the hat down on the bureau, apparently satisfied that the veil was undamaged.

"He and his brother—Giles, isn't it?—both have reputations for debauchery. Do you remember how Mama wouldn't let their names be mentioned at the table until we had turned sixteen?"

"The Stanhope brothers are enough to ruin anyone's appetite," Abigail said in an uncharacteristic heated tone. But after a glance in the mirror and a twist of one gold-tipped lock, Abigail announced she was ready for lunch.

Mandy would not serve Abigail until Matt appeared. "I cooked this creamed lobster for the rest of the family once and I won't heat it up twice. I'll let it curdle before I dish up extra for Master Matthew-Most-Mighty. Business in Boston, my foot! I remember when he had longer curls than either of you two!"

Huffing back toward the pantry, Mandy was still grumbling when Abigail sank onto a chair in the family dining room. "I'm famished," she gasped. "Can't you see if Matt is almost finished talking to your father?"

Serena said she'd find out; sure enough, the door to the study was ajar as she hurried down the hall. From within she could hear her father and brother speaking in tones which indicated their discussion was drawing to a close.

"Well done," Marcus was asserting in an expansive voice. "I was only twenty when your grandfather first sent me on business to Boston. I remember it well, facing all those gray-beards with their shrewd eyes and gnarled hands. Or so they seemed to me. I suppose they weren't much older than I am now." He chuckled richly and Serena heard her brother's answering laughter.

"I still don't think they believed me when I told them Captain Parnell wouldn't run any blockade whether he's your son-in-law or not," Matt said. "In Boston, he's something of a legend for boldness and daring."

"I wouldn't have him seeking Serena's hand if he weren't," Marcus replied. "Though I don't think we'll need to run any blockades if all goes well. I expect to hear from Washington in a few weeks about the uniform contracts. If I need any arm-twisting there, I'll send Brant. He knows some people who might prove useful. Though," Marcus added in a voice so low Serena almost didn't catch the words, "not as useful as your sister, if she can be made to see reason."

Serena didn't wait to hear her brother's reply. Hand over her mouth to keep from shrieking her indignation, she raced back down the hall, up the carpeted staircase, and into her room, where she slammed the door and threw herself on the bed. So that was why Brant Parnell had requested permission to court her! Now she knew why Cousin Josiah had withdrawn his earlier decision to have her start work September first. It was not a test at all, but a carefully conceived plan between her father and the charming but opportunistic whaling captain with his wary sea-blue eyes and rugged features and the aura of adventure. Serena sat up and clutched a satin-covered pillow against her bosom. Neither her father nor her so-called suitor would manipulate her into a marriage of convenience. She had a far different future in mind for herself, utilizing her talent and inspiration to change a world that sorely needed guidance from men—and women—of conscience. Which, she thought grimly, neither Marcus Farrar nor Brant Parnell seemed to own. They would not, she vowed, own her, either.

The silver tea tray sat on the low mahogany table, its empty cups and crumpled napkins mute evidence of a social rite duly concluded. Marcus and Lydia Farrar had discreetly withdrawn, "to let the young people have some time alone," as Lydia had graciously stated.

Brant was seated in a wing-backed armchair, legs crossed, one booted foot propped up on a petit-point–covered stool. He was dressed with unaccustomed formality, in a dark frock coat, matching trousers, and a deep blue vest with a white cravat. His manner, however, was that of a schoolboy whose teachers have just left the room. The polite if casual control he had exerted in the presence of the Farrars fled as soon as the door closed behind them.

Serena sat stiffly on a straight-backed chair, hands clasped in her lap, feet planted firmly together on the parlor's braided rug.

"I have to congratulate you, Serena," Brant said. "You're very adept at hiding your excitement."

She tried to keep from glaring at him. But he seemed quite serious—until she plumbed the depth of his blue eyes and caught the glint of sardonic humor. "I'm compelled to be honest with you, Captain. I find it appalling that my parents would consider my marriage as a commercial venture. Indeed, I'm quite certain that my mother disapproves as much as I do."

If Brant were surprised by Serena's knowledge of Marcus Farrar's intentions, he gave no sign. "But your father usually gets his way." Brant watched her closely, observing how the slanted brows seemed to draw more closely together. "You know, Serena, there are—incredible as it may seem—any number of young ladies who'd fairly foam at the mouth to be in your position."

His blatant conceit shocked Serena into animation. Her hands gestured in rapid movement, her body leaned forward so far that she almost slipped off the edge of the chair. "That's very crude. I must assume you're referring to harbor doxies and seaport slatterns rather than respectable young women of impeccable virtue."

Brant allowed his eyes to roll back in his head. "Good God, Serena, do you memorize drivel like that or do you actually make it up as you go along?" He didn't pause for her angry defense. "Look, I'm not some ruddy-cheeked Bowdoin boy who thinks all young ladies are to be worshipped from the base of a pedestal. I'm almost thirty years old, I've seen half the world, and most all of human nature in its varying forms of frailty and goodness. Maybe I've been exposed to more of the former than the latter, but I'm not yet a total cynic. I'm getting there, but a sable-eyed wife like you and a couple of children just might reform me. Have you considered what kind of service you'd be performing for society if you married me?"

"No!" Serena realized she had shouted the denial and blushed. "I'm going to Springfield where I can truly do something for social reform. I don't care what you or Matt or my father say, there is much good I can accomplish for a great many people through newspaper work. Why should I limit myself to you?"

Now Brant did look completely serious, even slightly saddened. He shook his head and stood up. "For most people, just helping one other person wage the war of life is more than enough. Maybe you're overestimating yourself, Serena."

She too had gotten up from her chair, trying to regain her dignity and poise, but aware that her voice and legs were both unsteady. "I'm not demeaning what other people do, I just feel that if a person has been given certain talents, they ought to be used. And used as fully as possible. I can't imagine, as a writer, writing only for an audience of one."

"Somehow, I wasn't thinking of writing." The bemused look had returned to Brant's craggy face. He stood very close to Serena, and the sheen of his satin waistcoat seemed overly bright. It also seemed to match his eyes. "In terms of us," he went on, putting his hand under her chin, "I was thinking of something else. You wanted me to kiss you that day in Livermore Falls, didn't you?"

Again, denial sprang to Serena's lips. But she didn't want to lie to Brant, nor did she need to when the truth was so self-absolving. "I was somewhat . . . tipsy."

"Being 'tipsy,' as you so quaintly call it, is always a wonderful excuse for acquiring the courage to do precisely what we want to do but under more sober circumstances would exercise rigid—if foolish—self-restraint." He tipped her chin up to his face. "You're quite sober now, Serena. Can you honestly say you don't want me to kiss you?"

He was so close, so confident, so in control, despite his apparent easygoing manner. And she still had never been kissed, had no thrilling secrets to write to Cecelia or whisper to Abigail. One kiss from Brant would give her ample ammunition to regale them both with titillating feminine confidences. On the other hand, it might encourage Brant to continue his suit.

"You may kiss me. Once." Serena closed her eyes and waited for the inevitable. It seemed to take a considerable amount of time for Brant to make up his mind, she thought with some impatience. Perhaps he was an honorable man. Was it possible that her father had coerced Brant Parnell into calling upon her? Was Brant faced with poverty because his whaling days were over? Was he actually to be pitied rather than condemned?

She opened her eyes just as Brant's mouth came down crushingly on hers, nipping her lower lip with his teeth, pressing her against him until she could no longer breathe. Serena felt his tongue delving into the recesses of her mouth, sensed the brute strength of him straining against her body, wondered if this were the proper moment to faint or merely to be outraged.

And then she wondered nothing at all, dazed with the ferocity of his kiss, reeling from the intensity of his embrace. It was not at all like the gauzy passages of the popular monthly women's magazines or even the more tempestuous novels she had read without her mother's knowledge or approval.

When Brant finally released her, she was caught off-balance and collapsed onto the wing-backed armchair. "So now we've kissed," Brant remarked idly and glanced at his watch which hung on a plain gold chain. "Do you want to discuss our future together or shall I be off to ready myself for the poker game at the Tontine Hotel?"

Serena clutched at the chair's beveled teak arms. "Poker! You're not only depraved, you're a gambling man! I can't believe my father would consider marrying me to anyone as contemptible as you!"

Brant leaned against the mantel, gazing with apparent curiosity at a miniature of Cecelia, painted just weeks before her wedding. "Your sister?"

"Yes. But don't you dare change the subject!" Serena had gotten to her feet again, stalking across the braided carpet to where Brant stood. "If you won't defend your character, then at least apologize for behaving so indecently!"

The broad shoulders heaved and the rough-hewn features tightened. "You wanted to be kissed, your first kiss, I'd imagine. Since your interest wasn't in romantic abandon, but intellectual investigation, I decided you might as well confront reality rather than some giddy, girlish notion about men's tender yearnings." His heavy dark brows drew together almost in a straight line as Brant snatched at Serena's wrist. "I am not material for an article in a ladies' magazine. I am flesh and blood, an honest-to-God human being. I even have feelings, Serena. And what you so piously call 'depravity,' I call ignorant naiveté on your part."

Serena had stood stockstill throughout Brant's glowering declaration. He still held her wrist, her forearm raised at an angle. "I don't want to marry you. I want to be a writer." The words came out in an impassioned whisper. She tried to pull her arm free but Brant's grasp was firm.

"You've said that. I hope your writing isn't as redundant as your conversation. Maybe kissing you is the only way to keep you quiet." He drew her close again, his face now relaxed though Serena could feel the tension in his body. She seemed to be enveloped in his arms, aware of her feminine frailty compared with his masculine strength. She was aware of something else as well, not unlike the sensation she had experienced from his nearness at the house in Livermore Falls. But she was quite sober now; why, despite her most earnest intentions, did she have no serious will to escape from Brant Parnell's embrace?

"You're not arguing," he said into her hair. "Does that mean you've surrendered or you're thinking that your silence will stop me from kissing you?"

"I don't know why you want to kiss me when you're only courting me because of my father's business connections," Serena said in muffled tones against Brant's waistcoat. "If you and Papa are so sure of yourselves, why don't we dispense with the formalities?"

He stepped back just far enough to put both hands on her face. "Oh, I don't know, Serena. Maybe I'm just bound by tradition. Or maybe I'd rather think about kissing you than about your father's business connections."

She didn't believe him for a moment, yet his words made her feel surprisingly light-hearted. She started to smile in spite of herself and then his lips caught hers. This time the kiss was more tender, though the arms that encircled her body seemed to force the air from her lungs. Serena found herself gasping, yet she didn't struggle to turn her head away. Her hands were pressing at his chest, fingers touching the smooth, sensuous satin of his blue waistcoat. She was kissing him in return, wondering vaguely why she felt more dizzy than she had when she was half-drunk on brandy and dazed from shock.

At last he released her, slowly moving backward but keeping his hands on her forearms. "Well? Was that more like what you'd expected?" He started to grin, but grew suddenly serious, letting his hands fall to his sides. "That's strange," he said wonderingly. "It wasn't what *I* expected." Brant kept staring at the huge, slanted brown eyes, the mouth with the lower lip that seemed to pout even when she laughed, the upturned nose, and the mass of lush, dark hair which had been tamed by a silver snood. Finally, his gaze shifted to the full, high bosom, decorously hidden under several rows of Belgian lace.

"You're making me nervous." Serena licked her lips which felt slightly bruised. "Aren't you going to be late for your poker game?"

"What? Oh, no, it doesn't start for another two hours." Now Brant did grin, that off-center, infectious white flash of teeth and snap of eyes that Serena was beginning to find unsettlingly familiar. "Don't worry," he added, adjusting his cravat and bending down to brush his lips against her temple, "I'll still have plenty of time to mark the cards and water down the whiskey."

She took a sharp, deep breath, but didn't reply. He was already at the door to the hallway, saluting her with a wave of his big hand as he turned to seek out her parents and bid them farewell.

From her window, Serena could just barely make out the shadowy form of the worn stone cherub in the garden. Had it not started raining again, she would have ventured outside to commune with the statue and relate her present, unquiet state of mind.

Although Abigail was now home to serve as a more responsive confidante, Serena was reluctant to express her churning emotions aloud. Uppermost in her mind was her resolve to work for Cousin Josiah come the new year. Unless some other unforeseen obstacle occurred, she had only to stall for four months until she could join the staff of the *Springfield Republican*.

Yet she could not deny that Brant Parnell's kisses had made her feel astonishingly happy. Perhaps kissing did that to a young lady, regardless of the gentleman who was partner to the act. Serena pried open the window a scant inch to let in the damp, fresh air. It was certainly not unusual to enjoy kissing, Serena told herself, since so many writers extolled the raptures of romantic love.

Yet Brant had alluded to something different, to what he termed "reality" and, on her part, "naiveté." Serena knew that married love was not the same as that of courtship. Her mother had told her and Cecelia about their wifely duties. It had sounded absurd at first, but Cecelia later told Serena she had actually spoken with a girl who had eloped to Augusta and not only had spent almost the entire night in bed with her bridegroom, but had been bold enough to talk about it. What was more, the exuberant bride had seemed to relish her duties as a wife. It was something to consider, Serena decided, and mused on how Cecelia managed as Mrs. Fitch Moncrief in New Bern, North Carolina.

Serena's attention was momentarily diverted by sounds outside. Voices, but whose? It was raining quite hard, as if washing away August and its dog days of summer. Serena shrugged as the voices drifted away and the raindrops began to trickle over the windowsill onto the floor. She closed the sash, wiped up the small puddle with her handkerchief, and glanced at the Dresden clock on her bureau. It was not yet nine-thirty—too early to go to bed, yet too late to start any serious task. She could read, perhaps, or write in her journal. Yes, she decided, that should have been her first inspiration. She opened the leather-bound volume and dipped her pen in the inkwell.

"August 31, 1861," she wrote with a growing sense of excitement. "This afternoon, I experienced the most delightful sensation when a certain young man from New Bedford called upon me and proffered a kiss." Serena stopped, frowning at the page. "Bilge," she said aloud and scratched out everything but the date. The kiss had not been "proffered," it had been an impassioned plundering of her lips and mouth. At least the first time. But she could hardly admit that, even in her private journal. Or could she? Wasn't truth what writing was all about? Serena was concentrating so hard on an accurate description of the experience that Abigail finally had to pound on the door to be heard.

"I was beginning to think you were asleep," she said in a low, anxious voice as Serena let her in.

"I was . . . lost in my writing," Serena asserted. She stared at Abigail, whose cloak was soaking wet and whose usually impeccable appearance was decidedly disheveled. Her cousin also seemed uncharacteristically agitated. "What's wrong? You look green."

"I feel green," Abigail replied, sinking onto the bed and kicking off her shoes. "Serena, I need your help."

Never, in all the years the girls had grown up together, had Abigail ever openly asked Serena for help. It had always been the other way around. Serena was speechless.

Even under duress, Abigail understood her cousin's reaction. Regaining her composure, she got off the bed and made a face at the damp circle caused by her rain-drenched cloak. "I'm sorry about your counterpane. Maybe it didn't go through."

"It'll dry," Serena said quickly. "What is it, Abby?"

Whatever urgency there was, Abigail apparently was prepared to take her time. She removed the cloak, shook it out, and hung it on a peg. Purposefully, she picked up the quilt which covered the cedar chest at the foot of the bed and laid it over the damp counterpane before sitting down again. She waited for what seemed to Serena like an excruciatingly long time before speaking. When Abigail at last began to explain her plight, it was in calm, measured tones.

"There is a man named Yancy Clarke in the stable. He has been shot and needs medical assistance. The law authorities in Boston are searching for him and it's possible that our local constabulary has been notified as well. Your parents must not find out he's here. No one must know, except the doctor who tends him." The green eyes seemed almost hypnotic, as if they were willing Serena to obey without question.

But the Serena who intended to work on a newspaper was not the same gullible girl of earlier times. "What has this Yancy Clarke done? Is he a criminal?"

Abigail placed the tips of her fingers against each other and regarded Serena speculatively. "He is not," she said firmly. "He is, however, believed to have shot Pembrose Stanhope."

"For that, he should be given a medal." Serena paused and shook her head. "I don't understand—that happened in Boston. Why is this man Clarke here in Brunswick?"

"He is from Texas," Abigail answered, averting her eyes, and twisting the silver ring beaten into leaf shapes, which she wore on her left hand. Deliberately, she stared down at her fingers, aware that she was betraying more than her inner turmoil. "He is also my husband."

"Oh, my God!" Serena reeled against the bureau, almost upsetting the Dresden clock. "Abby, are you serious?"

"Of course I'm serious," her cousin replied, with a touch of her usual pert manner. "Even I wouldn't joke about the man I married." She waited until a shaken Serena had settled into the rocking chair by the bed before continuing: "I never went to France. I went to New Orleans. Your father sent me there because I was going to have a baby—Pembrose Stanhope's baby. I stayed with my relatives and met Yancy. We were married after my child was born—dead. I can't tell you the whole story now, Serena, because it's Yancy's story too, and there are things that I'm not certain he'd want me to reveal even to you. But at the moment, the important thing is that we get help for Yancy as soon as your parents have gone to bed and that we keep him hidden until he can safely leave town."

"Oh, my God," Serena repeated, this time on a hushed note. "This is . . . incredible! But Pembrose's baby? I thought you loathed him!"

"I did. I do." Abigail stood up, her petite figure somehow looming tall under the shadow of the canopied bed. "He raped me. Do you remember the picnic at Topsham last year?"

Serena nodded. It had been a very pleasant occasion, under the elms at the edge of town, with several Bowdoin College undergraduates, and hampers filled with cold lobster and crusty bread and slabs of corned beef. Such an ordinary day, with the sun filtering through the leaves and a raucous game of croquet and the high-pitched laughter of young girls mingling with the deeper chuckles of their escorts. And Pembrose Stanhope, forgotten until now by Serena. In her mind's eye, she could see but a single image of him, uncorking a wine bottle with his long, thin fingers, and brushing the pale blond hair off his forehead as someone handed him a glass.

"I didn't know you were with him," Serena said, as Pembrose's slightly puffy features faded in her memory.

"I certainly didn't intend to be. I had started to get one of my headaches and had gone toward the river to find some quiet. He followed me . . ." She stopped, listening intently. "Your parents—are they going to bed?"

Serena got up from the rocking chair and tiptoed to the door. "Yes," she whispered. "Do you want me to fetch Dr. Kirby?"

Abigail was already putting her cloak back on. "Please. I must get back to Yancy. He's very weak." For the first time, the deep concern which Abigail had kept so carefully under control rose to the surface. Her face seemed to crumble momentarily, then she lifted her head and fastened the cloak at her neck.

Serena was getting her own wrap out of the closet along with a pair of stout boots. "Isn't this Saturday night?"

Abigail thought for a moment. "Yes. Why?"

"Because," Serena said with a trace of irritation, "every Saturday night since Mrs. Kirby died, the good doctor plays poker at the Tontine Hotel." With a resolute flip of her scarf over one shoulder, Serena marched from the bedroom, paused to make sure no one was in the hallway, and hurried quietly toward the staircase.

Five minutes later she was halfway to the Tontine Hotel while the steady rain obscured her vision. She could just barely make out the Town Hall with its clock tower. It chimed ten-thirty as she headed up Main Street toward the hotel.

Very few citizens were out on such a wet night, but Serena was just as well-pleased. She wouldn't have wished to be stopped by friends and neighbors inquiring about her errand. She did not, however, relish the prospect of facing Brant Parnell in the middle of a poker game with several of Brunswick's more affluent citizens. Indeed, her father had been known to join the Saturday games at the Tontine, though usually only during the winter months.

But Serena was presented with another problem: Summoning Dr. Kirby would provoke the interest of the other players. She had not considered this until she was in the palm-flanked lobby. Perhaps she could resolve her predicament by sending the vacant-eyed young man behind the desk to the card room. She eyed the clerk surreptitiously from behind one of the potted palms. He was one of several sons whose father worked as a steward in Marcus Farrar's Number One mill on the Androscoggin River. But Serena could remember neither his first nor his last name.

She approached the desk with her scarf clutched around her and the wet cloak dragging over the Persian carpet. The clerk's vacant stare flickered to life as Serena started to speak. "I'm seeking a Captain Parnell," she announced in imperious tones. "I believe he is playing cards."

The young man all but smirked. "Could be. You want to wait in his room until he's finished? It might be a while."

"I need to see him at once," Serena replied, somewhat puzzled. "Shall I send a note with you?"

"A note?" The young man now looked puzzled, too. He shrugged. "If you like. But I can just tell him you're here." He looked around the lobby to see if any of the guests might need his immediate assistance, apparently saw no one except an elderly man dozing in an armchair by the door to the dining room, and put out a printed sign which read "Temporarily Off Duty." Pushing open a wooden gate at the side of the desk, he turned to Serena. "Sorry, I forgot to ask if you were Molly or Polly."

"What?" Serena peered at the young man and then gasped. "Oh, good grief! I'm neither!" She felt her anger rising along with her embarrassment. "I'm— Never mind who I am, just tell Captain Parnell it's urgent!"

"If you say so." He shrugged again and loped across the lobby toward a double door beyond the winding staircase.

Serena bunched up her cloak in her hands and began pacing in front of the desk. Was it possible that the man who was courting her actually had loose women visit him in his hotel room? It seemed incredible, even monstrous. She almost walked into one of the palms just as Brant Parnell appeared in the lobby.

"I had no idea I'd made such a favorable impression," he said, waving the desk clerk away and attempting to take Serena's hand. "But next time can you wait until I've filled out my spade flush?"

Serena pulled her hand away. "I can't wait at all—there's a man in our stable with a bullet in him, you beast. Now go get Dr. Kirby with as much discretion as possible. This is a most serious secret."

Brant stared in confusion at Serena. "Hold on, I think you're trying to tell me six things at once. Including the fact that you're a mite put out with me. Would you care to start over?"

Serena took a deep breath; it wouldn't help Abigail or the man she called her husband to let personal feelings stand in the way. The important thing was to get Dr. Kirby. "A man who has been shot is hiding from the law in our stable. No one must know. But the bullet must be removed."

Brant scratched his head but looked slightly less mystified. "All right, except Dr. Kirby is in no shape to do the job. He passed out half an hour ago."

"Oh!" Serena put her hand to her mouth and the brown eyes widened in distress. "What shall we do?"

"'We'?" Brant's wry smile twisted at the corners of his mouth, but he guided Serena by the elbow toward the main entrance. "As a sea captain, I've had some experience with medicine. And I'm a hell of a lot more sober than Dr. Kirby. If you'll excuse me until I collect my winnings and get my hat, I'll go back with you."

Serena was so relieved that her anger fled. "Oh, thank you, Brant!" she said, unaware that she'd used his given name. "But please don't tell anyone where you're going."

"I won't." He was already halfway across the lobby. "I'll just mention a certain amorous lady and an unexpected assignation in a hayloft."

"Just so you don't mention Molly or Polly," Serena retorted, flushed again, and saw the desk clerk gaping at them both. She turned her back on the curious young man and examined a Hudson River school landscape which hung over the lobby's massive fireplace. If Brant had been surprised by her parting sally, he never broke stride as he went through the double doors to the hotel card room.

On their hurried walk back to Pleasant Street, the rain let up to a mere mist. Serena was surprised when Brant neither asked who the wounded man was nor how she had come to learn about Molly and Polly. They did converse, however, but mostly about the poker game and Dr. Kirby's unexpected inability to hold his liquor.

"Sometimes a man will pretend he gets drunk to throw off the other players," Brant explained, "but the poor old doc was all too genuine. He fell right off his chair onto the hotel cat."

"He's always seemed a most temperate man," Serena said wonderingly. "Perhaps he was deeply affected by his wife's passing." She stopped just as the brick chimneys of the Farrar house appeared between the trees. "We had better go around the long way," she told Brant, lowering her voice to a whisper. "Mama is a light sleeper."

The soft whinny of Hera, Lydia Farrar's hunting mare, greeted them as they entered the stables. All lay in darkness except for the glow of a lantern halfway down the row of stalls. Serena led the way, suddenly apprehensive about what she would find. For the last quarter of an hour, she had put everything out of her mind except the need to get help to a man she'd never before laid eyes on.

The man now lay inside one of the stalls, the quilt from Serena's bedroom thrown over his big, shambling body. He was unconscious, smears of dried blood on the callused hands which lay inert at his sides, the brown beard matted, the breathing slow and labored. It appeared to Serena that he wore Western garb; at least she could see a leather vest and black shirt above the quilt's edge. He seemed to be the most unlikely possible choice of a husband for the fastidious Abigail Beaulieu. Fleetingly, Serena wondered if her cousin had concocted the whole story.

But Abigail's concern was genuine. She was already conferring in a whisper with Brant, describing the wound, relating what she had done so far to make Yancy more comfortable. Brant listened in silence, nodding once or twice. Then he pulled off his frock coat, rolled up his sleeves, and set to work.

The bullet had entered Yancy Clarke's body just under his lower left ribs. "It's deep, I'll need some sort of instruments." Brant rocked back on his heels, heedless of the damage already done to his trousers and white linen shirt.

"I'll get whatever is needed," Serena volunteered. The boiling water, culinary utensils, and medical supplies were all rounded up as fast as Serena could manage. Fortunately, the fire had not yet died out in the huge stove which took up at least a quarter of the kitchen. Tea kettle in one hand and the other items in a basin balanced precariously against her side, Serena trudged back to the stable. A quick upward glance told her that Matt was still up; she could not see her parents' bedroom window from the rear of the house.

Yancy Clarke was still unconscious when she returned. Brant and Abigail were busy putting some of the horse blankets under him. At last, Brant began to probe for the bullet. Abigail, now under tight-reined control, assisted as if nursing were second nature to her. Serena could not watch. Instead, she went to the adjacent stall to stroke her little grey mare's head. It was very quiet in the stable, only the horses' breathing and occasional pawing, a muffled word from Brant, an even less audible response from Abigail—and then a deep, heartrending cry from the Texan before he passed out. Serena put her head down next to the little mare and prayed.

It seemed to take hours, but Abigail later said only about five minutes had passed. Brant, his chiseled features grim, blood covering his shirtfront, beads of sweat on his forehead, produced the bullet between red-stained thumb and forefinger.

"That's all I can do," he said tersely. "The rest is up to the man himself. He seems strong enough, but it depends on how much blood he's lost." Brant looked down at the Texan's still form. "There seems to be a lot—how are you going to keep the family and your help from finding out what's happened?"

Serena had not thought past extracting the bullet. She glanced questioningly at Abigail, who was gathering up the old bandages which had once been her petticoat. "There's a dollhouse by the root cellar," Abigail said. "It's small but there should be enough room if I take out some of the doll furnishings. We can make a pallet. But we'll have to move him, of course."

"Of course." Brant sighed. "He's heavier than I am. He must weigh well over two hundred pounds." Brant paused, pondering their next step. "We shouldn't move him until we have to. When will anyone come out to the stable?"

"Probably not until just after six when the stable boy usually comes to feed and water the horses," Serena answered.

Brant nodded and was silent for another moment. "All right. I'll stay here with him until about five. You two get everything cleaned up. The rain has washed away the bloody tracks outside, but you're going to have to do some scrubbing in here."

Both Serena and Abigail protested that Brant Parnell did not need to put himself out any further. He must, Serena insisted, return to the Tontine Hotel. But Brant brushed their words aside, ordering them to get busy with their own chores while he figured out a way to make himself comfortable. When Serena suggested bringing pillows and blankets from the house, Brant again dismissed her offer. There was no point in complicating their subterfuge. He was, after all, a seafaring man who had slept in far worse accommodations than the Farrar stable.

And so Abigail and Serena stealthily returned to the house to wash the kitchen utensils and to fetch more boiling water and rags. It was almost one in the morning when they finished, and both were weary. Serena told Abigail to go straight to bed. She protested, but only for the sake of form. The strain showed in the pinched corners of her mouth and the shadows under her eyes.

Brant had already made himself a bed in the hay and was stretched out just a few feet from the still-unconscious Texan. "No one saw you?" he asked, leaning on one elbow and taking the lantern from Serena.

She shook her head. "No." Serena dropped down beside Brant and let her shoulders slump with fatigue. "You were very professional. Why haven't you asked who he is and why he's here?"

Brant stifled a yawn with his big hand. "If you wanted me to know, you'd have told me. Besides, neither you nor your cousin strikes me as the type who does wildly unusual things without a reason. In this case, I presume our victim over there is also Cousin Abigail's dearly beloved."

Serena gaped at Brant. "How—why do you think that?"

Brant shrugged and stretched, his long arms almost touching the low beams of the stable. "Their rings. They're both beaten silver leaves." He gave Serena an ingenuous yet self-deprecating look. "That's not too hard to figure out. At least not for a poker player who watches hands as much as faces."

Serena felt chagrined. As an aspiring writer, she ought to have been observant enough to have noticed the same thing. But, she told herself, the last few hours had been so full of shocks and surprises that her mind had only been able to concentrate on one topic at a time.

Nor did she dare confirm Brant's assumption. Instead, she turned on him with a renewed spurt of energy, prepared not only to divert him from further speculation about Yancy and Abigail, but to reproach him for whatever he had intended to do with Polly and Molly.

"Would I be incorrect if I guess something about you?" She watched as the rugged features displayed mild interest. "Is it true that you entertain women of an unsavory reputation in your hotel room?"

"No." He looked quite appalled at the idea, but began to grin in his twisted, off-center manner. "Well, sometimes. But I prefer to think of them as entertaining *me*."

"Oh!" Serena's hands tightened into fists and it was all she could do to keep from raining blows on him. "How could you? You're supposed to be courting me!"

He held up his hands, as if to defend himself from her wrath. "But Serena, I thought you didn't want to be courted. Kissed, maybe, but not courted."

This time Serena did strike him, the blows glancing off his chest while he laughed and finally took both hands firmly in one of his. "Well? Did you change your mind?"

Glaring up angrily into the sea-blue eyes, Serena suddenly felt as confused as she was tired. "No. I still intend to have a career. If I'd ever considered marrying you, what I learned this evening about your flagrantly immoral behavior makes it impossible for me to become your wife."

Brant stared for a moment up into the rafters, as if seeking solutions to the problems she had posed. He still held her hands, which she was trying unsuccessfully to disengage. "Now see here, Serena," he said, with only the flicker of amusement in his eyes detracting from his otherwise sober countenance, "I came to Brunswick with only two changes of gear. I caught my other trousers on a nail in the waiting room at the train station. Molly and her sister Polly are both excellent seamstresses. The Quinn girls—you know them?"

Serena thought for a moment, her hands now slack in Brant's grasp. She knew some Quinns, but they lived by the toll bridge. Or the Gulf Dam. Offhand, she couldn't quite place them. Serena gazed dubiously at Brant. He seemed quite sincere, and she wanted to believe him, if only because he had been such a help to Abigail's alleged husband. Looking at Yancy Clarke's quilt-covered form, she noted that his breathing seemed more even. Surely if Brant hadn't been able to extract the bullet, Yancy might now be dead.

"The Quinn girls," she repeated, gazing at Brant again. "Well, I think I know who they are..."

"They came highly recommended by Mr. Cabot, who is a friend of your father's." Brant gave her hands a little squeeze and then released them. "It's late, you'd better head in if we have to get up so early to move our patient."

"Yes," Serena agreed, wondering if she had the strength to move at all. It was tempting to consider just curling up next to Brant in the hay and going to sleep. But it was also wildly improper. Serena started to get up, but Brant reached out to hook his arm around her neck.

"There's another variation, the good-night kiss. You might as well go for three of a kind. It beats a pair any day." Serena opened her mouth to protest, but Brant's lips caught hers to stifle the sound. This time it was a deep, lingering kiss as both of them stayed very still. Serena found herself savoring Brant's warmth, learning the taste and feel of him, responding as if she'd always belonged in his arms. When Brant released her mouth, he pressed her face against his chest. "Go to bed." He sounded rather gruff. As Serena tried to raise her head to look at him, he stood up, lifting her with him. "Go on. If you don't, we might do something that will raise the semi-dead."

Serena felt the color rising in her cheeks, but the set of Brant's jaw told her she mustn't dispute his orders. Feeling somewhat foolish, she gave him a halfhearted wave and headed out of the stable, skirts clutched in her hands.

It had grown chilly outside, the rain having left a damp autumnal nip in the air. Serena shivered as she hurried past the vegetable garden— and let out a startled little cry. Three men were coming through the open space of the laurel hedge which adjoined the Pembertons' house next door. One of them signaled with his hand for her to stop.

"Miss Serena?" came the voice as the men skirted their way around fat cabbages and a row of corn that hadn't quite come up to Mandy's expectations.

"Sheriff?" Serena answered back, torn between speaking loudly enough to warn Brant and softly enough to keep from rousing her family.

Sheriff Scott and his two deputies stamped wet earth from their boots as they reached the walkway. "Aren't you up pretty late?" Scott inquired, his broad features friendly, if curious.

"Oh, I am," Serena replied, licking her lips and stalling for time. "It must be well after one. What are you doing here, Sheriff?"

He shook his head and chuckled. "On a fool's errand, probably. There's an escaped criminal supposedly in the Brunswick-Topsham vicinity, on the run up from Boston. Somebody reported seeing him in Harpswell and somebody else said he was lurking around over on Oak Street. Cranks, no doubt, but we have to do our duty. At least," he added with a grimace. "it stopped raining."

"We needed a good rain, though. At least Mandy's corn could use it." She smiled as innocently as she could. "Do you want to look around here, Sheriff?"

Scott shook his head. "No, not if you've been out and about."

"Very well." She smoothed the folds of her cloak over her breast, aware that her heart was thumping too fast. "Good night."

Just as she started to turn toward the back steps, the sheriff called out in a low voice: "Miss Serena—wait up." She moved around slowly, feeling the eyes of all three men boring into her very being, as if the secret she was keeping had suddenly become transparent. "Yes?" she said, and her voice sounded very odd.

"Unlikely as it may be, you didn't come out here because you heard or saw anything unusual, did you?"

Serena forced a little laugh. "Oh, heavens, no. My little mare isn't well. I stayed with her until she went to sleep."

The sheriff nodded with understanding. "I'm sorry to hear that, but I wouldn't have wanted you to worry about an outlaw hiding out here. More to the point, I wouldn't want you running into him at night by yourself. He's said to be dangerous."

"Dear me! Thank you for the warning." Serena nodded rapidly at all three of the men, then hurried toward the sanctuary of the house.

Chapter 4

NEITHER SERENA nor Abigail had slept well for what was left of that night. By contrast, Brant averred that he'd dropped off as soon as he heard the sheriff and his deputies leave. Yes, he told Serena, he'd listened to the exchange, standing motionless just inside the stable door. There was an admiring glint in his eye that told her he was proud of the way she'd handled herself, and Serena was unaccountably pleased that he'd noticed.

Shortly before six, Brant had managed to haul the still unconscious Yancy Clarke the thirty yards to the dollhouse. It was already light out but Serena had stood guard to make sure no one was about. It being a Sunday, none of the tradesmen were making their rounds and even Mandy slept in until at least six-thirty.

Abigail, drawn and pale, had set up a pallet, brought food and drink and a change of bandages, which she set about applying as soon as Yancy was once again lying down. And though he had not regained consciousness during the arduous move from the stable, just as Abigail unwrapped the old, blood-soaked bandage, Yancy's eyes flickered open briefly. Serena thought he seemed to recognize Abigail before he heaved a great sigh and sank back into unconsciousness.

"That's some encouragement," Brant said, adjusting his clothes and smoothing his hair into place. "He ought to come around later today, I'd guess."

"He will," Abigail asserted tersely, settling herself onto a purple tasseled cushion she'd managed to pilfer from the Farrars' guest room.

Abigail insisted she would spend most of the day in the dollhouse. Serena must tell the rest of the family that her cousin had one of her headaches and couldn't be disturbed. Serena was also to avoid coming out to the dollhouse until at least midafternoon, lest anyone become curious as to why the long-neglected haven of their youth should suddenly beckon once more. Brant told Serena he'd return to the hotel for breakfast but would come back later, under the guise of paying a courting call.

"You don't need to," Serena said as they cautiously walked around the far side of the house, keeping in the shadows of the laurel hedge. The clouds had blown out to sea and the sun was up, promising a warm first day of September. "Abigail and I will manage perfectly well."

"No doubt," Brant remarked absently, looking toward the drive to make certain no early risers were in the neighborhood. "On the other hand, I *am* in Brunswick to press for your hand. I'd rather expect your parents to invite me for Sunday supper."

Lydia Farrar had mentioned doing just that, but in all the excitement of the previous evening, Serena had forgotten. No doubt Lydia would send an invitation to the Tontine Hotel right after church. Such an occasion would give her father and Brant an opportunity to discuss their proposed business ventures, Serena thought with annoyance.

"Well?" Brant stopped just as the elm-lined street came into full view. "You aren't arguing. Are you still tired?"

"Yes," Serena answered querulously. "I am. If I didn't have to fib for Abby, I'd take to my bed for the rest of the day."

Brant put his wide-brimmed black hat on his head and tilted it back a bit. He seemed disappointed that Serena wasn't easily provoked this morning. "What a waste," he sighed in an exaggerated manner and made as if to go.

"Waste? What waste?" Serena felt a breeze stirring the hedge behind her and the chestnut tree which stood at the front of the house.

Brant made a gesture of dismissal with his hand. "Oh, nothing. Just a waste for you to spend the day in bed—alone."

"That's not funny!" Serena hissed, suddenly glancing up toward the dormer window where Mandy and Dorcas shared a room. They would both be up by now, getting ready to go down to the kitchen and prepare the family's breakfast. "You are truly tasteless! Now please be on your way, the Pembertons next door may be up."

Brant made a show of looking hurt, was unable to keep from grinning, and touched the brim of his hat in salute before walking briskly but silently down the drive toward Pleasant Street.

Brant's prediction was accurate: Yancy Clarke regained consciousness for at least half an hour late that afternoon just after Serena had gone to check on Abigail. During the course of the next two days, his recovery seemed remarkable and Abigail was able to return to the house for long stretches at a time. Caught up in their weekday routine, no one seemed to notice any irregularities in Abigail's behavior. But ironically by Wednesday, when Yancy was starting to chafe about his confinement, the strain had taken its toll on Abigail and she actually did succumb to one of her demonic headaches.

Serena took over tending Yancy, though except for bringing him food and a change of bandages which he could now apply himself, there was little to be done. If Serena had hoped to learn more about the astounding tale Abigail had told her, Yancy proved to be even more discreet than the woman who called herself his wife. Indeed, he was probably the least talkative person Serena had ever met. The low, rumbling Texas drawl seldom was made up of more than monosyllables, and the heavy-lidded gray eyes revealed even less. If Abigail had actually married the man, Serena could not possibly guess why.

As for her own would-be wedding, the courtship had abruptly been derailed when Marcus had announced at supper the previous Sunday that Brant must accompany him and Matt on a three-day tour of the Farrar empire, from Yarmouth up the Kennebec River. It seemed to Serena that Brant accepted with a hint of reluctance, but if Marcus noticed, he gave no sign.

Not that it mattered, Serena told herself for the dozenth time as she got dressed Thursday morning. She and Abigail had not needed to summon Brant again to help with Yancy. A good thing, too, since Brant was scheduled to leave Brunswick that day for New Bedford. She assumed he'd call on her to bid farewell. If he didn't, she wouldn't be distressed, of course, though she wondered why she wasn't more relieved that he was going away. Perhaps, she told herself, it was because Yancy was going to move off the Farrar premises soon and she would feel more secure if a man were on hand to help ensure his safe escape.

At least Abigail was up and about that morning, looking pale but otherwise pert. Serena, smearing butter on a cornmeal muffin, relaxed a little; being solely responsible for Yancy Clarke had been a strain.

"A fine fellow, your Captain Parnell," Marcus asserted, turning to Serena as Mandy proffered a platter of fresh-baked doughnuts. "Good business head, sound instincts. He's going to Washington soon about those government contracts."

Serena paused briefly with the strawberry jam crock in one hand and a small silver spoon in the other. "I presume you knew that all along or you wouldn't have coerced him into courting me," Serena said. Never a cheerful early riser, she was often more blunt—and less patient—at the beginning of the day.

Marcus bit into a doughnut and guffawed, spewing crumbs on his vest while Lydia pursed her lips in displeasure. "'Coerced'! Now, now, Rena, what makes you think any man would have to be coerced into marrying you?"

"It's I who will have to be coerced," she murmured just as Matt arrived at the table, shirttail not quite tucked in and hair uncombed. "Pardon me, I overslept." He waited just long enough for both parents to nod acknowledgment of his apology, then speared two doughnuts and let Mandy pile fried potatoes on his plate. "Um, muffins, too! And my favorite pork sausages. Mandy, I've only been away three days, but I suffered mightily from the cooking of strangers. Will you marry me?"

Mandy made a noise that was half-grumble, half-giggle. "Go on with you, you'd eat a cedar shake if you were hungry enough." She made as if to slap his shoulder, gave him an affectionate look, and went back to the kitchen to refill the chafing dish with fried potatoes.

Matt was chewing with gusto while Serena stared glumly at her muffin. Brant had come to Brunswick to court her and they'd spent precisely half an hour alone together, not counting the unexpected time during which they'd been more concerned with Yancy Clarke than themselves. The real courtship, it seemed, was taking place between Brant and her father.

Not that she wanted to be courted, she reminded herself, finally tasting the muffin and letting the butter and jam mingle on her tongue. What she wanted was to put off any commitment until she could get to Springfield. If Brant went to Washington, there would be a delay of at least a month. By then it would be October, and even if Marcus pressed for their engagement, Lydia would want at least three months to plan the wedding. And to avoid any speculation about a precipitous marriage. That meant the date couldn't possibly be set until after the New Year. By then, Serena was determined to be working on Cousin Josiah's newspaper. Surely even her father couldn't pressure Josiah Holland into endless delay.

She was roused from her deep thought by Abigail, who was exhibiting unwonted enthusiasm for something Matt had proposed. Serena gazed from brother to cousin, puzzled but curious.

"It promises to be a fine evening," Abigail was saying as she dabbed at the corners of her mouth with a linen napkin. "And I think Clarence Prendergast has a marvelous idea. For once." She threw Serena a sly little glance before continuing: "Of course, I'm sure the sheriff is right, that dreadful man couldn't possibly be anywhere near Brunswick by now, but looking for clues as to his whereabouts is far more ingenious than just an ordinary hayride and scavenger hunt."

Serena swallowed the rest of the muffin. "Is there a description?" she asked cautiously, not altogether certain she knew what was happening.

"There's a good one, since old Chadwick at the depot talked to somebody who saw him on the Boston train," Matt replied. "Unless he changed gear, he won't be hard to find. He's wearing some Western get-up and he's a great big bugger."

Serena thought she saw Abigail wince slightly, but Matt was still talking. "Chadwick said whoever told him about it said he looked as if he were hurt. Or drunk. Judge Stanhope has put up a thousand-dollar reward."

"That would certainly make it worthwhile for some enterprising, courageous soul," Abigail remarked, wrapping a strand of gold-tipped hair around her finger. "I presume we're pursuing this person merely for our own amusement?"

Matt shoved his fork into the fried potatoes. "Hey, I wouldn't sneer at a thousand dollars for spending money! Split six ways, I mean." He grinned boyishly at Abigail. "You, me, Rena, Clarence, and Jack and Nora Pemberton."

"You could take all of it, propose to Nora, and take her on a honeymoon," Serena put in, wondering why Mandy's muffins didn't taste quite right this morning.

"Nora Pemberton may have designs," said Lydia, "but your father and I don't encourage her in any way." She plucked at the high collar of her dress, furling the lace just so to set off the onyx brooch at her throat. "And while I have never been an admirer of Judge Stanhope or his sons, it would seem more fitting to me if you young people showed more concern for Pembrose's recovery than for making a game out of capturing his alleged assailant."

Matt attempted to look contrite; Abigail appeared expressionless, studying the beaten silver ring on her left hand; Serena frowned, realizing that in truth, neither she nor Abigail—nor Brant, for that matter—had given even a passing thought to Pembrose Stanhope's fate. Glancing at Abigail, she knew that her cousin might even wish the loathsome man dead. And, Serena thought grimly, she not only had dismissed Pembrose from her mind during the past few tense days, but had given almost no consideration to Abigail's horrifying tale.

She was still dwelling on her cousin when she returned to her bedroom. It hurt to think that Abigail had not confided in her; it also hurt her pride that she'd been so unaware of what was happening around her. Her self-chastisement was interrupted by Abigail, who rapped only once before entering. She wore a madras shawl over her indigo blue dress and though she seemed in complete control, the green eyes were troubled.

"I've just been to see Yancy," she said, sitting on the bed and removing her shawl. "He agrees he must leave town as soon as possible. He's still weak, but insists he can manage." Abigail paused, suddenly looking very bleak. "You must help him. Tonight, while I'm on the hayride with the others."

Serena swiveled on the bench in front of the dressing table. "*I* must help him? But why?"

It was as difficult for Abigail to seek help as it was for Serena to be expected to give it. But just having reproached herself for being self-absorbed, and having been hurt because Abigail had not sought her aid during her earlier time of distress, Serena stood up and waved her hand. "Never mind, of course I'll help. What do you want me to do?"

Abigail's eyelids closed for just a moment, as if in relief. "Yancy needs a change of clothes—Matt's probably, he's not as large, but he'll do. Yancy also needs a gun."

Serena couldn't suppress a shudder, but she nodded. "Papa will never miss one from his collection. At least not right away. When should he leave?"

"The eight-fourteen to Boston would be just right. We'll be on the hayride then so that I can direct everyone in the opposite part of town. Just get him to the depot area. He can jump aboard as the train pulls out."

Serena regarded Abigail with skepticism. She had not seen Yancy since the previous day, and while he had improved considerably, she couldn't imagine he'd be able to clamber aboard a moving train. "It sounds too risky," she declared and began pacing the bedroom. Abruptly, she stopped by the commode where the large china pitcher and basin stood. "Brant—he's supposed to leave for Boston tonight. We'll ask him to help."

Abigail didn't look directly at Serena. "I already did. He's gone. At least," she amended, "he's not at the hotel this morning."

The slanted brown eyes momentarily raked Abigail. So she had considered Serena only as second choice in helping Yancy Clarke escape. But Abigail read her thoughts and also stood up, laying a delicate but firm hand on Serena's arm. "I agree, it *is* risky, it may even cost Yancy his life. That's why I went to Brant. A man could manage this much better than either of us. As for wondering why I'm not going with Yancy, I can't, not just now. Nor can I explain—it pertains to matters I mentioned earlier that have nothing to do with me, really. And I would help Yancy myself except that I have pleaded illness, real and feigned, for so long, I sense that the family—especially Mandy—is beginning to get suspicious." She took a deep breath, pulled her hand away, and turned to the window which looked out at the peaceful vista of Pleasant Street. "Besides, I don't think I could do it, at least not effectively. I would be too concerned, too cautious, too . . . much in love."

Serena stared at the small, graceful silhouette framed by the French voile curtains. Abigail's words both surprised and baffled her. Yet, when she thought them through, Serena began to understand: Even the cool, composed Abigail might allow the loving protectiveness she felt for Yancy Clarke to stand in the way of thinking swiftly and acting prudently.

"So you do love him," Serena said at last and sounded rather lame.

Abigail turned, smiling faintly. "Of course. I wouldn't have married him if I didn't love him."

"Of course." Serena shook her head, as if to clear away the conflicting thoughts and ideas which seemed to be pummeling her brain. "All right," she said, forcing herself to grapple with the situation in the most efficient manner possible. "I'll get the clothes and the ... gun. It'll take us at least twenty minutes to reach the depot since Yancy can't hurry. You must see that the hay-ride is set for no later than seven-thirty."

Abigail nodded. "I suggested a supper afterwards. At Pembertons'."

"Good. Oh, boots—Yancy must wear a down-easterner's boots. Those Texas hand-tooled ones won't do."

Abigail pulled a face. "He wouldn't give up his boots—even if his life depended on it." Her laugh was but an echo of its usual musical, untrammeled sound. "I was afraid he'd even wear them in bed. But he didn't."

Serena regarded her cousin's wistful expression with unabashed embarrassment. To further disconcert her, she had a sudden image of Brant's black-booted feet, casually stretched out on the braided rug in the parlor. And suddenly she wondered why he was not at the hotel and if that meant he'd already left town without bothering to say good-bye.

The past two days had been quite warm for September. Late that afternoon, it had grown very close and the clouds had begun to gather on the horizon toward the sea. Matt had talked about canceling the hayride, but Abigail had teased him, saying that a brief thunderstorm would only add excitement to the chase. Clarence Prendergast, beardless and round-faced, had diffidently begged Serena to join them.

"I've not felt well today," she told him, trying to look languorous from her place on the sofa. "It may be this unseasonable heat."

Clarence pouted, his features as unformed as a baby's. Then he launched into one of his scientific explanations about why the weather was unusual and how the pattern would change come the fall equinox. Serena hoped he took her bored expression for physical discomfort.

The thunder began to roll in the distance not ten minutes after the little party had left the Farrar house. By seven-forty, the rain was pelting the walkway between the garden and the dollhouse. Serena was upset at first, but then realized the bad weather would keep most people inside.

Yancy was wearing a heavy wool jacket Matt had discarded the previous winter and the Western wide-brimmed hat had been replaced by a knit watchcap. He seemed fit and capable of traveling.

They followed the railroad line toward the depot, walking slowly and in virtual silence. Yancy's big shambling frame seemed to move

with effort, and when a gust of wind whipped the trees on both sides
of the track, he swayed against Serena.

"Are you all right?" she asked in alarm, quaking under his weight
and the force of the wind.

"Yes, ma'am," he replied, the gray eyes half-hidden by the heavy
lids. "Just a mite taken aback."

They resumed walking, more slowly this time. Serena strained to
see the clock in the depot's short, stout wooden tower, but the leaves
were blowing so hard they obliterated everything from view. Lightning
crackled close by, making Serena jump as it illuminated their immediate surroundings—and themselves. As the rain streamed down
so hard that Serena couldn't see more than six inches in front of her,
she felt Yancy stumble at her side and catch his breath.

"Damn," she heard him breathe, stopping to put a hand over his
face. "I've got to jump aboard that train somehow."

"Yancy," Serena said firmly, "you can't go chasing a moving train.
If you're going to get out of Brunswick, you'll have to do it the usual
way."

The gray eyes regarded her questioningly. "No . . . There's no way
I can go into the depot . . . The stationmaster is the one who talked to
whoever saw me."

"Never mind. Just do what I say." Serena propped Yancy's elbow
with her hand and guided him along the tracks. At last she could
make out the depot clock; it read exactly eight o'clock. The platform
was deserted, though the wind was starting to die down and the rain
was already letting up. The spidery lightning which rent the evening
sky was now farther away, toward Harpswell.

Serena looked in every direction; only the waiting room seemed
occupied, with some half-dozen people inside. The rain ran in rivulets
along the edge of the platform but now that the wind had let up, the
air seemed fresh and mild. Serena's summer cloak was soaking wet
and very heavy. Her thick coiled hair had long since tumbled down
inside the sodden hood. She moved to the shelter of the freight room
door, Yancy following with slow, heavy footsteps. "Stay here," she
told him as he wiped drops of water from his beard. "I'll go get us
tickets to . . . to Boston, I suppose."

"Have you money?" he inquired, looking down at her from the
half-hidden gray eyes. "I don't."

She felt for the leather drawstring purse inside her cloak. "I've
enough. I'll be right back."

Nervously, she entered the waiting room. Hector Chadwick, who
had worked at the station for over forty years, was rolling a cigarette
behind the counter. He looked up and stared with surprise at Serena.

"Miss Farrar," he said in his raspy old voice, "what might you be doing here at such an hour?"

The buck-toothed baggage boy glanced up; so did the brakeman who had been dozing on a bench. The trio of passengers, all men of middle age and dressed like lumberjacks, stopped talking to observe the newcomer.

Serena put a finger to her lips, gathered her courage and her wits, and tried to smile engagingly. "I'm eloping, Mr. Chadwick. To Boston. I need two one-way tickets."

Hector raised the cigarette paper to his lips and licked with great thoroughness. His job was more than a source of income; it was also a veritable fountain of information about the comings and goings of Brunswick inhabitants. "Well. I'll be. Are you sure about taking a big step like this one, Miss Farrar?"

"Oh, very sure. But my parents aren't. Though," she added as she saw the flicker of disapproval pass across Hector's wrinkled face, "they'll realize I'm doing the right thing." She opened her purse and started to take out the money. "How much?"

"You paying for the wedding, too?" Hector looked more negative than ever.

"No. No, this is my dowry." She tried to keep the smile in place but felt her lips tremble. The clock behind Hector said five minutes after eight.

Hector was shaking his head slowly while he fumbled for a match. "I don't know, Miss Farrar, you're not the first runaway bride I've seen in my time. Seems to me these things don't always work out so well. Where's the groom?"

"He's with our belongings. Please, Mr. Chadwick, how much?" Serena's legs were beginning to shake and she felt faintly dizzy. After the buffeting wind and rain, the station, with its glowing pot-bellied stove and bright lights and prying eyes seemed insufferably warm and closed in.

The cigarette paper spurted flame as Hector puffed vigorously. "Well, it's not my business, though I'd be able to give you better advice if I knew who your intended was." Seeing Serena's stonelike expression, Hector sighed, picking a piece of tobacco from his lower lip. "It's eight-fifty for the both of you. And good luck, that's all I can say."

Serena counted out the coins and took the tickets from Hector. With great effort, she walked back to the door which led to the platform, ignoring the stares of the onlookers. In the distance, she could hear the whistle of the incoming train and felt a sudden sense of relief. Yancy was still standing in the freight room doorway; he hardly seemed to have moved since she'd left him.

"In case anyone asks, we're eloping," she whispered as the brakeman emerged from the station. "Are you sure you're all right? You look . . . tired."

"So do you," he drawled and managed a vague sort of smile.

Through the heavy rain, the locomotive light shone hazily down the track. The train had slowed and was inching its way toward the platform. The three lumberjacks and the baggage boy had come outside now, all of them cursing the weather. Serena and Yancy began to edge slowly out of the shadows just as the engine came to a halt.

Only two passengers got off. The conductor bade them a hearty good-night and waved his hand at the lumberjacks who clambered aboard. An unexpected, powerful gust of wind caught at Serena's cloak, almost knocking her down. Yancy grabbed her arm, slipped in a puddle, and just managed to right himself.

Marcus's revolver slipped from Yancy's belt and thudded onto the platform. "Damn," Yancy murmured but before he could bend down to retrieve it, the doors of the station flew open and Sheriff Scott stood outlined against the light.

"Stop! Stop or I'll shoot!" His own gun was in his hand, pointed directly at Yancy who stood only ten feet away.

Yancy and Serena both froze; the sheriff's two deputies were right behind him. From somewhere which seemed like a long way off Serena heard what sounded like a deep sigh of resignation. She turned slightly and saw Yancy put his hands up over his head. And then she rebelled, not knowing if it were for Yancy or herself or injustice in general.

"Sheriff," she called out in a voice which was amazingly strong and clear, "you have no right to interfere! I'm eloping!"

The slight hesitation on the sheriff's part was all Serena needed. She reached down and picked up the revolver, ignoring its weight, hefting it in front of her and taking direct aim at Sheriff Scott and his men. "You won't shoot me, Sheriff. But I might shoot you. I'm tired of being thwarted. Now please go away and leave us to our wedding."

Scott still held his gun pointed at Yancy but he looked more puzzled than threatening. "You mean to tell me you're marrying an outlaw? Have you lost your mind, young lady?"

"He's not an outlaw, you don't even know him. He's a French-Canadian fur trapper. He can't speak English." The gun was growing unbearably heavy in Serena's slim hands. She knew she couldn't keep up this pretense much longer.

"I tell you what," Scott said as the train let out a huge gasp of steam, "if you let me talk to you both for just a couple of minutes, I'll let you go ahead. I came down here to see if the storm had damaged the tracks and Hector told me about your plans. I'm not saying you're not telling the truth, Miss Farrar, but now that I see this fellow, it seems to me he looks a lot like Yancy Clarke's description. But if he can say a couple of French words, I'll let you both go. I wouldn't be doing my duty as an officer of the law if I did any less."

Serena had run out of ruses. She was also running out of strength. Yet she could not give in. The revolver was beginning to shake; it was difficult to catch her breath. And she was completely unprepared for Yancy Clarke's reaction: *"Je t'aime, ma cherie. Tu a mon coeur toujours."*

The sheriff and his deputies gaped; so did the conductor and the brakeman. Scott's own gun wavered and Serena finally let her weapon fall to her side. She was struggling to speak in a casual manner when Brant Parnell strode out onto the platform and stopped to stare at the strange tableau. "What is this, the Boston train or Bull Run?"

"I'm eloping with Pierre," Serena answered. "Sheriff Scott seems to think my fiance is Yancy Clarke."

Brant never changed his expression as he glanced from Serena to the sheriff to Yancy and back to Serena again.

"Oh, damnation, Sheriff, poor Pierre's had enough trouble with the Farrars as it is." Brant slapped Yancy on the shoulder. "Sorry, old pal, I knew they'd send someone after you two but I still think you're doing the right thing. Right, *mes amis?*"

Scott and his deputies were exchanging bewildered glances. "I take it you know this man, Captain?" Scott finally asked.

"Slightly. As rivals know each other. But I'm a good loser, I'll go drown my sorrows in some seedy tavern east of Java. Well, is it all aboard or is Serena going to take a potshot as a farewell gesture?"

The sheriff conferred briefly with his men in low, muffled voices. Though the wind had subsided again, Serena began to shiver uncontrollably. Gratefully, she let Brant take the gun out of her hand.

"All right," said Scott with a mixture of reluctance and relief. "It still sounds crazy to me but so does everything the younger generation does these days." He touched his hat and motioned to his men to go back into the station. Yancy gave Serena his arm and helped her climb aboard the train.

Brant followed them and before they had settled into their seats, the locomotive had begun to chug off down the tracks.

The handful of passengers who were in their car had been watching with anxious, terrified fascination. But no one dared ask the newcomers what had happened. Brant, noting that Yancy seemed to have used up his reserves, steered the Texan into an empty double seat where he could sprawl out and sleep. But before she sat down, Serena could not resist asking the question which obsessed her: "Yancy," she whispered, "where did you learn to speak French?"

The weary, heavy-lidded eyes regarded her with amusement. "That's all I know. Abigail taught me." He watched the sudden compassion on her face for just a few seconds before he dropped off to sleep.

Chapter 5

SERENA HAD NOT been in Boston for almost five years. The city fascinated her with its Bulfinch-designed statehouse dome, the handsome brick houses in Louisburg Square, the Old North Church, the bustle of traffic in the business section, and the contrasting quiet of the Common and the Garden just a few streets away.

There would, however, be no sight-seeing this time. The connecting train for New Bedford would pull out in less than half an hour. Yancy Clarke was heading west, to a still undisclosed destination. His train was already in the station.

Brant had warned both Serena and Yancy that it was possible they would be met by law enforcement officials at the depot. If Sheriff Scott had spoken to Marcus Farrar, the story of Serena's supposed elopement would be shattered. The only chance Yancy had to get away without further trouble was if the sheriff had decided he'd had enough for one night and had gone home to bed. And if he believed Serena, that was probably what he would have done. Meddling in the Farrar family's affairs could prove costly.

Yancy had slept straight through until the train began its slow stop into Boston just after nine in the morning. He was looking rested and seemed fit. Serena had dozed off and on, but Brant had remained awake.

Only Brant had any luggage. The three of them stood at the platform's edge as passengers and baggage carts moved briskly past them from every direction.

"So far, so good," Brant said, the blue eyes more wary than ever. "Scott must have gone home. Your train's over there, you can buy a ticket on board." Brant reached into his pocket and pulled out a worn leather wallet. "Here, take this, it'll see you through to wherever you may be going. As long as it isn't China."

Yancy hesitated; he'd accepted as much charity in the last week as he ever had in his entire life. Still, he had no choice. "I'll pay you both back. I don't know when but I will."

"We'll wait." Brant put out his hand and Yancy took it and smiled in a lazy, yet open manner. "You'd better go," Brant urged, hearing the conductor call out above the noise of the station traffic.

"So I had," Yancy agreed. He turned to Serena and reached out a huge hand to touch her cheek. "I'm not sure why the two of you folks did all this, but I got a mighty good guess." He hesitated, aware of Brant's sense of urgency lest the westbound train leave Yancy behind. "Do tell Miss Abigail to take care, you hear?"

"I will." Serena smiled warmly up at him. Yancy was such a paradox, so big and shambling and powerful and indolent and gentle— and yet possibly violent. She scarcely knew him but she felt a surprising sense of kinship. But then he was family. On impulse she reached up to hug him, her chin brushing his beard. "Good-bye, Yancy. Good luck."

He chuckled softly, gave a vague sort of wave to them both, and ambled off toward his train just as it began to move. Serena and Brant watched until Yancy managed to haul himself aboard the next to last car and disappear from view.

Rain showers chased the southbound train out of Boston all the way to Brockton. It was Brant's turn to doze for a while after they started the last half of their journey and Serena watched the gentle countryside with fascination. It began to occur to her that she had very likely cut herself off from her family. She could not imagine either of her parents being anything less than horrified by her complicity in hiding Pembrose Stanhope's assailant. And the mere idea of menacing Sheriff Scott with a gun was sufficient cause for Lydia to disown her younger daughter.

"Oh, Brant, what have I done?" she suddenly wailed as the train seemed to tilt precariously close to the edge of a large lake. "I think I ruined my whole life!"

Brant had just awakened from a half-hour nap. He sat up, hat tilted back on his head, blue eyes trying to adjust to a sudden burst of sunlight. "I thought that was what you intended to do." He shifted his long legs and grimaced. "Who did they build this train for anyway, circus midgets?"

Serena had heard only the first half of Brant's remarks. She stared straight ahead, seeing but not taking in the papier-mache roses on the hat worn by an elderly lady in the next seat. "Did I?" she asked more of herself than Brant. "Is that what I've done?"

"It looks like it." Brant checked his watch. "We should get to New Bedford in another hour. God, I'm starving!"

Serena was suddenly angered by Brant's ready acceptance of her plight. "It's one thing to have plans and dreams which ought to work out," she said heatedly, "but it's something else to have your family turn against you. And they will, I know it. Abigail's in for it, too."

"Abigail will manage just fine and dandy from what I've seen of her," Brant asserted. "You will, too, if you don't lose your head. I'm not even convinced your parents won't forgive you. At least your father."

Serena vaguely noted a group of small children who were standing outside a neat white farmhouse waving at the passengers. Perhaps Brant was right, perhaps her father might even find something admirable in what she had done. Serena smiled faintly at Brant, noting the strong jawline which needed a shave. "I was stunned when I saw you at the station. I thought you'd left town."

"No, I didn't come back to Brunswick with your father and brother. As a shirttail relation of the Stanhopes, I decided it would be fitting for me to visit the judge in Livermore Falls and inquire about his son. Unfortunately, his idea of consolation is to drink large amounts of your father's whiskey. I didn't get back to Brunswick until early last evening."

Serena felt strangely mollified; at least Brant hadn't deliberately avoided making a formal farewell. "If you hadn't come along, I thought Yancy was going to be hauled off and I'd be arrested as his accomplice. You were very quick to figure it all out."

"It wasn't very hard," he answered dryly. "My biggest worry was that Yancy would get pneumonia and we'd have to take him to New Bedford. My Stanhope sister-in-law would have been put out with me. Even more than she usually is."

"Peggy?" Serena saw Brant nod as she stifled a sneeze. The rigors of the previous night's storm apparently had brought on a cold. "Oh, my," Serena exclaimed suddenly, shielding her eyes from the sun which was peering out from behind the scudding clouds, "now what shall I do? Take the return train home?"

"What?" Brant sat up straight, banging his knees against the seat in front of them which caused the sharp-nosed woman to stare back from under her rose-covered hat. "Don't be silly, Serena. You eloped, remember?"

The slanted brows came close together. "I seem to be missing a groom," she remarked with a grimace. "Do you think my parents will believe I went to Boston to trap muskrat?"

Brant regarded Serena as if she were somewhat dull-witted. "Your groom is at your side. Would you settle for a gopher?"

The papier-mache roses bobbed in the seat up ahead. Serena motioned for Brant to speak more quietly. "Don't talk nonsense," she hissed. "I've never consented to marry you!"

Brant shrugged. "I never asked," he said offhandedly. "But," he went on, grimacing as the cluster of roses edged closer against the upholstered seat, "I'll sweeten the pot a little. What about a job on the *New Bedford Mercury* instead of the *Springfield Republican?*"

The brown eyes grew wide under the slanted brows. "You mean

the paper your brother works for?" Serena licked her lips and shoved the hair off her forehead with her hand. "Are you saying that if I marry you, you'll get me a job on the *Mercury?*"

"It's a fine paper, used to be owned by the Lindsey family until Ben the Younger went to Brazil last summer. Kirk has some reservations about the new owners, but he thinks they'll work out." Brant paused, watching Serena's little nose all but twitch at the prospect. "Well? Do you smell printer's ink?"

Her head jerked up suddenly, eyeing him squarely. "I smell a rat. Is this some plot you and my father concocted?"

Brant looked as innocent as possible for a man steeped in cynical experience. "Hell, no." He paused as a young couple with twin boys moved past them down the aisle. The sun withdrew behind a heavy gray cloud bank as their route took them close to Buzzard's Bay and New Bedford. "See here, Serena," Brant said with a touch of impatience and a glare at the sharp-nosed profile which he glimpsed between the gap in the seats ahead, "even if everybody in Brunswick knows by now that Yancy isn't a French fur trapper, your reputation is sullied, to say the least. Old Chadwick doesn't know I wasn't the future groom for sure. Even the sheriff may think it was all a ruse of some kind. Everybody will be so confused they won't know who was marrying who. But what matters is that you marry *somebody* before your mother succumbs to a case of town gossip."

Serena leaned back against the upholstered seat. Everything was indeed a muddle, including her own future. But Brant was right about one thing—she could never face Brunswick—or her parents—again unless she made good on her claim of elopement. And if Brant lived up to his promise to get her a job on the *Mercury,* she would get her dearest wish after all. Becoming Mrs. Parnell suddenly didn't seem like the worst of all possible fates.

"I'll consider it," Serena said with a smile. "Given time, I might be able to sort out everything you've said."

Brant scowled and pulled out his watch. "It's five after nine. You have not quite ten hours to make up your mind. The minister at the Bethel performs evening wedding ceremonies at seven on weeknights."

The papier-mache roses jutted half a foot above the seat. Two small eyes stared at Serena and Brant before darting away. "You old biddy!" gasped Serena and flushed. She twisted in her seat to look at Brant but sneezed loudly before she could utter another word. "Damn!" she said between clenched teeth, holding one hand over her nose while she groped for a handkerchief.

Brant pulled out his own, handing it to her with a sardonic expression. "Don't tell me you're going to claim to be too ill to consummate our union tonight?" he asked in a low, droll voice.

Serena felt her flush grow even deeper and wondered if she were running a fever. "This is insane," she whispered, pausing to blow her nose with an unladylike, trumpeting sound. "We can't get married so quickly! That in itself will cause scandal!"

"Which will be easily disproved when no baby appears within the calculated period of time," Brant reminded her. He leaned forward, a hand on her knee. "Why argue about it? You're getting exactly what you want—and me, as well."

Serena was about to declare that she didn't want Brant, just the newspaper job. But the strong clasp of his fingers on her flesh caused her to falter; if she were going to have to struggle to remain single while still battling to begin her career, the cards—as Brant might say—were stacked against her. And certainly Brant Parnell was a far better choice than Clarence Prendergast.

"My father always gets his way," Serena said bitterly. "He may not have arranged things, but he'll surely be pleased."

Brant sank back at an angle in the seat, trying to find room for his long legs without letting them block the aisle. "No doubt," he commented with a yawn. "But," he added, a spark in the sea-blue eyes, "have you considered that we'll please each other?"

For over forty years, Seamen's Bethel had been the place of worship for New Bedford mariners and their families. The solid, unimposing wooden structure stood on Johnny Cake Hill, its jutting pulpit carved in the shape of a ship's prow. How spare it is, thought Serena, her eyes not quite focusing properly in the dim, lantern-lighted aisle of the church. Fleetingly, yet with regret, she remembered Cecelia's lavish wedding at St. Paul's with its beamed ceiling and whitewashed walls. It had been high summer, with clusters of gladioli and marigolds and dahlias festooning the pews and flanking the altar. Cecelia, in miles of tulle, had carried three dozen white roses; Serena, as maid of honor, had almost as many yellow roses to match her hand-stitched gown. The reception, held on the lawn of the Farrar house, had hosted more than four hundred people who exclaimed over the extravagant feast laid out on trestle tables. The guests had danced to a string quartet from Bowdoin College, the sun had smiled down on bride and groom, while Marcus Farrar beamed his blessing on the finest wedding money could buy.

How different this ceremony was, with the empty pews, the echoing voice of the sunken-cheeked minister, the fog creeping in from Buzzard's Bay to touch the Bethel's square tower, and the little nosegay of chrysanthemums Serena held in her unsteady hands. Her wedding dress, purchased ready-made that afternoon in a New Bedford dry goods store, was of cream-colored cotton with a flounce of lace at the scooped neckline and hem. Brant wore the same black outfit he'd had on when he came to call less than a week ago in Brunswick. It didn't seem possible, Serena thought, shaking her head suddenly and aware that the minister was watching her with curiosity. Had so much happened in so short a time to change her life forever?

But it had. She and Brant faced the minister at the front of the church, repeating their vows while her new in-laws, Kirk and Peggy Parnell, stood up for them. She had met them only moments before entering the church and scarcely recalled what either of them looked like. Kirk was almost as tall as his brother and Peggy had reddish hair. But if Serena saw them on the street, she wouldn't recognize them.

In less than ten minutes, the ceremony was over. Brant slipped the plain gold band on Serena's finger and gave her a perfunctory kiss. Kirk shook his brother's hand. Peggy kissed Serena's cheek and uttered effusive if unmemorable good wishes. The registry was signed, Kirk was dispatched to send a telegram to the senior Farrars in Brunswick, and Peggy waved Brant and Serena off in the jitney hired for the occasion.

The house on Cove Road had belonged to Brant's parents. Both had been dead for almost ten years, and when Kirk and Peggy were first married, they had moved in to set up housekeeping. It was a white clapboard two-story home with a widow's walk and a large front porch. Comfortable but unimposing, Brant had described it that afternoon. When Peggy had prodded Kirk to purchase a grander home for their growing family, Brant had moved in and hired a couple named Tilford to care for the house while he was away.

Serena wore a forced expression of pleasure as she greeted Mr. and Mrs. Tilford in the narrow hallway. Gaunt and expressionless, they seemed more like twins than husband and wife. If they were surprised that Captain Parnell had brought home a bride, their reaction was carefully suppressed. After a few polite words, they withdrew, saying that a cold supper was waiting in the master bedroom.

"That means chicken and pickled pears," Brant told Serena as he guided her up the stairs. "Let's hope Mrs. Tilford felt the occasion worthy of wine."

She had. A dusty bottle of tawny port sat on the aged dressing table next to a plate of cold fried chicken. Serena glanced about apprehensively, noting that if either the late Mrs. Parnell or Peggy had made their feminine marks upon the bedroom, Brant had managed to stamp it as his own. A converted ship's lantern stood on the nightstand, its light wavering feebly. The big four-poster bed was covered

with an intricately pieced but worn and faded quilt. The only adorn-
ment on the bureau was a piece of scrimshaw. One wall displayed a
very good French landscape, the other, what Serena considered an
ugly sketch of a clipper ship.

"It's usually not this tidy," Brant admitted, taking off his frock
coat and making a conscious effort to hang it carefully over the back
of the room's only chair. "But Mrs. Tilford must have spun around
in her tracks cleaning today." He frowned and ran a hand through his
crinkly dark hair. "This is actually a hell of a place for a picnic. Want
to sit on the bed?"

Serena all but jumped. "The bed?" She gazed around once more,
as if she were hoping a second inventory of the room would magically
reveal a set of chairs and a table.

Brant pulled a droll face. "There's the floor, of course."

"The bed's . . . fine." Serena turned away to pick up the chicken
and the dish of pickled pears. "We'll put these things on the nightstand."

From behind her, she heard Brant chuckle. "Aren't you going to
take off your cape, Serena? Or don't you plan to stay?"

"Oh!" Serena set the food back down on the dresser. Mechanically,
she began to undo the clasp of her light woolen summer cape. But
her fingers were trembling and she cursed under her breath.

Brant ambled over to where she stood by the dresser. "Here, let
me." His grin was off-center, half-teasing, half-encouraging. But though
his own hands were steady and confident, the clasp would not come
undone. Brant's grin faded and the black eyebrows drew together.
"It's stuck. What did you do, sew yourself into your clothes?"

"Certainly not!" Serena felt herself flush. "I was so rushed putting
it on at the dry goods store, I must have done it wrong." She backed
away from him, attacking the clasp with renewed vigor. Her efforts,
however, resulted only in flustering her further and she began to
sneeze.

"Oh, hell!" Brant whipped out his handkerchief and gave it to
Serena. "Can you pull the damned thing over your head?"

"No!" Serena wiped her nose angrily, the brown eyes snapping at
Brant, the lower lip in full pout. "I mean, I don't know, I've never
tried it!"

Brant shifted his weight from one leg to the other and sighed. "I
suggest we try it now, Serena. I know modesty should be respected
in a woman, but making love to a fully-clothed wife somehow lacks
excitement."

For the first time, the impact of being a married woman struck
Serena with hurricane force. The day had been so filled with activity,
her mind so glutted with new impressions, her body so fatigued from

the flight to New Bedford, that she had not had time to reflect seriously upon anything but the legal implications of her union with Brant. But now, as he stood before her, hands on hips, booted feet planted firmly on the old rose-patterned carpet, and wary eyes disturbingly determined, Serena recognized the source of her anxiety. "Don't shirk your marital duties," her mother had admonished Serena and Cecelia and Abigail. "Submit and think of pleasant things."

But Cecelia had seemed an eager bride and Abigail had wistfully mentioned Yancy in bed. There was the couple who had run away to Augusta, too, with the young girl expressing delight over the nuptial bed. But, Serena reminded herself, in all three cases, there had been a decided similarity: Each of the brides apparently had been in love.

Resignedly, Serena started to pull the cloak over her head. But the clasp miraculously opened. Startled, Serena let it fall to the floor and stood staring at Brant, who was gazing at the ceiling in mock surprise.

"I'll get the food," Serena said hastily and started to turn again toward the dresser. But Brant reached out to take her by the arm.

"A cold supper doesn't get any colder," he said wryly. His glance moved from the wisp of a veil which sat atop the coils of thick brown hair, to the hint of bosom which swelled above the lace-edged neckline, to the wide sash which encircled the slender waist, and down to the toes of her shiny new brown buckled shoes. Slowly, he extricated the veil from her hair and reached around her to place it on the dresser. His hands lifted her face toward his and he kissed her very gently. "You don't understand much of this, do you?" he asked quietly. Seeing the mute answer of her helpless gaze, he kissed her again, this time more lingeringly, forcing her lips apart, making her pulses quicken and her arms hold him tight.

Serena allowed him to probe her mouth with his tongue, felt his hands move searchingly from her back to her waist to the curve of her buttocks. But within her brain, a small voice was questioning their ardor: Was this love or merely lust? Was their precipitous marriage ceremony binding or just a sham? Except for a few kisses, where was the romantic aura of a courtship which led to lifelong happiness?

With a suddenness that caught Brant off-guard, Serena pulled free and dodged out of his arms. Her hair had come loose, tumbling about her shoulders. She felt slightly feverish and wondered if her cold had worsened. Backing away, she braced herself against the dressing table, taking heavy, deep breaths and trying to regain her composure.

"This isn't right, it's not real," she asserted, wishing Brant didn't look so suddenly stormy and yet mystified at the same time. Still, she told herself, he was a reasonable, practical man. "We've gone through the motions. My parents have been notified, a scandal is avoided, and Yancy is safe. I hope. Wouldn't it be better for both of us if we considered the marriage just a temporary convenience?"

Brant's strong, wide mouth clamped into a narrow line; the sea-blue eyes glinted under the black brows. The mystified expression changed to incredulity, but the anger only intensified. Serena shivered and actually flinched when Brant spoke:

"That was a real marriage, Serena," he stated in hard, clipped tones. "You understood that from the start. I don't like cheats, at cards, or at life." He took two purposeful steps toward her and stopped just a few inches from where she stood mute and motionless. "You also seem to have forgotten why we were going to be married in the first place. Your father and I have a business arrangement, remember?"

In truth, Serena had forgotten. In all the anxiety and activity of the last twenty-four hours, she had not considered the real reason why Brant had begun his courtship. Caught up in the dizzying events that had engulfed her, Serena had not thought beyond the immediacy of the moment.

"You're cruel," she blurted, holding up her hands as if to fend him off. "You don't want me, you want my father's partnership! That's vile, demeaning, even corrupt!" Serena was all but shouting.

"It's called business and I intend to do it damned near as well as your father." Brant had raised his own voice but apparently considered the possibility of the Tilfords lurking nearby. When he spoke again, it was on a lowered note. "Damn it, Serena, I don't believe you don't want me!"

The slanted brown eyes shimmered with unshed tears and the full lips trembled; Serena was desperately confused. She didn't know *what* she wanted, nor could she believe that Brant wanted *her*. Even less credible was the idea that Brant could possibly be disconcerted by her rejection of him.

"It's . . . so mixed up," she mumbled at last. "Give me time . . ."

Brant could be a patient man when the circumstances warranted it, but his reservoir of self-control had run dry. He disdained the use of force unless it was absolutely necessary; will power and persuasion were his more comfortable allies. Serena could not plumb his character deeply enough to know these things, but she sensed that the time she asked for had already ticked away. She met the steel grip of his embrace with a sudden stiffening of her body and a stifled cry of protest.

His mouth clamped down on hers, hurting the trembling lips, making the tears trickle down her cheeks. One hand was in the masses of her hair, the other pulled the back of her wedding dress apart. Serena's arms were trapped against his chest and she could hardly breathe. She felt her feet stumbling across the floor as he moved her roughly to the bed.

They went down together onto the faded quilt, and only then did he release her mouth if not her body. As they lay cross-wise on the bed, his grasp was still tight and she felt his hand against the bare flesh of her back. "Does it have to be like this?" he demanded in a fierce voice that sounded as if it belonged to a stranger.

Overcome by his strength, frightened by his anger, Serena desperately wanted to know what he was talking about. It was impossible to relate whispered innuendoes and her mother's precise account of the marital act with Brant's unleashed ardor. Given his relentless determination, Serena was tempted to surrender.

Yet until these past few weeks, she had always surrendered: to her mother, to her father, to her brother and her sister, even to Abigail. Their wills had always superseded her own. But at least they were family. Even though Brant considered himself her husband, he had no deep-rooted ties to Serena, save for the cursory wedding ceremony amid strangers in the Bethel.

The uncertainty which clouded her tearstained face was not lost on Brant. He buried his lips in the curve of her shoulder as his hands pulled the fabric of her dress and camisole down over her breasts. Serena writhed against him, feeling with shock the cold touch of his shirt studs against her bare flesh.

"I didn't consent!" she cried, but her voice was almost inaudible as she twisted about on the quilt-covered bed. If Brant heard her, he gave no sign, his lips pressing kisses along her bare upper arm, her throat, and the curve of her breast. At last he paused to look at her body. The lamp was burning low, casting deep shroudlike shadows over the bedroom. Serena recoiled as he gazed at her with that familiar bemused expression. But there was something else in his eyes this time, something different and somehow exciting. Still, Serena moved to cover herself with her hands but Brant swiftly took each wrist and pinned her arms down on the quilt. In that moment, she saw herself as never before, lying on her back, arms stretched wide, her breasts seemed to arch in high, pointed mounds, beckoning Brant's mouth.

As if mesmerized, Serena watched his dark head come down across her bosom; his tongue flicked at each breast in turn until she grew distressingly aware of how hard and tight her nipples had become. The sensation traveled down into the very core of her being, setting off an alarm of denial.

Serena tried to draw up her knees in a feeble effort to shove him away. But his grip was unbreakable. His mouth roved down to her waist and with his teeth, he tugged the skirt band of her clothing just enough to expose her navel. Again, the quick, darting motions of his tongue probed until Serena thought she would scream in protest. Her eyes were tight shut now and her arms were beginning to ache. Then, with a deliberate movement, Brant let go of her and sat up as he began to undress. Dazed, Serena watched him as he carelessly tossed the shirt onto the floor and unbuckled his belt. His shoulders were very broad, the torso more muscular than she would have imagined. But then, she told herself vaguely, she'd never thought about what Brant would look like without his clothes. Perhaps while he was taking off his trousers, she could reach the door to the hallway. But what if she did, Serena asked herself angrily; she could hardly flee half-naked through her husband's house with the Tilfords nosing about. She was powerless.

As Brant's hands moved to pull off his trousers, she closed her eyes once more. Seconds later he had hooked his fingers in her skirts, sliding them over her hips. Serena desperately tried to summon up the last remnants of her will to resist, but knew it was useless. She was trapped in this house, trapped in this bedroom, trapped in this sham of a marriage with a man who considered her not a wife but an acquisition. The only weapon Serena had was indifference. Lying rigid on the bed as Brant took off her stockings, she kept her eyes shut and prayed that the alarm she had felt reverberate through her body would strengthen her self-control.

In her innocence, she was completely unprepared for the shock of his hands between her thighs. As if by reflex, she tried to keep her legs pressed together, but it was too late. His fingers were taunting the vulnerable flesh even as his mouth explored her belly. Serena stifled a gasp but could not prevent the wild stirring of her senses.

Don't let him know, she commanded herself as he fell upon her and drove the brute strength of his masculinity into what seemed her very soul. The first thrusts were painful and jolted Serena momentarily out of her private war. Then she felt a wrenching, savage thrust which evoked a cry even her stubborn will could not subdue. Still, she welcomed the pain, certain that it would armor her against further betrayal by her body.

Serena was wrong. Within seconds, Brant's assured invasion rocked her in a dizzying motion until she felt him erupt within her as the night shattered into a thousand shimmering shards.

But though Brant had called out, Serena had kept her word. Elated with her monumental act of self-discipline and released from emotional turmoil, Serena rolled over and pressed her face against the quilt. She had won a great personal victory, and if she felt strangely empty, that was due to sheer exhaustion. Slowly, she moved her head just enough to peek out at Brant.

He was still naked, standing with his back to the bed and going through his bureau. Serena could not resist studying him for just a moment, noting how trim he was, yet how strong, and she was reminded of a fleet Baltimore clipper. To her surprise, Serena discovered she was smiling.

"Did you buy a nightgown?" Brant still had his back to her and was pulling garments out of the top drawer.

"What? Oh . . . no, I forgot." Considering how little time they'd had to shop, Serena was lucky to have come away with two dresses, underclothes, stockings, and a pair of shoes. And now one of those dresses lay ripped down the back in a pile on the floor.

"Here," said Brant, turning around and throwing a flannel nightshirt at her. "I don't wear the things unless it's twenty below so you can have it for now."

Serena blinked as she saw him completely naked for the first time. To hide her embarrassment, she hurriedly pulled the nightshirt over her head. The sleeves seemed about a foot too long and it smelled as if it had laid tucked away for years.

Brant had gone into the adjacent bathroom. Serena picked up her clothes, sorted them out, and then, for the first time, noticed with shock the bloodstains on the quilt. She'd have to scrub them away in the morning, before Mrs. Tilford came in to do the room. Serena scrambled into bed as she heard Brant open the bathroom door. He moved swiftly to the nightstand, blew out the light, and got under the covers next to Serena. She inched toward him just enough so that he could kiss her good-night.

Brant, however, was lying on his back, hands entwined behind his head. "I wasn't going to Washington until next week," he announced in a heavy, strained voice. "But I might as well leave tomorrow, if I can make the arrangements. I'll talk to Kirk about your job on the newspaper, of course."

Serena sat halfway up in bed, leaning on her elbow. "But why? I mean, now that . . ." She floundered, not knowing what she meant, but suddenly upset by Brant's detached, impersonal declaration of his change in plans.

He didn't even look at her. "You were right in the first place. We made a mistake, you and I. And in the game of life, I always cut my losses." He stretched, yawned, and rolled over, turning his back to her. "Good night, Serena."

Very slowly, Serena sank back down on the pillow. Brant's aloofness was devastating. She had grown used to his wry humor, his affable if impatient manner, his disarming candor, and, she had to admit to herself, his masculine attentions, whether they were real or feigned. Now she would be stranded in a strange city, not knowing if her parents would ever welcome her home again, abandoned in the house of a man who seemed determined to desert her. She would, of course, have her newspaper job. At least Brant had promised as much. Serena clutched the blankets up around her chin and reprimanded herself for feeling so upset. After all, it was her career which had been paramount. Now it lay within her grasp. She ought to feel triumphant.

Instead, Serena felt bewildered and distressed. In the quiet of the night, she heard Brant's deep, even breathing next to her. Through sheer force of will, Serena had kept him from realizing how he had aroused her senses. Perhaps that had been a mistake. But, she argued silently, how could she let him know her body had been ignited by his kisses and caresses? He had only possessed her because she was her father's daughter. And, she reminded herself, it was only her body which had responded. Her heart, like his own, had remained untouched.

Serena nodded once against the pillow, as if to reaffirm the rationality of her thoughts. Despite the surprising twists and turns she had taken in the past few weeks, Serena had almost reached her destination: A newspaper job lay in wait for her, possibly just hours away. She would prove herself as a writer and as a person. Freed from the smothering influence of her family, Serena had gotten what she wanted most.

She stared up into the canopy's gloom and wondered why she felt so sad.

Chapter 6

THE *NEW BEDFORD MERCURY* had been founded as a weekly newspaper in 1807 by Benjamin Lindsey Sr. His son, Benjamin Jr., had joined the paper some twenty years later and had become publisher after his father's retirement in the 1830s. By that time, the *Mercury* had become an influential daily newspaper. When Ben Jr. left the *Mercury* in the summer of 1861 to become the American consul in St. Catherine's, Brazil, the new owners, C. B. H. Fessenden and William G. Baker, took over without much money or any serious journalistic experience. But their enthusiasm and ambition satisfied Lindsey, who sailed off to South America, confident that the *Mercury* was in good hands. His optimism was further buoyed by the presence of Kirk Parnell, a diligent, talented editor.

Kirk had managed to ease Baker and Fessenden through the transition period, convincing them that the *Mercury's* lively, hopeful tone should be maintained even with a war raging through the heart of the country. Anxious to keep up the paper's standards and circulation, the new owners heeded Kirk's advice. They also acceded to his request concerning his new sister-in-law; Serena was informed that she could begin work the following Monday.

Serena, clutching at her fleecy lambs-wool scarf as the wind picked up off the mouth of the Acushnet River, was effusive in her gratitude. Kirk, however, was self-deprecating. "Brant can be very convincing. I think I've spent a lifetime trying to say no to him and I've never done it yet."

Serena threw Kirk a sidelong look. His tone was ironic, yet it contained brotherly affection. Two years younger than Brant, Kirk was an inch shorter, a trifle leaner, but almost as dark. His features were more angular and his eyes were hazel. He had an engaging, boyish grin, with little of Brant's cynical wariness, but the physical resemblance proved their mutual bloodlines.

In truth, Serena was glad of the differences: She would not want to be reminded of Brant any more than she had to be. The chilling, swift manner of his departure still rankled. He had left on the train for Washington the night after their wedding, speaking to her only in the presence of the Tilfords. He'd discussed the running of the house and the arrangements he'd made with Kirk regarding the newspaper job. And he left without saying good-bye.

Still, as she and Kirk paused along the brick walkway to lean against the iron rail and look out over the maze of masts in the harbor, Serena could not resist asking which one was Brant's.

"There," he said, pointing to a large schooner with seven masts. *"The Irish Rover.* She's a fine ship, out of Boston. But Brant wishes he'd gone into steam."

"I don't like the look of the new steamships," Serena declared, squinting against the sun. "Do you remember *The Fair Rosamonde?"* She saw Kirk nod. "My grandfather built her, she was his favorite clipper. They called her *The Rarin' Rosie* because she was so fast."

"She was lost in the North Atlantic," Kirk said, looking solemn. "I knew her captain and several members of the crew." His lips tightened for just a moment as the hazel eyes rested on Serena's face. "That was when I decided to quit the sea."

"Oh." Serena turned away, resting her hands on the cold, smooth railing. "Have you ever regretted it?"

"No. Not really. It wouldn't have been fair to Peggy and the children. For me, the newspaper is just as great a challenge."

Serena thought he sounded convincing, yet she wondered. Having grown up so close to the sea, she knew how men fell victim to its lure, and once having succumbed, could never remain on dry land forever.

"We were the fourth generation of seamen in the family," Kirk went on, taking a deep breath of salt-tinged air. "Maybe our father thought the strain was weakening, maybe he was just a good prophet." Kirk's hazel eyes narrowed into the wind as they turned away from the harbor. "He sent us both to college, Brant to Dartmouth, me to Amherst. I liked writing, I worked on the yearbook. It seemed natural to go to work for a newspaper. The *Mercury* had an opening and it was a stable paper. At least it was then."

They were passing a tall, narrow four-story house which was surrounded by a weathered wooden fence. The ghostly stalks of long-dead hollyhocks lay between the boards like mourners at a bier. A rusty anchor was propped against a large stone next to the garden gate.

Deliberately, Serena avoided looking in the direction of the Bethel and Johnny Cake Hill. Instead, she concentrated on the outline of the Whalers' Hotel, and beyond, to the well-tended homes which flanked the commercial section of New Bedford. Kirk and Peggy lived only a short distance from Brant's home on Cove Road but Serena declined their supper invitation. Peggy's openheartedness had been a great help to Serena, but she had no wish to become entwined in her in-laws' lives.

"You're sure?" Kirk asked after Serena had politely refused his offer.

"I am," she said and smiled up at him. His face seemed very open, as if the story of his life were written there for all the world to see. Yet, she noted for the first time, the hazel eyes might not be wary like Brant's, but there was something very private, almost secretive about them, as if there were a part of Kirk Parnell's soul which was shuttered from everyone but himself.

"What's wrong?" he asked, putting a hand on her arm.

Serena had not realized she was staring. "Nothing!" She laughed in a forced sort of way. "I was just hoping Peggy hadn't chosen tonight to make dumplings. You said hers were excellent."

"They are," he asserted and patted her shoulder. "She's a wonderful cook. She's a wonderful housekeeper, too, and a wonderful mother." Kirk started to laugh and shook his head. "You'll get the impression I think Peggy is quite a wonderful wife."

"I do at that," Serena said and discovered she was anxious to be alone. Kirk had never asked why she had married his brother or the reason Brant had left town so suddenly. Immersed as he was in the joys of his own domesticity, Kirk would never understand—or approve of—the marriage his brother had made. Bidding Kirk what she hoped wasn't too hasty a farewell, Serena walked briskly away in the direction of Cove Road and the home she would have to learn to call her own.

The letter had been sitting on a tiny teakwood table in the hallway. There was no mistaking Marcus Farrar's big, bold handwriting. It was jarring, however, to note that he had addressed her as "Mrs. Brant Parnell." It was the first time Serena had thought of herself in that way and her hands shook as she carried the letter into the privacy of the bedroom.

"Dear Serena," Marcus began, "Your mother and I were astonished, yet pleased, at the news that you and Captain Parnell had eloped. Much confusion ensued in the wake of your departure for reasons I won't detail herein, but upon learning what had happened from a telegram dispatched to us by Captain Parnell's brother, we were assured as to your safety and happiness. Naturally, your mother and I had hoped to give you the same kind of splendid wedding we gave Cecelia, but we'll assume you young people preferred a less elaborate ceremony and perhaps that's as well. I placed the order for your nuptial gift only this morning and as it will come from England, it may be some time before you receive it. Meanwhile, your mother, Matt, Abigail, and I all wish you every happiness in your new life as Mrs. Brant Parnell."

Serena reread the letter, this time much more slowly. Apparently, there had been enough of the truth in her flight from Brunswick to at least camouflage Yancy Clarke's escape. And even if Marcus Farrar had not been fooled, he had gotten his way about marrying Serena to Brant. Yancy, after all, was of no importance to Marcus. As for Lydia Farrar, Serena wasn't convinced that the elopement met with her mother's approval. There would be talk, which Lydia would ostensibly ignore, but which would rankle deep down, and probably require not just apologies and explanations from Serena, but a considerable amount of time before forgiveness would be granted.

But Serena wondered most about Abigail. She would, of course, carry out her role of innocent party with flair. As long as the dollhouse had been scrubbed clean, no one would ever make the connection between Abigail and Yancy Clarke. Yet under her flippant, unruffled façade, Abigail must carry the burden not just of separation from Yancy, but of not knowing where or how he fared.

Serena folded the letter and put it in the nightstand drawer. She stood there by the bed for a long time, thinking of Abigail and realizing with an unsettling awareness that she actually sympathized with her cousin, not just out of affection, but of understanding. For Serena wondered where Brant was and what he was doing, and felt her own heart grow heavy.

The completed series on the half-dozen New Bedford widows came to thirty-one handwritten pages. Serena had placed them on William Baker's desk with a sense of pride and accomplishment. She was utterly devastated to find them torn in two and pinned to her blotter with a note that said: "Too solemn. Perk these stories up and never use the word 'dead' in the *Mercury*."

An hour later, Serena was still downcast as she sat on the edge of a pier overlooking the cove while Kirk Parnell tossed bread crusts at the sea gulls. "I don't understand—how can you show these women triumphing over sorrow if you don't say their husbands died?"

Kirk gave a short laugh, for once looking almost as cynical as his older brother. "You write around it. 'While the winter winds swept Mrs. Arbuthnot's dreams out to sea...' Sentiment without sadness. Baker's doing his damnedest to follow in Ben Lindsey's footsteps. Look how optimistically we've handled the ineptitude of Union leadership. It isn't chaos in the commanding ranks, it's challenge. General Scott isn't a doddering old fool, he's a venerated hero." He tossed the last scrap of bread onto the wet sand and watched two gulls tussle for it. "I'm sorry, Serena," he said, turning to pat her shoulder. "Baker gets into these moods sometimes, he and Fessenden are still unsure of themselves. Their main concern is bringing new industry here before the town dies out along with the whaling trade."

"That's so." Serena sighed. "Do you think their campaign to arm the slaves is sound?"

"God only knows." Kirk watched a lobster boat fighting the incoming tide. It was a fine October day, though scattered clouds were gathering on the horizon. Turning to Serena, he smiled, helping her adjust the new dark green cloak she had purchased just the previous day. "I like that color on you, you look like a forest creature with that brown hair and your big eyes."

Serena smiled back at Kirk. His compliments rested easily on her, as he had a knack of phrasing them offhandedly and with more of an intent to please than to flatter. "I'm going back to the office to rewrite that damnable story," she said. "I don't want to lie awake tonight fretting about all those widows."

Kirk glanced at his watch chain. "It's almost suppertime. Don't stay too late."

"I'll stay until I'm finished," Serena asserted. "But I *have* done some good articles and I'm proud of them. I don't intend to let Will Baker's criticism upset me."

"Good for you," Kirk said and gave her a quick hug. "Remember," he added as they walked along the pier past a little shack where an elderly man was selling fresh shrimp in paper bags, "I intend to be proud of you. You're my protegee."

"I suppose I am," Serena answered with amusement and made no protest when Kirk took her hand as they headed away from the water and back into town.

"Never a day goes by that I don't feel my husband's loving shadow beside me and know his indomitable spirit guides my every step."

Serena set down her pen and reread the last sentence. Well and good for Mrs. Grosvenor to say; Serena didn't even know where her own husband was. Brant had now been gone almost a month. Perhaps he was still in Washington; government dealings could take a long time. Not that it mattered, she told herself, trying to concentrate on her scribbled notes. If and when Brant appeared in New Bedford, they would have to sort out the tangle of their lives in a way which would satisfy all parties concerned, including Serena's parents. For now, she didn't even want to contemplate what might happen.

The bells in Christ Church chimed six in the distance. Serena was alone in the *Mercury* offices, more than halfway through the new version of her widows' article. She felt that if she wrote one more word about faith, hope, and optimism, she'd fairly gag on her own treacle.

Serena didn't hear the front door open nor the light footsteps of the man who suddenly loomed over her desk. But she heard his voice and looked up in surprise. Pembrose Stanhope was smiling at her in a most unpleasant way.

"I only just learned you'd married Captain Parnell," he said in his light, smug voice. "How ironic to discover we're related through the saintly Peggy!"

The intricacies of family relationship seemed to defy Serena's mental process. But of course it was true: Peggy was a cousin of Pembrose's, and a niece to Judge Stanhope. But Peggy had a passle of aunts and uncles and cousins in New Bedford; she rarely, if ever, mentioned her Boston and Maine kinfolk.

"Distantly related," Serena pointed out, unconsciously backing away from him in her chair. "Have you come to visit Peggy and Kirk?"

Pembrose removed his hat and smoothed his pale blond hair. His countenance looked benign, with its neat, thin moustache and rather pointed nose, but the pale blue eyes were cold. "I think not," he replied agreeably enough. "I've spent the past weeks putting a puzzle together. It seems you are part of the final solution."

"I?" Serena stood up, busying her hands with the stack of papers which comprised her widows' story. "How might that be?" she inquired innocently, though the sudden pounding of her heart told her she already knew the answer.

Pembrose flicked at an imaginary piece of lint on his impeccably cut waistcoat. "A certain Mr. Yancy Clarke of Austin, Texas—I believe you know him?"

"Clarke? From Texas?" Serena licked her lips and shook her head. "I'm afraid I haven't met everyone in New Bedford yet. It just seems like it." She spread her hands in what she hoped was a disarming gesture.

"You are a passable liar, but insufficiently convincing." Pembrose put a well-manicured hand on Serena's arm. "I dont know what compelled you to go so far as to marry Brant Parnell in order to protect Yancy Clarke, but I've managed to ferret out enough information to know that's precisely what you did. I also know it had something to do with your charming cousin, Abigail." He gave Serena's arm a sudden, hard jerk that almost upset her balance. "Do you recall what happened to Abigail?"

Serena stood completely still and met Pembrose's menacing gaze head-on. "Get out. Get out before I have you thrown out!"

Pembrose merely threw back his head and laughed. "Nonsense, there's no one here but ourselves. I already did a bit of stalking from the outside." In three quick strides, he moved around the desk to stand toe-to-toe with Serena.

"The bullet wound in my shoulder is healed," he said, his voice low and controlled. "But no man—or woman—gets the best of Pembrose Stanhope. And," he added, giving Serena's arm a vicious yank, "that includes you." He clutched her shoulders in a brutal grip, driving her up against the wall which was covered by a large map of New Bedford and Fairhaven. Serena tried to kick, scratch, claw—but Pembrose's strength was no match for her own; he was forcing her down to the floor and as she leaned as far away from him as she could, the Spanish comb in her hair caught the flimsy map and ripped the paper down the center.

Serena felt her head bump on the floor as Pembrose held both her wrists with one hand, the other seizing her bombazine dress by the collar and tearing it wildly. In panic and horror, she saw the demonic look in his pale eyes and knew she was fighting a madman.

"You are as stubborn as your silly cousin," Pembrose said between clenched teeth. "Perhaps my seed will bear living fruit in you. Abigail failed me!" He raised his hand high and brought it sharp against her cheek; Serena saw flashes like sparks and tasted blood in her mouth.

Pembrose had now ripped away the chemise, leaving her breasts exposed. He laughed low, smirking appreciatively and nodding just once. "Your teats are too delectable for that arrogant swine you married, Mrs. Parnell. Do they taste as sweet as they look?" In answer to his own question, he pounced upon her, burying his face between her breasts. Serena was whimpering, pleading, sobbing, and shaking. He had let go of her wrists but they were pinioned under him. She felt his hand pulling at her skirt band, tugging and tearing until the fabric gave way. He straddled her thighs, his fingers now kneading her belly.

"Flat," he murmured. "How convenient—as if you were waiting for me to fill you." He uttered that low laugh again. "I wonder," he mused, "what words are needed to coax the Farrar and Beaulieu women into submission?"

Serena had been working to free her hands but his knees pinned them to her sides. She stared up at him, blood trickling from her lips, head aching, breasts sore, heart pounding. "You're a monster," she gasped. "A fiend!"

Pembrose laughed, this time on a haughty note which seemed to reverberate off the walls. The diversion gave Serena her chance: Drawing upon every ounce of strength she possessed, Serena lifted her entire body, catching Pembrose off-balance. The laughter died on his lips as his shoulder struck the desk. Her arms free, Serena went for his face, clawing at his eyes with one hand, reaching blindly for the sharp-edged pica rule which lay somewhere under the litter of foolscap paper. Pembrose cursed obscenely, grabbing at her waist; now standing, Serena swerved away, finally feeling the pica rule between her fingers.

But Pembrose had also scrambled to his feet, curses still raining from a mouth twisted by venomous fury. Backing toward the door, Serena lashed out with the steel rule.

"Don't come near me!" she shrieked. "I'll kill you! I swear it!" Her naked breasts heaved and her hair streamed down her face. Pembrose lunged at her, ducking to avoid the wild slashing of the sharp steel rule. His foot skidded on the oak floor and he crashed into the wall behind Serena. She whirled around just as a sickening crash rent the air.

In his way, Ben Lindsey Sr. had been a sentimental man. He had kept the first printer's stone from the *Mercury*'s maiden edition as a souvenir. For well over half a century, it had rested on a ledge in the editorial office, a thick, heavy, rough-edged monument to freedom of the press. Now it lay beside the motionless form of Pembrose Stanhope. One horrified glance told Serena he was dead.

She had no idea how long she stood there clasping the pica rule with one hand, the other clutching her skirts around her waist. A few seconds, perhaps, but it had seemed like hours. She was barely conscious of Kirk Parnell opening the door and exclaiming in shock. Only when he cradled her in his arms did she seem to rouse from her stupor and realize that he was trying as hard to avoid the sight of her bare breasts as the sight of the body of the man on the office floor.

Dropping the pica rule with a clatter, Serena fumbled at her clothes, trying to cover herself. In stammering phrases, she recounted the terrifying story to Kirk, gathering her wits sufficiently to omit the part about Yancy Clarke and Abigail.

"Good God," Kirk murmured, still holding her close. "I only met Pembrose once, at our wedding. He seemed a bit . . . unbalanced even then."

"He was obsessed," Serena declared, at last feeling her composure return. Gently, she pulled away from Kirk, but still kept her torn dress clasped tightly over her bosom. "What shall we do now?"

Kirk forced himself to look at Pembrose's body. A small puddle of blood was drying on the floor next to the dead man's head. "We could throw him off one of the piers," Kirk said, but sounded dubious. He frowned and turned back to Serena. "I wish I'd come sooner. I was uneasy about you staying so late. I might have gotten here in time if I hadn't dropped off some of Peggy's peach jam at Mrs. Wilson's."

"It's all right, you couldn't have known." Serena attempted a reassuring smile, but her lips felt stiff.

They both jumped as the door opened again. This time it was Will Baker, his square jaw and boxlike body going rigid at the sight before him. Serena was somewhat more coherent as she repeated her story. Will listened intently, the occasional tic over his right eye more apparent than usual.

"I'll be damned," he said at last on a low whistle, gazing with revulsion at Pembrose Stanhope's body. He shook his head at Serena and made a vague gesture as if he wanted to offer comfort, but was held at bay by her disheveled state. "Well. I'll have to talk with Fess about this. Does anybody besides us know Pembrose Stanhope was in town?"

Serena and Kirk glanced at each other. "Peggy didn't," Kirk said at last. "But they weren't close. The last time she mentioned him was a year or two ago when he sent us a creche from Mexico for Christmas." Kirk frowned as if it were impossible to reconcile his children's cherished nativity set with the brutal man who lay dead on the office floor.

Will rubbed his square jaw and looked thoughtful. "Some of the other Stanhopes might know. Still," he went on, his lapis-blue eyes taking in the damage to the editorial offices, "he probably arrived from Boston on the five thirty-six."

"The Tilfords," Serena said suddenly. "He must have talked to them or he wouldn't have known where I was. Kirk, shouldn't we report this? How can we avoid it?"

It occurred to Serena that in the past few months, she had become involved in one too many incidents which ignored the channels of legal authority. But Kirk was shaking his head vehemently. "It's not just your reputation I'm thinking of, Serena, it's the *Mercury*. My God, a scandal could ruin this newspaper and its new owners." He paused, fingering his long chin, then abruptly moved with a brisk stride to get Serena's dark green cloak from a peg on the far wall. "Let's go, we can't let this wretch lie here all night." He turned to Will. "You talk to Fess. I'll take Serena home before she collapses."

"I was on my way to Fess's house when I saw the light on in here," Will said, looking at Serena in puzzlement. "It doesn't make sense—unless Stanhope was just plain crazy."

Kirk had bundled Serena into her cloak and was propelling her toward the door. "That's what he was, crazy as a loon. Peggy always said so."

Seconds later, Serena felt the salt-tinged breeze caress her face and soothe her spirit. "Did Peggy really say that?" she asked as they walked away from the *Mercury* office to the accompaniment of a concertina which played in a nearby boardinghouse. In the month that she had known Peggy Parnell, she had never heard the other woman say an unkind word about anyone.

"No," Kirk admitted flatly. "But Will was getting suspicious." He gave Serena a sidelong glance. "I think he has reason to be, but I won't pry."

A protest formed on Serena's lips, but instinct told her it would be wrong to hide the truth from Kirk Parnell. Yet she could not betray Abigail or Yancy. "Are you going to tell Peggy what happened?"

"Not unless I have to. Given Will's attitude, it might not be necessary. I suspect both Mr. Baker and Mr. Fessenden are going to play this one close to their chests."

"What do you mean? Will and Fess wouldn't *really* cover up what happened, would they? Good heavens, they're newspapermen!"

"They own a newspaper, you mean. They're not Ben Lindsey." Kirk's mouth twisted in irony. "I told you, they've just gotten started here in New Bedford and there's nobody alive in this town who remembers when a Lindsey didn't run the *Mercury.* You'd be surprised how many people resent Will and Fess just because they aren't Ben Jr. or Ben Sr." They turned a corner and saw the trees lining Cove Road in the distance. Kirk halted in midstep, causing Serena to stumble slightly. "Careful. Serena, I think maybe you should stay at our house tonight."

She shook her head vehemently. "No. Then you would have to explain to Peggy. And I'd have to tell those sourpuss Tilfords. I'll be fine, truly I will."

Kirk scanned her face and though he didn't look entirely reassured, he gave in. After all, the menace to Serena was lying stiff as a spar. But he knew that the real terror of the night lay with Serena herself.

The same haunting thoughts plagued Serena. Pembrose's death had been an accident; indeed, her assailant had already escaped death once very recently. Perhaps Pembrose had eluded perdition on other occasions. Yet Serena found little comfort in such logic and knew that her battered, bruised body would not rest easy that night in the big, cold, canopied bed.

"I think it best at this time to visit Washington. A change of scene will help fill the void left here by you and others who have fled the Brunswick scene." Abigail's letter had arrived in the early post and its contents did nothing to ease Serena's troubled mind. Abigail had written that there had been talk about the elopement and the strange incident at the train depot, but news of the war and the plight of local businessmen faced with defaulting Southern borrowers had soon taken precedence.

"Your father makes allusions to the fine match with Captain Parnell," Abigail had written. "Your mother is less enthused. Still, she speaks of you in her customary maternal style, usually wondering if you have mastered certain domestic tasks."

How like Mama, Serena thought, and sighed. She would never consider that Serena might spend more time in the *Mercury* office than in the Parnell kitchen. And how like Papa, so effusive in getting his own way without ever reflecting upon Serena's personal happiness. Certainly he of all people must know that Brant was in Washington and not hovering devotedly at Serena's side.

Awkwardly, Serena rolled over in bed and reached for the other, more surprising letter she had received that morning. Miraculously, mail had gotten through from North Carolina; Serena perused Cecelia's letter now for the third time. While it was couched in her sister's usual flamboyant style with the parade of daily events a mere showcase for Cecelia's beauty and charm, the fact was that Abigail's subtle wording conveyed more real news. Still, the last lines of Cecelia's letter held an oddly poignant note:

"Though Uncle Luke and I are both Yankees, we are treated with the utmost courtesy and deference. New Bern has not really been touched by the war, of course, yet I must confess to a feeling of being on enemy ground. I have learned that this city was founded by the Swiss, who are famous for being politically neutral. But Uncle Luke says there are never three sides to any war, only two, and in time, we may find ourselves on the wrong one. How strange that would be, having been feted and entertained in the most gracious manner possible since my arrival, yet I occasionally find myself yearning for Mandy's molasses cookies and a good gossip with you and Abigail in our cozy kitchen on Pleasant Street."

The admission of loneliness and the sense of foreboding were not like Cecelia. Serena refolded the letter and laid it next to Abigail's on the nightstand. Surely if hostilities broke out in New Bern, Uncle Luke and Cecelia would be safe. Luke Farrar, after all, had lived in North Carolina for almost fifteen years. Nor was the state itself in the vanguard of anti-Union feeling, having been the last to secede. Hadn't Uncle Luke written only a year ago to say that he thought most of his fellow plantation owners would eventually free their slaves without coercion by the federal government? While he had been wrong, North Carolina had certainly been reluctant to go to war.

Serena thought about the matter for a long time, finding it easier to contemplate far-off political and military issues than to worry herself sick over what was going on at the *Mercury*. She had sent Mr. Tilford to the newspaper office that morning with a note saying she was ill. Certainly she was stiff and sore, her mouth still swollen and her face blue with bruises. She could hardly make an appearance in such a state.

Shortly before noon, Kirk Parnell was announced by Mrs. Tilford. He was solicitous about her physical well-being, but seemed uneasy and moved restlessly about the bedroom. Growing equally unsettled, Serena finally demanded to know what Will and Fess had decided as their course of action.

Kirk sat down on the room's only chair. The angular features looked sharper this morning, and he appeared to have not slept any better than Serena. "Will and Fess dumped Pembrose off the lobster pier last night," he said without further preamble.

Aghast, Serena stared open-mouthed at Kirk. "But that's criminal!"

Kirk rested his chin on his hand and gave Serena a weary half-smile. "No, not the way they figure it. Pembrose was the criminal, committing his crime on their property. Will and Fess argue that far from violating any principles of our esteemed profession, they were protecting the newspaper." He sighed and smoothed his hand over the straight, dark hair which had a tendency to fall down over his right eye when he was distressed. "Frankly, Serena, neither Fess nor Will was very pleased when I asked them to hire you. The fact that you were young was bad enough, but when they saw you . . ." His voice trailed away and his sudden boyish grin seemed to pounce at Serena. "Hell, they ought to have known Brant wouldn't marry a homely woman!"

Serena drew back among the pillows, and in an unconscious gesture, one hand flew to the bosom of her cotton robe. Her first reaction was to deny that Brant had any interest in her as a woman at all, but she held herself in check, aware that Kirk's words may have been intended to distract her from his real message. "So?" was all she said and pursed her lips in a manner which would have done Lydia Farrar proud.

The grin faded from Kirk's face. "The townspeople are critical enough as it is," he said, sounding harsher than he meant to be. "A couple of our big advertisers have expressed displeasure. If the story gets around that some man tried to attack you and ended up dead on the *Mercury* floor, it could be the end of Fess and Will. It could be the end of the *Mercury*." Kirk sat back in the chair, legs crossed at the knee, hands clasped over his belt buckle. He looked like a man who had just completed a repugnant duty, but was proud of his accomplishment.

The slanted brown eyes narrowed as Serena leaned toward Kirk, fists on hips. "Do you mean to tell me, Kirk Parnell, that I am no longer working for the *Mercury?*"

Kirk nodded once and looked infuriatingly self-righteous. "All of us are acting in the best interests of the paper."

"You sanctimonious pig!" Serena picked up the copy of *Moby Dick* she'd been plowing through and hurled it at Kirk. It fell short of his knees by about six inches. Kirk seemed more shocked than startled. Sighing deeply, he bent to retrieve the book and set it down carefully on the aged quilt.

"I'm sorry, Serena, I really am," he said and his hazel eyes were sad.

Against her will, she took pity on him. "Maybe you are," she offered, beginning to simmer down. "But I'll be in hell twice over before I can see how two men who throw bodies off piers in the middle of the night can run a newspaper that stands for truth and justice."

"They can and they will," Kirk asserted. "But they have to be given a chance to try. There are lots of other newspapers right here in New Bedford. Besides, when Brant comes back, he can help you see things more clearly."

Serena had to clamp her teeth together to keep from telling Kirk what she thought about her errant, indifferent husband. Instead, she tossed her head in an imperious gesture, the foxlike mane spilling over her shoulders almost to her waist. "I think not. When—and if— Brant comes back, I won't be here."

Kirk stared, his hands clenching on his knees. "You don't mean that, Serena."

"I do." She lifted her chin, the turned-up nose pointed toward the canopy. "I have a sister who needs me," she announced and paid no heed to the inner voice which told her she was a reckless, obstinate fool. "I'm going to North Carolina."

Brant Parnell had dined on broiled cod, fried potatoes, and a medley of carrots and peas. It had been an adequate meal, topped off with hot coffee and an excellent port Brant had picked up two years earlier in Trinidad. The evening had boded well, with a poker game to follow in Fairview at a hotel near the wharves.

Not that Brant was a carefree man these days. Less than a week after Serena had left for North Carolina, Brant returned to New Bedford from Washington. He had been surprised to find his wife gone, but upon reflection, realized it was typical of the bullheaded girl with the one-track mind. Still, it baffled him that she'd deserted her coveted job. Questioning a tight-lipped Kirk only confirmed Brant's suspicions.

In their youth, Brant had used the threat—and sometimes the reality—of force to make his younger brother reveal the secrets he could keep so well. In manhood, Brant had found an easier, even enjoyable, way of eliciting information from Kirk: Vast amounts of Irish whiskey loosened Kirk's tongue, though this time Brant had been sure he'd either be unconscious or too drunk to care by the time Kirk told him the story of Serena and Pembrose Stanhope. The violent, bizarre tale had sobered Brant considerably. He was glad the wretched Pembrose Stanhope was dead. It had saved Brant the trouble of killing the bastard himself.

As for Serena, Brant could hardly blame her for running away from a terrifying experience or a potential scandal. But were those Serena's real motives? Or was she escaping from their marriage, from him, Brant wondered grimly—or from herself?

Most husbands would have rushed after her. But then he wasn't most husbands, nor was Serena like most wives. Brant had already admitted that their marital union seemed doomed. It was not unlike the Union itself, with the Confederacy cast in the role of rebellious bride. Brant considered the high price the Union was paying to retrieve its errant other half. It could cost him almost as dearly to go after Serena. And once having dragged her back into the fold, what were the odds of making a happy home life together? About as good as the Union's chances of peaceably reconciling with the Confederacy, he figured. He and Serena would never live in harmony until she returned to him of her own free will.

So, despite the fine dinner he had consumed and the pleasurable evening which lay ahead, Brant's soul didn't rest as comfortably as he would have wished it to that chilly, damp winter night. But he was distracted from his inner thoughts as he entered the familiar gaslit hotel room with its heavy rose-colored draperies. Brant was puzzled: The poker table was set for six, not five. Of course, in seafaring towns such as Fairview and New Bedford it was hardly out of the ordinary to find players in transit. Kirk wasn't able to play, being needed at home to nurse Peggy and one of their boys who were both ill with stomach cramps. Tom Collier, a longtime fisherman friend of the Parnell brothers, had told Brant just that afternoon that no one else would be sitting in.

Tom was setting out the chips, cards, glasses, and three bottles of whiskey when Brant threw his hat onto the rack by the door. "We've got company?" he inquired mildly.

A stack of white chips seemed to skitter out of control in Tom's thin hand and roll across the green baize table cover. "Unexpectedly," answered Tom with an uncertain, gap-toothed grin. He was a lean man of medium height whose years of fishing for sturgeon, haddock, cod, hake, turbot, and herring mackerel seemed etched one by one in the creases of his skin. "I wasn't sure . . . but he claimed to be a friend of yours."

"I never trust that type," Brant said with irony as he cracked open a new deck of cards and spread them expertly across the table in an even arc. "What's his name?"

"Giles Stanhope. Some shirttail relation of Kirk's wife. You know him?" Tom looked anxious, obviously afraid he'd somehow committed a social error in permitting the newcomer to join the game.

Brant's dark eyebrows drew together but he gave Tom a forced, if reassuring, smile. "I know him. I don't like him, but I know him." He sighed as he pulled the cards together in one hand and riffled their edges. "Just watch how he plays. And we'll tell Jack and Dunc and Press to do the same."

Giles Stanhope, however, did not cheat at poker. Giles might cheat at some other aspects of life, but never at cards. Poker, after all, was

a lot more serious than real life. It took Brant exactly three cuts of
the cards to perceive that. It took longer, however, to learn why Giles
Stanhope was in the New Bedford area and why he had asked to play
poker with Brant and his friends.

It was close onto midnight when Giles, his dark cravat loosened
and his neatly parted hair falling just slightly across his forehead,
leaned toward Brant between hands of six-card stud and proffered a
package of French cigarettes. "How is your charming bride?"

Brant's hand tightened over his ante before he carefully placed it
on the baize table cover. "She's on a little trip." He glanced at Press
Prescott, who was dealing out the first three cards of the hand. "Your
ten's high, Giles."

Giles peered at the two facedown cards and put a dollar piece into
the pot.

The etiquette of the game demanded that he withhold any further
nonpoker comments until the hand was over. It soon was, with Press
and Jack folding immediately, Dunc going out on the next round, and
Brant and Giles surrendering the pot to Tom, who had a pair of queens
showing.

"Is Mrs. Parnell returning soon?" Giles asked as Jack shuffled the
cards.

Brant looked unconcerned. "You know how women are—they
change their minds along with their clothes."

A spark seemed to ignite in Giles's cool eyes. "You've been away
for quite a while, I hear. How's your brother?"

"In the pink." Brant picked up his cards and hummed a few notes
of a sea chanty.

But even as Giles took in his hefty winnings from the hand a few
minutes later, he seemed impatient. "Ever played poker with a French
fur trapper?"

"No," Brant replied, still wearing a mask of innocence, "but I've
played with a lot of skunks." He leaned his head to one side and
regarded Giles with irony. "Why don't we skip the quilting-bee gossip
and play poker? I'll check the bet. It's up to you, Press."

The game lasted almost another hour, with the whiskey bottles
empty and the gaslights so low it was difficult to see the cards. None
of the men won a great deal, so none lost much. After the cards and
chips had been put away and the cigar and cigarette ashes were dusted
from the baize table cover, Giles suggested that Brant walk with him
part way to his own hotel.

The fog was thick over the harbor and the two towns which flanked
it. Looking at ease, but inwardly on guard, Brant fell in step with
Giles. If Brant hadn't known his way so well, Giles would probably
have gotten lost in the course of the quarter-mile trek. As it was,

Brant guided the other man all the way to his lodgings by the bridge which crossed the Acushnet River to New Bedford.

"You're staying on?" Brant asked casually. His voice seemed to echo off the fog bank.

"Maybe." Giles looked ghostly in the heavy mist which fell between the two men. "It depends on how informative you are." He paused and Brant could have sworn that the cool eyes glinted even through the fog. "I want the truth, Parnell. What happened to my brother, Pembrose?"

Brant scowled, no longer attempting to mask his impatience with Giles Stanhope. "I haven't seen your brother since I was at the judge's house two years ago. I hardly know Pembrose, I hardly know you, and I don't think I've suffered because of it. You came to New Bedford to play poker—fine. Now why don't you head back to Boston or wherever you live and forget about the Parnells and New Bedford?"

Giles's nostrils flared, his eyes now looking as if they could burn off the fog, and his hands tightened into fists. "My brother's disappeared! He came to see your rich Farrar wife! Did somebody kill him? Did you? Your wife? Or was that Texan around?"

"Christ Almighty." Brant swore on a low breath, shaking his head and backing away from Giles just enough to be out of easy reach. "I wasn't around, that's for damned sure. Maybe Pembrose got swallowed by a whale. Maybe you're boring me. Go home, Giles. It's late." Brant turned around purposefully, but braced himself for the assault he was certain would occur. He hadn't taken more than two steps when he felt Giles's weight on his back and an arm around his neck. Brant locked his knees to hold his balance, then suddenly shifted his whole body, pulling Giles over his shoulder and dumping him onto the sidewalk. Stunned, Giles lay facedown, gasping for breath. Brant put a foot in the small of the other man's back and pressed down just enough to assert his authority. "Keep out of New Bedford. Stay away from the Parnells." Slowly, Brant lifted his foot, retrieved his broad-brimmed hat which had fallen to the ground, and began walking away at a pace that was almost leisurely. He didn't bother to turn around.

PART TWO
NORTH CAROLINA
1862–1863

Chapter 7

THE CONTRAPTION had two motor-driven metal hands and a tin container at the bottom. Serena scrutinized it closely and shook her head. "I'm sorry, Uncle Luke, I can't see how you'll ever refine it to actually roll the cigarette papers."

"Takes time, my dear, always plenty of time down South. Maybe we've got more than usual while we wait for the Yankees." He took a screwdriver and adjusted something on the base of his latest invention. "Strange, isn't it, Rena, that I call my own people 'Yankees' and yet not mean it the way the Southern folks do. One has to make accommodations—yes, that's what life is all about—refinements and accommodations. Can you please give me those pliers?"

Serena obeyed and smiled fondly at her uncle. He was not as dark, not as tall, not as broad as her father, and even his facial features seemed scaled down somehow. Yet there was a definite resemblance. In other ways, however, Marcus and Lucas Farrar were as different as two men could be.

It had been two months since Serena arrived in New Bern. When Serena had asked Kirk to help her find a way to sail south, he'd refused—until she threatened to tell the story of Pembrose Stanhope's death to the rival *Standard*. If Kirk had doubted that she'd carry out her threat, he was no more skeptical than Serena herself. But neither dared take the chance she wasn't bluffing. Ten days later, Kirk had made the arrangements for Serena's passage on an English merchant vessel which was prepared to run any Union blockade.

The voyage had been uneventful, though a Federal steam frigate had been sighted off Cape Hatteras. The greatest excitement had been Serena's arrival at her uncle's home in New Bern. Luke Farrar's astonished delight had been matched only by Cecelia's shrieks of surprise. Aunt Kathleen and Fitch Moncrief both seemed more puzzled than pleased.

It was Cecelia, however, who had monopolized Serena's time. Privately, Cecelia related her latest social triumphs and the precocious activities of her six-month old son, while publicly exhibiting Serena at an endless round of holiday gatherings. At first, Serena enjoyed the novelty, but after being introduced by Cecelia as "my dear sister, the New England writer," for the fiftieth time, she began to feel like a circus freak. Following dutifully in Cecelia's shadow, smiling pleasantly at New Bern society while answering polite if sometimes awkward questions, Serena felt as if she were just another of her sister's accessories. She wondered if Fitch Moncrief had a similar reaction when escorting his wife.

Cecelia and Fitch lived in a fashionably decorated house which adjoined Uncle Luke and Aunt Kathleen's property. The tobacco plantation, called Wexford by Kathleen's late father, Thomas Prendergast, was located just a mile outside of New Bern. It was run by Fitch, with Luke occasionally emerging from the shed where he worked on his inventions long enough to reassure himself that all was well.

It was of Fitch that Luke Farrar spoke after he had finished toying with the pliers and seemed satisfied with his efforts. "Poor Fitch, he's in between a high creek and a low wall these days. His cronies think he ought to be off shooting Yankees, but he's not keen on signing up, especially since he married one."

"Somehow I can't imagine Fitch as a soldier," Serena said, fascinated by the metal hands which were now clickety-clacking at the empty air.

"Look at that little devil go!" Luke nodded in pleased wonder. "But you're right, I can't yet make it hold the paper tight enough. Well, I don't think a man should fight if he doesn't want to. Besides, the South seems to be holding fast."

Uncle Luke appeared to be correct. By the winter of 1862, the Confederacy had scored at least one major victory, near the Manassas railway junction in Virginia. However, the Union's naval blockade along the coast of the Carolinas threatened to cut off badly needed supplies.

"I wonder," Serena mused, reflecting upon her uncle's words and her own plight, "just how long this war will continue. Do you expect the Union to give up now that President Lincoln sees the Confederacy is willing to fight?"

Uncle Luke took out his tobacco pouch and sprinkled some of the crumpled, brown leaf into the tin container. "Maybe. Maybe not. I think Mr. Lincoln is serious about restoring the Southern states to the Union. And freeing the slaves. Or does he want to make colonies for them? I forget."

"I just wish the fighting would stop," Serena sighed as her uncle stared fixedly at his invention. "I don't think the local papers want a Yankee working for them after all."

Uncle Luke was so absorbed in his experiment that Serena was certain he hadn't heard her. But when he finally looked up, he smiled in kindly reproach. "Our newspapers here are more pro-South than the people. Your idea of writing articles to present a different point of view is fine, but no local will publish Union sentiments."

Serena put a hand on her uncle's arm. "I guess I wasn't being realistic," she said, gazing at the bizarre contraption and wondering if she had inherited her penchant for ignoring grim reality from Uncle Luke. Certainly her proposal to compose a series of pieces describing the attitude of Northerners toward the war had been met with responses ranging from outrage to derision. Serena had been shocked; it had seemed possible that people who looked the same, spoke the same language, attended the same churches, and had lived under the same government could be so different. But they were, and Serena's sense of being in an alien land would have overwhelmed her in those first weeks had she not been living in the circle of her own kind.

"Funny thing," Luke mused, rolling up the pouch and putting it in his pocket, "nobody knows how the other fellow feels until he hears him speak from the heart instead of the mouth." A sudden gust of wind from the Neuse River banged the shed door behind a collie which had nosed its way inside. "I'm kind of mystified, though," he went on in his mild voice, "since I would have thought you'd want to go back home while you could still get out of New Bern."

"I've considered it," Serena replied with a bite in her voice that dismayed her. "I intend to do that as soon as the worst of the winter weather is over." And, she told herself, when I know where my home is. Reluctant to return to her parents, she could not possibly go back to Brant's house in New Bedford. It seemed to Serena that he was no more anxious for them to live together than she was.

"I wouldn't wait too long," Luke advised, with a little shake of his head. "It won't be easy. You'll have to find a foreign vessel as you did when you came South. I hear only two have docked since you've been here."

The collie was nuzzling Serena's ankles, hoping for a treat. "My visit isn't a nuisance, is it?" she asked, patting the dog's head in a distracted manner.

Uncle Luke chuckled. "No, no, it's a delight. I enjoy your company so much I'm afraid I'll prolong your stay until you get trapped for the duration." He fingered his short-cropped beard and studied the collie's wagging tail. "Can you forgive a blundering old uncle for asking why you never speak of Captain Parnell?"

Cecelia, of course, had put the same question to Serena the very day of her arrival. Serena's answer had been terse: She had been forced into a merger, not a marriage, and it suited neither Serena nor Brant Parnell. Accustomed to Marcus Farrar's awesome will, Cecelia had merely shrugged and allowed that their father's meddling could go too far.

Serena's hesitation went on too long. Uncle Luke was smiling fondly at her. "I remember you as a little girl, Rena. You'd sit out there in the garden by that Guardian Angel of yours for an hour at a time and hardly move. I'd think, there's our little dreamer, with more of me in her than her papa. My little fox, all soft and sleek and clever like those furry fellows. But so unsure of herself, wishing you had Cecelia's looks and Abigail's brains. I never knew how to tell you that being Serena was enough. But what does Serena want?"

"To be Serena," she answered with a lift of her chin. Strange, she thought, a year ago, even six months earlier, she would not have been able to give that reply. "And I want to write for a newspaper. I enjoyed the *Mercury*. But," she continued more slowly, "it didn't work out precisely as I'd hoped."

Uncle Luke sat down again, pressing his fingers against the bridge of his nose. He looked more solemn, if still sympathetic. "Don't grow old and cold writing about other people's lives." He cleared his throat and shook his head. "When I was young like you, I dreamed of inventing something wonderful—another steamboat, a second cotton gin, a marvel the world would remember me by. I knew I was no man of commerce like your father. But I had my own talents and I was determined to make my mark, too. Then along came your Aunt Kathleen, visiting her Yankee relations in Brunswick. I forgot about being Robert Fulton or Eli Whitney. All I wanted was to be Kathleen Prendergast's husband. And she wanted to be Lucas Farrar's wife, thank God. So there we were, and along with our twins and all that tobacco, we've done well enough for ourselves. Oh, I still putter around with contraptions like this"—Luke gave the would-be cigarette rolling machine an affectionate tap—"but it's just to pass the time. With all the field hands, there's not much for me to do except watch the blasted stuff grow."

Serena shuffled her feet under her calico skirts and pondered Uncle Luke's words. She could refute neither his well-meant intentions nor his innate wisdom. But it occurred to Serena that perhaps he had been able to resolve his life far more easily than she could: Marcus Farrar had been his brother, not his father—and Luke and Kathleen had fallen in love. She and Brant had not been so fortunate.

Even if Serena had felt it appropriate, there was no chance to make these comparisons aloud. Cecelia was outlined in the shed's doorway, dressed in a handsome maroon riding costume, the jet-black hair piled under the veiled crown of her hat. "Don't take Serena's advice about your inventions, Uncle," Cecelia admonished in her husky voice. "She never was the least bit scientific. It's clearing off, why don't we ride out to the plantation, Rena? I must talk to Fitch."

Serena wasn't dressed for riding but Cecelia said she'd wait. Fifteen minutes later they were astride two fine chestnut mares and cantering down the dirt road toward Wexford. Cecelia nodded a greeting to a couple driving a buckboard. The woman had stared back with disapproval; ladies did not usually ride astride in New Bern. After a quarter of a mile, Cecelia slowed her horse to a walk and Serena reined in beside her. The wintry sky had brightened to take the January chill from the air. The earth smelled damp and fertile, the tall oaks which lined the road stood like an honor guard. Soon they were almost to the plantation itself and could already see the vast expanse of scorched black earth, burned before the spring planting could begin. Serena could make out colorful specks on the horizons as the slaves went about their routine of readying the soil for the early harvest. Some one hundred Negroes worked Wexford. Most of the adults were second-generation slaves born on the Prendergast plantation.

Serena couldn't get used to the idea of people being in bondage, no matter how just their master, but she knew better by now than to raise the issue with Cecelia, who had no interest in social reform.

Thomas Prendergast's original plantation house had been built of brick and limestone forty years earlier. But substantial as it had appeared, a summer lightning storm had set it afire shortly after Thomas's death three years earlier. Kathleen wept over the ghostly hulk of her childhood home but Luke saw no reason to rebuild. Instead, he had the shell razed, used the brick to build new housing for his slaves, and left only the east wing as offices and visitors' quarters. It was here that Fitch Moncrief ran the plantation.

Serena and Cecelia were greeted by a young, gangling black boy with crooked teeth. He seemed to regard Cecelia with awe as he helped her down from her mare. "Well, Otis," Cecelia said, adjusting her brown felt riding hat, "is Master Fitch receiving visitors?"

"That he is," Otis answered, offering a long, thin hand to Serena. "He be working this afternoon."

Cecelia nodded, as if reassuring herself. Serena glanced curiously from her sister to the young slave. It was obvious that they understood something between them which eluded Serena.

But Cecelia spoke frankly as they approached the double door of the east wing. "Fitch is not always alone. He enjoys acting like the lord of the manor in more ways than one."

Serena paused in midstep. "I . . . I see. But you don't . . . mind?"

Cecelia shrugged. "It keeps him out of other mischief." She stopped to allow Otis to open the doors for them. "I'm not complaining," Cecelia went on, lifting her skirts to avoid a clump of wet earth which someone had tracked into the hallway. "Since he lets me have my way in almost everything. Of course he'd better, if he wants to keep his pockets well-lined."

Serena's slanted eyebrows lifted slightly. Certainly she had noticed a change in Cecelia and Fitch's attitude toward each other, but assumed it was due to the natural mellowing which occurred in married life. When Fitch had come North in the spring of 1860 to make shipping arrangements on Luke Farrar's behalf, he had been dazzled by Cecelia's opulent beauty. She, in turn, had found his courtly manner and golden-haired good looks intriguing. Fitch devised one reason after another to prolong his visit, and within two months, Marcus and Lydia Farrar had announced the engagement of their elder daughter. The following August they were married, and Cecelia, armed with a trousseau which filled four steamer trunks and ten suitcases, bade her family a fond farewell as the newlyweds sailed off for North Carolina.

Even then, Serena had found Cecelia's choice puzzling. She could understand her sister's fascination with Fitch's wheat-colored curls and dapjper wardrobe. She could also appreciate the elaborate courtesies and artful flirtation expended upon Cecelia; indeed, it was a talent Fitch used with women in general. Yet Serena perceived him as unctuous, perhaps even sly. He did not seem to be the right sort of man either to work for Uncle Luke or to marry Cecelia Farrar. There was no denying, however, that Fitch had done both. Now Serena wondered if her sister regretted her whirlwind romance and marriage.

They had covered the length of the hall and come to a handsomely carved door with an elaborate lintel. "This was saved from old Prendergast's study, I think," Cecelia said and opened the door without knocking.

The room was surprisingly small, even cramped. Books and ledgers lined the walls, a mediocre painting of an Arabian mare hung above a fireplace which had been sealed off, and the sparse furnishings were old and worn. Fitch Moncrief sat behind an ancient desk littered with papers. The finish was scratched and lusterless, and one leg appeared to have been replaced with a mismatched piece of wood. Fitch looked up from something he was writing and smiled. He was just over average height, hardly taller than Cecelia, but his trim physique emphasized his masculinity. The carefully tended moustache was just a shade darker than his cluster of golden curls, and, as always, he was impeccably groomed.

"Welcome, ladies, an unexpected pleasure. I was just jotting down instructions for Mr. Saile." Fitch glanced at Serena. "He's the overseer, you know." He opened a drawer and pulled out a half-empty bottle of whiskey. "Drink?"

"No, thank you." Cecelia spoke decisively for both herself and Serena, who wondered how much of the bottle Fitch had already consumed that day. Yet, Serena noted, he was clear-eyed and his hands were steady.

"To what do I owe this visit?" Fitch asked smoothly, putting the bottle back and closing the drawer.

Cecelia and Serena had both sat down in chairs which looked as if they belonged in a kitchen rather than a study. Cecelia had gathered her skirts close, as if she weren't quite sure that something small and silent might not crawl onto her clothing. Serena, who had still not grown accustomed to the active insect life of the Carolina coast, glanced hastily about her own hem but saw nothing alarming. Perhaps the Southern fashion of pantalets was not a whimsy, but a deterrent.

"I've been thinking, Fitch," Cecelia began, both hands loosely holding her riding crop, "it's absurd for Serena to stay holed up here in New Bern. I want to go home with her on a visit. Surely this stupid war isn't so serious that I can't get back to New Bern after a few months up North."

Though he smiled, Fitch was slightly condescending. "The war seems serious to the soldiers fighting it. What were you thinking of, sailing from here or going to New Orleans?"

Cecelia shrugged her broad shoulders. "Whichever way is most expedient. And safest." She gave Fitch an arch little smile. "You have . . . contacts in various places, Fitch. Surely you could make inquiries."

Fitch sighed and again opened the drawer, pulling out the whiskey bottle along with a chipped shot glass. "It would be expensive," he said and frowned as he poured the liquor into the glass. "Think of the risk, Cecelia, two women and a baby. And the mammy. And your maid." He eyed Cecelia over the rim of the glass, as if offering her a challenge.

"Everything *you* do is expensive, Fitch," she replied matter-of-factly. "It has to be, since you know I can afford it."

The brief spurt of laughter that emitted from Fitch's throat was almost a cackle. But before he could reply, there was a single rap on the door. "It must be Otis. Come in," he called, gulping down the last of the whiskey and putting the glass away.

Otis scurried inside, out of breath and waving his long, thin hands. "Mr. Fitch, sir, there be a rumpus at the warehouse. Big Jed and Roscoe is at it again."

"They both need a good hiding," Fitch declared, standing and putting on his jacket. "I wish to God your uncle weren't so faint-hearted," he added, glancing at Cecelia as he propelled Otis out the door. "I'll be back as soon as I can."

The pokey little room was silent for a long moment. And for the first time since entering the plantation office, Serena spoke: "Why didn't you tell me about your plan to go home?" she demanded.

Cecelia stood up, swinging the riding crop in one hand and pacing the width of the small room. "I just assumed you wanted to leave. I certainly do. But we have to find out if it's possible." She stopped abruptly and swung around to face her sister. "See here, Rena, I've no intention of spending my life in a Southern backwater, living with a nasty snake like Fitch Moncrief!"

"Well," Serena said, trying to take in all the nuances of her sister's ardent declaration. "I wondered. But you've only been married a year and a half, you have a child. What do you propose to do—divorce him?"

"Of course. I have ample grounds." Cecelia gave a little laugh. "Oh, don't look so shocked, people *do* divorce in this modern age. Maybe it wouldn't even come to that, Papa could probably get Judge Stanhope or someone to find ways of getting an annulment." She returned to her chair and sat down again, leaning close to Serena. "Sometimes I think I only married Fitch to get away from Mama and Papa. Sailing off down South sounded so romantic and Fitch *was* . . . persuasive. But I made a mistake. I don't love him and I don't think he loves me." Her onyx eyes glistened. "I think that little weasel just married me for my money!"

Serena blinked. The irony struck home like a blow in the stomach. Could both Farrar daughters, particularly the handsome, sought-after Cecelia, have been targeted by fortune-hunters?

Forcing herself to face the matter at hand, Serena finally spoke. "Uncle Luke thinks we might be able to sail from New Bern if we go on a foreign ship," she offered. "A few are still risking the blockade."

"Maybe. Fitch will find out." Cecelia looked down at Fitch's littered desk. "Such a mess, I wonder how he keeps things straight." She turned back to Serena, obviously not caring much about how or if her husband coped with Uncle Luke's plantation holdings. "Big Jed and Roscoe must have had a real showdown this time. We don't need to wait for Fitch. I've told him all he has to know for now."

Serena rose to follow Cecelia to the door. But her sister halted and a curious smile played across her wide, thin lips. "Now you know why I wasn't too surprised to learn that your own marriage was a bit of a sham. Did you let Bruce make love to you?"

"Bruce?" Serena flushed, taking a backward step away from Cecelia. "His name is Brant! And it's none of your business!"

Cecelia shrugged her wide shoulders and looked amused. "I suppose not." She turned to push the door open. "One thing I'll say for Fitch, he's rather accomplished in the bedroom. Until he becomes . . . eccentric." She flashed Serena a knowing glance over her shoulder. "I'd hate to think that Bruce was dull as well as greedy."

"Brant," Serena all but growled, watching Cecelia move with graceful self-assurance down the passageway ahead of her. There was no reply from Cecelia, and Serena had a sudden urge to tell her that Brant wasn't dull at all, he was quite exciting and certainly ten times smarter and more attractive than Fitch Moncrief. But since she was not in the habit of defending Brant Parnell in her mind, it seemed absurd to defend him from Cecelia's errant tongue. As they emerged into the wintry sunlight, it seemed ridiculous to think of Brant Parnell at all.

* * *

A light snow had fallen over New Bern the last week of January. It was not the sharp cold of Brunswick, but a dampish chill which seemed to permeate every nook and cranny of Uncle Luke's and Aunt Kathleen's townhouse on Pollock Street. The Farrars had cancelled their al fresco fish bake; the inclement weather would not permit holding it in the enclosed courtyard at the back of Uncle Luke's house. Instead, the dozen or so husbands had come for an evening of cards in the gentlemen's parlor while their wives tatted and did other needlework in the retiring room.

Serena had wished to beg off from what appeared to be an evening of local gossip and—for her—uneven stitchery. But Cecelia had already made her excuses, pleading an upset stomach, and Serena felt obliged to attend.

She stifled a sigh of tedium, wondered why she had ever volunteered to make a petit-point cover for Aunt Kathleen's piano-forte stool, and let her mind wander while the others fell into a discussion of the much-admired Southern general, Robert E. Lee, and if he would share his command with General Longstreet and General Johnston, or if Jefferson Davis would appoint a single leader for the Confederate forces.

It had been over two weeks since Cecelia had demanded that Fitch find a way to get both Farrar sisters back to Brunswick. So far, nothing had happened. When Serena had asked Cecelia about the plan the previous day, her sister had simply shrugged her shoulders and remarked that such things took time. But rumors of increased Union naval activity in the vicinity made Serena anxious to leave. The war suddenly appeared to be edging dangerously close to New Bern.

From out of the corner of her eye, Serena saw Leonard, her aunt and uncle's houseman, discreetly open a door built into the room's paneling. To Serena's surprise, he gave her an almost imperceptible nod. She put down her needlework, murmured her excuses to Aunt Kathleen, who seemed totally caught up in Mrs. Carr's chirruping account of General Longstreet's youth in the Edgefield District, and followed Leonard into the hallway.

"A message from Mrs. Moncrief has arrived," Leonard announced in a voice which bore almost no Southern accent of any kind. Indeed, Leonard would have been more at home as the butler in a stately English mansion than as a plantation slave in North Carolina. Sometimes it seemed to Serena that the faintly haughty, impeccably correct Leonard would have been just as at ease as the master of a vast estate. He was no darker than Cecelia, his features were refined, and only the slightly fuller mouth and curly hair betrayed his Negro heritage. Leonard was said to be the illegitimate son of a Haitian slave and one of Aunt Kathleen's distant cousins. That in itself was not unusual, but his obvious education and superb dignity set him apart from the other slaves. Serena would have liked to learn more about Leonard but Uncle Luke seemed evasive on the subject.

"Cecelia wants me to go over to their house," Serena said, refolding the brief note. "Is it snowing very hard?"

"It's stopped for the time being," Leonard replied, "but the footing is uncertain, Mrs. Parnell. If you'll permit me, I'll accompany you. Young Calvin is abed with a stomach complaint."

Young Calvin was the houseboy, a rotund ten-year-old prone to mischief but the source of much amusement to Uncle Luke. "He probably overate again," Serena said. "I'll fetch my cloak."

She returned from her upstairs bedroom within three minutes to find Leonard, also attired in a warm cape, waiting for her outside the gentlemen's room. The muffled sound of laughter and a hearty hoot from one of the card players indicated that the men were enjoying their game.

"I wonder who's winning," Serena commented as Leonard held the front door open for her. As always, she felt an almost obsessive desire to make Leonard speak more freely. "Is Mr. Moncrief playing?"

"I believe not, Mrs. Parnell." He cleared his throat in a disapproving sort of way. "Mr. Farrar preferred to keep the gathering to his own age and peer group tonight."

"Oh." Clearly, Leonard did not feel that Fitch Moncrief was fit company for Uncle Luke's more intimate friends. Serena stopped while Leonard picked up a lantern from a post outside the door and began to make his way down the gravel walk. The snow was sticking only on the lawn which reached to the road, and after twenty winters in New England, Serena didn't find it difficult to keep her footing.

Three of the front windows at the Moncrief house showed lights burning behind them. The nursery upstairs and the front parlor on the main floor were lighted, Serena noted and wondered if something were wrong with the infant, Mark. She quickened her pace, drawing alongside Leonard, whose pointed eyebrows twitched ever so slightly. Serena knew it was not proper to walk beside a slave; ordinarily, they followed behind at a respectful distance, except in an instance such as this when Leonard was lighting the way for her. But Serena was still having trouble accepting the nuances of Southern social behavior.

Within a few paces, however, they were up the steps and at the front door with its brass knocker. Leonard rapped just once; Hannah, Cecelia's maid, let Serena in while Leonard discreetly withdrew to head back to his master's home.

Hannah smiled warmly at Serena and took her cloak. "They be in the parlor, Miz Rena," she said, nodding in that direction. The pink ties in her kerchief danced like little pigs' ears.

"They?" Serena noted that the parlor door was closed. Before

Hannah could reply, Cecelia stepped out into the hall in a swish of crinoline petticoats and crimson taffeta.

"Hello, Rena," she said and glanced at Hannah. "You may go." She paused while the slave ambled down the hall. "Fitch has found someone who can find us passage home. Via New Orleans." Cecelia grabbed Serena's arms and all but jigged in triumph. "He's a Confederate soldier, but he's willing to help. Come in, you must meet him."

Suppressing her skepticism, Serena followed her sister into the parlor. Two wall sconces provided the only light except for a fitful fire which burned in the grate. Fitch Moncrief lounged in an armchair; standing by the heavy portieres was a large man wearing the jgray uniform of a Confederate captain. He was clean-shaven and, at first glance, seemed to possess the very essence of military bearing. But the indolent move he made toward Serena and the sleepy gray eyes startled her into sudden recognition: The man was Yancy Clarke and his drawled greeting was unmistakable.

"Hullo, it's Mrs. Parnell now, I hear." He put out a huge hand which shook Serena's with surprising gentleness.

But it was Cecelia's turn to be confounded: "Fitch! You didn't tell me Captain Clarke knew Rena!"

"I didn't know," Fitch replied, equally astonished. He stared at Yancy. "You never told me, Captain."

"You never asked," Yancy said in his laconic manner. Cecelia was clearly flustered and much put out. She glowered at Fitch, looked curiously at Serena, and then scowled at Yancy Clarke. "This is a fine kettle of fish! Not that it matters, I suppose, as long as Captain Clarke can get us home."

"Can you?" Serena couldn't help but smile up at Yancy, who looked much younger without his beard and far less like a gunslinging Texas outlaw. Still, Serena noted, there was something definitely untamable about Yancy, with or without the beard, in uniform or frontier garb. She wondered when, if ever, she'd get the chance to tell him about Pembrose Stanhope.

"I reckon I can manage your passage. It's only fitting, after all, isn't it?" The gray eyes had a secretive but amused gleam. He hesitated, his voice dropping even lower than usual. "How is Miss Abby? Have you heard from her?"

Serena heard Cecelia's short intake of breath but ignored it. "Abby was going to Washington the last I heard," she replied. "But that was in October. I haven't seen her since . . . since I left Brunswick."

"Ah." Yancy paused and the eyelids seemed to all but shut for just a moment. "A lot of things have happened since then."

"So they have. Who'd ever dream I'd meet you again here in New Bern?" Serena laughed and realized she sounded faintly giddy.

"The whole world's upside down," Fitch put in agreeably. "But then New Bern's a natural stopping place, with all the railroads and ships." He picked up a cut-glass decanter and refilled the whiskey tumblers from which he and Yancy had been drinking before Serena's arrival. Fitch and the Texan made a striking contrast in masculine appearance: the slender, blond-haired Fitch in his carefully cut evening coat with an English cravat, and the hulking, dark Yancy whose plain gray uniform exhibited no decoration except for the captain's braid on his sleeve. To Serena, it seemed that the world must indeed be upside down to bring these two men together in the dimly lighted parlor of a North Carolina plantation manager's home.

"How soon, Captain?" Cecelia asked, impatient with talk of old acquaintances and philosophical musing. "How do we get to New Orleans?"

"The train from Goldsboro," Yancy replied. "Two, three weeks to arrange it, I'd reckon. Figure on leaving about the first of March or so."

Cecelia nodded eagerly and turned to Serena. "Perfect. Won't Mama and Papa be surprised to see us?"

"I'm sure they will," Serena answered dryly but smiled in an effort not to spoil her sister's enthusiasm. She turned back to Yancy. "Of course I'll pay my own way."

Yancy set his empty glass down on the mantel and picked up his hat with its black ostrich plume. "Let's not fuss over that just now," he said and bowed to Cecelia. "I'd better be off to the camp, it's getting late." He looked down at Serena. "I might as well walk you home, Mrs. Parnell, if you please."

"Oh, certainly. My cloak's in the hall." Serena bade her sister and Fitch a rather hasty good-night and a few moments later was outside, with Yancy's hand guiding her by the elbow.

"Yancy—Captain Clarke—whatever happened to you after Boston?" She craned her neck to look up at him but his features had turned uncommonly grim.

"That doesn't matter now," Yancy responded as they squelched their way down the walk. The snow had turned to slush and the water could be heard running off the rooftops. "I've got some other news for you, ma'am." Yancy paused and looked up into the dark night sky as if seeking inspiration. "We captured a spy this afternoon in Bayboro. At least Colonel Campbell thinks he's a spy."

"Well? That's not so amazing during wartime, is it?"

Yancy gave a deep, hollow laugh. "No, that it isn't. But the so-called spy is your husband."

Chapter 8

THE WARMING BREEZE from the south rustled the branches of the myrtle trees which lined Pollock Street. From nearby, a dog howled dolefully, begging to be let inside his owner's house. The air smelled of damp decay as Serena gasped for breath.

"Not Brant," she whispered at last. "I don't believe it."

They had stopped midway between the Farrar and Moncrief houses, two motionless figures merging into the shadows of the night. Yancy put a hand on Serena's shoulder and gave her a kindly look. "I don't know just how it happened except he must have sailed a ship into Pamlico Sound through the blockade somehow and dropped anchor before he took a smaller boat up the Neuse River. I heard he was picked up by a patrol near Bayboro and New Bern."

"I have to see him, there must be a mistake. Brant doesn't give a fig about the war, North or South. Please, Yancy, take me to . . . where is he?"

"In the stockade at the camp, madder than a new-branded steer. But I'd better not, Mrs. Parnell, at least not now."

Serena stamped her foot and splattered slush all over her hem. "Damnation, Yancy, don't call me Mrs. Parnell! If you and I are going to make a habit of helping each other escape from half the country, let's not be so formal!" She realized she was shouting, glanced in the direction of Uncle Luke's house, and lowered her voice. "Will they shoot him?"

"I doubt it." Yancy clutched at the saber which hung at his side and frowned. "Seems to me your husband can probably talk his way out of most any tight spot, and after what he did for me at the railway station in Brunswick, I'll help him. Not that I'm any talker, but Colonel Campbell tends to listen when I do."

"I still want to see him," Serena asserted and never stopped to ask herself why. "If not tonight, tomorrow?"

Yancy paused before answering. "We'll see. I've already told the colonel that Captain Parnell no doubt came to fetch you."

Serena eyed Yancy quizzically. Of course that was the logical answer, at least as far as the rest of the world would be concerned. But Serena wasn't convinced. Still, she had to let Yancy—and every-

104

one else—believe that Brant Parnell had risked his life to rescue his bride from the clutches of the Confederacy.

"I'll meet you tomorrow. At eleven, by Tryon Palace," Serena declared in a tone which left little room for argument.

Yancy sighed deeply. "I don't know . . . I'll come if I can. If not, I'll send a message."

Serena nodded her acceptance. Yancy would come, she was sure of that. Yancy Clarke might be a gunslinging outlaw, but he was also a man of his word.

Serena had spent a restless night, falling into a deep sleep just before the late winter dawn crept across the stormy eastern sky. She had dreamed of a picnic at Kennebunk, with Matt skipping pebbles into the sea and Cecelia preening as she strode along the shore and Abigail building a sandcastle that looked exactly like Tryon Palace. Upon awakening, Serena realized that she herself had not been in the dream, at least in an active sense. The eternal observer, she told herself sleepily, and was startled into full consciousness by the face of three-year-old Liberty, a mulatto child Leonard had taken under his capable wing.

"You sick, Miz Rena?" Liberty asked, limpid brown eyes sympathetic. The child was standing on top of three wooden steps which led up to Serena's chintz-draped bed.

"Oh—no, no, Liberty," Serena said with an uncertain smile. "Just tired. What are you doing in here?"

"Mizzer Luke say you must be sick. You not at breakfast." Liberty teetered dangerously on the step and cocked his head to one side. "You sick, Miz Rena?"

"I told you I'm *not* sick," Serena answered, still smiling but with a touch of impatience. Liberty had the irritating habit of asking the same question over and over. Peering at the tiny pendant watch she rarely wore but always kept next to her bed, Serena let out a little cry. "Good Lord, it's almost ten! Liberty, run along, I must get dressed."

Liberty was studying his right hand, which seemed to have acquired a great smear of raspberry jam on the palm. "I help if you sick."

Serena suppressed a sigh and tapped Liberty's small nose. "You go find Young Calvin. He *is* sick. At least he was last night."

The little nose wrinkled in disgust. "He not sick, he *fat*." But after only a moment's hesitation, he climbed backward down the three steps and scampered out of the bedroom.

The snow had disappeared during the night but a steady drizzle fell over New Bern. Serena had hoped to avoid the rest of the family before she left, but her excursion into the kitchen for toast and a steaming mug of coffee brought her face to face with Aunt Kathleen.

"Glory be, child, I thought you'd come down with grippe! You went off last night in the middle of the evening and we haven't seen hide nor hair of you since!"

Serena added just a touch of coarse brown sugar to her coffee and avoided her aunt's keen eyes. "Cecelia sent for me. She wasn't feeling well, you know," Serena lied, suddenly feeling as if everyone on Pollock Street had succumbed to illness, real or imagined. "I was tired when I came back and went straight to bed. I'm sorry if I appeared rude to your guests." She tried to look abject.

"Oh, they were all so fired up with county talk and war rumors they didn't notice," Aunt Kathleen said, plying Serena with butter and jam. "I was just worried, that's all. I'll call on her today myself."

"She'd like that," Serena replied glibly, thinking that Cecelia could fend for herself—and no doubt would manage it very well.

Ten minutes later, Serena was bundled into her cloak with the hood pulled down to keep the rain out of her eyes. Serena followed Hancock Street toward the Trent River and then turned due west toward Tryon Palace. On a rise overlooking the Trent just before it joined the Neuse, the old colonial governor's mansion stood deserted, a derelict from its days of pre-Revolutionary glory.

The rosy brick had faded, pieces of the wrought-iron fence had been torn out by the Revolutionaries to make bullets, the local citizenry had removed brick after brick to build their own homes, and the ornamental gardens had long since withered from neglect. Serena had passed by the ghostly palace shell many times since her arrival in New Bern and always had felt a pang of sadness that such a handsome building should have been allowed to deteriorate. Much of the interior had been destroyed by fire in 1798. But on this drizzly morning Serena did not pause to reflect upon the palace's aura of defeat and dejection; instead, she hurried up the overgrown drive and passed through the open gates.

She stopped, not knowing precisely where she would find Yancy Clarke. The palace grounds were vast. As she stood anxiously in the unrelenting rain, Serena heard the bells of First Baptist Church on nearby Middle Street strike eleven. Serena had received no message so Yancy must be here—somewhere.

"Serena!" The voice was low but distinct. She whirled around, taking in both round brick sentry houses which flanked the gateway. Her name was repeated, this time more loudly, and Serena knew it came from the guardhouse on the left—and that it was not Yancy Clarke who called to her, but Brant Parnell.

She all but stumbled on the uneven bricks as she hurried across the scant twenty feet to see Brant standing there just inside the ruined guardhouse, shaking his head. The grin he flashed at her did not seem quite real, as if it belonged to the ghost of a Revolutionary patriot. "Where did you think I'd be, in the old governor's bedroom?"

Serena reached out to touch the hand which pulled her inside the small curved guardhouse. Brant was chuckling, his dark blue seaman's jacket and cap both wet from the rain.

"How did you get away?" she breathed, flustered at the sight of him, amazed at her own thudding heart.

"I didn't, exactly," Brant replied, studying the wide-eyed, astonished face under its heavy hood. "Relax, Serena, nobody's after me—yet. Yancy has sort of let me out on parole. I'm safe until his sergeant comes back on duty. Davis is a stickler for rules."

"Is he related to Jefferson?" It was the first thing that popped into Serena's head and she realized it sounded inane under the circumstances.

"I don't think so." Brant let go of her hand and leaned out the door. "Any chance we could go inside that monument and talk a bit?"

"I don't know—oh, maybe, I think Aunt Kathleen has said the twins and their friends sometimes play inside." Serena gazed questioningly at the long-neglected rain-blurred image of the palace. "We could go to Uncle Luke's. It's not far from here."

Brant grinned in that familiar, ironic way Serena had almost forgotten. "I don't know, Serena, I'm not sure I'm ready to meet the rest of your family. This branch might shoot me." He took her arm. "Let's try our luck here. By God, those old Royalists knew how to live, even in the far-flung colonies."

"I'm sure you've seen grander sights than this in your travels," Serena said carefully, making her way along the circular driveway. At each side of the palace stood piles of rubble, mute evidence of the original adjoining wings which had been connected by colonnaded walkways. Some dozen broken steps led up to the battered front door. Sure enough, when Brant touched the splintered wood, it creaked inward on rusty hinges.

Their quick intakes of breath sounded simultaneously in the musty, mildewed entrance hall. Dust and cobwebs clung to the walls and cornices; the hardwood floor groaned and sagged while startled spiders fled to safety between the cracks in the molding. Serena picked up her skirts and gritted her teeth. "I don't like this place," she whispered. "Please, let's go to Uncle Luke's."

Brant tipped back his cap and surveyed the decaying walls and ceiling. "A grand building a century ago," he said in appreciation, steering Serena around a pile of statuary which had apparently been toppled from a pedestal long ago. "We don't have much choice," he remarked, noting that only one remaining room seemed intact. "Let's try this, it looks as if it must have been steeped in officialdom."

Serena found herself in a large chamber with tall windows, most of them broken and partially boarded up but at least untouched by the long-ago fire. A few sticks of furniture lay scattered about on the bare hardwood floor and the paint was peeling from the walls. Gaping holes in the ceiling indicated that elegant chandeliers had once provided diadems of light as the governor's guests toasted King George the Third.

"It's not a ballroom," Brant noted. "Probably not a dining room either. I'd say it was the governor's office."

"The council chambers, perhaps," Serena said, wrinkling her nose at the smell of damp and decay. "Uncle Luke told me about it and how William Tryon summoned the royal council here to celebrate the building's completion."

"Poor old bastard would turn over in his grave if he could see it now." Despite the harshness of his words, Brant shook his head in commiseration. "Well, have a seat Serena; the window embrasures seem our only choice."

Serena crossed the room and paused to brush dust, pieces of paint, and cobwebs from the faded, fragile silk upholstery. She seated herself cautiously, wondering if the wood might give way under her weight. But even when Brant sat down beside her, the windowseat only seemed to sag slightly.

Now that Serena found herself settled with Brant inside the council chamber, she realized that her reluctance had not been caused by a desire to avoid the ravaged palace, but to prevent a private confrontation with her husband. Absurd, she told herself. Serena cleared her throat, folded her gloved hands in her lap, and spoke in a voice that was somewhat less assured than usual: "How did you get here?"

Brant's dark brows drew together as he took off his cap and put it down on the windowseat. "Oh, I was just cruising around Pamlico Sound and I thought I'd stop by to pay you a visit." The corners of the strongly etched mouth turned down as he gazed at her. "Your parents asked me to bring you home. Matt's gone to war."

Serena jerked back in astonishment, the hood slipping from her head. How typical of her parents to find their nest suddenly empty and decide to replace at least one chick to reaffirm themselves as figures of authority. "Is that what you think I should do? Go home to Brunswick and live with my parents?" The question was carefully phrased, as bereft of emotion as Serena could make it.

Brant was equally guarded. "If that's what you wish. Kirk tells me things didn't work out too well on the *Mercury*. As a matter of fact," he added casually, "Kirk isn't working there anymore, either. He joined a Massachusetts regiment just before Thanksgiving."

Serena was momentarily distracted from her own plight. "How surprising! I thought he was dedicated to the *Mercury.*"

"So did I." Brant lifted one broad shoulder in a baffled gesture. "They say a happy man never volunteers. There are times when I don't understand my own brother. But then I don't expect he always understands me, either." He paused and rested the sea-blue eyes on Serena. "Well? Do you want to go home or not?"

Serena brushed at the damp strands of hair which hadn't been protected by her hood. "Did you get the government contracts for Papa?"

Brant inhaled deeply, his mouth setting into a tight line. "No. Not yet." One big hand cut through the air in impatience. "Hell, Serena, every grafter and leech in the Union is slithering around Washington these days. It's going to take some time to make the right people listen. Never mind that, I asked you a question."

Serena, however, had only half an answer. She didn't know if she wanted to go home or not. But she was certain that she could not remain in New Bern. Spending any more time there was not merely useless, but potentially dangerous. "Both Cecelia and I plan to return North. Where I'll settle once I get there is something I haven't sorted out quite yet."

Serena's cool, noncommittal manner was stretching Brant's patience to the limit. He snatched up his cap and got to his feet. "I don't suppose it ever occurred to you that you have a home in New Bedford?"

"Why should it?" Serena snapped. "It never seemed to occur to you!"

The look Brant gave Serena was searing in its intensity. At last he turned away for a moment, then regarded her levelly: "All right. I suppose I deserved that. Now would you mind telling me if it matters to you whether it occurred to me or not?"

Brant's unexpected appearance at Tryon Palace had surprised her; his announcement that her parents wanted her to come home had unsettled her; his question about her return to New Bedford had confused her. Indeed, if there was one emotion that Brant seemed consistently to arouse in Serena, it was confusion. Having spent almost twenty years living a balanced, routine, predictable existence, Serena felt that from the moment Brant Parnell had entered her life the previous summer at Plunkett's Pond, her world had been in chaos.

Serena stood up, wringing her gloved hands. "I don't know what matters to me," she admitted, her voice peevish in its frustration. "Why should I, when you left me the day after we married, and it seemed as if you never planned on coming back? There I was, alone

among virtual strangers, trying to find my way on the *Mercury*, and
then Pembrose Stanhope comes along and . . ." She was forced to halt
in midsentence, the memories she had kept at bay for so many weeks
suddenly returning all too vividly. Pembrose, with his pernicious
smile, masking an interior that was far more rotten than the timbers
of the once-proud governor's palace . . . Serena turned her back on
Brant, staring with blind eyes through the jagged windowpanes.

"Ah, yes—Pembrose Stanhope." Brant spoke quietly, the anger
gone. "He and his brother Giles were always just on the wrong side
of loathsome. I'm sorry about what happened, Serena. I truly am."

"Are you now?" Serena rasped, still facing the tall, shattered
window. "You were off wining and dining men of great influence in
Washington! It didn't matter to you if I had to fight for my virtue—
and my life!" She whirled on him, gesturing wildly with her hands.
"Pembrose was an animal, a vicious beast! You can't imagine what
it was like!"

Brant reached out to catch Serena's darting hands. "You're right,
I probably couldn't guess. But I said I was sorry. Stanhope's dead as
a beached bass and it's over." He tugged her back toward the windowseat, all but dragging her down beside him. "Frankly, neither of
us has exhibited a lot of consternation over the other's ghastly ex-
periences." He paused to offer a rueful grin. "So in answer to your
next question, no, I wasn't brutally tortured or savagely beaten."

"By whom?" The words toppled from Serena's lips, as if her brain
had temporarily become disengaged from her speech.

Brant was surprised to find himself unamused. "By the enemy, or
whatever you call my captors." His reply held a faint growling sound.

"I should hope not!" Serena was sincere and also embarrassed. "I
mean, you're a civilian, after all, and there is at least a veneer of
gallantry attached to the Confederate soldiers."

For all the common sense Serena paraded with such pride, Brant
found her occasional lapses into unreality more than a little aggra-
vating. Especially when they pertained to him. The sudden silence
between them unnerved Serena further. She wished for some distraction—a howl of wind, the crumbling of plaster, a groan from the
aged walls. Brant wore an uncommonly stern expression, as if he
were waging war within himself to keep his temper in check.

"I *was* worried, I envisioned all sorts of horrid things happening
to you." She avoided the wary eyes, instead frowning into her lap,
where her hands couldn't seem to stay still. "Outside just now—why,
I was genuinely relieved to see you safe. And well. And . . . uh, all
in one piece." She stopped fumbling for words and swallowed hard.

"Prove it." The words came out on a weary sigh.

At last Serena looked at him. "Prove it?" She was confused as much by his instransigent manner as by his curt demand. "Well, Yancy knows I was concerned. He'll vouch for my feelings."

"Yancy!" Brant leaned back against the windowseat, eyes turned up in disbelief to the decayed ceiling. Serena stared in bewilderment, wondering what she'd done now to annoy Brant. He was making her feel foolish. If she weren't an independent, grown-up woman, she'd cry. At least then he might offer to dry her tears and make her feel better.

Her lower lip was quivering dangerously and she started to turn away when Brant yanked her into his arms, covering her mouth with his. Serena went rigid in his embrace, as unyielding as she was amazed. But Brant's body pressing against hers felt so reassuring, so solid, so confident of being in command, that her resistance melted like butter on hot toast. With only a vague sense of hesitation, Serena put her arms around Brant's neck. His kiss deepened, making Serena aware of his right to possession. Fleetingly, she thought of Pembrose Stanhope's brutal embrace and instinctively recognized the difference between uncontrolled madness and untrammeled masculinity.

She was about to pull away when she felt Brant's hands move under her cloak, slipping down to her slim waist. His tongue searched inside her mouth as strong fingers smoothed the fabric of her gown against the flat of her stomach. His lips moved to her ear and Serena took a deep, grateful breath, only vaguely aware of how eagerly she was straining against his probing hands. Brant inched downward, setting off that alarming sense of betrayal by her body.

The window embrasure creaked ominously as Brant shifted her in his arms to caress her thighs. Serena cried out, but was too befuddled to recognize whether it was from such sudden intimacy or a fear that the floor was about to give way beneath them.

But Brant was now sitting up straight, withdrawing his right hand from the little valley he'd made in Serena's skirts. "This old relic of a palace isn't made for passionate reunions," he remarked, not quite as coolly composed as usual. "I'd hate for the walls to fall down around us and have half of New Bern gather outside watching our amorous encounter."

Serena stifled a giggle and blushed. She felt almost as giddy as she had been on Judge Stanhope's brandy in Livermore Falls. But while Brant seemed relaxed, the blue eyes wore an unfamiliar, serious expression. For one searching second they stared at each other, and then Brant spoke again, more lightly this time. "You see, Serena, that was a hell of a lot more eloquent than a testimonial from the ineloquent Captain Clarke." He straightened his coat and brushed back his hair, then stared beyond Serena's shoulder. "Speak of the devil," he murmured.

Serena turned to see Yancy Clarke framed in the doorway. If he'd overheard the reference to himself, he gave no sign. "Pardon me, ma'am, Captain," Yancy said apologetically, plumed hat in hand, saber at his hip, "but Sergeant Davis is getting nervous. He's afraid the colonel is going to decide we have an escaped prisoner."

Brant picked up his watch cap from the windowseat, then got to his feet. "You'll have to excuse us, Yancy. Mrs. Parnell and I were just having a little domestic discussion." He saw Serena bristle at his ironic tone.

But when he put an arm around her she made no effort to shake him off. "Let's get out of this place," Brant said. "I'm beginning to feel like a ruin myself."

Brant allowed Serena to precede them out of the room and down the hallway. After the dank and musty odors of the old palace, the rain seemed fresh and fragrant. Serena peered out from under her hood to let the dampness revive her. She avoided Brant's gaze, trying to mask her feelings until she could gauge his.

As they walked down the drive in silence, Serena noted a gray gelding tethered to one of the remaining wrought-iron railings. Yancy's, she thought, and then saw a man and two more horses by one of the guardhouses. Sergeant Davis, she decided, noting the insignia on his gray uniform. He tipped his hat and saluted Yancy.

"Do we give the lady a ride?" Brant asked of no one in particular.

"No!" Serena gave a vehement shake of her head, then bit her lip and offered Yancy a bleak smile. "I mean, it's not far and I don't mind the rain. Truly, I'd rather walk."

Yancy reached for his horse's bridle. "Good enough. I'll keep in touch." He tipped his hat and climbed into the saddle.

Brant signaled for Sergeant Davis to wait, then turned back to Serena. *"The Irish Rover*'s tied up in Pamlico Sound. Unless you get word to me otherwise, I'll assume that when I'm able to get out of here, you'll go with me." He kept his voice low and level, allowing no indication of his feelings.

Serena vowed to be equally unemotional. "My sister and her baby must come, too."

Brant shrugged. "Bring the whole blasted family, we've got plenty of room." He scowled briefly, then made as if to touch her face under the hood, but let his hand fall to his side. Serena watched him turn away and stride toward Sergeant Davis. "The prisoner's back in your hands, Sergeant," he called out cheerfully. "Remember, I still intend to charge you with cruel and inhuman punishment. I drink Irish whiskey, not that gutless bourbon you Southerners swig down."

Serena heard the clip-clop of Yancy's horse crunching the gravel under its hooves. She walked the street, her hood shielding her face from the rain—and concealing her distressed expression from the three men. She muttered an oath that would have curled Lydia Farrar's hair, and wondered why Brant Parnell was the cause of her perpetual consternation.

Chapter 9

LEONARD WAS LAUGHING. Serena realized she had never heard the houseman laugh before and actually froze in place as she watched him toss a fabric-covered ball to Liberty, who was all but bouncing up and down on the lawn outside the Farrar townhouse.

"Throw it back," Leonard urged the youngster, motioning with his long, thin fingers and trying to suppress his mirth. It occurred to Serena that Leonard was not nearly as old as she had surmised. His rigid demeanor added years to his appearance, but seeing him now in a relatively relaxed and jocular mood, Serena guessed that he was probably no more than thirty. He was bending down, hands patting his knees in a coaxing motion. "We take turns, remember, Liberty?"

"My turn," declared Liberty, tucking the ball into his stomach and doubling over on the grass. "Every turn my turn."

Serena couldn't help but laugh—and thought that it had been some time since she'd felt so lighthearted. Leonard glanced toward the portico where she stood, a big straw hat shading her face, the yellow dimity dress blowing slightly in the March breeze. "I'm teaching Liberty to play ball," Leonard explained, almost apologetically. "It seems I must also teach him to share."

Serena held on to her hat as she walked down the path toward Leonard and the child. "He does well playing, but he needs more practice at sharing. Or so it seems," she added hastily, always somehow afraid of offending Leonard's dignity.

"It does indeed." Leonard spoke with unusual affability as his pursed lips puckered into a smile. "But he's making progress. You would never recognize him from the poor little creature who first came to us."

Serena gazed quizzically at Leonard. "Oh? How long has he been here?"

Leonard's face stiffened into its customary stoic expression. "Quite some time," he replied and gestured to Liberty. "Be a good child, throw the ball back."

Liberty stood up and rolled the ball toward Leonard, who trapped it against his foot. Serena watched them continue the game for a few minutes and then started back indoors. There was a new softness in the air, heralding spring's official arrival in another week or so. But without her shawl she felt chilly, and it would be foolish to risk catching cold just now: Tomorrow she and Brant and Cecelia would be leaving New Bern on *The Irish Rover*. The blockade had tightened in recent weeks, but Brant felt there was a chance of escape on a Yankee ship.

The plans had only come to fruition the previous day. For over three weeks there had been no word from Brant or Yancy. Serena's anxiety mounted steadily; she was certain that Brant had been taken to a Confederate prison somewhere or even shot. If, she thought grimly, Brant wanted real proof of her concern for his welfare, he would see it in the circles under her eyes. Neither Fitch nor Cecelia had been able to offer any reassurance, and in fact Cecelia had been on the verge of resurrecting the New Orleans plan if Brant didn't act soon.

Uncle Luke and Aunt Kathleen had been told about the departure plans that same night. Aunt Kathleen had cried, pleading for them to change their minds, but Uncle Luke had thought the matter over in silence for more than an hour and finally given his nieces the family blessing.

"You belong up North," he'd said, eyes shamelessly misty. "Maybe I do, too. But this is my home, my wife and children are here. I feel compelled to stay in New Bern."

Fitch, however, had seemed surprisingly subdued. Serena asked her sister whether or not Fitch might be upset if he suspected his wife and son would not return to New Bern. But Cecelia had scoffed. "He knows it wouldn't be easy at best for me to come back. He may even be afraid that some of the county folk will snicker behind his back at his Yankee wife running away, but in a couple of weeks he'll forget about me. At least about me as his wife," she added with a little snort of contempt. "As for little Mark, Fitch isn't precisely a doting father."

Serena recalled that conversation as she made her way up the stairs to her room. Before she reached the landing, however, Cecelia's voice called out from the hallway. Serena turned, hand on the balustrade with its miniature gargoyles, one of the many whimsies Uncle Luke had incorporated into his home.

"Rena, we must talk." Cecelia stood in the middle of the parquet floor, a spring vision in floral-patterned lavender, saffron, and green bombazine, with a matching parasol.

"Of course." Serena waited for Cecelia to glide up the stairs. They went into the bedroom where Cecelia alighted on a bergère chair after setting her parasol on the credenza. Serena pulled up a crewel-covered footstool and noted that her sister's olive skin seemed darker than usual and her black eyes were bright as onyx.

"Final plans," Cecelia announced, a smile playing at the corners of her wide mouth. "You're packed?"

"Oh, yes, I just finished a bit ago." Serena indicated the luggage stacked on the far side of the bed.

Cecelia glanced in that direction but raced on to the matter of most importance: "Yancy has relayed the final plans. The crew was forced to move *The Irish Rover* away from an area of possible conflict. She's anchored off Cape Fear."

The very name seemed ominous to Serena. "Do you mean *we* have to run the blockade?"

"No, no." Cecelia's wide shoulders all but shook with merriment at her sister's foolish idea. "We'll sail south for a while, then east— and north to home." The gracefully draped arms stretched wide. "No roundabout, endless railway journey through the entire damnable South, no months and months to wait before we're back in Brunswick. Of course we'll have to take the train as far as Beaufort but that's all of two hours. Brant told me we ought to be home by the end of April."

Serena considered this alteration of their plans. As long as Brant had found a way to leave the clutches of the Confederacy, and his ship was nearby, it was a simple, no doubt risk-free, solution.

"What time will we leave?" Serena asked.

"Noon." Cecelia rose, posing langorously against the credenza. "You haven't asked how—or if—Captain Parnell has extricated himself from captivity. Don't you care?"

"Certainly I care," Serena retorted vexedly. "I just assumed that glib son-of-a-seaman would figure a way out. He has Yancy to help him, in any event."

"That's so." Cecelia picked up her parasol and patted the ruffle which adorned its edges. "But Sergeant Davis wasn't so willing to bend the rules and Uncle Luke had to intervene with Colonel Campbell to insist that no Farrar kin would stoop to spying."

Serena all but snorted. "I'm not sure what Brant wouldn't stoop to, if he thought it would serve his purposes." She heard Cecelia's sharp intake of breath, but refused to soften her words. "Brant Parnell is as ruthless as Papa—and as unscrupulous as Fitch. You and I don't seem to be very lucky with the men in our lives."

Cecelia shrugged. "At least none of them is keen on being poor. Neither am I." The statement somehow seemed to tickle Cecelia's fancy and her throaty laugh echoed in the bedroom. "I must be off, I have to see to Chloe and Hannah's packing."

"You're taking both the nurse and the maid?" Serena asked in mild surprise.

"Why not? They'll be a great help to Mandy and Dorcas. Chloe is particularly excited, never having been out of New Bern." Cecelia put her hand on the brass doorknob. "It will be a nice change for them; maybe I'll emancipate them or something."

"What a fine idea," Serena said blandly. She watched Cecelia wave a white-gloved hand and disappear down the corridor. And then Serena stifled a bitter laugh, kicked the crendenza, and wished it were Brant Parnell.

Serena was not superstitious, but somehow the idea of leaving for Cape Fear on the morning of March 13 struck her as vaguely foreboding. To exacerbate her anxiety, the fine weather of the previous day had changed to a drenching rain. Serena gazed from her bedroom window after a restless night and watched the downpour pummel the myrtles which had leafed out in the garden below.

It was only a few minutes after seven. Uncle Luke was already seated at the table in the family dining room, reading *The Daily Progress* and sipping coffee. From somewhere in the distance thunder rumbled, causing Serena to jump just as she entered the room.

"Hold on, Rena, just a pre-equinoctial storm." Uncle Luke smiled in reassurance as Leonard came out from the kitchen. "Mrs. Parnell needs some coffee, Leonard. She's off to an early start today."

Leonard produced a steaming silver pot and a china cup and saucer from the sideboard. He did not usually wait on table and in fact, Serena had discovered, often sat in familiar conversation with his master in the mornings before anyone else had come downstairs.

Serena poured a bit of cream and half a teaspoon of sugar in her coffee. Leonard had left the room, apparently heeding the call of Liberty, whose youthful shrieks could be heard coming from the direction of the pantry.

"I want to let you and Aunt Kathleen know how much I appreciate your kindness and hospitality," Serena said, raising the cup to her lips. "It's really been wonderful to get to know you both after all these years."

"It's been pretty wonderful having you here, Rena. And Celia, too, despite her occasional lapses." Luke's eyes crinkled at the corners. "Once this idiotic war is over, we'll have a big reunion of all the Farrars."

"That would be marvelous." Serena paused while Leonard returned, bearing a plateful of smoked ham, deep-fried bread, and pickled pears. Never having grown quite used to the heaviness of Southern cooking, Serena found the meal particularly overwhelming on this anxious March morning. But she knew she ought to eat something and began to cut up the ham while the thunder continued to roll out toward the seacoast.

"Strange," she commented, "I left Brunswick by train in a storm, now I'll leave New Bern the same way."

Uncle Luke nodded and then sat bolt upright. "Odd. Leonard, listen."

Leonard halted in midstep, a white linen napkin over his right arm. "Sir?" He and Uncle Luke stared at each other as the rain continued to splatter against the windows and the thunder kept up its steady, distant beat.

Uncle Luke stood up abruptly, an unfamiliar scowl on his face. "That's not thunder, by God. Those are guns." He marched around the table to the window which looked out toward the east. Leonard joined him as Serena sat rigidly watching their backs, her fingers digging into the dainty holes of the lace tablecloth.

"You're correct, Mister Luke," Leonard declared. "But quite far off. Slocum's Creek area, I'd estimate."

"You have a good ear, Leonard," Uncle Luke said, and turned to look at Serena. "You're pale, my dear, don't be alarmed. It's probably only some of the militiamen practicing. Or are they called the 'malish'?"

"In a derisive way," Leonard said. He gestured discreetly at the folded newspaper which lay on the table. "I believe *The Daily Progress* took the citizenry to task for referring to the soldiers as such and for ridiculing their military preparations."

Uncle Luke walked back to the table and looked down at the newspaper. "So they did, I'd forgotten. About a month ago, wasn't it? Well," he went on, reseating himself and lighting a brown cigarette, "I have to agree with the *Progress*—if you're going to fight a war—God forbid—you have to make ready for it. Some of the men I've talked to don't agree, though."

Serena's stomach was churning in a most alarming fashion. She pushed away her uneaten breakfast, which lay congealing on the plate, and took a deep drink of coffee. "I don't understand that attitude," she said, hoping her voice sounded normal and that her stomach would hear and be reassured. "It isn't because they don't believe in the war, is it?"

"Who knows?" Uncle Luke fingered the moistened end of his cigarette, which apparently had been rolled by his latest invention. "Some don't, that's why North Carolina was the last state to secede. Many do, but somehow they find the—what's the term, Leonard?—the 'malish'?—laughable because it's something different—and maybe frightening." He stopped talking and fingering his cigarette to sit very still. "The cannons are quiet now. I'll have to admit, it's an inconsiderate hour of the day to make noises like that. A lot of people out at Slocum's Creek must have had a rude awakening." Uncle Luke chuckled at his play on words and gave Serena an encouraging look.

"Don't fret, Rena, in a few hours you'll be on board *The Irish Rover*, safe and sound."

Serena smiled back at her uncle and tried to nod with conviction. "I know, it's just that I've always been the sort to assume that if something can go wrong at the last minute, it will."

Leonard had moved out of the room once again, with the innate grace and noiseless tread which seldom caused others to note his arrivals and departures. Uncle Luke was puffing away, somewhat obscured from Serena's view by blue clouds of smoke. "Interesting folks here in Craven County," he said through the haze, "and good folks, all told. While some of them may poke a bit of fun at the soldiers, perhaps it's because the ones who've signed up are poor, mostly farm boys. That sixty-five dollars the Confederacy is offering sounds like a lot of money to those young fellows."

Serena's stomach had begun to calm down but she still had no appetite. "Didn't you tell me that some of the county folks have complained because most of the North Carolina men who joined the army have been sent to Virginia?"

"My, yes. But that's where the action is. Still, it leaves us undermanned and . . ." Uncle Luke shifted in his chair at the sound of voices in the hall. Serena peered through the blue smoke to see Leonard ushering Brant Parnell into the room. He was dressed exactly as she had seen him almost a month ago, in his seaman's garb and cap. To Serena's surprise, her heart turned over in her breast. Or perhaps it was her upset stomach. Surely, she told herself, it could not be a reaction to seeing Brant Parnell.

Leonard began to speak but Brant cut across his words: "I'm Brant Parnell, sir, and I don't have time for formalities." He reached down to wring Uncle Luke's unsuspecting hand and then turned to Serena. "The goddamned Union army is encamped on the banks of the Neuse River. We haven't got an iceberg's chance in hell of taking a train to Cape Fear. Excuse my language."

Serena froze in her place. Prepared for the worst, she had not actually expected it. "Dear God," she murmured and was hardly aware that Brant had moved to her side to put a comforting arm around her trembling shoulders.

"The cannon . . ." Uncle Luke stubbed out his cigarette and waved away the smoke clouds. "You mean, those were *Yankee* cannons?"

"That's right." Brant's voice was tight. "*Only* Yankee cannon fire. The Federal forces met no opposition. What in hell kind of war are you people fighting?"

Uncle Luke could not suppress a short laugh. "I'm not fighting any sort of war, Captain Parnell. Nor is Leonard. As a fellow New Englander and, I might add, a shirttail relation of yours, I'm doing my best to remain neutral at the moment. As for Leonard, I hardly think he'd care to defend the concept of slavery." Uncle Luke turned to Leonard, who was looking positively prunelike with indignation. "Well, would you, Leonard?"

"I believe I made my views quite clear in my treatise on William E. Wilberforce, sir." The words were all but spat through clenched teeth.

"A fine treatise it was, too," Uncle Luke declared, nodding with approbation at Leonard. "Wonderful theoretical work on the comparison between Wilberforce's antislavery views and his Catholic emancipation advocacy . . ."

"Uncle Luke!" Serena actually screamed. She felt Brant's grip tighten, and put both her hands on her head. "I'm sorry, but we can't sit here and talk about Wilberforce, we're about to be captured by the enemy!"

Uncle Luke stared at Serena. "The enemy? Dear Rena, these are our people. Let's not lose our heads."

Brant nodded at Uncle Luke. "That's true, but they don't know that. If the Union army approaches through New Bern, they won't stop to ask who was born where or who believes in what." Brant sat down in the chair next to Serena's. "I didn't say we couldn't leave, I just said we couldn't take the train. But we're going to try to go by horseback tonight, after dark. If anyone else wants to go with us, that's fine. As long as there aren't more than a dozen." He turned to Uncle Luke. "Sir? Is there any chance you'd consider going North?"

Uncle Luke was going through the motions of searching for his tobacco pouch, matches, and whatever else he pulled out of the recesses of his clothing. The room was silent, except for the rain pelting the windows and the rivulets of water running off the roof. "You're right," Uncle Luke said at last. He gestured toward the windows. "That's not the sound of battle, is it? So I must presume it's the sound of surrender." His chuckle was hollow as he got to his feet, suddenly looking almost as impressive as Marcus Farrar himself. "I believe I'll stay, sir. This is my home." He glanced at Leonard. "These are my people now. If I must, I'll fight for both. God forbid."

Brant and Yancy—and the Confederate forces in New Bern—had learned of the Union invasion late the previous night. Warning fires along the Neuse River sent up billowing black smoke as the word passed along the Southern outposts. But by the time Sergeant Davis returned to camp with a full report, it was well after midnight.

There had been no point in conveying the disastrous news to either the Farrar or Moncrief house until morning. Brant had gone first to see Fitch, since he was Yancy's original contact. Cecelia had become hysterical and Fitch had asked to go with them should they devise a new escape route. That request had halted Cecelia's outburst; she had shrieked at Fitch that if he even considered going North she'd divorce him immediately upon setting foot in Brunswick and cut him off without a penny. Fitch had looked stricken but Cecelia had calmed down enough to remind him that with a war on, Uncle Luke would need his services more than ever. God only knew how the slaves would react, no one could predict the outcome of the conflict, who would protect the plantation—and Uncle Luke's own fortune—if Fitch turned tail and ran.

Whether it was the threat to his wallet or the appeal to his manhood which made Fitch retract his request, no one would ever know. But Brant had left the Moncrief house with a sense of relief before he'd gone next door to confront his wife and Uncle Luke. Serena had finally managed to compose herself after Uncle Luke had made his moving declaration to stay in New Bern. Aunt Kathleen and the twins had appeared, however, adding considerable confusion to the gathering. Under the guise of seeing Brant out, Serena extricated herself from the family melee. Brant gave her tentative instructions: to be ready by nine but not to be surprised if they left somewhat later; to take only what was absolutely necessary; to rest up and be prepared for a long, difficult ride. The roads were a quagmire. It would not be possible to take a wagon, so everyone must ride astride.

"I know you can do that, Serena," Brant said, a hint of amusement in the blue eyes. "Just pay attention to the footing this time, all right?"

Serena had too many other matters on her mind to let the reference to her tumble in Livermore Falls annoy her. "What about little Mark?" she asked.

"I can carry him part of the way and I've got a couple of crewmen who've come ashore to join us. Unless we get some other volunteers, it'll be four women, three men, and the baby. Yancy can't spare anyone to give us an escort."

Serena brushed at the stray hairs which trailed down her forehead. She caught Brant's gaze on her bosom and flushed. "I don't know . . . Are you sure it's safe?"

"What? Oh—no, actually, I'm not." Brant forced himself to meet her troubled gaze and bring his mind back to the business at hand. "See here, Serena, I'd be a liar if I said otherwise. But I think we have a good chance. So we'll take it."

And so they would. The rest of the day had been spent sorting out the luggage, deciding what to wear, and coping with Cecelia, who made at least ten flying, rainsoaked dashes between her home and the Farrar house. She was angry, she was terrified, she was impatient, she ran a gamut of emotions which left Serena exhausted and yet unable to sleep by late afternoon. Aunt Kathleen fidgeted and fretted, conjuring up every possible danger which might beset them. Every word of the impending battle which filtered inside the Farrar house was brought to Serena by the older woman. By nightfall, however, the only real news was that the Federal force was sizable, more troops were going to land, and the first contingent had fought a few skirmishes with the Confederates along the Neuse River.

When the mantel clock in the retiring room struck nine, Serena was standing by the fireplace, dressed in a pair of one twin's trousers, a heavy flannel shirt, and an ancient hooded sou'wester Uncle Luke had brought from Maine. She wore her own boots and gloves, and her luggage had been reduced to one canvas bag.

Leonard appeared in the doorway to announce that Captain Parnell had arrived. Serena was surprised and suddenly afraid. She had been certain that they would have to wait well into the evening, half the night, perhaps. But Brant's prompt appearance jarred her into facing the reality of flight. She caught a glimpse of him with another man who had picked up her bag in the hall and was taking it outside. Then Brant was in the room, shaking Uncle Luke's hand and making a brief bow to Aunt Kathleen, who offered him a somewhat coquettish smile.

"It's time, Serena," Brant said and his voice was strangely gentle, as if he were reassuring a skittish mare. Brant took her gloved hand but she was forced to withdraw it to hug Aunt Kathleen tight. Her aunt began to weep and Uncle Luke pried the two women apart.

"I never did like farewells," he asserted. "Good-bye. Good luck." He leaned down to kiss Serena's cheek, stepped back two paces, and turned to stare into the fire in the grate. "Take care of her, Captain," he called without looking back. "Take care of them all."

There were a dozen horses outside, seven for the riders, five for their belongings. Cecelia had been adamant about taking her ball-gowns North. Having had to forsake a great portion of her elegant wardrobe, Cecelia balked at leaving the dresses she'd had specially made by New Bern's finest seamstress.

Fitch Moncrief had already bade farewell to his wife and the baby. "Fitch wanted to keep dry," Cecelia remarked with a touch of scorn. She lowered her voice and leaned toward Serena: "He told Uncle Luke he was going to help protect the city, but I doubt that Madame Eugenie's bawdy house is of strategic importance."

Serena had no reply, but could not have voiced it if she did: Brant was introducing them to his crewmen, Jake Carew and Dennis O'Malley. O'Malley's brogue was so thick that Serena assumed he had just arrived from Ireland, but in fact the young man with the carrot-colored hair had been in America for over five years.

Serena observed the deference both men showed Brant despite his easy manner of authority. He must, she decided somewhat irritably, have a more winning way with men than with women.

O'Malley led the way down Pollock Street, heading due west to Queen Street and onto either the Trent or Pollocksville Road. While the early stages of the route would take them several miles in the opposite direction of Cape Fear, Brant had determined that they must circumvent the Union army and any possibility of walking into a military confrontation.

Brant, with the baby cradled in his arms and well-wrapped against the cold, damp air, rode behind O'Malley. Cecelia followed him, then Serena, Hannah, Chloe, and Carew, who kept one eye on the pack horses and the other on anyone who might approach the rear of their small caravan.

They weren't the only people abroad on this inclement night. Dozens of other New Bern citizens apparently had decided to move to safer ground. Carts, wagons, mules, and horses were loaded down as families fled to sanctuary in the adjoining counties. Just off Forbes Alley they had to stop and wait when a buckboard toppled over and its owners argued volubly about whose fault the accident had been and who was responsible for reloading.

Half an hour later, the small band reached the Pollocksville Road. In the distance they could see the flicker of a few Confederate camp-fires. Nearby, the waters of the Trent River mingled with Lawson's Creek to rumble seaward in the night. The guns, however, were silent. For some reason, it had never occurred to Serena that soliders had to sleep, too; she thought that once they began a battle, they didn't stop until it was over. But then Serena had not thought much about sol-diers—or war—until this very day.

Toward midnight, they crossed the Trent and found the footing more difficult. The deluge of the past day had turned even the best roads to mud, but there, on the edge of Hood's Creek, the country byway was a virtual marsh. Serena huddled inside Uncle Luke's sou'wester and squinted into the darkness as the rain pummeled her face. Her mare was balky, the baby was crying, and Chloe had kept up a steady whimper for the last half-mile.

Cecelia's temper finally snapped: "Chloe, do hush! You wanted to have an adventure and this is it!"

"But I'd never had no notion it'd be such a wet one!" Chloe sneezed and began to whimper again.

"Don't you dare take cold," Cecelia barked. "You'll pass it on to Mark when you nurse him!"

Loud as she was, Cecelia's cries were all but drowned out by the baby's squalling. Brant signaled for O'Malley to stop. "All right," Brant said as the little group sat their horses in varying stages of discomfort, "we'll rest a bit. I assume the baby's hungry?" He shifted in the saddle to look at Cecelia who had put on a canvas windbreaker over her finely cut riding habit.

"He may be." She glanced reproachfully at Chloe. "I thought you said he'd been sleeping all night since before Christmas."

"Some nights do, some nights don't," Chloe murmured into the recesses of her ample bosom.

Brant dismounted and the others did too, except Cecelia, who suddenly seemed quite unable to move off her horse. Brant carefully passed the baby to Chloe before reaching out to take Cecelia's hand.

"I've never believed that Southern gentlemen are more gallant than Northerners," Cecelia declared, allowing herself to lean against him for just a few seconds. "Hannah has brought some chicken and black-eyed peas. Is anyone besides my darling Marky hungry?" She gazed up at Brant, a radiant look on her face. "Isn't he a handsome boy, Captain?"

"Handsome, yes. And loud. Very loud." Brant wore a fixed smile as Carew put out a large piece of tarpaulin, O'Malley unrolled more canvas to make a tent, and Serena gave her a sister a quizzical, side-long look.

They had stopped in a grove of pine trees which provided some shelter from the rain. Chloe was already seated on the canvas, nursing the baby, and Cecelia was munching on a chicken leg Hannah had unpacked.

"This is quite the strangest picnic I've ever been on," Cecelia said between hearty bites. "Not at all like the ones at the shore in Maine."

Serena stood apart from the others, nudging a pine cone with her foot and deciding that she would refrain from eating rain-soaked chicken. How different, how desolate the forest seemed this strange, dreary night, she thought, a far cry from how it had been the day she had taken a stroll with Uncle Luke and the twins the first week of her arrival. They had walked over four miles, with the scent of the pine trees heavy on the late autumn air, the shafts of sunlight slanting down between the boughs, and the ground firm beneath their feet.

Carew and O'Malley had the tent up, a sorry-looking affair which seemed to sag dangerously in the middle. Chloe moved inside with the baby as soon as the men were finished. Cecelia plucked another chicken leg out of the hamper and followed the nurse and the baby under cover.

"Aren't you eating, Rena?" Cecelia asked as they unrolled their blankets.

"Is there any left?" Serena inquired more archly than she'd intended.

"I had a very light supper," Cecelia replied defensively. "Only some ham and collard greens and potatoes. Oh, and souffle."

Serena tentatively reached up to test the tarpaulin roof of the tent. "Well, you can always end up wearing this if it falls down."

"Serena! I don't want to hear your wicked tongue when we're practically on the edge of a battlefield!" Cecelia, always sensitive about her opulent stature, had whirled on her sister, startling the baby, who stopped nursing and began to cry again.

"You weren't concerned about that when you were stuffing yourself just now," Serena said affably.

"You know I always eat when I'm troubled! Oh, hush, Marky! Chloe, make that child be quiet!" Cecelia tossed the rest of the chicken leg outside the tent, catching O'Malley in the left knee. He swore in surprise and Cecelia turned on him: "Your language isn't fit for ladies' company! Please be more of a gentleman in my presence!"

"Holy Mother, I was not expecting a chicken to fly after it be dead," O'Malley declared. "Beggin' your pardon, Mrs. Moncrief, I meant no harm."

Brant had come up behind O'Malley and put a hand on the Irishman's shoulder. "We may all be a little testy this evening," he said mildly. "Is something wrong, Mrs. Moncrief?"

In reply, Cecelia burst into tears and, all but toppling O'Malley, hurled herself into Brant's arms. "I've been trying to be so brave, for the sake of the others! Now Serena is being nasty and all I want to do is get some rest!" Cecelia darted a baleful look in Serena's direction. Clamping her mouth shut, Serena refrained from asking her sister why she had suddenly turned into such a namby-pamby.

Brant patted her back through the thick canvas jacket while she continued to sob heavily against his chest. "Just lie down, ma'am. Here, let me fix this blanket for you, it's pretty lumpy."

Cecelia seemed to shudder as she watched Brant bend down to straighten the blanket. "I know you won't let anything happen to us, Captain, but I still get these . . . twinges of fear. I'd feel much better if you'd stay next to me."

"I don't have much choice," Brant said with a grin, "since this tent is only about ten feet square. All right, you settle in here and I'll keep close." He smiled reassuringly as Cecelia knelt rather timorously on the blanket and looked up through her lashes.

"I'll put little Marky between us—for his protection." Cecelia turned to Chloe. "Here, the baby must sleep by me."

Chloe's round brown eyes grew even rounder. "Sleep by you, Miz Celia? Why, sakes' alive, you ain't never had that baby sleep—"

"Hush, Chloe!" Cecelia's tone had suddenly grown strident again. "We've had enough foolish chatter for one night."

Chloe dutifully handed over the baby who was now asleep; Cecelia cuddled him against her breast, gave Brant a grateful smile, and laid down beneath the blanket.

Brant had prepared his own place and within a few minutes, the lantern was snuffed out and all was quiet within the crowded tent, save for the sound of concerted breathing and the relentless rain striking the tarpaulin. Serena was on the opposite side of the tent, next to Hannah, who was already snoring softly. Indeed, within a quarter of an hour, everyone seemed to be asleep. Except Serena. Her feet had gotten tangled in the blanket; the ground felt extremely uneven under the canvas; the sou'wester encumbered her movements and she would have taken it off except that then she would have been too cold. So she lay on her back, looking up into the sagging tarpaulin and listening to the rain.

As typical as Cecelia's theatrical behavior had been, it annoyed Serena more than she'd realized. In the year and a half that they'd been separated, she had forgotten just how obvious Cecelia could be—at least to Serena. Somehow, her sister's male victims rarely seemed to see through her overblown affectations.

Certainly Brant was too experienced to fall prey to Cecelia's wiles. Yet he had humored her, even comforted her with his arms. He couldn't do much else, of course; given their precarious situation, only a cad would have attempted to put Cecelia in her place. It was even possible that Cecelia was genuinely frightened. A young mother fleeing the war-torn countryside with a small baby was bound to feel vulnerable. Serena kicked at her blanket, accidentally striking Hannah, who gave a little jump and immediately stopped snoring. The maid, however, was still asleep, Serena noted as she cautiously rolled over. The rain had finally let up to only a tap-tap-tap above her head. She got to her knees and crawled outside, heedless of the wet ground soaking into her trousers. She stood up, leaned against the trunk of a pine tree, and realized it had stopped raining altogether.

She also realized that she was extremely angry. Frightened, indeed—Cecelia had more nerve than a peanut merchant. In the past few months since Serena's arrival, Cecelia had fluttered and flirted among the gentlemen of New Bern, but she never—ever—hurled herself at any of them as she had done this very night with Brant.

Furthermore, Serena reminded herself as she left the haven of the pine tree and began walking aimlessly over the muddy ground, Brant hadn't even bothered to ask what her own future plans were. After the questions he'd posed in the crumbling audience chamber of Tryon Palace, he hadn't seen fit to trouble himself to inquire again. Sometimes Serena felt she'd imagined that searing kiss at Tryon Palace;

certainly it did no good to dwell on what must have been a mere show of masculine bravado on Brant's part.

Serena's feet all but stuck in the mud as she plodded among the trees. Brant and Cecelia had just met that morning. Was it possible that her sister, aware that there was no love lost in Serena's marriage, would dare make a play for Brant? Surely not—Cecelia might be an outrageous flirt, but she possessed enough honor to stay away from her brother-in-law.

Nor, Serena reflected, should it disturb her—it wasn't as if she were madly in love with Brant Parnell. Cecelia could make a fool of herself twice over and it wouldn't make the slightest bit of difference, other than what the usual gossip-mongers might say. So why was she wandering about in the middle of the night with a war going on and getting herself mud-soaked all the way to her knees? Certainly it wasn't a matter of jealousy. She didn't care enough about Brant to be jealous of Cecelia. Yet Serena's agile mind wasn't put to rest so easily. If, she questioned herself, I don't care, why did I let Cecelia upset me so? Could I care and not know it?

"I must sort this out," she murmured aloud, and had an unexpected longing to stand before the little cherub in her parents' garden and tell him her troubles. Instead, she stood before a creek which was running high, almost spilling over its banks. Serena frowned and stared into the darkness. Had she walked back to Hood's Creek? No, this rush of rumbling water was too wide; there was a much bigger creek to the east, she had seen it last November with Uncle Luke and the twins. Price's Creek or Brice's Creek or something like that . . . She felt a surge of panic for she knew she had lost her way.

Sternly telling herself she must not lose her wits as well, Serena stood very still and tried to think logically, but her inner turmoil was now surpassed by the anger she felt with herself for being such a heedless ninny. She could almost hear her mother's voice saying, "Now, Serena, where is that good common sense of yours? Don't tell me you let emotion rule your brain!"

But that was precisely what she *had* done and it served her right to have gotten herself so miserably lost. It didn't serve the others right, however; Brant would undoubtedly take Carew or O'Malley and start searching as soon as they awoke and discovered she was missing. And that delay just might ruin their hopes of getting away before the countryside was swarming with soliders from both armies.

Following the creek was her only chance, Serena decided grimly. She wondered what time it was—probably around three o'clock. Certainly there was no sign of dawn, though she might not have been able to tell, as a heavy mist had moved in after the rain. Serena began to follow the cresting creek as it plunged in what she hoped would be a short distance to the Trent River.

I must be going north, she told herself, but there was still no river in sight. The mist had turned into a thick fog as the creek's waters appeared to be dropping slightly. Yet to Serena's dismay, the creek was taking a great many twists and turns. Over an hour later, walking in mud up to her ankles, cold and shivering, exhausted and hungry, Serena sat down on a tree stump and cried.

She had no idea how long she remained there, feeling desolate, distraught, and extremely sorry for herself, but when she finally brushed the tears away and peeled the dried mud off her trousers, she realized it had grown lighter. Through the fog, she could make out the framework of a small wooden bridge. If there was a bridge, there must be a road; at least she had found some sort of direction. Assuming, she thought with a sense of chagrin, it was the *right* direction.

The road, however, provided only slightly better footing than the forest. It was almost like walking in a swamp, and Serena suddenly remembered how Uncle Luke had warned her about the many snakes which inhabited this part of the country. But since it was growing lighter, she would be able to see them, she told herself, and then wondered if that fact actually gave any comfort. It didn't make much difference, if only her weary, shaking legs would hold her up.

And then she heard voices through the drifting vapors. Serena saw a dozen men, all wearing the blue uniform of the Union army. Was it a dream—or a nightmare? Surely she could explain, tell them she was a Yankee woman homeward-bound to Brunswick, Maine.

The soliders were having their own difficulties making headway on the muddy road. They did indeed seem dreamlike, appearing and reappearing as the gray mists floated past.

But this was no dream. Serena raised her hand to wave, then stood very still. Union men or not, they wouldn't know that she wasn't the enemy. The fog thickened, completely obscuring the little group, and the dampness tingled against her cheeks as her feet sank deeper into the mud. She could hear the men's voices, just a few yards away. Pulling hard, she managed to dislodge one of her feet, only to feel the other being sucked further into the mire. Tears of panic, fright, and frustration spilled down her cheeks. It would be better, she thought bitterly, if the soldiers discovered her and fired their weapons. Being shot would be a more merciful death than dying of starvation and exposure in a North Carolina swamp.

The startling buffet of another human being's body against hers sent a chilling shriek from the depths of Serena's lungs. Afraid to look and not sure she could see through her tears, Serena found herself leaning against the solid form which stood next to her. At least he's too close to shoot me, she thought in a daze of fear, and closed her eyes as her knees buckled.

"If you faint, I'll boot you from here to the Trent," Brant Parnell muttered and gave her a sharp little shake. He steadied Serena with one arm and raised his voice: "I found her, men. Head back to the footbridge."

Serena vaguely heard the sounds of the soldiers' voices, no doubt cursing wayward women who managed to complicate the masculine privilege of war. She didn't care. Brant was holding her safe in his arms and she craned her neck to stare up at him, offering a tremulous smile. "I'm sorry," she said, and knew it was the voice of a penitent child.

"Sorry, my hind end." His craggy face looked as if it were etched in Vermont granite. He grabbed her by the shoulders and yanked her straight up. Both feet came free with a hollow sucking noise. "Now hang on to me and start walking. This way," he urged, giving her a none-too-gentle nudge, "toward the bridge."

Again the fog's curtain parted just enough so that Serena could see the men slogging up ahead in a straggly line. Wiping away her tears with the back of her hand, Serena gritted her teeth and let Brant haul her along through the mud.

"I know it was stupid . . ." she began, but Brant waved a hand for silence.

"Don't waste words on the obvious. Any chance we had of escaping is gone, not to mention that we might all have been killed. You, especially, staggering around this goddamned swamp."

"I thought I knew my way," Serena protested. "I said I was sorry. If you don't care what happens to me, why didn't you just keep going?"

Dawn's weak March light waged its own battle against the fog, outlining the men up ahead and the trees on the horizon. "The horses couldn't manage it," Brant admitted with reluctance. "And your delicate sister, despite her Amazonian proportions, refused to walk. Good God, between the two of you, I married the one who walked too far!"

Serena thought she detected a hint of Brant's familiar ironic humor and felt a faint sense of relief. "What do we do now?"

Brant snorted as they reached the wooden footbridge across the creek. The roiling waters rushed dangerously close to the underside of the bridge but the soldiers had already crossed safely.

"I'll go back to my ship and on to New Bedford. You sit here on that pretty little backside of yours until I can figure out another way to bring you home. Of course," he added, giving her a wry sidelong look, "it may take a year or two, but maybe that'll teach you not to act like a spoiled brat."

"Brat!" exploded Serena, stumbling slightly on the last board in the footbridge. "That's not fair! And spending what sounds like forever in New Bern is a punishment that doesn't fit the crime."

"I'd commute the sentence if there wasn't a war on. Head this way, Rena, the men are waiting for you over here. I've got to go back to the others."

"What? Why can't I come?" The petulant note was back in her voice.

Brant looked down at the small figure enveloped in the sou'wester and grinned. "It's at least a mile and I want to be quick about it. Don't worry, those fellows will take you to the Union camp and you'll have ample Parnell protection." Brant paused as Serena's eyes widened in puzzlement. "My brother, who occasionally has fewer brains than you do, is part of the Massachusetts contingent."

"Kirk!" Serena put a hand over her mouth. "How . . . coincidental. Have you seen him?

Brant shook his head. "These boys belong to his regiment. They'll take you to him, it's not far from here. Now march, Serena, I've got to move along."

"But . . ." Serena licked her lips and tried to find the right words. "Will I see you before you leave?"

"Probably. I can't just point your sister and the rest of them toward New Bern and wave. Go on, Rena, those men have a war to win." He poked at her with a forefinger, but she was reluctant to turn away. "Well?" He wore a rueful look.

Serena moved clumsily in the muddied boots, shifting from side to side like a listing ship. "Well." She cursed the squeak in her voice. "Well, good-bye. And good luck." Inwardly, she asked why she was prolonging this awkward moment.

Brant seemed to be struggling with a desire to laugh. Or was he damping down his impatience? Serena couldn't be sure, but either way, his reaction unsettled her even further. Damn, she thought, the man is so infernally disturbing; why do I always feel so blasted uneasy around him? Except, she reminded herself, when I'm in his arms . . .

And suddenly she was, with his lips claiming hers and the feel of his unshaven chin against her face. Serena let his tongue roam at will inside her mouth, let her own arms hold him close, let her body strain as near to him as layers of oilskin and wool would permit.

Dimly, Serena recognized that it wasn't just comfort she sought from Brant, but something more—a testimonial to her survival, an affirmation of her womanhood. She had spent dark dangerous hours alone and afraid, behaving like a child in her fit of pique, but emerging with common sense intact. Her mother would have nodded in approval; her father would have slapped her shoulder in congratulation; but from her husband, Serena wanted—and needed—much more.

Yet even as Brant kissed her eyelids and the end of her nose, she reminded herself that this was neither the time nor the place. Which perhaps was why she *could* admit her need for Brant to prove she was a woman, not a girl. It was impossible for that to happen— therefore, it was safe. Serena allowed herself to playfully nip Brant's lower lip with her teeth and saw the blue eyes spark with surprise.

"Well." Brant glimpsed swiftly back over his shoulder at the waiting Union men, saw them clustered together by the bridge exchanging speculative comments, and shrugged. "Oh, what the hell," Brant breathed and kissed Serena again, bending her so far back she was certain she'd fall in the mud. But that was unimportant; she realized, with a happy glow building inside, that she was very happy, despite the war, the fog, the terror of the night. She was sinking not into the mire, but drowning in Brant's kisses, oblivious to everything except that strange, detached realm where only the two of them mattered . . .

It was only when Brant pulled away just enough to look into her dazed, slanting eyes that Serena came back to grim, damp reality. "Is that what you were waiting for?" Brant asked, but saw the confusion on her face and shook his head. "Don't answer. If you lie, I might believe you. If you tell the truth, I'll probably think you're lying." As the befuddled expression deepened, Brant sealed her mouth with his finger. "Never mind, the real problem is, you don't know the difference either." Abruptly he let her go, and Serena felt her feet start to sink back into the mud. She had no idea what Brant was talking about, she only knew that for a few magic moments she had been elated in his embrace, and that soon he'd be gone again, leaving her to wonder if she'd imagined their mutual ardor.

Brant was already gesturing to the patient, if curious, soldiers, but he wore his familiar wry grin as he turned back to Serena. "If I didn't know you look a lot better than this, I might not come South again. It's not just that this get-up is so unbecoming," he went on, lowering his voice and pulling her out of the mire by both arms, "but I do recall what you look like with no clothes on at all." The grin faded; he was suddenly serious, even concerned. "For God's sake, Rena, be careful!"

Before she could reply, he was moving swiftly away, disappearing across the footbridge and into the fog.

Chapter 10

SERENA WASN'T SURE which was more nerve-racking—Aunt Kathleen's anxious wails or her peals of relief. When Serena finally got home that evening, both Uncle Luke and Aunt Kathleen had been astonished to see her. Indeed, Aunt Kathleen had all but swooned at the sight of the Yankee escort provided by Kirk Parnell to ensure his sister-in-law's safety. Finally, she had calmed down sufficiently to hear Serena's story, but had begun to lament anew over the fate of Cecelia, the baby, and the others. Their return the following morning evoked joyous shrieks from Aunt Kathleen which threatened to give Serena a worse headache than any Abigail had ever endured.

"Excitable, I take it," Brant said mildly as he guided Serena out onto the veranda. His unshaven face was weary, but the blue eyes remained alert despite the rigors of bringing his little party home without mishap. Serena examined the patches of muddy dirt which still clung to his clothes and the left sleeve on his coat which had unraveled at the cuff. She repressed an uncharacteristic urge to suggest that she mend the sleeve and vigorously rubbed at her throbbing temples instead.

"It's strange," she remarked, grateful for the reviving breeze coming off the river, "I would have thought Aunt Kathleen might flee New Bern. Many of her friends did, I'm told, running away out along the railway tracks with nothing but the clothes on their backs. No wonder she's so . . . distraught."

"And shrill." Brant made a face, then sighed. "A crazy time, a crazy war, a crazy bunch of people." He gave a little shake of his head and turned to watch half a dozen Union soldiers march down Pollock Street in slack formation. As they disappeared around the corner, Brant looked back to his wife. "You managed all right, I see."

Serena lifted one shoulder. "Certainly. Kirk and his men were very kind." Major Kirk Parnell of the 21st Massachusetts Regiment had been not merely gallant, but genuinely glad to see his sister-in-law. While she still felt his role in her precipitous departure from New Bedford had been somewhat shabby, their reunion virtually at the edge of the battlefield made her personal grudge seem small. "It was good to see him again." She offered Brant a peaked smile. "I suppose we've no chance to get out of here now?"

Brant rubbed at the dark stubble along his jaw. "Probably not. No betting man would take the odds." He saw Serena's face fall and grimaced. "All right, Serena, just to make sure you won't blame me in that convoluted, contrary way of yours for being exiled to New Bern, I'll go see the Union high command today." His mouth was set in a tight line of resignation.

Inside the house, Serena could still hear snatches of Aunt Kathleen's unbridled joy. Trying to turn a deaf ear, she assumed an abject look. "I know it was my fault, but I didn't mean to ruin it for everyone else." Perhaps if she let him hold her or kiss her, he'd say she really wasn't to blame.

But Brant didn't attempt to come any nearer. Instead, he passed a hand over his eyes, shook his head, and yawned. "What's done is done." Brant squared his shoulders and glanced at the window where he glimpsed Uncle Luke and Leonard speaking to each other in solemn tones. "I'd better try to find Kirk." He lifted a hand in a halfhearted salute. "I'll see you later, Rena."

She started to say something which would detain him but thought better of it and clamped her mouth shut. Feeling empty, inadequate, and very much alone, she watched Brant walk with less than his usual vigor toward Pollock Street. He was almost to the drive when Serena started down the steps, stopped, and then, with feet that felt like bricks, made her lonely way back into the townhouse.

The bandage around Fitch Moncrief's head matched the taupe cravat he wore at his neck. It seemed to Serena that he was striking a pose as he leaned against the Farrar mantelpiece, brandy glass in hand. Serena wondered idly how much of Fitch and Cecelia's married life had been spent with them posing for each other.

"Of course I could have been killed outright," Fitch was saying for the third time. "If the larger piece of mortar had struck me instead of that smaller one, I'd have been a war casualty."

Cecelia didn't attempt to conceal the disdain she felt for her husband. "If you hadn't tried to chase after the Carr boy when he took your favorite Borsalino hat out of the establishment you were visiting while an invasion was under way, it would never have happened."

Fitch didn't even bother to look chagrined at Cecelia's reference to his spending the night in a bordello while his fellow citizens were besieged by the enemy. "He had no right to take my hat! It was thievery!" Fitch looked indignant, glancing at Uncle Luke as if for masculine support.

"Everybody was taking everything they could find, it seems to me," Uncle Luke said amiably. "It was that kind of night, what with fires being set and all. So many people have fled, too. The city seems deserted." His face appeared more deeply lined as he gazed out the window toward Pollock Street where the air was still smoky from the burning buildings and exchanges of gunfire in the heart of the town. "Besides being undermanned, our soldiers had damned few weapons. Excuse my language, ladies, but our men were using bricks to defend themselves."

"Most short-sighted," Cecelia said with contempt, rearranging her Irish linen skirts from her place on the settee. "Think of it, the actual battle for New Bern took only four hours! And now we're stranded for the duration!"

For once, Serena had to agree with her sister. The deployment of so many North Carolina troops to Virginia had been a tragic error in Confederate strategy. Fewer than four thousand men had been left to defend the city against an invading force of fifteen thousand Union troops. The only consolation was that the brevity of the battle had resulted in few casualties on either side and damage to the town itself had been minimal. The largest of the fires, which had threatened the commercial area, had been put out by the invaders.

Uncle Luke was gazing at the clock on the mantel as Aunt Kathleen stifled a delicate yawn. "You young folks ought to be abed and so should the rest of us. We've had a rugged past few days." He stood up as Cecelia glumly rose from the settee. Out in the street, they could hear the tramp of soldiers as the Union watch passed by. Serena gave a little shake of her head, still not used to being under siege— and by her own people at that.

A few moments later, Cecelia and Fitch had gone home while Uncle Luke was extinguishing the lamps. "I hope the Yankees won't arrest Celia and Fitch for breaking curfew." He smiled and sighed. "Such an upside-down world we live in! I don't even know who I want to win this war."

"I do." Aunt Kathleen, her emotions now under control, spoke with surprising vehemence. "You may be a Yankee, Mr. Farrar, but I'm a Southerner going back to 1772."

Uncle Luke stared at his wife and chuckled. "Such patriotism, my dear! And such a confession! I had no idea you were so old!"

Aunt Kathleen stared back and then giggled. "Lucas Farrar! Now aren't you the one!" Arm-in-arm, they bade Serena good-night and headed toward the gargoyle-studded staircase.

Serena picked up the copy of Goethe's *The Sorrows of Young Werther* which she'd been reading before Fitch and Cecelia had arrived. For once, she had not minded the interruption; Werther's romantic unrealism was more irritating than heartrending. She moved quietly out of the room, just in time to see Leonard extinguishing the hallway lamps.

Serena nodded at Leonard and started to say good-night, but remembered something Aunt Kathleen had said during the course of the evening, "Leonard—is it true that Uncle Luke freed his slaves?"

Leonard paused, a long, thin hand on one of the wall sconces. "No, Mrs. Parnell. He intends to, however, unless the Federal forces do it for him."

The faint note of disapproval was not lost on Serena. "You would oppose lawful emancipation, Leonard? I find that puzzling."

"I foresee grave difficulties," Leonard said somberly. He drew himself up to his full height and pursed his lips. "If the Confederacy is to be an independent, separate government, the North has no right to impose its will. I believe, Mrs. Parnell, that is the real issue."

His calm, precise words had the effect of making Serena feel as if she'd been scolded severely by her mother. "That's so," she answered, somewhat flustered by Leonard's keen-eyed gaze. "But surely you don't condone slavery."

"I do not. But there is more than one kind of slavery. I find it ironic that people in the North criticize people in the South when the working conditions in your factories are every bit as harsh and demeaning as what takes place here. You also employ children, which we do not, at least until they are twelve. It's true that some younger ones join their parents in the fields and some are trained in helpful tasks, but they are not expected to work long hours in wretched conditions such as I expect exist in your own father's factories in Maine."

Serena suppressed a little gasp. Leonard's outspoken diatribe had affronted her. While she was aware of shocking conditions in many Northern factories, at least Marcus Farrar didn't employ children.

"My father employs only able-bodied workers and pays a fair wage," she replied, forcing her voice to stay calm. "He firmly believes that a well-treated employee will help him achieve a better profit." She waited for Leonard to respond but his only reaction was the slight quivering of his V-shaped eyebrows. "As for you, I would think you'd be most pleased when you're eventually given your freedom."

Leonard's eyebrows now seemed to actually stand on end. "I?" The pursed lips drew down at the corners, the high forehead creased. "Why, no, Mrs. Parnell. I've never been a slave."

Serena felt herself flush and was glad there was so little light in the hallway. She began a stammered apology but was cut short by a knock at the door. Leonard brushed past her to find Brant Parnell standing on the veranda. He exchanged a brief greeting with Leonard before coming to Serena's side. "I've got a small army of my own in my hotel room. At least the half of the hotel that's still standing," he said irritably. "Our conquering heroes have taken over the place and I decided I'd better impose on your uncle's hospitality if I wanted any sleep tonight."

Serena informed him that Uncle Luke had gone to bed. Leonard stood with rigid patience, waiting for them to leave so that he could put out the last of the lamps. "There's a spare room next to mine," Serena said. "I'll have it made up for you."

Brant's eyes flickered in Leonard's direction before he spoke to Serena. "Fine. Are you going up now?"

"Yes." She looked past Brant's shoulder to ask Leonard if he could see to having the spare room taken care of. At his affirmative reply, Serena led the way upstairs and down the hall. "There," she whispered, pointing to the door next to hers. "Good night."

But Brant made no move to leave her side. "Serena, I want to talk to you." When she just stood there regarding him curiously, he opened the door and virtually pushed her inside. The room was in total darkness. Serena tersely informed him that if he took three paces to his left, he could light the lamp on the credenza. A few seconds later, a golden glow filled the chamber. Serena stood tensely, her hands folded in front of her, waiting for Brant to speak.

Brant had taken off his cap and wore his familiar ironic expression. "I had a long talk with Kirk tonight," he began. "The Union occupation has been deemed an official success. In fact, they expect to release Confederate prisoners on parole shortly."

"With three times as many Yankees as there are local citizens, I shouldn't think there'd be much of a problem," Serena remarked.

"Maybe not. But that doesn't take into account a possible counterattack by the Confederacy or even guerrilla warfare around the outskirts of the city." Brant paused, frowned and turned his head slightly so that the lamplight outlined his craggy features. "According to Kirk and General Reno, General Burnside wouldn't object to letting me sail *The Irish Rover* back home. But getting four women and a baby from here to Cape Fear is too risky. At least until the situation stabilizes."

Serena uttered a sigh of resignation. "I can't say you didn't warn me. How long until it's stabilized?"

Brant shrugged. "Nobody knows. But I can't allow my crew to remain anchored off the coast any longer. They've already been delayed for over a month. I'm going to have to leave as soon as Kirk can provide an escort for me and the two crewmen who came ashore."

The bedroom grew very still as Serena considered the implications of Brant's words. Finally she looked up at him with a poignant expression. "I suppose it would be highly unlikely that you would come this way again until the war is over?"

The blue eyes never wavered. "Probably not. I took a big chance coming this time. A sea captain is at a distinct disadvantage in terms of knowing what's happening on land. And what took place last week proves that even when you're not at sea, there's no way of predicting the fortunes of war."

"True." Serena lowered her eyes, staring at the hem of her cream-colored eyelet dress. "My God," she murmured, "how long will it be?"

A twisted smile touched Brant's face. "How does that Irish ballad go? 'It may be for years, and it may be forever . . .'" He saw the stricken look on Serena's face and looked contrite. "Hell, Serena, it won't be *that* long. I don't even know why the silly song came into my head. It may have been the luckiest thing in the world for New Bern to have fallen so easily—and so early—in the war. You may all be able to sit out the duration in relative comfort."

She put her hand to her forehead, wishing she could be as sanguine as Brant. It was easy for him to say how well off they would be in New Bern; he would be safe and sound up North, free as a bird to profit financially from the war. She had intended to tell him so, too, but the glint of amusement in his eyes blotted out her words. "What's funny?" she demanded. "What could possibly be funny about being stranded here forever?"

"Nothing." Brant suddenly wore his ingenuous look. "I wasn't thinking of that at all, Serena." His tone had an edge to it. "I was considering how disarming you are."

"Disarming?" Serena all but spat out the word. "Like Cecelia?"

Brant shook his head. "No. You're not like Cecelia at all."

"Did she continue playing the frail flower of motherhood after I got lost?"

"As I recall, she progressed to martyrdom. Joan of Arc in a Savile Row riding habit. Charming, if somewhat incongruous."

Serena could not suppress her laughter. So Brant had not been deceived. She wasn't sure if she were amused or relieved. "Cecelia's a dear, in her way, but she does sometimes go too far."

Brant lifted an eyebrow. "Oh? I wondered about that."

The hint of a blush touched Serena's cheeks. "Did you now? I'm sure your curiosity would please Cecelia enormously. But then," Serena added spitefully, "everything about Cecelia is enormous."

Brant's eyes glinted with amusement, though he was trying to keep a straight face. "Don't tell me you've had a change of heart, Serena."

"I? About what?" She blinked at him, feigning ignorance. The sudden shift in conversation disconcerted her.

"About me. About us." He had moved back enough almost to block out the lamp's amber glow.

"Why should I?" she demanded, armoring herself with anger. "You've never cared about me, all you want is my father's money!"

Except for Serena's erratic breathing, the room was silent for a long time. Brant's statement fell between them like the rumble of cannon fire: "Your father has no money."

At first, Serena thought Brant had gone as mad as Pembrose Stanhope. Slowly, she moved around to face him, almost afraid that she'd discover Brant had turned into a wild-eyed, raving beast. But he was standing precisely as he had been a few minutes earlier, arms folded across his chest, booted feet planted squarely on Aunt Kathleen's hooked rug.

"Don't be silly," she said in a wispy voice. "Papa is immensely rich."

"Was. But like a lot of other Northern businessmen, he relied on Southern money. He also had a great deal of capital tied up in banks which have failed because Confederate planters defaulted on their loans. Right now," Brant went on matter-of-factly, "I don't need your papa as much as he needs me."

She frowned at him, wishing she could read what lay behind that bland, rugged face. "Papa can't possibly be poverty-stricken," Serena declared, reminding herself that whatever Marcus Farrar's present financial state might be, it didn't change Brant's original reasons for marrying her.

"I didn't say he was," Brant replied equably, shrugging out of his seaman's coat and setting it on the credenza next to the lamp. "I just said he wasn't rich as Croesus anymore. If I can get those government contracts, he'll recoup his losses and then some. But I can't do that while I'm cooling my heels in this Southern backwater."

"Then I'm surprised Papa wanted you to neglect your pressing business ventures to fetch me home," Serena said with some asperity as Brant came to stand directly in front of her. "Surely your valuable time would be better spent in Washington."

"It would," he agreed, sounding irritatingly congenial. "But the one distraction your father apparently has always permitted himself is his family. He genuinely wanted to see that at least one of his offspring wasn't living on a battleground. And then there's the matter of timing, as far as the contracts are concerned. He feels—we feel— that many of the suppliers who jumped on the uniform bandwagon early weren't prepared. There'll be a fair share of shoddy goods. When their contracts are canceled, we'll be able to leap into the breach and look like a couple of heroes."

"Heroes!" Serena breathed the word on a note of scorn. "Matt will be the hero, risking his life in some godforsaken place . . . Where *is* Matt?" she demanded, wishing Brant weren't standing so close.

"Virginia, I suppose." Brant shook his head. "Your brother's as foolish as mine. Both Kirk and Matt could have sat out the war, even if there's a draft. They could have paid a dozen poor farm boys or factory workers to go in their places."

"They're gallant, brave men, both of them!" Serena's slanting eyes narrowed. "It's you who are foolish, thinking only to make money off this war!"

"War is foolish," Brant asserted, his voice still pleasant. "Worse than that, it's wasteful. There are a lot of things worth living for, but nothing worth dying for. More to the point, there's nothing worth killing a lot of other poor bastards for in the process." He put his hand under Serena's chin, but she jerked her head away. "No more talk, Serena. We only seem to argue when we do. It's time I got an answer to my question. But there's only one way to make sure it's honest."

"What question?" Serena tried to slip between Brant and the bed, but his hand on her arm held her fast.

Brant's steady gaze unnerved Serena. "I think you know," he said, without inflection.

Serena's long lashes dipped against her cheeks. She had managed to conceal her response to him on their wedding night; she was not about to let him tarnish that victory. But before she could think of a suitably devastating retort, Brant bent to crush her mouth in a searing kiss. Serena pulled her arm from his grasp; to her surprise, he made no effort to stop her. He didn't need to, since her lips still clung to his. They stood there, motionless, only the kiss binding them together, until Serena felt her knees buckle and she sagged against Brant's chest.

"You must go now," she whispered, mentally berating herself for being such a spineless ninny.

"Not yet." He sounded almost laconic, yet there was an ever-present undertone of command. Was it the authority he exuded as a sea captain, Serena wondered hazily, or an intrinsic attribute he masked under a sometimes amiable, so often arrogant manner? Whatever Brant Parnell possessed, it seemed to be turning her will to water.

Serena swayed slightly as Brant's lips sought hers once more. She opened her mouth to let his tongue probe hers, dug her fingers into the linen shirt, felt his knees against her thighs. The kisses moved to her forehead, her temple, her throat. He caressed her back, then lifted her in his arms and carried her to the chintz-covered bed where he laid her down on her stomach.

"Hooks and eyes? Whatever happened to buttons?" He was unfastening her dress and she could imagine his bemused expression.

"One of the local seamstresses always uses hooks and eyes," she said in a muffled voice. Serena took a deep breath as he slid the dress from her shoulders and began undoing the cotton camisole. At last she felt his hands slide under her to cup her breasts. Serena raised her upper body just enough so that he could feel their full ripeness. He moved them slowly, sensuously, making Serena aware of a throbbing sensation between her thighs. His thumbs began to flick at her nipples which had already grown tight and pointed.

"By God," he said in a low voice, "I think you've missed me!" Brant turned her over, savoring the expectant look on her face as much as the rosy glory of her breasts.

Serena knew she ought to give him a swift, stinging retort, but it died on her lips. So many times in her life she had been afraid of not meeting her mother's expectations or her father's demands, of never being as handsome as Cecelia, as clever as Abigail, or as likable as Matt. Serena had not just lived in the Farrar family shadow, she had been eclipsed by it. Now, she suddenly realized, she no longer bore the Farrar name; she was a Parnell, and the only person she needed to please was the man whose body hovered over her in such sensual, intimate contact. In many ways, Brant was still a stranger, yet he was her whole world.

"It's insane," she said aloud and startled them both.

Brant stood up, starting to take off his clothes. "Most things are," he replied dubiously. "Did you have anything specific in mind?"

"I . . ." Serena folded her arms over her bare body. "Well . . ." She made an uncertain, all-encompassing gesture. "Us. And . . . life."

"Probably." He grinned at her, then dropped down beside her on the bed, firmly prying her arms away from her breasts. The sea-blue eyes did a devilish dance. He leaned down to kiss the hollow of her throat while his hands worked at her skirt and petticoats. Sliding the garments down to rest on her thighs, he pressed his face into the soft mat of curling hair.

"Oh!" Serena gasped, but allowed him to nudge her legs apart. His tongue sought the tender cleft, making her shiver with a demand for deeper, more searing exploration. She moaned when Brant paused to finish removing her clothing and shoes, and slowly he let his palm cup the throbbing mound and felt her writhe under his touch. His fingers caressed and probed, inward, upward, setting off every nerve in Serena's body. He tantalized her eager, throbbing flesh while Serena groaned with excitement, consumed by her need for possession. With an almost frantic, primeval instinct, she reached out for the source of her ultimate pleasure and grasped Brant's hardened masculinity in both hands. An elated sort of growl sounded in his throat as their caresses brought them both closer to the precipice.

Hazily, Serena felt him slip from her clasping fingers; for one split second, she panicked. But when Brant clutched her shoulders and she felt him plunge inside her body, Serena cried out with relief—and ecstasy. Face pressed against his chest, eyes squeezed tightly shut, Serena's entire being clamored for the melding of their flesh into one. Moving in a frenzied rhythm, they exploded together in joyous fulfillment.

Serena was amazed to realize that her cheeks were wet with tears. Brant still lay buried inside her, his breathing heavy, his lips in her tangled hair. When he finally withdrew and sat up to rest on one elbow, the ironic gaze had never been more apparent.

"What the hell do we do now, Serena?"

Serena attempted to move up toward the pillows but discovered she felt quite stiff. "What do you mean?" she asked in an odd, wispy voice.

Brant laughed and ran a hand through his crinkly dark hair. "I don't know. And I'm not in any frame of mind for deep thought." He tipped up her chin and stared into the slanting brown eyes for a very long time. "We may have been married for almost six months, but we sure as hell don't know each other very well, Rena."

"How could we?" she demanded, sounding more like herself. "I could practically count on both hands the hours that we've spent together."

"I thought you wanted it that way. You tried to bluff me, didn't you, Serena?"

"No. Yes." She nestled against his chest, not wanting him to see her face. "I had to."

"Why?"

Serena let out a long sigh. "Because we weren't in love."

"Hmmm. I see," he said, sounding as if there were a chance he didn't. "I suppose I don't need to tell you now that being in love or not, we make love very well together."

Slowly, Serena edged away from him, lying back among the pillows and carefully pulling the sheet up over her breasts. Was it possible that she could take such pleasure from Brant even if she didn't love him? All the romantic ideals of her youth told her that could not happen. But then she had not known what this sort of pleasure was until he had initiated her into the rites of the flesh. "I'm muddled," she confessed, a lame smile touching the corners of her full lips as he brushed the thick hair from her forehead.

"Probably. You had me 'muddled' on our wedding night. I was damned near convinced you found me repulsive. Hell, I *was* convinced. That came as a shock." He stood up, the amber light of the lamp giving his tanned body a bronzed glow.

"Is that why you left town?" Serena's voice sounded strangely like an echo.

"As a matter of fact, it was." He started to reach for his clothes. "I thought I'd lost my boyish charm."

Serena regarded him with a quizzical expression, wondering if Brant were serious. But the very offhandedness of his tone suggested he wasn't teasing her. Perhaps he had been hurt, even humiliated by her refusal to admit that his lovemaking had aroused her in the most amazing, unimaginable way.

"Wait," she called to him as he shook out his trousers, "why don't you stay here tonight?"

Brant turned around, eyeing her curiously. He shrugged. "Why not? After all, we *are* married."

Serena couldn't suppress a wide smile, no more than she could tamp down the triumph she suddenly felt rising out of what was probably not part of her better nature. But for once, Serena wasn't going to worry about that; instead, she was thinking of the neat, unused bed in the spare room next door and how the servants would comment on it to their friends in the Moncrief house and how Cecelia would find out that Brant Parnell had slept with his wife.

Serena was still smiling after Brant had turned down the lamp and had slipped into bed beside her. But as he put his arm around her, and she nestled against him, it occurred to her that she wasn't merely suffering from a fit of sisterly spite—she was genuinely pleased to be lying in the sanctuary of her husband's embrace.

Brant had just finished dressing when Serena woke up. The morning light which filtered from behind the chintz curtains was weak, indicating another wet, foggy day. Serena glanced at the little watch on the nightstand: just after seven.

Brant heard her set the watch back down and turned to give her a sleepy grin. "I didn't mean to wake you."

"That's all right." She rubbed her eyes and pushed the hair out of her face, momentarily forgetting that she was naked. Flustered, she jerked the sheet up under her chin.

Brant moved to the bed. "Don't do that, you're a pleasurable sight in the morning. At least as much as I can see at this time of day." He sat down next to her, taking her hand in his. "Frankly, I intended to leave before we had to say good-bye. I thought it might be better. At least we wouldn't have a chance to fight."

She regarded his droll expression and smiled. "I'm never alert enought to argue this early. When will . . . when are you leaving New Bern?"

He clasped her fingers more tightly, the blue eyes never leaving her face. "Today, if everything goes well. Though first there's the matter of seeing to Yancy's parole. It's my turn, this time." He forced a grin. "I wonder which of us will come out ahead of rescuing one another before the war's over?"

His diversion was lost on Serena. "I'm coming with you," she announced, surprising herself more than Brant. "Cecelia belongs here. I don't."

He let go of her hand and sat with his fingertips perched on his knees. "I can't let you come with me," he said solemnly.

"Why not?" She sounded breathless, the brown eyes wide and searching.

"Because there's a good chance I'll get shot between here and Cape Fear." He saw the protest forming and shook his head. "I know, I'm supposed to have a safe conduct or some damned thing but who's to know that out in the woods or the swamps or wherever I'm headed? All it means is that I've got an answer if anybody asks a question. But people tend to forget their manners when there's a war on."

From somewhere off in the distance, a bugle sounded as if to confirm Brant's statement. Serena shivered and threw herself into Brant's arms, heedless of the sheet which slipped down to her waist. "Then you mustn't go either!"

Brant looked down at the curve of her back and the mass of rich, brown hair which cascaded over his arm. "The odds are in my favor, five to two. That's not bad. But if I take you with me, it's fifty-fifty. For both of us."

Serena started to ask why—and suddenly Abigail's words came back to her: Abigail, unable to help Yancy escape as effectively as Serena could; hampered not because she wasn't capable, but because she loved Yancy. Serena didn't dare put the question to Brant. She was suddenly afraid of his answer.

"I understand," she said in a controlled voice, trying to look up at him steadily. "You have Carew and O'Malley to worry about, too."

"They left last night." Abruptly, Brant pulled her close and kissed her hard on the lips. "Nothing lasts forever," he said, but his voice lacked its usual humor. He stood up and turned away quickly, snatching his watchcap off the credenza. "Keep an eye on Kirk. He's the only brother I've got." Again, the lightheartedness was labored. And then he was gone with only a brief grin over his shoulder as he went through the door.

Serena sat on her haunches in the bed, still half-naked, distractedly running her fingers through her hair. She realized she hadn't written any letters to send home to her parents or to Abigail in Washington. Perhaps there was still time to jot down a few lines and somehow get them to Brant before he left New Bern.

Disconsolately, she tugged at the quilt and pulled it free. Flinging it over her shoulders, she walked to the window which overlooked the curving drive to Pollock Street. The fog was already lifting and the azaleas were beginning to bud along the walk to the carriage house. Brant had just come out the front door with Leonard, who was calling to Young Calvin to bring the visitor's horse.

The two men stood talking amiably, Brant nodding, Leonard making a gesture toward the street where a Union sentry paraded by and disappeared in the fog beyond the Moncrief house. Serena couldn't gauge Leonard's expression from two stories away, but she saw Brant throw back his head and laugh. Afraid that he might look up and see her peering at him and Leonard, she ducked back from the window, still clasping the quilt around her body.

But the image of Brant's tall form and easy laughter didn't go away. It remained fixed in her mind's eye, almost as if he were still in the room with her. *Oh, damn,* Serena thought, pressing one hand over her eyes as if she could staunch the tears which seemed about to burst forth, *I love that big, overbearing, scheming rogue.*

Dragging the quilt behind her, Serena fell facedown on the bed. She cried then, but there was joy mingled with her shock and sorrow: For in that one insightful moment when Abigail's words about Yancy had leaped into her brain, she knew there was the possibility that Brant loved her, too.

Chapter 11

THE NEW BERN LYCEUM had scheduled a lecture for April 3, 1862, on "Flora of the Coastal Plain: Transplanting Procedures Ordained by the Quarters of the Moon." A professor of botany from the state university in Chapel Hill was to deliver the presentation at the New Bern Academy. Unfortunately, he had been shot in the thigh by an overly vigilant Union soldier.

"At least the lecture would have been something to do," Cecelia fretted, pulling off her kid gloves and flinging them on a mahogany end table. "I swear I shall get blisters from sitting out this stupid war in this stupid town."

"We may have mail from home soon," Serena said hopefully. "Brant promised that if there were any way we could get letters, he'd see to it."

"He's only been gone a little over a week, it'll be ages before we hear anything. And when we do, what's the difference? Mama will tell us that Nora Kingsbury has the pip and that Mrs. Pemberton replaced her portieres and that Matt is ever so patriotic."

Serena couldn't help but smile. "Mama would talk of duty, not patriotism. I wonder if Matt joined up for the excitement or—"

"Papa won't write at all," Cecelia went on, ignoring her sister's comment, "and here we are, with all social activities restricted, all the more interesting young men off in Virginia, a curfew, a lot of preachers bellowing about hellfire and damnation, and Aunt Kathleen whining constantly about the 'loathsome Yankess.' Doesn't that silly woman know she's married to one of them?" Cecelia was stamping about the retiring room, almost upsetting a jardiniere from its pedestal.

"Be quiet, Celia, she may come in at any moment! Have some peanuts." Serena indicated a cut-glass comfit dish on an inlaid table next to the settee. Cecelia scooped up a handful but continued to stalk the room. Serena didn't really blame her sister: Since the reality of the occupation had set in, life in New Bern had acquired a stringent, tedious pattern. Brant had left on March 24, sailing for New England without any further discussion concerning their marital status. Perhaps it was just as well, Serena told herself, since the whole world seemed to be in a state of uncertainty. With Brant gone, she did not have to face up to the discovery of her love for him. Such a newly found emotion was too fragile—and frightening—for Serena to fully comprehend.

Instead, common sense asserted itself, dictating that the best be made of a bad thing as far as her virtual incarceration in New Bern was concerned. "It just occurred to me," Serena said, rearranging a cloisonné bowl of camellias, "that there might be some activities we could take up, some sort of liaison we could provide between the local residents and the Federal forces."

Cecelia finally stood still and gave her sister an inquiring glance. "Are you talking about spying?"

"Good Lord, no! I don't know what I'm talking about yet, just that as Yankees living in a Confederate town, we might be of some assistance."

"It sounds harebrained," Cecelia said, but her voice lacked its usual incisiveness. She picked up another handful of peanuts and munched thoughtfully. "It's important that we keep busy, Celia. At least you have your baby and your husband, while I . . ." Serena faltered as she saw her sister's sudden, inquisitive stare.

"It seems you had your husband—in more ways than one. Or was that idle gossip I heard?"

Serena lifted her chin in defiance. "I have no idea. Nor do I see what business it is of yours what my husband and I do in our private moments."

Cecelia smirked. "Don't play the priss with me. Your Brant is quite an intriguing animal. I suspect you'd like to tame him, Rena."

Serena felt her heels dig into the Oriental carpet. Cecelia was baiting her, but to what purpose? Was her sister merely prying? Or was Cecelia embarking on a serious rivalry? As a child Cecelia had always been the more aggressive and outgoing of the two girls. As the years passed, Cecelia seemed to take her victories over Serena as her due. Her attitude seemed simple enough: I came first. But Serena no longer found Cecelia's dominance acceptable.

"I don't know what you mean by 'tame,' Celia," Serena said calmly. "It seems to me you've not 'tamed' Fitch—you've castrated him."

A strangled sort of noise boiled up out of Cecelia's throat. "I ought to slap you silly, Serena Farrar!"

"Serena *Parnell*," Serena corrected her, still standing her ground but wondering if she'd pushed the apparently apoplectic Cecelia too far.

But Cecelia backed off a few paces and took a deep breath. "You seem far too touchy about a man you don't love," she went on, waving a gloved finger at Serena. "I wonder who you're trying to fool—yourself, maybe?" She paused just long enough to let her message sink in, then swished out of the retiring room and headed for the front door.

Serena collapsed on the couch. Cecelia had marched on dangerous ground. If she continued to probe and needle, life could become very disturbing. Serena didn't want to face up to her feelings for Brant yet, nor would she have to, as long as he was out of sight—and out of her arms.

A noise in the doorway invaded her troubled mind. It was Liberty, riding a stick horse. "Me General Lee," he announced, skittering across the carpet. "Me free slaves."

"Your politics are confused," Serena said with a smile, though Liberty wasn't entirely wrong. Robert E. Lee had freed his own slaves some time ago. He had pledged his allegiance to the Confederacy only after the most excruciating examination of conscience and loyalties. Lee was an advocate of state's rights but not of slavery, a position which reminded Serena of Leonard. In the wake of all that had happened since, Serena had forgotten that Leonard had told her he had never been a slave. Who was Leonard? And who was Liberty, for that matter? She scrutinized the child: He was a handsome little fellow, perhaps with as much white blood as Leonard himself. But there was no noticeable resemblance between them.

"Why you look at me, Miz Rena?" Liberty's lower lip protruded and his little face puckered in a scowl.

"Oh, I was just thinking about how you've grown in the last few weeks." Serena patted his cheek and watched his eyelids all but close in disapproval of her touch. "Now, Liberty, I'm not frightening you, am I?"

The lower lip remained thrust out, but he shook his head from side to side. Serena folded both hands in her lap, to make sure he knew she would not touch him if he didn't wish it. He reminded her of the birds she used to watch from her window as a child; as long as she kept her hands behind her back, they'd stay close by, hopping about in the laurel hedge and the lilac tree. But if she made a sudden motion, they'd fly away in panic.

Liberty's small features softened and he gave her a slow, enchanting smile. For a fleeting instant, he did remind her of someone—certainly not Leonard, but someone she knew. Who? She had no idea, and was suddenly disturbed. Liberty, however, was again his cheerful self, galloping about the retiring room and making whooping noises. Serena shook off the momentary sense of unease, and allowed his antics to amuse her. He was truly a charming child. For the first time in her life, Serena wondered what it would be like to have babies of her own—and quickly banished the thought. If ever there were a time when she must not consider that possibility, it was now, when her heart was as uncertain as her future.

Aunt Kathleen had been utterly aghast at the idea of having a man in Union Army attire cross her threshold. "Have you heard what some of those vicious brutes have done?" she cried, fanning herself in agitation. "Looting, pillaging, setting fires, and . . . the good Lord Himself only knows what as far as our poor ladies are concerned! If that man comes here, I shall faint!"

Serena had tried reason and failed. Uncle Luke had tried coaxing and been turned aside. Fitch had tried complete agreement—and Aunt Kathleen had suddenly changed her mind.

"Major Parnell *is* your brother-in-law," she told Serena after Fitch had left the house. "And any man that Fitch Moncrief finds offensive must have some redeeming qualities."

"He's a very nice man with a lovely wife and three children," Serena asserted. "Truly, Auntie, I'm sure it's men like Kirk who keep most Union soldiers in line."

Aunt Kathleen absently patted Serena's hand. They were sitting out in the bricked courtyard, with a soft June breeze stirring the pink petals of the myrtle trees. "Perhaps, perhaps. And I know that you and Cecelia are anxious to get your letters from the North. Oh, your uncle is, too, he's never stopped longing to hear news of what he still calls 'home.'"

So Kirk Parnell came to supper that last night of June, bearing the correspondence which had been sent from Brunswick through official Federal channels. Etiquette was dispensed with for once, as Serena, Cecelia, and Uncle Luke eagerly read their letters over a postprandial fruit punch flavored with peach moby. Aunt Kathleen sat as if starched for the first quarter hour, but began to unbend as Kirk plied her with stories of his children's latest adventures and his wife's heroic efforts to set up shelters for war widows and orphans. Fitch reclined in sardonic silence, as if such homespun goodness were somehow basically suspect.

"Good grief," exclaimed Cecelia, who held her mother's letter, "Matt's in Virginia, with General Hooker!"

Serena's hand flew to her breast. "He's so close! Oh, if only we could see him!" But Serena glanced at Aunt Kathleen, who wore a look of disapproval that would have done Lydia Farrar proud.

"I think," Kirk said gently, "your niece meant a social visit, not as an invader."

"A fine fellow, Matt," Uncle Luke said directly to his wife. "You recall him, Mrs. Farrar, he was a cheerful sort, with good manners."

Aunt Kathleen murmured something no one but Uncle Luke could hear. Clearly, she would have said more but her role as hostess dictated discretion in front of their guest, even if he were a major in the Union army.

Serena turned back to the letter from Marcus Farrar. Cecelia's prediction had missed the mark: The letter was two pages long and the gist of it confirmed Brant's words—business was bad. Marcus railed at the sudden cutoff of trade between North and South, he decried the fact that debts and bonds incurred by Southerners before the war were not being made good, he lamented how several banks had failed, and denounced the farm surplus. Shipbuilding had all but ceased in Brunswick; only Pennel and his brother had a new frame under way. Marcus cursed the day that Fort Sumter had been fired upon.

On a calmer note, he stressed Brant's determination to recoup the Farrar empire's losses. "When Brant was here last week he had plans to visit Washington again and contact his Federal connections."

Well, thought Serena, at least she knew where her husband had been as of a month ago. Not that it mattered, she told herself ruefully, giving Cecelia her letter from Marcus in exchange for the one from Lydia. Lydia's concern for Matt's safety was carefully veiled, but still evident. There was talk of organizing a town militia. "I cannot imagine that we would have to defend ourselves in these far reaches but William Field and Augustus Spollet seem eager to make sure our bastions are secure. Of course they are anticipating the drafting of men which will no doubt begin before long."

Never one for idle gossip, Lydia Farrar sketchily recounted the comings and goings of their friends and neighbors. Births, deaths, and marriages were listed in crisp, chronological order. Only her last paragraph caused Serena any consternation:

"Judge Stanhope has not been well lately. Some say it is because of the mysterious disappearance of his nephew, Pembrose. At this late date, one must assume some tragic accident befell him. All things considered, perhaps that is just as well. His escapades of the last few years have been said to be unsavory."

Serena frowned at the finely wrought words. How much did her parents guess about Yancy Clarke and her own role in his escape? But of course they could know nothing about the terrifying night in New Bedford.

The others were now chattering with animation over the shared contents of their correspondence. Serena, however, sat in silence, thinking how far away the trim, orderly streets of Brunswick seemed and how long ago it had been since she and Abby had conspired to save Yancy's life and get him safely out of town. Less than a year, but the intervening events made it seem much longer and almost unreal.

"We'll all go home someday, Serena. You know that." It was Kirk Parnell, speaking low and moving from his caned armchair to sit next to her on the settee. He looked very handsome in his military uniform, with the gold epaulettes and matching sash. Older, too, Serena noted, and wondered why he had left his happy home to volunteer.

She gave him a grateful smile. "I have to believe this won't last forever. But it's all so strange, like being in limbo."

"It's stranger yet to be killing people," Kirk asserted, the angular features grim.

A furtive glance told Serena that her relatives were too wrapped up in their own conversations to pay any attention to her and Kirk. "Can you justify it, inside?" she asked in a voice that was almost a whisper.

"No. Not down deep." His eyes turned shadowy, then he leaned closer. "Pembrose Stanhope's death was an accident. Just as your mother presumes in her letter."

Serena regarded Kirk's somber face in silence. That whole nightmarish episode was buried within her, yet often in the empty gloom of night, she could still hear the sickening thud of the printer's stone and see Pembrose's body lying on the *Mercury* floor.

"He was mad," she said at last, no longer able to meet his gaze. "Was . . . did anyone make inquiries?"

His smile was slightly crooked, but his dark eyes were kind. "No. Not in New Bedford. There was quite a stir in Boston, though. The authorities seemed to think the man who shot Pembrose had come back."

Serena shivered despite the warm evening. She pressed her palms together in the supplicating gesture which was so unconscious to her and noticed that Cecelia was watching them. "Kirk, let's go outside. It's uncomfortably close in here." Serena ignored her sister's stare as she excused herself to Aunt Kathleen, who barely seemed to notice.

Out in the bricked courtyard, the night was heavy with the scent of jasmine and honeysuckle. There was no hint of breeze to stir the myrtle trees and rhododendron bushes. From not far away, Serena heard the strains of a mournful Negro spiritual, defying the curfew.

"Life is more complicated than I thought," Serena said, leaning against one of the pillars which held up the roof over the courtyard. "Growing up, everything seemed so simple."

Kirk rested his hands lightly on Serena's shoulders. "Parents make sure of that for us. Don't worry, Serena, Brant told me about Yancy. I was the one who had him paroled."

"I see." Serena blinked and licked her lips. "If you know about Yancy, you must also know why I married Brant."

The slaves' distant voices had taken up a livelier, more raucous tune, but suddenly were silenced. Their master, or perhaps the sentries, had enforced the curfew.

Kirk's expression grew guarded. "It was time for Brant to marry," he said somewhat stiffly.

Serena's eyes narrowed. Time for Brant, perhaps, at almost thirty, but not for Serena, who was ten years younger and had a future planned that didn't include a husband. Kirk had been noncommittal on purpose, or else he was ignorant of why Serena and Brant had married.

"Were you surprised that he married me?" she asked bluntly.

Kirk had moved a few paces away, standing by a windowbox full of daisies and periwinkle. "Nothing Brant does ever surprises me."

Serena's features relaxed slightly as she cleared her throat. "I gather you're fond of Brant, though." The statement sounded tentative; Serena wished she hadn't uttered it.

"Of course I am," Kirk replied heartily, stepping toward her and taking her hand. "We've had our bad times, like any pair of brothers, but basically, Brant is a good man."

Serena's smile was weak. Kirk's reassurance wasn't quite what she wanted to hear. She had hoped he would confide that Brant had married for love, not money. But that, Serena reminded herself, was the silly, romantic dream of youth; mature reality told her something very different.

Brant Parnell's first mate, Press Prescott, had a younger brother who had been plagued by seasickness all his life. In a family which had spawned three generations of sea-faring men, Elmer Prescott had become obsessed with his malady, fearing that he would disgrace the family. But in his attempts to find a cure, he discovered he was more intrigued by the search than the result. Consequently, he had studied medicine and was now a physician to the fashionable in New York City, where he lived with his family in a fine house above the East River. Whenever Brant and Press dropped anchor in New York harbor, they stayed with the Prescotts and, as Brant put it, listened to Elmer tell how he made the wealthy healthy.

There were, however, occasions when Brant tired of Elmer's endless medical recitals and his catalogue of well-to-do patients. It was just such an evening which finally sent Brant out into the fresh June air for a brisk walk before retiring to the solitude of his room overlooking Mill Rock and Hell's Gate.

He enjoyed gazing up at the lighted windows of the fine four- and five-story mansions and musing upon the doings of their inhabitants.

Though in fact, he told himself with characteristic realism, they were all probably damned near as boring as Elmer.

Still, from a nearby house he heard the sound of a pianoforte and some hearty laughter. He also heard the sound of footsteps behind him. They had been there virtually since he'd left the Prescott house but only now after a quarter of a mile did he decide there might be some cause for concern. He kept walking at the same pace, reasoning that a thief would have attacked him earlier on, where the neighborhood was more isolated. After another two blocks, he turned purposefully around a corner and into the doorway of a carriage house. A few seconds later, his pursuer rounded the same corner and paused. Brant stepped swiftly back out into the street and stood stockstill not more than three yards from the other man.

"I only take walks with people I know," Brant remarked in a conversational tone. "Who the hell are you?"

The man's face was obscured under a slouch hat, but though he was shorter than Brant, he was considerably broader. "I know you already, Parnell," the man said in a faintly accented voice. "You come with me, you will be grateful."

"I can't think offhand why," Brant replied equably. "Do I guess or beg for clues?"

The man seemed puzzled by Brant's comments. "You know Mrs. St. George?"

"St. George!" Brant relaxed and grinned. Gloria St. George had started life in New Bedford as Gladys Jones, the daughter of an Irish scrubwoman and a Welsh deckhand. Raised with a passel of brothers and sisters while both parents drank themselves into an early grave, Gladys had run away from home at the age of sixteen to find a better life in Boston, and eventually in New York. But before leaving New Bedford, she had made an indelible impression on fifteen-year-old Brant Parnell by initiating him into the realm of sexual delight. Ten years later, Brant had not recognized Gladys when he met her at an elegant, if illegal, gambling salon in New York City. But the woman who called herself Gloria St. George had an extraordinary memory for faces. She had lured Brant away from a quixotic roulette wheel to renew their acquaintanceship in her black and purple boudoir. As Gloria told the story, she had married a wealthy, arthritic banker who had conveniently died within a year. Shrewdly investing her money in various legitimate enterprises, she had also used a portion to back a gambling establishment which had ultimately earned more income for her than all the other investments put together. She had also acquired a string of lovers, one of whom was Pembrose Stanhope. Brant and Pembrose had never crossed each other's paths in New

York, and in truth, Brant hadn't visited Gloria much in recent years, though he enjoyed her frank eroticism.

"You're right," Brant said at last. "This is where Gloria lives. That corner by the park."

Without a further word, the man led Brant down the street to a large, elegant brownstone which sat behind a splendidly detailed wrought-iron fence. Brant's curiosity mounted with each of the wide stone steps which led to the handsomely carved front door.

Gloria St. George was in the sitting room off her boudoir, wearing black as she often did. The style, however, was not as somber as the color: The elaborate peignoir bared her white shoulders with a trail of raven feathers from bodice to hem. She wore slippers trimmed in jet, held a black lace fan, and had a matching ribbon entwined in her golden hair. She was not a tall woman but carried herself so well that most people described her as such. Now that she was over thirty, Gloria St. George's opulent beauty was at its zenith.

"My, my," she said in a carefully cultured voice as Brant and the man appeared in the sitting room door, "look who washed ashore!"

"I feel more like I've been beached." Brant's grin was ingenuous.

Gloria St. George smiled charmingly. "Nonsense. It's just fortunate I heard you were in New York. Run along, Spiro," she said to the foreign man. "You performed your task well."

A flicker of Spiro's eyes was all that betrayed his appreciation to his employer. He backed out into the hall and closed the door behind him. Gloria was laughing, a rich sound that caused her gorgeous bosom to move under the black silk of the peignoir.

"Do sit, Brant," she said, indicating a chair next to her chaise longue. The room was not large but furnished entirely in black and white with purple accents. Everything was covered in cut velvet and all the wood was painted a virgin white. "A drink perhaps?"

"I'd rather have an explanation," Brant replied, crossing his legs at the ankles and stretching his frame out over the chair as best he could.

Gloria reached for a plum in a crystal fruit bowl next to the chaise longue. "You knew Pembrose Stanhope?" The question was devoid of inflection.

"Only through his father, the judge. But Pembrose seems to have been relegated to the past tense. Do you know what happened to him?" Brant asked blandly, watching with mild fascination as Gloria took a tiny silver knife and cut the plum in two, extracted the pit, and offered him one of the halves.

"He disappeared on a trip to our old hometown." She chewed thoughtfully on her half of the plum, then slowly licked her lips. "He's dead, no doubt, which is rather a pity. Pembrose was marvelously inventive in bed." The emerald eyes glistened at Brant. "His brother, Giles, came to see me a while ago." Gloria's shoulders shook with a mirthless little laugh. "A silly person, actually, devoid of Pembrose's amorous creativity. Still," she went on more briskly, "Pembrose considered him clever enough to make him a business associate. For some reason, Giles thought I was involved in their venture, and after Pembrose disappeared, Giles came to ask what I knew about all the money Pembrose had made." Gloria turned her white palms face up. "I had no idea, of course. Pembrose never confided in me about such things, nor did I ask."

As Gloria paused, Brant started to speak but stopped. He didn't know what the woman was talking about. While Judge Stanhope might be implicated in some questionable dealings, the man was no criminal. His sons, however, were a different matter.

"Giles had done some investigating, on his own, and by hiring others." Gloria twisted a golden curl around her finger and arranged it artfully behind her right ear. "Pembrose went to New Bedford to see a Parnell—I thought it was you or your brother. But that was before I knew you'd behaved so recklessly and gotten married." She gave him a smile of fond reproach. "In any event, Pembrose was never seen alive again. And now it turns out that your wife's cousin was in Boston when someone shot Pembrose earlier on."

"All I know is I wasn't near Pembrose on either occasion." Brant flexed his neck muscles, which had grown stiff while he listened to her rambling account. "Look, Gloria, Pembrose was a bit of a heel. I suppose Giles might want to get revenge and maybe I ought to see Judge Stanhope the next time I'm in Maine and ask him. But I wasn't in New Bedford when Pembrose was there."

"He went mad, I'd wager." Gloria looked up at Brant through her lashes. "They're all quite mad, you know."

"All? Well, the judge seems sane enough when he's sober."

"I don't know the judge, only Pembrose and Giles. But if I were you, I'd be more than interested—I'd be on guard."

Brant frowned. "I've had one run-in with Giles which should be enough. I appreciate your warning, Gloria, but it's a closed chapter for me." And for Serena and Kirk, too, Brant told himself with an optimism he didn't feel.

"It's not that way with Giles," Gloria said slowly. "He wants his share of the money they earned. And he can't get it until they find Pembrose. Or his body. It's quite a large sum."

"Oh." Brant shrugged. "That's tough luck for Giles. Hell, Gloria, I don't know a damned thing about their 'business.'"

Gloria's mouth formed a circle of surprise. "I thought perhaps you did. Though I can see why they didn't advertise it." She gave him a sidelong glance from the emerald eyes. "They captured runaway slaves and returned them to their owners down South. Very profitable, at least until the war started."

"God." Brant stared across the room, his unseeing eyes fixed on a floor-length rococo-edged mirror. "What a pair of leeches. No wonder they always made my skin feel like I hadn't had a bath in six months."

"It was all perfectly legal," Gloria pointed out calmly. "Many Northerners engaged in it. Slaves, after all, are private property, like cattle or carriages."

Brant shook his head vehemently. "Only in the South, and that's why we're fighting this damned-fool war. People—if I can use the word—like Pembrose and Giles Stanhope are unscrupulous bounty hunters."

"Perhaps." Gloria had stopped smiling, apparently now bored with the topic of Pembrose and Giles Stanhope. "I only wanted to warn you. I never liked Giles." She pouted prettily, flipping a blond curl over her shoulder. "But I've always liked you. A lot."

"I like you, too, Gloria." Brant grinned a bit sheepishly. "I appreciate your . . . concern." He made an effort to avoid the gleaming mounds of ripe flesh, which rose above the black peignoir's tantalizing neckline. "I'm married now, you know."

Gloria stood up, the raven feathers fluttering gracefully. "You sound apologetic, my dear. Being a husband isn't a fatal flaw." She leaned toward Brant, a hand lightly touching his chest. "Some of my best friends are husbands."

Her words caught Brant off-guard; he was mesmerized by the emerald eyes, the opulent flesh, the golden curls. Gloria was beautiful, willing, provocative. She had often given him great pleasure. But tonight he found her eagerness more irritating than stimulating. He thought of Serena, of the smoky brown hair and the slanting, big eyes and the delightfully sensuous body with its innocent passion. They'd only made love twice, and given the kind of marriage they had, there was no telling when—or if—they'd ever make love again.

And here was Gloria, openly wanting to pleasure him in any way he wished. But he hesitated, unaccustomed to the sense of restraint which seemed to weigh him down.

"Sorry, Gloria, I think I've got a headache." He gave her a lame sort of grin and, with almost grim determination, picked up his hat and started for the door.

"Brant." Gloria breathed his name, low and incredulous. "I think you're in love."

Brant paused, hand on the doorknob, feeling a sudden weariness come over him. "I think I'm insane. Like the Stanhopes, maybe."

Over his shoulder, he gave her a smile of regret. "Maybe I'll kick myself all the way back to Boston. Or New Bedford or New Bern or Brunswick or Bombay," he added thoughtfully. "So far, she hasn't gone there. Yet."

"Who?" asked Gloria, obviously puzzled, "Where?"

But Brant had already clicked the door behind him.

Being in New Bern under the Yankee occupation was indeed like being in limbo, Serena thought, and said the word aloud. She closed her eyes, aware that even such a small gesture cost her an unusual amount of energy. The July air felt so thick it seemed to press down on the city, slowing the pace, paralyzing the war, enervating even the mental processes.

The field hands hardly seemed to move; only the bright bandanas among the tobacco leaves verified that, somehow, no matter how slowly, work went on at Wexford. Serena knew that slaves belonging to other owners had run away since the outbreak of war and that some of the farms and plantations around New Bern had already been ravaged by Union soldiers. But the long years of benevolence on Uncle Luke's part had earned him the loyalty of his people: At Wexford, the slaves continued to labor despite the oppressive heat of a North Carolina summer.

Serena was equally astounded by her own lack of judgment in coming out to the plantation on such a hot day. She had gotten up that morning determined to go beyond the confines of Uncle Luke's townhouse and the well-guarded streets of New Bern's commercial district. Living under siege had not yet proved intolerable, yet so many residents had fled that New Bern seemed to echo with the ghosts of a dead era. The once-bustling crossroads for land and sea had assumed the air of a well-mannered prison camp.

Kirk Parnell had signed the permission card for Serena, Leonard, and Liberty to leave the confines of the town. They had driven a carriage out to Wexford that morning. Now, standing outside the brick plantation office watching Liberty chase a half-dozen chickens, she cursed herself for ever leaving Pollock Street.

She batted at some flies and wondered how long it would take Leonard and Fitch to conclude their business. While Fitch was competent at making commercial transactions and reasonably efficient in running the plantation with the help of an overseer, he had little talent for keeping the books. It was Leonard who was called in twice a month to go over the accounts and keep the ledgers in order. The two men had already been at work for over an hour; surely, Serena thought, they must be done. It was well after noon.

The sound of hooves made Serena turn slowly. A horse was plod-

ding up the drive, its rider taking off his straw hat and wiping his
forehead with a kerchief. The newcomer was Harold Saile, Uncle
Luke's overseer, a rigid man in his middle years with wavy auburn
hair and a bristling moustache.

"Mrs. Parnell," he greeted her, with the hint of a bow from the
saddle. "Is Mr. Farrar here?"

"No. Mr. Leonard is here." Serena noticed that Saile's face puckered at her form of address for the Negro servant. Under ordinary
circumstances, she might have been embarrassed. But with her gingham
dress sticking to her back and the perspiration trickling down her
neck, she didn't much care if she'd called Leonard "His Majesty."

Saile dismounted, tied up his horse next to the trough, made certain
the animal didn't drink too much too fast, frowned at Liberty who
had just tossed a hen into the air to see how far it could fly, and
walked toward the plantation office. It occurred to Serena that Harold
Saile looked a bit like a rooster, with his bandy-legged strut and
coxcomb of hair. So self-important, she thought hazily, and with so
little reason.

"Liberty," she pleaded, "you must come in. Now you've scared
the chickens. They won't be able to lay any eggs tomorrow."

"Eggs sicky." Liberty blew out his cheeks and wrinkled his nose.
"I like fried mush."

"Fried mush is very tasty. Now behave yourself and come with
me. If you don't, I'll go inside without you." Serena expended the
effort to walk toward the office building. After a few steps, she glanced
over her shoulder to see Liberty warily approaching Harold Saile's
horse. "Liberty!" The sound rasped out, Serena's temper ignited by
the heat far more than by the child. "You come here or I'll thump
you!"

Startled, Liberty stood stockstill. The brown eyes grew enormous,
the little body went stiff, the mouth clamped shut. Liberty stared at
Serena in frightened shock.

Astonishment overcame Serena's inertia as well as her anger. She
half-stumbled to Liberty, scooping him up in her arms. "Don't be
silly, Liberty, I didn't mean it, I'm just so hot! And wet and sticky
and uncomfortable." The litany of her complaints seemed to have a
soothing effect on the child, who relaxed slightly in Serena's grasp.
Behind them, she heard men's voices—Fitch and Saile, both sounding
agitated.

"It's your responsibility," she heard Fitch say as the two men drew
closer. "But Luke Farrar wouldn't like it."

Saile lowered his voice. "What Luke Farrar don't know—and
that's plenty, considering—don't hurt him." There was a pause. Serena

kept patting Liberty, hoping that Saile and Fitch would think she was too absorbed with the child to notice.

"Well?" Saile demanded, the coxcomb of auburn hair glistening under the brilliant sun.

Fitch let out a heavy sigh. "I always say you know your own part of the business. But it might have repercussions."

Saile snorted. "Whatever those are!" He walked past Serena to his horse, saw that the animal was still lathered, and headed on foot toward the edge of the tobacco fields. With Liberty still cradled against her bosom, Serena heard Saile call to Roscoe, one of the few slaves she knew by name. He was a big·man, completely bald though probably no more than thirty. He emerged from a sea of golden-leaved plants to stand before the overseer.

Their conversation was conducted in tones Serena could not hear. She released Liberty, who no longer looked terrified but exhibited none of his usual youthful exuberance. Taking his hand, she led him to where Fitch was leaning against a rotting fence post, studying his fingernails.

"What's Saile up to?" she asked without preamble.

"He's doing his job," Fitch answered, avoiding Serena's head-on gaze and sounding defensive. "It's hotter than Hades out here. Why don't you and the pickaninny come inside? Leonard and I are almost finished."

The oppressiveness of the midday heat dulled Serena's reaction to Fitch's insulting reference, but she shook her head. "We'll wait here since you're nearly done."

Fitch shrugged, turning back toward his office. "Close to it, but you'll bake out here." He gave Serena·a patronizing smile.

Ignoring her brother-in-law's insupportable manners, Serena stood up very straight until Fitch disappeared, then abruptly sat down on an old barrel. Liberty began chasing the chickens again, gray dust flying everywhere. In Serena's dull-witted state, it took her some time to realize that she could hear Saile and Roscoe talking nearby. They had moved closer, standing under the shade of a myrtle tree. Roscoe looked grim; Saile wore a determined grimace.

"They got to understand," Saile declared, emphasizing his point with a ·slashing gesture of his right hand. "No work, no water. Hot weather's never been no excuse for shiftlessness at Wexford."

"I tell you, Mr. Saile, they's droppin' like flies." Roscoe's heavy eyebrows drew together in a deep scowl. "'Specially the young'uns. They all start runnin' away if you be harsh."

"They got it too good here, always have. And those young'uns don't work much anyways," Saile said. "I don't want none of their elders to take this war as an excuse for getting uppity. You go tell all of 'em that, you hear? Or," he added, his hand making a fist, "they learn the whip whether they're used to it or not."

For one brief moment, Roscoe's scowl looked malevolent. Then he turned away, heading slowly back toward the tobacco fields. Saile remained under the shade of the tree, taking out a plug of tobacco and putting it inside his cheek. Until now, Serena had not given Harold Saile a thought. Stern, rigid, inarticulate—that had been her superficial impression of her uncle's overseer. But now it dawned on Serena that he was also horribly inhumane—and foolish. Slaves were controlled far more by a cultivated dependency than by the whip. Besides, Serena thought with a shudder, cutting into a Negro's flesh also cut into profit.

Serena's mind was functioning again. She was not bound by Southern idiosyncrasies about women not meddling in plantation matters. Immediately upon her return to town, she would tell Uncle Luke what was happening. As she watched Saile strut back toward the horse trough, she heard a mewing sound and started to tell Liberty to go look for kittens.

Except that it wasn't mewing at all: Beyond the jutting wing of the plantation office, she saw a slow-moving rainbow weaving its way toward the slave quarters. Straining for a better view, Serena realized it was mostly women, all of whom were carrying children. Some of the youngsters were no more than infants.

The plaintive cries goaded Serena into overcoming her inertia. Careful not to alarm Liberty again, she gently took his hand. "We must go see if Leonard is ready to leave. You must be hungry."

"We eat hush puppies?" Liberty asked, hopping along at her side.

"I don't know." Serena hoped not; the heat had taken away her appetite.

Neither Fitch nor Leonard seemed pleased at the intrusion. But Serena informed them in the primmest of tones that she had to leave the child in their care for just a few moments. Annoyed, Fitch bluntly reminded her where the privy was located while Leonard did his best to conceal his dismay at such a lack of propriety.

Outside, the heat seemed to strike Serena like an ocean wave. But after noting that Saile and his horse had both disappeared, she hurried over the dry, caked ground which led to the slave quarters.

The buildings directly behind the plantation office were made of leftover brick from the old house. While small and crowded, they were better constructed than many of the wooden shacks where the poor whites lived.

The door to the first dwelling was open and Serena could hear the mewing sobs again. She stood on the threshold, taking in the sight

of a half-dozen women with almost twice that many children, all of
whom seemed to be in extreme agony.

Serena decided on coming straight to the point: "Do you need
water?"

A half-dozen heads swathed in bright bandanas swung around to
stare at her. Distrust, fear, anger—and hope—all emanated from the
six pairs of black eyes. At last, one woman, no older than Serena,
stood up and wiped away a tear. She was tall, with high cheekbones
and a strong jawline. "Our babies are dying," she said. "My Rufus,
he be only three."

Serena looked at Rufus, lying on a pallet, his eyes closed, his
small body motionless. "Show me the well," Serena said. "I don't
know where it's located."

But the woman shook her head. "Massa Saile sealed it off. There
be a well down the road, but he got men watching it."

A frenzied howl erupted behind Serena where a little girl about
ten years old struggled to sit up. A stout woman clutched her close,
wailing uncontrollably. Serena's face tightened as yet another child
began to cry out in hysterical hallucination. The room was a bedlam
of cries and heat and color and despair.

"What's your name?" Serena finally asked, hoping that the prosaic
question might anchor her own wavering sensibilities.

There was a long pause, as if the woman could not remember.
"Cora," she said low, and the tears began to spill down her cheeks
once more.

"All right, Cora," Serena said briskly. "I can get a bit of water
immediately and then have more brought very soon. If Saile—or
anyone else—interferes, I'll kill them with my bare hands."

Cora was so startled that she regained her composure. "You crazy,
lady?"

"Probably," Serena replied, already out the door. "Just pray for
me."

Serena knew that Fitch did not always take his whiskey neat, nor
did his guests. He kept a fresh jug of water in the office, along with
a siphon and spoon.

This time Fitch greeted Serena with a smile. "Another quarter of
an hour," he began, but Serena brushed past him and Leonard, the
wake of her flying gingham skirts scattering papers on the floor. "Say,
hold on there, what's the all-fired hurry?"

"I want the water jug." She already had grabbed it, giving Liberty
a quick smile of reassurance. "Leonard, you go into town right now
and bring back water, as much as you can get. Hurry!"

Leonard's brow puckered. Fitch, however, was on his feet, one
hand on Serena's arm as she kept a fierce grip on the glass jug. "Are

you meddling with matters you don't know a rat's ass about, Mrs. Parnell?"

"I know about dying children," she snapped. "I just saw a dozen of them. God only knows how many others there are in the fields. Leonard, go!"

Leonard, however, was torn between his habit of doing the Farrar family bidding and the potential need to intervene, however discreetly, in what appeared to be a confrontation between Mrs. Parnell and Mr. Moncrief. Liberty watched with excited round-eyed anticipation.

Fitch chuckled, patting Serena's arm. "You're a Yankee gal, you've no notion how to deal with darkies. Why, your poor uncle would be out on the street corner with a beggar bowl if this plantation were run strictly according to his whims and fancies."

"He'd prefer begging his bread to having children die of thirst." Serena glared at Fitch. "Get your hand off my arm and give me the siphon and spoon. Leonard, get going!"

Leonard stood up, but made no move for the door. Still amused, Fitch stepped away from Serena. He pulled open the drawer but shook his head. "No, Mrs. Parnell, I can't let you do this. Now be a good girl and put that water jug down." The smile was now coaxing, even patronizing. Fitch seemed confident that Serena would obey.

Serena did. She set the water jug on the desk by the open drawer. But before Fitch could utter a word of approbation, Serena had pulled out the small, short-muzzled revolver which had rested next to Fitch's drinking utensils. The slanted, foxlike eyes bristling with outrage, she pointed the weapon directly at Fitch's chest. "You and Leonard fetch that water now! If you don't, so help me God, I'll shoot!"

Fitch's smile remained fixed though his eyes looked anxious. "Oh, Serena Parnell, you are quite the self-righteous Yankee! Now be sensible and calm down. We're just all overheated and out of sorts."

"I'll count to three." Serena's voice was shatteringly sharp. From somewhere, she saw herself in a similar situation, shaking from the cold and rain, knowing she could no more pull the trigger than soar through the clouds to New Bedford.

The smile faded from Fitch's lips. "Serena, I'm running out of patience. Leonard and I have work to do." He took a step backward, in the direction of the wide-eyed Liberty.

"One." The word edged through Serena's clenched teeth. Fitch moved back another step, within reach of the transfixed child. "Two." Serena had no doubt what Fitch intended to do. "Three."

Fitch reached down to grab Liberty just as the gun exploded in the hot, heavy confines of the small room. Leonard gasped, Liberty shrieked, and Fitch fell face forward, upsetting a chair. Although jarred by the revolver's report, Serena plunged ahead. "Leonard, take Liberty and get out of here!"

Leonard had turned pale around the lips. He was bending over Fitch, searching for a heartbeat. "He's still alive." The words were spoken with cautious relief.

"Of course he's alive." Serena gestured with difficulty at the painting of the Arabian mare behind the desk. "I missed him entirely and blew a hole in that dreadful picture. I daresay Mr. Moncrief has fainted from fright."

For one brief second, Leonard's eyes locked with Serena's and the merest hint of an admiring smile touched his pursed mouth. Then he grasped Liberty by the arm and hurried out of the room.

Without so much as a glance at Fitch, Serena slipped the revolver into the pocket of her dress, gathered up the siphon, spoon, and water jug, and headed out of the plantation office.

To Serena, it had seemed like hours since she'd left the slave quarters but, in fact, it had been only about ten minutes. The sobbing and wailing died down when she entered the room. Cora stood aside as Serena tended to the unconscious Rufus. Just a few drops between the lips, then a cool cloth on his forehead. The other women followed her example, working quietly and efficiently, until each child had been treated.

"More water is coming," Serena said. "Cora, would you show me where the others are?"

Cora, however, demurred. "I need stay with Rufus." She looked down at the small figure of her son, whose breathing had become more regular.

"I'll come," offered a spare, dark-skinned woman who wore enormous hoop earrings in her pierced ears. "I'm Josepha. My two be more well than the rest."

Serena nodded as Josepha picked up the water jug. An awed murmur followed her out of the cabin. Plodding alongside Josepha, Serena was filled with a sense of exhilaration, then she felt the revolver in her pocket bump against her thigh, and shuddered.

Oh, my God, did I mean to kill Fitch? Only a few feet from the cabin door, she stopped abruptly, dizzy with emotion.

"Missus!" Josepha cried in alarm. "You sick, too?"

But Serena had no opportunity to reply. Harold Saile, astride his weary horse, was riding toward her, a puzzled, angry shadow darkening his features.

"What's going on?" he demanded, his right hand jabbing at the water jug Josepha carried.

Serena's vision blurred, her legs felt unsteady, her mind scattered into fragments. Can't stop now ... children dying ... water, more water ...

Through a haze, she saw Saile brandish his riding crop at Josepha. "Pour it out! Hear me, bitch! Dump it!"

Serena dropped the siphon and spoon. She fumbled in her pocket and, with a shaking hand, pulled out the gun. "Go away," she muttered, wondering fuzzily how long she could remain standing. "Go away, you wretched man."

If Fitch Moncrief had been patronizing, Harold Saile was just plain furious. "I don't take orders from females, not of no color."

"You'd better," Serena said, her voice gaining strength. "I've already shot at Fitch Moncrief. What's one more bullet to me?"

Josepha emitted a small squeal and for an instant, Serena was afraid the other woman would drop the jug. Saile still brandished the crop, but gaped incredulously at Serena. "God almighty!" he breathed, glancing back toward the plantation office. "You're lying!"

"No." Serena shook her head; it felt like a puppet's, moving loosely on a string. "I won't shoot you if I don't have to. I'll take you as a prisoner of war instead."

Saile's expression clearly stated that he knew Serena was out of her mind. The moustache twitched as he sucked in his breath, trying to figure out how to handle this preposterous situation. Heat-crazed, no doubt; Northerners often succumbed to Southern weather.

"Well, that's your right." He eased the riding crop onto the saddle. "Let's go someplace and talk about it. That stable, maybe?"

Serena's grasp on reality was ebbing away, as if melted by the sun which blazed down from the cloudless sky. The gun was slipping out of her hand, the parched ground was coming closer, the overwhelming brilliance of the afternoon was suddenly turning to twilight ...

Josepha was making noises, whimpering, perhaps, like a kitten. Saile had dismounted from his horse. But someone else had, too, someone very large and familiar. Liberty was laughing and Leonard said, "Shock, one must presume." But Serena didn't care any more; it was night and she was asleep with the sound of the ocean in her ears.

Chapter 12

SHE HAD BEEN CERTAIN that it was Brant who had been sitting by her bed when she awoke the next morning. But it was Kirk instead, his resemblance to Brant accentuated by Serena's unfocused eyes.

Uncle Luke had joined them almost immediately, and while Serena sipped at mint tea and wondered if she could keep it in her stomach, the two men explained what had happened after she'd lost consciousness.

Leonard and Liberty had gone only about a half-mile when they'd encountered Yancy Clarke on the road into town. Yancy, on parole and wearing civilian clothes, was taking his sidekick, Sergeant Davis, along to inspect the Union camp where Confederate soldiers were still held prisoner. Knowing the whereabouts of a nearby well, Yancy, Davis, and Leonard had filled two barrels and headed back to the plantation just in time to find Saile trying to beat Josepha with his riding crop. It took Yancy only a few seconds to break the overseer's jaw while Leonard and Sergeant Davis began distributing the water. Josepha had tended to Serena while Liberty cried for fear that she was dead.

Yancy had declined to return to town with Leonard and Serena, but hauled Saile off to the Union camp. As a Yankee, asserted Yancy, Serena was within her rights to take Saile as a prisoner of war. Sergeant Davis had argued at length about the legality, morality, and rules of military conduct involved, but Yancy was adamant. Unconvinced, Sergeant Davis was still shaking his head when they rode away from Wexford.

Uncle Luke had been horrified when his unconscious niece was brought home and the story unfolded. Aunt Kathleen fainted dead away. Cecelia, however, was amused, setting off to receive her "cowardly cavalier," as she called Fitch, at their house next door. The family physician, Dr. Hooper, was a sanguine man who cheerfully took time off from helping tend the local military to predict a rapid and complete recovery for Serena.

Aunt Kathleen, sipping fruit punch laced with gin, rallied long enough to upbraid Luke for summoning Kirk Parnell in a time of family crisis. But Kirk had rushed to the Farrar townhouse, spent the night in a guest room, and gotten up early to sit by Serena's side until she woke up. He had not slept well and was growing convinced that the apparently conventional, sheltered girl his brother had brought from Brunswick was somehow fatally bent on attracting violence.

She was hollow-eyed and pale this warm, humid morning, listening to her uncle and brother-in-law relate their account of the previous day. "Is Cecelia mad at me?" she asked at last.

Uncle Luke's eyes twinkled as he shook his head. "Not at all. Fitch's cowardice gives her one more thing to hold over him. I wouldn't be surprised if poor Fitch signed up just to get away from Celia's tongue-lashings. Of course," Luke continued, suddenly thoughtful, "I'd dismiss him as my manager if he weren't kin. I won't tolerate cruelty."

"He's an unpleasant sort, Uncle Luke. Why did you ever hire him?"

"Because he was so unpleasant." Luke looked rueful, glancing from Serena to Kirk. "Fitch was a bayou brat, full of sneaky tricks and nasty ideas. He needed somebody to believe in him. I wanted to do that for him—while he did what had to be done for the plantation. Hell's fire, I couldn't even *ask* my people to work, let alone *make* them. That didn't bother Fitch at all—and maybe I closed my eyes to some things. I can't do that anymore."

Kirk seemed to read Luke's thoughts. "You've been in a strange situation for a Northerner, sir. Slavery just doesn't mesh with our way of thinking."

Luke looked rueful. "I know—up North, we pay our slaves."

Kirk's shoulders straightened. "They have the right to strike," he responded, sounding both defensive and annoyed. "Look at those shoe factory workers just a couple of years ago . . ."

"Now, now." Uncle Luke held up his hands and smiled. "Let's not argue among ourselves. We don't want to disturb our sick little lady here."

"I'm not sick," Serena asserted. "Just tired."

"We're all a little tired," Uncle Luke said, getting up to pour himself a cup of tea. The window stood open, a weak breeze attempting to stir the humid morning air.

Uncle Luke frowned into his teacup. "Who made this foul brew?" He put the cup and saucer down on the floor. "Medicinal, I suppose. I don't know how long Fitch has been letting Saile have a free hand with my people, but I'd guess it hasn't been too long or I'd have heard about it."

The sunlight streaming through the window caught the gold braid on Kirk's sleeve as he turned to Uncle Luke. "Has Saile been at Wexford long, sir?" Kirk's tone was respectful, but Serena knew from

hearing him interview people on the *Mercury* that he had a knack for
eliciting information in an unobtrusive, tactful way.

"Just a year. Maybe a little more, I forget." Uncle Luke scratched
his head. "Highly recommended by a couple of county folks he'd
worked for. Good souls, too—but maybe not too bright." He sighed
and suddenly looked old. "I never was any judge of people, at least
Marcus always told me that." The smile he gave Serena was a travesty
of his usual good humor. "Guess I tend to think most folks are basically
well-intentioned. I don't want to stop believing that, despite the Harold
Sailes and Fitch Moncriefs of this world."

"No, of course not." Kirk looked at the crease in his uniform's
trouser leg. "But," he went on, glancing at Serena and back to Uncle
Luke, "how will the local people react to Serena's interference?"

A short guffaw erupted from Uncle Luke. "You're starting to sound
like Leonard. First off, since we're under military occupation and
Serena is a Yankee, she could gun down the whole town and nobody
would arrest her."

Kirk pulled thoughtfully on his long chin. "In other words, she's
not going to be very popular. Will she need Federal protection?"

"No!" Serena's reaction cut through the air with a report almost
as sharp as the bullet she'd fired at Fitch Moncrief. Both men sat bolt
upright, staring at the seemingly depleted creature who now was
leaning forward in the bed, slanted eyes snapping, up-turned nose
virtually twitching with determination. "You're both talking about me
as if I were sitting out on a raft in the Neuse. I don't need anyone to
protect me. And at the first hint of criticism, I'll defend myself—in
any way I have to."

Kirk appeared dubious, Uncle Luke seemed pleased. Serena flopped
back onto the pillows, arms folded across her bosom. The door flew
open and Liberty raced across the room, thrusting himself between
the two men to all but fly up the three steps to Serena's chintz-covered
bed. "You 'wake?" he asked, beating his small hands on the counterpane in excitement.

"My yes," Serena replied and smiled at the child. In her mind's
eye, she saw other children, wailing in agony, writhing from thirst,
helpless, innocent, only a step from death. But they, like Liberty,
were alive this morning, safe in their mothers' arms, and she, Serena
Farrar Parnell, had saved them. Reaching out, she hugged Liberty so
tight that his gurgle of pleasure quickly turned into a squeaking plea
for release. "I'm sorry, I'm just so glad to see you," she said and
kissed him on the cheek. He giggled and scrambled about on the
counterpane, his small backside bounding with exuberance.

Kirk had stood up. "I'd better get back to camp," he said, extending
his hand to Serena. "I'll stop by tomorrow, if I may."

"Certainly, certainly," said Uncle Luke rather absently. Kirk was almost to the door before the other man stopped him. "I'll see you out, I have to look for something." He turned to Serena, who was smiling at Liberty's antics. "I'm coming back, don't nod off."

With Liberty trying to climb the bedpost, that was hardly possible. But within five minutes, Helen, the ramrod mammy who had brought up the twins and was second only to Leonard within the household ranks, arrived to haul Liberty off to breakfast.

The bedclothes had grown heavy as the sun rose to its zenith. Serena wasn't inclined to lie about; that was acceptable for Southern ladies but unsuited to a Yankee temperament. As she was about to get out of bed, Uncle Luke came hurrying into the room. "I found it!" He seemed pleased with himself as he brandished a tattered book at Serena. "Talk about defending yourself—you've got a better way," he declared, sitting down in the shoofly chair with its overhead fan to ward off heat and insects. "If you stay in New Bern, you might as well make yourself useful. Listen to this," he said, opening the book and flipping through the pages. "'At the North, we willingly publish pro-slavery arguments, and ask only a fair field and no favor for the other side. But you will not even allow your own citizens a chance to examine this important subject. Your letter to me is published in Northern papers, as well as Southern: but my reply will not be allowed to appear in any Southern paper. The despotic measures you take to silence investigation, and shut out the light from your own white population, prove how little reliance you have on the strength of your cause. In this enlightened age, all despotisms *ought* to come to an end by the agency of moral and rational means. But if they resist such agencies, it is in the order of Providence that they *must* come to an end by violence. History is full of such lessons.'" Uncle Luke nodded his head in decisive agreement and slapped the book shut. "What do you think of that?"

Serena brushed her hair from her forehead and smiled. "I think you're a very good man who wants very much to make me feel better. Thank you."

Uncle Luke waved the volume at Serena and shook his head. "Not quite. Do you know who wrote that?"

"No. But whoever he was, he had a convincing style."

"'He,' my foot!" Uncle Luke pressed the book on Serena. "That's Lydia Maria Child, writing to some Southern nitwit—female variety, they do come in both sexes—about the evils of slavery. Those are all Mrs. Child's letters, published—oh, I'm not sure, a few years ago and hard to come by down here, but I sent up North for them. Now—do you know what else Mrs. Child has done?"

Serena ought to know, knew, in fact, that she'd heard the name during discussions at the family dinner table. "Oh! She was one of the early abolitionists! Even before Mrs. Stowe."

"Long before Mrs. Stowe. But that's not all," said Uncle Luke. "Some years back, she edited a newspaper in New York." He paused and rocked back and forth in the shoofly chair. "You've heard about some of the Yankees wanting to publish a paper here?"

Serena put the book down on the counterpane and regarded her uncle levelly. "Oh. I see." They exchanged a long, understanding look. "But how?"

"All you need is a printing press. And whatever else, I don't know much about newspapers. And Kirk. A man away from his family needs something to do besides twiddle his thumbs in an army camp. At least that one does. But then as I said, I'm no judge of people."

The silence which filled the bedroom all but obliterated the heavy heat of mid-morning. At last Serena spoke, slowly and cautiously. "If people in New Bern—at least some of them—already regard me as the enemy, won't publishing a newspaper make me even more so? And won't that endanger you as well?"

"Maybe." Uncle Luke shrugged. "Hell's fire, Serena, this is war. We're all in danger. I may be a slaveholder, God help me, but I'm opposed to the system and always have been. The only reason I never freed our people after I married your aunt was because her father's will had a codicil about keeping slaves. Old Prendergast knew there could be problems with a Yankee son-in-law. If I'd freed the Negroes, the plantation would have gone to some cousin in Savannah who's already drunk himself to death. Oh, I love the land and a lot of things about the South, but slavery never was one of them."

"I never knew about the will." Serena shifted in the bed, trying to ease a backache she felt coming on. "But Uncle Luke, will anybody but other Yankees read what I write?"

Uncle Luke fingered his chin. "Oh—maybe, maybe not. But truth is kind of like time—they both have a funny way of sneaking up on people."

"So they do." Serena closed her eyes, suddenly reminded of Brant's confusing words about truth. Brant, hovering at the edge of her mind as he so often did, momentarily obliterated Uncle Luke and his talk of newspaper publishing. But there had been a time when newspapers had come before Brant. With effort, Serena thrust him aside and tried to concentrate on becoming Serena Parnell, New Bern editor and publisher.

Aunt Kathleen had thrown up her hands in despair when Serena insisted on going out to Wexford alone. "It's just not proper, especially these days," Aunt Kathleen had asserted, wringing her skirts and shaking her head. "I'd go with you, but I feel quite vaporous."

There was no point in arguing with Aunt Kathleen, who seemed to derive emotional strength from physical frailties. As for Serena, she felt cooped up, oppressed by the heat and the Union siege. Still, an air of normality was returning to New Bern: Some of the residents who had fled in March came back by midsummer. A few businesses had reopened and repairs were being made to damaged buildings. If former slaves roamed the streets and blue-clad soldiers stood at almost every street corner, the city had resumed a surface calm.

So, after three days marking time in the townhouse, Serena responded to the humbly worded request sent by Cora and the other women at Wexford. They had asked Leonard if Serena would come to the plantation so they could show their gratitude for what she had done to save their children.

Roscoe was waiting for Serena when she arrived in Uncle Luke's trap. It was another hot day, but the hint of a breeze lightened the summer air. Within moments, the women and children materialized as if by magic. Cora and Rufus stepped forward, each carrying a bouquet of tiger lilies.

Serena took the brilliant orange blooms first from Cora and then from her little son, who refused to look up. "Thank you," Serena declared, brushing Rufus's fuzzy head with her hand. "But I only did what any Christian person would have done." She caught Rufus looking at her and quickly bent down to the child. "Here," she said in an unsteady voice, "keep this." His small hand reached out to take the lily from her before he toddled away to his mother's side.

The women and children seemed to disperse as swiftly as they'd come. Even Roscoe had disappeared. Serena started toward the trap just as Josepha emerged from the plantation office building, her dark skin beaded with perspiration.

Serena set the lilies down on the seat of the trap. Curious as to why Josepha had been in the plantation office, Serena walked over to the other woman and motioned for her to stop.

"Thank you for the flowers," Serena said with a smile. "You weren't here when Cora and the others gave them to me."

Josepha's great black eyes looked beyond Serena's shoulder. "No, I be inside." She pulled at the neckline of her worn dress, the dark forehead creased by a frown.

Serena's eyes narrowed with sudden intuition. "With Mr. Moncrief?"

"He done have his way with me. He always do." Josepha's big hoop earrings swung, catching the sunlight.

"Did . . . does he hurt you?" Serena's voice was low and tentative.

Josepha shook her head. "He not cruel, he . . . spooky."

"Spooky?" Serena peered more closely at Josepha. Josepha was no beauty, but she possessed the wonderful, limpid eyes of her race, a firm, full figure, and perfect white teeth. It occurred to Serena that she also had two children who bore no trace of white blood.

Josepha was nodding. "Massa Fitch, he do strange things. Why, one time, he tell me to chain him up and use the whip. I call that spooky!"

"I would, too," Serena replied with feeling, unable to keep from shaking her head. "You . . . don't object?"

The big eyes grew bigger. "Object? Why, Miz Parnell, I be a slave."

Josepha's response momentarily silenced Serena.

"You may not be a slave much longer," Serena said after a moment, her tone almost challenging. "Many of your people have already deserted their owners."

"I hear 'bout them." Josepha was looking beyond Serena. "My man and me, we done talk it over." She nodded at someone, causing Serena to turn and see Roscoe coming back from the fields. "Roscoe say we wait."

The bald head gleamed under the sun as Roscoe greeted Serena deferentially before speaking to Josepha. "You done in there?" The black eyes darted toward the plantation office, as if he had to force himself to look in that direction.

"He be through." Josepha spoke as matter-of-factly as if she'd just completed a minor household chore instead of what—to Serena—must have been a degrading act of sexual submission. So confounded was Serena that she didn't realize Josepha and Roscoe were patiently waiting for dismissal.

"Dear me," Serena finally said with a lame smile, "I must get back to town and see how my aunt's getting along. She tends to have the vapors, though I think she exaggerates. But who am I to judge, at her age she may suffer from . . . uh, certain maladies . . ." Serena's babble trailed away as she saw the two slaves staring. She flushed and licked her lips. In all the etiquette lessons from Lydia Farrar, the subject of how to converse with a race held in bondage had never been discussed. With a rueful shake of her head, Serena murmured a garbled good-bye and walked hurriedly toward the trap.

Chapter 13

MARE'S-TAIL CLOUDS swept across the sky behind the national Capitol, promising rain before dusk. To Brant Parnell, Washington was aesthetically unimpressive. The new Capitol dome was emerging along classic lines, and the monument dedicated to General Washington was supposed to be spectacular—if either ever finished abuilding. For all its orderly planning, the city wore the air of an elegant dame who has just begun her toilette and been interrupted by squabbling scullery help. In the autumn of 1862, Washington suffered not just from the threat of enemy attack, but from a period of stymied expansion. Yet if construction slowed on the more decorative additions to Washington, work crews could hardly keep pace with the need for barracks, bridges, gun emplacements, and bureaucratic offices.

While Brant might fault Washington's sprawling, makeshift, military atmosphere, he couldn't criticize the city's response to his most recent proposal: Finally gaining access to Secretary of War Stanton, Brant had secured the coveted uniform contracts for Farrar and Company's four mills in Maine. Marcus would recoup his losses within a year and Brant would receive a healthy share of the profits. While neither man would have chosen to make his money in such a way, both had agreed that if people couldn't resolve their differences without resorting to violence, then it was foolish not to take advantage of reality. If soldiers had to fight, at least Farrar and Company could promise that the Union army would wear quality.

But fine uniforms wouldn't alleviate pain and sorrow and suffering, thought Brant as he walked along the C&O Canal in Georgetown where two young soldiers helped a third who had lost a leg. The streets were full of Union men; no, Brant corrected himself—boys—beardless, guileless, brainless. You had to be, he thought bitterly, to throw your life away just because rational men couldn't also be reasonable.

A few yards away, a pair of mules hauled a barge laden with heavy crates down the canal. Brant saw the bridge just ahead, crossed over, and finally sighted the spire of St. John's Episcopal Church. The Catholic Convent of Mercy must be close by. It occurred to him that war also had a way of uniting factions at odds in peacetime. To provide a hospital in Georgetown, the two religions had banded together, their differences dissipated by the wounded and dying men of various faiths and no faith at all.

Black-clad nuns and somber-garbed laywomen moved briskly among the crowded beds. The odor of chloroform filled the air and the sound of pain pierced the ears. Brant removed his hat as a very short, stout nun blocked his path.

"Pardon me, Sister," he said in a quiet voice, "I'm looking for a Miss Abigail Beaulieu. Do you know where she is?"

The nun tapped a pudgy finger against a crinkled cheek. *"Ja,"* she replied in a heavy German accent, "go to dispensary down hall, at left."

"Danke," Brant responded without thinking. He made a little bow and followed the nun's directions. The first door on the left turned out to be a storage closet, but the dispensary was next and Abigail was there, readying a tray of medical instruments.

"Brant, how nice to see a man come here in an upright position." Abigail may have been surprised to see Brant, but her welcoming smile didn't betray it. She offered him her hand, then gestured to a stool. "Sit, I can talk while I finish getting these ready for the surgeons. How long have you been in Washington?"

"A week." Brant tested the rung on the stool, found it wobbly, and planted both feet on the bare floor. "Your letter arrived the day before I left Brunswick."

"I was afraid it might not reach you in time. The mail is so slow and I only learned last month that you were coming here." She paused to count the items on the tray. "I thought perhaps you'd sail."

"No. It was more expedient to take the train." Brant watched with fascination as Abigail took out another tray and deftly sorted through a strange-looking array of shining steel. "You seem to know what you're doing."

"It's not difficult." She sat down on another stool and arranged her dark blue skirts. "Now—I've had my fill of Washington after almost a year. Enough is enough. Will you take me to New Bern?"

"New Bern?" Brant drew back the dark eyebrows drawing together. "I thought you wanted to go home to Brunswick."

The green eyes danced. "Oh, heavens, no! I never said any such thing! Did I?"

"Well—no, everyone just assumed . . ." Brant broke off, grinning at Abigail. "But that's your stock in trade, I gather, the art of assumption?"

Abigail's mouth formed a silent O. "Shame on you, Brant Parnell, you seem to have presumptions regarding my assumptions."

"Do they let you talk to the patients? Or only the ones who are already delirious?"

"No. Or yes, as the case may be." Abigail sobered, the smooth forehead furrowing slightly. "It's really quite simple. I feel an obligation to continue helping with the wounded, but I've never liked politics. Washington is the last place on earth I'd ever care to live, war or no war. So," she went on, adjusting the lace fichu at her neck, "if I must go where the fighting is—or at least the soldiers are— then New Bern is my logical choice because I already have family there." She smiled ingenuously at Brant and folded her hands in her lap.

Brant nodded twice. "That makes sense. I think. But," he inquired, getting up from the stool and taking a step toward Abigail, "how do you know I plan on going to New Bern?"

The smile stayed in place. "Because you're taking old printing equipment from the *Mercury* there at your brother's request. I finally got a letter from Serena."

Abigail's alert eye caught the fleeting change in Brant's expression, but she couldn't discern what it was. Anger? Concern? Pain? Brant's voice was tinged with its customary good-humored irony when he spoke: "Yes, it seems that my wife and my brother are going into the newspaper business together. He was on leave in August and we talked about it while he was in New Bedford. When he wasn't helping build an extra room on the house for Peggy's widows and orphans."

"I think that's wonderful of Peggy," Abigail said and ignored Brant's faint grimace. "Now tell me how and when you're going to New Bern."

Brant, in fact, wasn't sure. By ship, of course, with permission to run the blockade, and certainly before the autumn weather turned to winter storms. But the dangers weren't limited to nature's whims; Confederate ships lurked in the coastal waters, avoiding the Union navy, willing to run great risks to cut off seagoing supplies to the enemy troops of occupation. Brant was no more anxious to take Abigail into North Carolina waters than he had been to take Serena and Cecelia out of them.

Stalling for time, Brant asked if Abigail would care to join him for supper at a nearby inn. She accepted, since her shift was over and she hadn't eaten since breakfast. "It's been a hectic day until now," she explained as they walked back down the corridor to the convent's entrance. "There's been fierce fighting reported at Antietam."

As if to prove her point, a wagon filled with bleeding, wounded men had just drawn up in what recently had been a carefully tended rose garden. The arbors still stood, but most of the bushes had been trampled into the earth. As the orderlies began to unload the men onto stretchers, Abigail walked by quickly with Brant following close behind.

"You never get used to it," she said, her fine lips scarcely moving.

"No," Brant agreed, wondering how Abigail had managed in the first place. Helping remove a bullet from Yancy Clarke had been relatively wholesome compared to the carnage of an army hospital. Such a fastidious young lady seemed out of place among the torn, butchered bodies of brave young men. But he knew there were many such equally elegant women doing the same thing in different places on both sides of the battlelines.

After they had been seated at an old trestle table in the inn, Brant commented on Abigail's fortitude. But Abigail merely lifted her slim shoulders. "It's work which must be done by someone. I would never have it said that the Beaulieus shirked their duty to the Union."

If Abigail had intended her comment as a barb, Brant ignored it as he accepted a mug of porter from an elderly black waiter. "Have you heard from Matt?"

"He was here in July." She touched the rim of her wineglass experimentally. "There's much frustration among the Army of the Potomac." Abigail looked away and frowned. "Matt complained most bitterly."

Brant's voice took on a harsh note: "Men like Matt are too eager to be heroes. I'd hate to see him grow so impatient that his next trip to Washington was in a cart like the one we just saw." Brant saw Abigail's green eyes flicker, but made no attempt to apologize for the severity of his words. He did, however, change the subject. "As far as serving the Union goes, I think you'd be better off staying somewhere closer. Maryland, Pennsylvania, maybe. There are plenty of wounded men to care for. Let's face it, Abigail, I don't think taking you to New Bern is a good idea."

His statement did not elicit the counterargument he was expecting. "Did you know Yancy has a farm?" The green eyes were clear and direct, the refined features calm and composed.

"Yes. Kirk told me."

"Someone named Sergeant Davis is helping him."

"And you want to be the farmer's wife?" Brant saw Abigail's lips tighten and wondered if he'd gone too far in invading her privacy.

"The agrarian life might have its charms." Abigail gave Brant a cool smile, then embarked on a new topic.

"Why didn't Serena go home when Kirk went on leave?" she asked as the waiter brought them a basket of thick-crusted bread and a small crock of butter.

"You've seen troop trains and yet ask that question?" Brant broke up the bread and handed Abigail a chunk. "Anyway, it's not allowed.

If I weren't on government business, I'd never have been able to take the train to Washington." He stopped long enough to chew a mouthful of bread. "Do the Episcopal sisters have a hospital at Catonsville?"

"I'm not sure. I'm not going to Maryland, I'm going to North Carolina." Abigail glanced about the wooden tabletop. "Is there any jam?"

If there was one thing in a woman that rendered Brant helpless, it was a lack of willingness to argue. Brant usually won arguments, whether with men or women. It was just that with women, sometimes it took a little longer. And often proved more enjoyable.

"Abigail, I'll bet you five dollars you haven't put jam on your bread since you were eight years old." Brant drained the porter and signaled to the waiter to bring him another.

"How did you know?" It was Abigail's turn to be taken aback, though Brant thought she concealed it very well. It was not, however, Abigail's style to let such perceptiveness deter her. "Did Kirk enjoy his leave?"

"Of course." Brant sighed as the waiter put the mug in front of him. It was almost six o'clock and the supper trade was beginning to pick up as government workers left their jobs and ventured out into the overcast September evening to try to forget the all-consuming dilemma of how to save the Union. "He misses the children. And dotes on pretty Peggy."

Abigail didn't speak until the waiter had placed two steaming pewter bowls of beef and vegetable soup on the table. "You don't like Peggy, do you?"

"I love Peggy. Everybody loves Peggy." Brant was growing vexed. "Oh, hell, Abigail, Peggy is a saint. How can anybody not love a saint?"

Abigail tested her soup; it was too hot. "All the verified saints I know are dead. Those are the kind that are much easier to love."

Brant grinned at her. "How true. So much goodness rolled into one person makes me suspicious. As my father used to say, 'Goodness, mercy, and truth shall follow me all the days of my life—but God help me, keep 'em at a distance.'"

"I think I would have liked your father. Was he a sea captain too?"

"Yes." Brant was about to launch into a brief history of his family, but decided it was time to cut Abigail's game short. "You can't go to New Bern. I won't take you."

Abigail had just swallowed her first mouthful of soup. She patted her lips with a napkin before speaking. "You know I must. You also seem to know why." The green eyes locked with his in a nearly hypnotic stare. "Well?"

Brant fingered the slight cleft in his chin and regarded Abigail speculatively. She was serenely tasting her soup. "I'll send you a telegraph message as soon as I decide when I'm leaving," Brant said evenly. "We'll be stopping here in Washington to pick up dispatches and whatever else we need to take for the army of occupation."

"Fine. I'll be ready." She pulled a face and put down her soup spoon. "This beef seems tough. But then I'm not fond of beef."

"We'll be lucky to have meat at all before this war is over," Brant asserted in an impatient tone. He leaned across the table and put a hand on Abigail's arm. "Listen, Abby, it's none of my business, but are you sure about Yancy? Farm or no farm, he's a footloose sort, a rambler. I know that type. He'll never really settle down. And he does shoot people."

Abigail picked up her wineglass and took a slow sip of the red burgundy. "Pembrose Stanhope wasn't *people*. Which is beside the point. Yancy didn't shoot Pembrose, I did. Do you think we could order some fish?"

Brant prided himself on seldom being surprised by what other people said or did. Yet Abigail was an exception. She would have made a hell of a poker player, Brant thought as he signaled for the waiter. If Serena was unpredictable, her cousin was unfathomable.

Brant asked for poached sea bass and leaned toward his companion. "Why did you shoot Pembrose, Abby? Did you have a real reason or was he wearing a tasteless cravat?"

Abigail was unruffled by Brant's asperity. "Pembrose and Yancy did not see eye to eye on a certain matter. There was an exchange of blows and Pembrose had a knife. Yancy went for his gun, but Giles appeared out of nowhere and attacked him from behind. The gun fell on the floor." She paused to rearrange her napkin. "It was dark. None of the men could see Yancy's gun but it had landed by me. I picked it up and shot Pembrose." Abigail gave a little shrug. "It was all very prosaic. And Yancy, being basically a very noble person, refused to let me take the blame. I was rather put out with him at the time, and downright annoyed when he got arrested and managed to get shot trying to escape." Her fine brows came together. "If only he'd let me tell the authorities the truth in the first place. I do find it vexing when men feel obliged to be so everlastingly noble."

Brant sighed. "Not a great failing of mine, actually." He looked up as the waiter removed their soup bowls and uncovered two servings of sea bass. "Have you told Serena all this?"

Shaking her head, Abigail remained silent until the waiter was out of hearing range. "Nor will I, unless I must. It's Yancy's personal situation, you see, and until he wishes for anyone else to know, I must keep it to myself."

Brant paused, fork in hand. "But you told me."

"So I did. But you were painting an unjust portrait of Yancy. I couldn't let you do that." Abigail smiled gently, then squeezed a drop of lemon juice on her fish.

Brant chewed thoughtfully. "You must love him very much."

"Yes." Abigail tasted the bass and brightened. "That's quite delicious. I much prefer fish to fowl or meat. Have you ever eaten octopus?"

"Once," Brant replied. He cast a surreptitious glance at Abigail, who seemed absorbed with her food. And he wondered why he suddenly felt resentful of Yancy Clarke. For one brief second, he asked himself if Abigail stirred desire in him. She was a charming, elegant little creature whose calm exterior no doubt masked a passionate nature. But it wasn't Abigail who unsettled his masculine aplomb, it was Yancy—and the fact that he was loved so willingly, so completely by this woman who was sitting across the table, serenely eating her fish. Did every man deserve to be loved like that? Did any man? Brant didn't know, and he wondered if he'd ever be lucky enough to find out.

Serena and Kirk had chosen the old *Carolina Sentinel* offices as their headquarters. The *Sentinel* had been shut down for some years and other businesses had leased the space from time to time, but the last tenants had fled New Bern when the Yankees invaded. Uncle Luke had argued that his shed could be converted into a newspaper office, but Serena had been adamant: She did not want him or the rest of his family to be connected so closely to her pro-Yankee endeavor. It was not at all unlikely that the newspaper offices would be a target for vandalism, possibly even violence. She refused to let her uncle risk the possibility of losing the cherished shed where he had spent so many hours working on his ingenious if impractical inventions.

Somewhat to Serena's surprise, Kirk had leaped at the chance to help her start the paper. He had gotten General Reno's permission without having to resort to the military bureaucracy. Reno was a shrewd man who knew the value of propaganda in time of war. His captured city was a captive audience for the voice of the Union.

In mid-September, Serena and Kirk set about cleaning and organizing their new offices, a task which took over two weeks. They worked well together, as they had in New Bedford. By early October, they were growing anxious for the promised printing equipment from the North. They were also arguing over a name for the paper. Kirk wanted to simply call it *The Union*, but Serena felt that was too blatantly pro-North. "We want to convert people, not berate them," she told Kirk one evening after they'd settled upon the paper's format and frequency. "What about *Unity?*"

Kirk shook his head. He wore his army uniform; not only was he still an officer, but he felt that retaining the military garb would help enforce authority. "*Unity* implies too much, as if we'd already accomplished what we've set out to do. We're not even close—Antietam is the first place we've really stopped Lee. He's brilliant. So's Jackson. Damn, if only we had the leadership the South has we could end this war in six weeks."

"Leader!" Serena snapped her fingers. "I like that, the *Carolina Leader*. What do you think?"

Kirk pulled at his chin. "It's got possibilities." He picked up a pen and piece of paper, writing the word several times in his big, sprawling hand. "It addresses the present—and the future." He looked at the word for a long moment. "Yes, I like it. Now," he said, getting up to survey the desks, chairs, filing cabinets, and a bookcase with several reference volumes, "all we need is a staff. Any ideas?"

"We also need a press." Serena sat with her head resting on her hands. Even for a pro-Union paper, staff might not be a serious problem. There were many men out of work in New Bern, men paroled from the Confederate army, men forced from their jobs in businesses or plantations that had been shut down, or rural men who had sought refuge in New Bern when the battlefields came too close to their homes. Nor were they all Confederate sympathizers; Serena had been surprised to learn how many people in North Carolina had opposed secession.

"I suspect the press will arrive before the end of October," Kirk said, examining a font of type he'd managed to unearth in Fayetteville. "Brant won't want to sail too late into the fall."

At the mention of her husband's name, Serena tensed. While she was extremely anxious to have the press delivered, she had wildly mixed emotions about seeing Brant again. Aware that Kirk was watching her with curiosity, she changed the subject. "I've been wondering—now that everything seems to be settling into a routine under the occupation and some of the men are sending for their families, will Peggy and the children join you?"

Kirk's reply came almost too quickly. "Oh, no. Peggy has her shelter to run. It's very important work. We talked about her coming here, of course, but as she said, we must all make sacrifices in wartime. Staying in New Bedford is hers."

To her surprise, Serena found Peggy's logic flawed. She was on the verge of pointing out that Peggy's decision only doubled Kirk's sacrifice but realized her own right to criticize another woman had been surrendered with the decision to come to New Bern. In any event, it was none of her business. "It's all so difficult," she remarked noncommittally. "Fitch seemed quite the dashing soldier when he went off west last month."

"He may just keep going," Kirk said with a hint of contempt. "Do you suppose your sister and your uncle forced him to sign up?"

"Not quite. Fitch was glad to go, in his way." Serena paused, recalling how Cecelia had described Fitch's varying moods of bravado and reluctance. But his primary motivation had been embarrassment, fearing what people would say about being bested by a mere slip of a Yankee girl. A Confederate uniform would vindicate his badly bruised masculine ego.

"Fitch will find ways to avoid danger," Kirk said at last, then got up and pulled at Serena's sleeve. "Come on, it's time to go home. We've had a long day."

"We've had a long two weeks." She smiled up at him, grateful for his constant support, his endless patience, his cautious enthusiasm. Now that everything was in readiness as far as their own duties were concerned, Serena was not only impatient to begin publication but exhausted from the physical and mental energy she had poured into getting her project under way. For the briefest moment, she closed her eyes and dropped her head on her breast. "Will all this work be worth it?" she murmured.

Kirk's arm was around her; she felt his lips in her hair. "Of course. It's the waiting that's hard. Are you all right, Serena?"

She opened her eyes and looked up at him. "Yes, just tired. Do I look peaked?"

His response was a great, hearty laugh which made his body vibrate against hers. "Good God, no," he asserted, looking down into her slanting eyes and lush, parted lips. "You look entrancingly..." He stopped, still holding her in the curve of one arm, his hand pressing just under her breast. Then he laughed again, a more hollow sound this time, released her, and patted her on the back. "A good night's sleep will fix you up fine." He handed over her cloak which she had unceremoniously dropped on the filing cabinet when she'd come into the office that morning. "Here, put your hood up, it sounds as if it's started to rain."

"We can use it," she said, making sure her pocketbook was inside the cloak. "It was such a hot, dry summer."

"Typical, I gather," Kirk said, extinguishing the sperm oil lamp. They walked out into the damp night, talking of the weather.

When Kirk wasn't able to accompany Serena to the Craven Street office of the yet-to-be-published *Carolina Leader*, he sent one of the men from his Massachusetts regiment instead. But on the first day of

November, the swarthy young major who showed up was from another contingent. His name was George Graham and he told Serena that the 21st Massachusetts was undermanned, having had to send a large number of soldiers to Goldsboro to disperse Confederate raiders.

The twins, Nathan and Jason, were agog over this latest combat report. At almost sixteen, both were steeped in military lore. Aunt Kathleen worried that it would not be long before they both asked to enlist.

"Two howitzers!" Nathan was exclaiming, his curly red hair dancing with excitement. "How many raiders are there?"

Major Graham had a raffish grin. "Now, now, you wouldn't be soliciting information for the rebels, would you, young man?" He turned to Serena, regarding her with frank approval. "You seem too pretty to be running a newspaper. Is it true you tried to gun down your uncle's plantation manager?"

Serena's chin jutted up. "I beg your pardon, Major, if you wish to know more about me, I suggest you read what I write when the newspaper is published. Shall we go?"

Graham did not seem unduly abashed by Serena's rebuke but made a bow as he let her precede him out the door. Leonard was standing in the drive, taking delivery from the one local dairy which had survived the occupation. He cut his conversation short to turn to Serena.

"If you please, Mrs. Parnell, I must get something I'd like to have you peruse." He nodded abruptly to Graham, moved silently but swiftly into the house, and returned almost at once with a sheaf of papers in his hand. "It's a treatise I've recently completed on the possible effects of emancipation. Should it come to that," Leonard added almost apologetically.

"Well." Serena flipped through the carefully written pages of Leonard's work. "You would like to have us use it in the newspaper? When we *have* a newspaper," she said with irony, and wondered where her husband—and the printing press—were about now.

Leonard coughed softly. "If you should deem it worthy." He avoided Graham's open stare and looked almost diffidently at Serena. "I would prefer, however, to have it printed under a name other than my own. Spartacus, perhaps."

"I like that." Serena's smile widened. "All right, Leonard, I'll read it this afternoon."

A few minutes later she and Graham were heading on foot into the commercial center of New Bern. It still grieved Serena to see the many vacant businesses, the fire-gutted buildings which had not been restored, the aimless men who wandered the ill-kept streets, the soldiers in Union garb who stood at almost each corner with bayonets at the ready. While the recent arrival of several Yankee families had piqued some interest, they had also aroused resentment.

Serena received her own share of hostile glances, though otherwise her passage was uneventful. There was a note from someone named Pigott seeking a job as a printer, but no word about the press—or Brant.

Graham smoothed his straight black hair and sat on the edge of Serena's desk. "You want me to wait until Major Parnell comes in?"

"No, I'm expecting one of my uncle's people to come by to do some painting." Serena attempted to absorb herself in Leonard's treatise, feeling increasingly uncomfortable in Graham's presence. He seemed to be inching closer on the desktop, his blue-clad thigh now only a scant foot away.

"I'd better wait, just in case." He took some coins from his pocket and juggled them expertly. "There were some rough doings last night over on Metcalf Street."

"Oh?" Serena professed curiosity, but wished Graham would desist.

"A couple of Southern ladies had been into the sherry wine and got to waving their fans at some Union soldiers. Our boys in blue took the little gals seriously and went in the house but it seems these two were just teasing and when the . . ."

If Serena's look of growing disapproval hadn't interrupted Graham, the arrival of Yancy Clarke did. "Yancy!" exclaimed Serena, getting up to greet the Texan as he shambled into the office. "Where have you been?"

The sleepy gray eyes barely seemed to notice Graham but Serena had the feeling that Yancy had sized up the other man, weighed his impressions, and decided he didn't approve. "Out yonder, near Drew's Creek, trying to raise corn." Yancy loomed over Graham, as if daring him to get off the desk.

But Graham was not easily intimidated. "What's an able-bodied Southerner like you doing not fighting for the cause?" he asked with his raffish grin. "You're not wearing the noble gray."

Yancy thoughtfully fingered the beard he'd grown back in recent months. "I was taken prisoner when the Yankees captured New Bern. I bought some land dirt cheap and I'm farming it, best I can."

"On parole, eh?" Graham looked up boldly at Yancy. "Don't you feel obliged to escape so you can fight another day?"

"No." Yancy strolled around the desk to where Serena was seated. "I just heard about your newspaper." He pointed at the sheaf of papers in front of Serena. "You write all that?"

"Lord, no, it's too tidy." She smiled at Yancy, grateful for his solid presence in the office. "It's a piece Leonard submitted."

"Leonard. Well, that's mighty imposing stuff," Yancy said with open admiration.

Graham had finally stood up. "Maybe you don't want to fight because you think slavery is wrong?"

Yancy's eyelids drooped just a fraction more than usual. "Maybe it's none of your business. Maybe you ought to stop asking me all those damned questions."

"Maybe I got my reasons." Graham leaned against the filing cabinet, his gaze insinuating.

"Maybe it's time you went back to your camp, Major Graham," Serena cut in sharply. "Mr. Clarke and I are old friends."

Graham's keen eyes raked over them both. "I see." His tone implied he saw more than mere friendship. Serena sensed the tension gathering in Yancy's big frame but before she could intervene further, Graham picked up his rakish hat and bowed low. "In that case, I'll leave you to his . . . protection." He nodded at Yancy and was gone.

"Maybe I should still go hit him, just for good measure," Yancy muttered, ambling to the window to see which way Graham had headed. "That one's a bad piece of goods, if you ask me."

"I've never seen him before and hopefully never will again," Serena said, taking out the coffeepot and filling it with water from a bucket next to the broom closet. "Tell me about your farm. I haven't seen you since that day at Wexford." Impulsively, she put a hand on Yancy's faded plaid shirt sleeve. "I never told you how glad I was that you came by to save Josepha and me from Harold Saile."

Yancy's mouth turned down at the corners into his beard. "I'd come round to inquire about some of them old bricks. Fortuitous, as it turned out."

"Yes. Fortuitous." Serena smiled, charmed by the strange drawling nuances of Yancy's speech. She wondered what the Texan and Abigail found to talk about. "Yancy, why New Bern?"

The big hands gestured loosely at himself. "For me?" He lifted one shoulder. "I was hoping it'd be the end of a long trail. Maybe it is."

Somewhat impatient, Serena concluded that Yancy and Abigail certainly had one thing in common—both were prone to obscurity. "Are we talking philosophy or reality?"

"Oh, it's real, all right." Yancy nodded slowly. "I came here to find my son."

"Your . . . son?" Serena placed both hands on the desktop and leaned toward Yancy. Abigail's child had been born dead. Yancy had not been the baby's father. Serena wished fervently that during those last tumultuous days in Brunswick she and Abigail had had more time to talk. "I didn't know you had a son. Abigail never mentioned him."

A flicker of warm light filtered through the sleepy gray eyes. "No," he said with a deep chuckle, "she wouldn't, bless her. I wouldn't either, except maybe you can help me find him."

"How? Through the newspaper?"

"I never thought of that." He paused, carefully considering the idea. "Shouldn't be necessary. I reckon you just have to ask some questions."

"Who do I ask?" Serena's impatience was returning.

"Start with your Uncle Luke." Yancy reached for his high-crowned hat which was apparently as close as he could come to Western-style headgear in New Bern. "My little Sam's about four years old now. He's half-black. His mama was a slave in Louisiana."

"Oh." Serena tried to conceal her shock. "You're certain he's not with her?"

The gray eyes opened as wide as Serena had ever seen them. "Certain as can be." Yancy swallowed hard. "She's dead. Pembrose Stanhope murdered her."

Chapter 14

IT WAS UNCOMMONLY warm for the middle of November. Serena had begun to perspire under her rust-colored bombazine dress as she watched Herman Pigott try to set type. He was a cheerful if not overly bright farm boy; his parents had owned land at Rattle Hill a few miles outside of New Bern, but their acreage had been ravaged by Union soldiers. With no trade and little concern for politics, Herman had let his sister, Emaline, talk him into trying for a job on the *Carolina Leader*. Neither Serena nor Kirk had been impressed, but when Emaline volunteered to run errands and clean for free if they'd hire her brother, Herman got the job. Kirk insisted on backing the gawky youth up with someone else, an experienced printer named Caldwell Smith from the First Rhode Island Light Artillery, who was anxious to exchange his life as a soldier for the more peaceable atmosphere of a newspaper office.

"Herman, are you left-handed?" Serena looked up from her list of things to do for the day.

"Yes, ma'am. Right-handed, too." He had a habit of smiling widely without ever opening his mouth.

"Are you sure?" But of course she'd seen him write; he'd had to prove he was literate to be a printer—and she wasn't certain which hand had held the pen.

"Yes, ma'am." He held up both hands, moving his fingers as if he were about to attempt a sonata on the pianoforte.

Serena sighed. "All right." She turned back to her list, wishing that it included a publication date. The calendar above the filing cabinet read November 16; was it possible that Brant had not eluded the Confederate ships which roamed off the Virginia and Carolina coasts? She shivered and shoved a stray lock of hair into the black net snood, trying to concentrate on the items she had yet to accomplish.

She'd given up on advertising, though. Few businessmen who were not ardent Confederate supporters wished to be branded as pro-Yankee by contributing money to a Northern cause. Not that it mattered; their financial situation was secure as long as the Union army paid for the cost of their operation. As for the office itself, Kirk could have commandeered it as occupied territory. Instead, he had offered the owner a fair rental price—and been refused. But after several glasses of Irish whiskey, the reluctant landlord had finally agreed that perhaps all was fair in love and war.

Serena put a checkmark next to the "paper supply." Kirk had brought an adequate amount from Raleigh earlier in the month. Next was Emaline; her duties had to be outlined more carefully. But Serena puzzled over Emaline. Both brother and sister had been taught to read and write in their Rattle Hill farm. Though Herman seemed somewhat slow, Emaline was very quick. Serena found it strange that Emaline, who might have found a better position for herself, seemed so determined to sacrifice herself for Herman.

The Southern mentality, Serena decided, always permitting the male to come first. Not that it couldn't happen up North, but somehow Emaline's offer to work for no pay at all struck Serena as far too subservient.

The final item on her list was etched in large block letters: WRITE. The order was directed at herself, to come to grips with her maiden editorial. Kirk had insisted that she have the honor of christening the *Leader*'s first edition. Serena wondered if it were his apology for terminating her short-lived career on the *Mercury*.

Thinking about those events of the previous year sent her mind back to the day Yancy Clarke had told her about his son and the woman he had married in Mexico. His tale had ended abruptly with the arrival of Mr. Beers, the stationer. She had not seen Yancy since, and her initial questioning of Uncle Luke had proved fruitless. He simply had no idea what she was talking about. Serena was equally stupefied about the wretched Pembrose Stanhope's involvement in the matter. Twice she had started to broach the subject with Kirk, but each time had decided to protect Yancy's confidences a little longer. At least the story was beginning to take on a hazy shape: Yancy's first wife had come from Louisiana; Abigail had gone to New Orleans to bear her child. Obviously, Yancy had been widowed by then. Perhaps it was their mutual hatred of Pembrose Stanhope which had first drawn Yancy and Abigail together. But when and why had Pembrose gone to Louisiana? Or Mexico, perhaps, since that was where Yancy had married his wife. Angelique, he'd called her. The boy was Sam, for Sam Houston. Mexico and Pembrose Stanhope . . . something stirred tauntingly at the back of Serena's brain but it slipped away when the office door opened and Brant Parnell strolled in, his jacket over his arm, the seaman's cap in his hand. He wore his perpetual tan, the craggy face seemed open and good-humored, but the blue eyes were ever-watchful.

"Do I need an appointment to see the editor?" he asked cheerfully, making an attempt to look self-effacing.

Herman had swiveled around, peering closely at their visitor.

Serena started to get up, changed her mind, and sat down again. "I thought you'd been sunk," she said and wondered why she felt suddenly weak. But Lydia Farrar's training came to the fore: "Brant, this is Herman Pigott, one of our printers. Herman, please meet Captain Brant Parnell. My husband," she added, almost apologetically.

Herman made no effort to conceal his surprise, though he put out a hand to Brant and gave him his closed-mouthed grin. "Howdy, a pleasure."

"Mine, too," Brant replied, his smile friendly. "How about going out in the backshop or whatever it's called and make sure everything's ready for the press?"

"Oh, it's ready, been ready for days and days." Herman was still grinning. When Brant made no comment but just continued to stare at him with that ironic sea-blue gaze, Herman all but jumped. "I see, oh, yep, I'll go look out back, I'm on my way."

When Herman had disappeared into the recesses of the newspaper offices, Brant came over to Serena's chair. He put his jacket and cap on the bookcase and set one booted foot atop the only uncluttered spot on Serena's desk. "It looks as if you're ready for business. Where's Kirk?"

"At the army camp. There was another skirmish last night, about five miles west of town." Serena lowered her lashes, trying to dredge up her recently acquired self-confidence. Surely she had been cultivating it long enough. Why should she be less assured around her own husband than in the company of his brother, Kirk, or even Herman Pigott?

"I suppose Kirk will give up soldiering when you start publishing." Brant's tone was casual and he appeared as relaxed as ever, but somehow Serena sensed an unusual restraint.

"I would imagine," she answered carefully, afraid that her voice might tremble. "But since we aren't actually in operation he still feels a duty to his regiment."

"A great man for duty is our Kirk," Brant said and took his foot off the desk. He moved about the office, noting the furnishings, the fresh paint on the walls, even the newly polished wooden floor. "It looks very professional," he remarked, touching the bald head on a small bust of Benjamin Franklin which Serena had found in Uncle Luke's attic. Brant came back to the desk and stood behind Serena. "Did you really think I'd sunk?"

He seemed to loom over her, like a mighty fir shadowing a fragile trillium. "I was afraid you might have," she admitted in a peculiarly small voice.

"And that the press had gone down to the briny deep along with me?"

Serena could not see his face but the jaunty tone seemed forced. "Yes. I mean, if you'd sunk, of course the press would have . . ." She twisted around in the chair to look up at him. Whether it was the aura of masculine strength he exuded even in repose or the compelling gaze in the wary eyes, Serena sensed that this was a time for candor. "I'm very relieved to see you. I was worried."

Brant appeared to weigh her words carefully. "I believe you," he said, looking quite serious. "But you certainly hide your enthusiasm well."

Serena frowned up at Brant, achingly aware of the craggy features, the crinkly black hair, the square jawline that needed a shave. "I'm surprised. I suppose I thought we'd hear something before you actually arrived." To her great astonishment, she actually uttered the words: "Are you going to kiss me hello or are you trying to memorize my face?"

Brant's heavy eyebrows lifted slightly. "I thought I had memorized it. Funny," he said, his tone softening, "I never remember exactly what you look like. But then you keep changing." He brushed his lips against hers, searchingly, then with an intensity which seemed to take Serena's breath away. She felt his arms go around her, parted her lips to accept his kisses as her hands clung to his back, feeling the hard-muscled strength of him. The rough beginnings of his beard scraped her neck as he kissed the curve of her throat, her ear, and finally the tip of her nose. Dimly, Serena heard herself making small, pleased sounds, like a kitten who has found the softest wool to paw. But Brant was now holding her at arm's length, looking both characteristically bemused and strangely bewildered. "I suppose there's no reason why I can't stay with you at Uncle Luke's, is there?"

"Of course there isn't," she replied boldly. "It would seem strange if you did not."

Brant's grin recaptured its usual brashness as he let her go. "You know, if we ever put our minds to it, we might like the idea of being married. We might even try living in the same town." He saw the hesitation in her face and paused in the act of collecting his jacket and cap. "Look, I didn't say we *had* to live together, it was just a passing thought."

Serena all but flung herself upon him. "No, no, I wasn't thinking about that. I mean, not in the way you mean." The slanted eyes held his, her confusion evident but inexplicable. "I just want us to . . . to be happy together while you're here."

He kissed her temple and nodded. "Living in occupied territory can't be a lot of fun. By the way, the press will be delivered by some of my crewmen tomorrow morning. Unless you've got something vital to do, why don't you ride back to Uncle Luke's with me and greet his guest?"

"Guest?" Serena looked puzzled as Brant went to the door of the backshop and called to Herman, telling him he could return to the office. "Who is visiting Uncle Luke?"

Brant looked as pleased as if he were about to present Serena with a diamond necklace. "A certain Miss Abigail Beaulieu of Brunswick and Washington. She says she's dying to talk to another female who can understand her when she doesn't always make sense."

"Abby!" Serena all but danced with excitement. "I don't believe it! But why is she here?"

Brant acknowledged Herman's return with a wave of his hand. "Abigail wanted a change of scenery," he replied airily. "I tried to stop her, but she's a very determined young lady."

"She is that," Serena said, starting to clear away her desk. Perhaps Abigail, like Yancy, had come to the end of a long trail.

The roast pork loin with parsley stuffing had been served on a bed of crisp celery leaves and spiced crab apples. Cheese biscuits, candied sweet potatoes, and coconut pralines rounded out the meal, while everyone grew quite merry as Leonard kept refilling the syllabub bowl. It occurred to Serena that this was the first supper she had enjoyed for some time—or was it that, given the high price of food and the increasing scarcities, meals had become less appetizing?

No matter, what counted most on that warm November evening was the company: Brant, Kirk, Abigail, Uncle Luke, Aunt Kathleen, the twins, and Cecelia were all gathered round the big mahogany dining room table. The reunion with Abigail had been filled with laughter and warmth, though the new arrival was fatigued from her journey and had been a victim of seasickness for two days out of Washington. There had been no opportunity for Serena to discuss Yancy and the child.

"I still find it curious how you managed to get dear Brant to bring you South when he couldn't take us North," Cecelia exclaimed, all round-eyed innocence above the rim of her lacquered Chinese fan.

"I gave him no choice," Abigail responded with a sweet smile of her own. "To be honest, as an army nurse, I am entitled to such privileges. Not," she added, turning to Kirk on her right, "that he was easy to convince."

Kirk was washing down a praline with Turkish coffee. "Brant seldom is," he said, grinning at his brother across the table. "I figured you stowed away."

Serena, too, had been puzzled. Perhaps her cousin would confide the secret of her success later. Knowing Abigail, it could have been anything from persuasion by the French ambassador to President Lincoln himself intervening on her behalf.

No matter, Abigail was there, the press was there—and Brant was there. Serena watched him surreptitiously over her syllabub cup as he discussed rumors of the Emancipation Proclamation the President was supposed to issue soon. Now shaved and wearing a dark frockcoat with a deep blue cravat, Brant looked ruggedly handsome as he held the attention of the other family members. Serena patted the upswept coiffure she'd so meticulously created and made sure that the pearl-edged combs were in place. She had chosen one of the gowns made the previous winter by Cecelia's dressmaker. Of rich crimson watered silk, it had bell sleeves, slashings of coffee-colored taffeta in the big skirt, and a decollete bodice which Aunt Kathleen deemed "inappropriate . . . except for New Year's Eve."

That had, in fact, been the only time Serena had worn it—until now. There had been little occasion in the New Year to don festive apparel as the cotillions and barbecues and picnics and fox hunts were washed away by the turbulent tides of war.

But tonight, Serena had wanted to look her most becoming. Even if she already knew that Brant wanted her, she had to be certain he understood that she also wanted him. It seemed to Serena that basic honesty was vital to sustaining the tenuous bond they had forged between them.

Aunt Kathleen was fussing with a lace-trimmed handkerchief. "Whatever will become of us if the slaves are freed?" she asked fretfully. "Will they run away or turn on us?"

"Most of ours won't do either," Uncle Luke asserted. "I can't speak for other plantations, but at Wexford, the people know they'll be cared for." He gazed for a brief moment at Serena. "They're grateful to the Farrars, though it's only their due as human beings."

"Colonel Suggs and Mrs. Murphy say they're not human," Nathan piped up in the uneven voice of adolescence. "At least not like us."

Uncle Luke gave his son a baleful look. "Old Suggs and Mrs. Murphy are nice souls, but they got their brains boiled by the sun a long time ago. You never learned those ideas in this house, young man." He turned to Aunt Kathleen. "Isn't it high time these boys were in bed?"

"My, yes," gasped Aunt Kathleen, noting the time on the tiny watch she wore on her Coburg lace-draped bosom. "Excuse yourselves and don't forget your prayers."

After the twins had gone upstairs, the talk turned to New Bern's vacant houses and commercial buildings, the farmland trampled under foot by soldiers of both armies, the runaway slaves and roving bandits who had become an ever-growing menace, the families who were on the verge of starvation as prices climbed and shortages grew commonplace.

"Preacher Roth has organized several of us ladies to provide food and clothing," Aunt Kathleen said in a sad voice. "But more are coming to the church every day."

"It's all so tragic," Kirk said, the angular features very solemn. "My wife writes that she may have to find new quarters for the widows and children in New Bedford. It breaks her heart to have to turn anyone away."

Serena heard a clock chime ten. Absently, she allowed Uncle Luke to refill her syllabub cup. While she admired the charity and generosity displayed by women such as Aunt Kathleen and Peggy Parnell, she was anxious for the evening to end and to feel the excitement of Brant's embrace. Sure enough, he winked at her while Aunt Kathleen explained in droning detail how a certain Pickens had disguised himself as a woman to beg food for a dozen children but had revealed his true identity by spitting tobacco as he was about to leave the church hall.

"So heartrending," murmured Cecelia in a tone which made Serena wonder if she'd been listening at all. "But it's late, I must be going home." Languorously, she allowed Brant to pull back her chair. Folding up her fan against her breast, she looked up at him from underneath her lashes. "I hate to trouble Leonard—could you walk me next door, Captain Parnell?"

It was an invitation Brant could hardly refuse. Serena clamped her lips tightly shut and told herself she'd concede Cecelia her small victory. As if reading her mind, Brant turned to his wife: "I'll be back in a few minutes. Excuse me, everyone."

When Uncle Luke and Aunt Kathleen returned from seeing their niece to the door, it was mutually decided that it was time for everyone to retire. Looking vaguely pinched and not a little peaked, Abigail agreed. Serena accompanied her cousin to the guest room, noting aloud that it was obvious Abigail was worn out—she'd been too quiet during the latter stages of the evening.

"True," Abigail said with a hint of her enigmatic smile. "But tell me one thing before I fall on my nose." She was leaning on the guest room door for support, her hand on the ornate brass knob. "How is Yancy?"

For once, it was Serena who didn't want to prolong the conversation. "Fine. He has some land near Drew's Creek. He's growing corn."

Abigail took in the information with studied composure. "That's very nice." She touched her lips with a finger as if to blow her cousin a kiss. "Good night, Rena." Abigail started to open the door, but glanced over her shoulder and the green eyes took on their familiar spark. "Happy night, Rena." The door clicked shut behind her.

Smiling to herself, Serena went to her own room and turned up the kerosene lamp. Her image in the mirror assured her that she had achieved her goal: The coils of smoky brown hair set off the contours of her face, the coffee-colored taffeta highlighted the slanting fox-like eyes, the crimson silk added color to her skin, the curve of her bosom rose fetchingly above the neckline of her gown.

There had been no opportunity for Brant to tell her how enchanting she looked before dinner, but Serena had seen the sea-blue eyes glint with approval when she came down the curving staircase. Recalling the delight she'd felt in his glance, Serena literally twirled across the room to the bed. The covers were turned down, the chintz hangings pulled back, the pillows plumped up. The window was open a few inches, a light breeze blowing away the unseasonably warm air.

The little clock which sat in an alcove said it was just after ten-thirty. Brant ought to be coming any minute. Serena wondered if she should send for champagne, but decided against it; she was already faintly light-headed, but whether that was from the syllabub or her anticipation of Brant's lovemaking, she couldn't be sure.

Perhaps she should undress. But, she had to admit, it would be more exciting to let Brant remove her gown with its frustrating hooks and eyes, to have him take down the carefully arranged coiffure, to watch his eyes as he slipped off her undergarments.

Serena frowned at herself in the mirror: Was she wanton? No, she told her image, she was only a woman who desires her husband. "A woman in love," she said aloud and her face lighted up with a smile. Now that Brant was here in New Bern, she could say the words, if only to herself. And hope that perhaps Brant loved her, too, at least a little. If she could prove to him that she cared, that he aroused her, that she truly wanted to be his wife, surely he would return her feelings in full measure.

Another fifteen minutes passed; Serena turned away from the dress-ing table, straining her ears for sounds in the hallway. Brant would arrive very soon. Of course there were nights when Leonard escorted Cecelia home and was gone for close to an hour. If Cecelia's servants were abed or only the women were up, she would ask Leonard to make certain the house was secure. That took some time with at least a half-dozen entrances and four times that many windows. With so many thieves and vagrants around, nobody could be too careful. The Union patrols did their best to enforce the curfew, but there was always a chance of someone slipping past them . . .

Serena picked up a book and sat down on the bed. It was Dickens's *A Tale of Two Cities*, which she'd read and enjoyed a couple of years earlier. Still, Dickens was always worth rereading. She flipped through the pages but realized the kerosene lamp did not cast sufficient light from the dressing table. She also realized she was growing anxious: It was after eleven o'clock.

Serena could not see the Moncrief house from her room. She wondered if Brant had returned but been waylaid by Uncle Luke for a chat over brandy and cigars. Kirk had left just before Serena and Abigail had gone upstairs. But Brant might have encountered Leonard. One of the twins could have sneaked downstairs to query Brant about his life as a sea captain. Any number of things might have delayed him. She tiptoed out into the hall and crept down the spiral staircase.

Only one lamp in the hallway remained lighted. The house was silent. She looked in each of the rooms but they were all dark and empty. Cautiously, she opened the front door which was not yet latched. Down the drive, she could barely make out two Union soldiers, going on their rounds. Through the trees now stripped of their leaves, she could see the outline of Cecelia's house but there were no lights showing behind the windows.

The eagerness which had given way to anxiety now succumbed to anger. Serena closed the door and turned to see Leonard standing in the hallway, a basin of water in his hands.

"I was about to retire, Mrs. Parnell," he said. "Shall I lock up?" As ever, his features were under complete control.

The innocuous question seemed to hang in the air like the ominous thunderclap of a gathering storm. "Yes," Serena replied at last. She gathered up her crimson skirts and forced herself to move toward the stairs. "Good night, Leonard. Thank you for everything this evening."

She did not hear his polite response. The staircase seemed to go on forever, the hallway appeared endless. When she got back inside her room, Serena began ripping off the elegant gown, not caring if she pulled out hooks and eyes, ripped silk and taffeta, or threw the pearl-edged combs onto the carpet. Hot tears streamed down her cheeks as she flung her undergarments into a heap, pulled on her faded cotton nightgown, and yanked back the bedding. Serena cried noiselessly for the better part of an hour, finally falling into an exhausted sleep in which she dreamed of a fox cub that had been abandoned in a swamp and was slowly but inexorably sinking in quicksand.

Chapter 15

"YOU'RE RIGHT about one thing," Serena said, her voice shaking with rage and humiliation, "there is nothing you could *ever* say to explain what happened last night."

"I'm beginning to see that," Brant replied, his anger almost matching Serena's. "But it's not really fair—I've told you before, I never lie."

"Unless you have to," she snapped, getting up from the bed and pulling her blue flannel robe more securely around her. It was shortly after seven, just a few minutes since he had tapped on Serena's door. When she realized it was Brant and not Abigail or one of the servants, she'd refused to open the door. But Brant had threatened to rouse anyone who wasn't yet awake, and as Serena knew that would probably include the exhausted Abigail, his request was finally granted.

"That's not what I mean," Brant asserted doggedly. "I've never lied to you. And I wouldn't. I haven't now." He saw the enraged, intransigent look on her face and threw up his hands. "I'll even be honest enough to admit I find your sister a ravishing piece of goods. But I keep telling you, we just talked. Or *she* talked. Forever. About Fitch. Her little boy. Your parents. War. Peace. Slavery. The woman never closed her mouth!"

"Ooooh!" Serena ran her hands in agitation through her uncombed hair. "You couldn't find any excuse to leave! You, so clever at government negotiations, so shrewd at the poker table! Even if I believed that Celia's mouth ran like a spring freshet, I couldn't accept the fact that you let her go on and on while I cooled my heels waiting for you!"

"For all of an hour." Brant glowered at Serena, the square jawline set like a cornerstone.

"An hour and a half! Leonard didn't lock up until eleven-thirty." She turned her back on him, feeling the tears once again well up in her eyes. "And you expect me to believe that when you couldn't get in this house, you slept in a spare room at Cecelia's?"

"I don't give a damn if you think I slept on the roof!" Brant's temper had finally snapped. He strode to the wardrobe to pick up the valise he'd had the servants bring up before dinner the previous evening.

193

Serena put her hands to her head, snatching in frustration at the thick strands of long, flowing hair. How could he shatter her dream like this, how could Cecelia conspire to ruin Serena's vision of marital bliss? Cecelia, with her imposing good looks and intuitive way with men; Cecelia, who had always come first; Cecelia, now without a man of her own, sufficiently brazen—and ruthless—to usurp Serena's husband. If Cecelia had been within reach, Serena was certain she'd gladly throttle her sister.

No man, including Brant, could resist her. Serena was absolutely certain of that. She'd watched Cecelia since they were children, observed how her older sister had always captured the attention of every male, no matter what his age or estate. Brant had admitted he found her attractive; he'd be less than human if he hadn't succumbed to her wiles.

But that didn't excuse him. Serena forced herself to stop pulling at her hair and act with as much dignity as she could muster. If she noticed that Brant was taking an unusually long time to get his valise out of the wardrobe, she didn't let on. Instead, she took a deep breath and spoke in cold, sharp tones learned at her mother's knee: "I don't care what you say about yourself, Brant Parnell. You're a cheat. A cheap, chiseling, underhanded cheat."

Brant dropped the valise and moved across the room with incredible swiftness for a man his size. Serena never saw the hand which crashed against her cheek. She stumbled backward, reeling against the bed, and her eyes were able to focus only after Brant had left the bedroom.

The balding man with the affable face and probing eyes was a few years older than Brant, but somewhat shorter and of a more wiry build. His Carolina accent was barely noticeable as he greeted Brant at Yancy Clarke's wooden gate. "Captain Parnell," said Sergeant Davis with a smart, if unnecessary, salute, "I see you're back down South again."

"For a very short time," Brant replied dryly. "I came out here to Drew's Creek to see Captain Clarke." He paused to squint into the noonday sun. "Is he home?"

Davis opened the gate which seemed in danger of falling off its rusty hinges. "Captain Clarke is in the barn," he said as Brant got down from his horse and tethered the reins to a hitching post. "We got a sick mule." Moving briskly, Davis led Brant around to the back of the small two-story house. A hound which had been dozing in the afternoon sun opened its eyes for just an instant. A few yards away, several geese pecked at insects in the winter cornfield. Just before

the two men reached the barn, Yancy emerged, looking mildly surprised at Brant's presence on his farm.

"I heard you were in town," Yancy said, putting out a huge hand
in welcome. "We got beer, you want to come inside?"

"Sounds good to me," said Brant. Yancy asked Sergeant Davis to
join them but the other man demurred, saying that he still had chores
to do.

"Conscientious fellow," Yancy said as they went through the back
door and into a kitchen which appeared to have suffered at the hands
of marauding vandals, but which Brant suspected was merely the
result of a womanless household. "Have a seat," Yancy said, picking
up a pair of old boots from a battered wicker chair. He went to the
ice chest to get the beer and poured it into two chipped, mismatched
glasses.

The two men talked for some time about the progress of the war,
Brant's voyage south, Yancy's efforts at farming, Sergeant Davis's
loyalty in refusing to leave his captain even after they had both been
paroled, and the prospects for the *Carolina Leader*.

"You married a spunky lady," Yancy said, wiping the foam from
his beard. "Your brother's got pluck, too."

"Oh, yes, those two are a real pair," Brant said, and the irony was
not lost on Yancy. "Oh, hell, I'm just a little put out today, Yancy.
Forget it." He let his host refill his glass before he spoke again.
"There's something I've been wanting to ask you for a long time. I
should have done it when I was here in March but somehow while I
was a prisoner, you and I never had much chance to talk alone."

"Then I was a prisoner." Yancy shook his head. "Nowadays life's
more mystifying than a two-headed heifer."

"It is at that." Brant rubbed at the cleft in his chin and looked
quizzical. "It's probably just as well we didn't talk then. I learned a
few things later." He paused, waiting for Yancy's comment, but there
was none. The Texan sat quietly, sipping his beer. "I have to conclude
you knew that Pembrose Stanhope and his equally detestable brother,
Giles, were involved in returning runaway slaves?"

"Yep." Yancy nodded once.

"I figured that. There couldn't be any other reason for a Texan to
track down a man in Boston. Oh, there *could* be, but it didn't make
sense otherwise and I'm a great one for wanting things to turn out
even."

The eyelids drooped slightly. Yancy removed one of his elbows
from the table and scratched his head. "That's fair enough."

"Look, Yancy, I don't have any hole cards because I'm not in the
game. But Pembrose's brother is pretty upset that nobody's ever found

a body, live or otherwise. If I were you, I wouldn't go back North after this damnable war is over."

"I didn't kill Pembrose Stanhope."

"I know that. But a lot of other people don't. Including Giles Stanhope." The wary blue eyes met the indolent gray stare. Neither turned away until Brant spoke again: "Maybe I'm overly cautious, but humor me. I'm going back to New England very soon and I wanted to make sure we had a chance to talk." Brant looked faintly rueful; as usual with Yancy, the talk was pretty one-sided. "As long as I'm here, I can tell you Miss Abigail came with me. She's at the Farrar townhouse."

Only the slight twitch of his mouth in the thick beard betrayed Yancy's surprise. His big hand was steady as he lifted the beer glass. "I'll be," he said, with the beginnings of a smile.

"And I'll be going," Brant responded, getting to his feet. "Thanks for the beer." He picked up his cap and started 'for the door. Out in the back yard, Sergeant Davis was feeding the chickens while the old hound scratched his fleas. Brant wondered how—and if—Abigail would fit into this unlikely setting.

Yancy had also stood up, his chair scraping on the floor. "Glad you dropped by." He paused as they shook hands. "I'm much obliged." The sleepy gaze was suddenly transformed, as if an intense fire had been ignited behind the gray eyes.

"Any time." Brant's casual irony failed him; the words sounded almost begrudging. What the hell, he thought to himself, Yancy and Abigail can stage an orgy out in the chicken coop when they have their passionate reunion. They'd been lucky and gotten dealt a better hand than he and Serena had. Or had they just played their cards smarter? Brant clapped Yancy on the shoulder and forced his broadest grin. "Abby's quite a gal—but she's no sailor."

Yancy's smile had finally succeeded in parting his beard. If he were surprised that Brant knew of his relationship with Abigail, he gave no sign. "That don't bother me. I'm a landlubber myself."

"Great. Good luck," Brant said, feeling dogged by the word. He touched his cap in salute to both Yancy and Sergeant Davis. But it was the old hound which had the final say, erupting into a mournful howl as Brant strode around the edge of the farmhouse to where his horse waited patiently by the hitching post.

Only the Advent season and Uncle Luke's inherent goodness could have persuaded Serena to accompany her sister and Major Graham on a tour of the Union fortifications. In the week that followed the bitter quarrel with Brant and his abrupt departure from New Bern, Serena forced herself to stay away from Cecelia. As the days dragged by, Serena's anger shifted. Though she had been furious with Brant, she'd originally blamed Cecelia. But now that Brant was gone, Serena found herself more inclined to believe that the burden of guilt lay with her husband, not her sister. It had been absurd of Serena to think Brant might love her, and if he didn't, then it was even more ridiculous to believe he would remain faithful. Disillusioned by her brief, tragic attempt at love, Serena reproached herself for being such a brainless ninny in the first place, and vowed to forget about the indifferent, dishonorable man she had been coerced into marrying.

It was impossible, however. Only in her preparations for getting out the first edition of the *Leader* could she at least shove him out of her mind's eye for a time, and even then, there was always Kirk, whose very presence served as a reminder of his brother.

She did not confide in Kirk. Somehow, it would not have seemed right. She wanted to pour out her heart to Abigail but her cousin had been reunited with Yancy Clarke, and while their meetings were secret from the rest of the family, Serena knew and was loath to spoil their long-awaited happiness. Uncle Luke would have listened to Serena's tale of woe with great sympathy, but she couldn't tell him the whole story without besmirching Cecelia's reputation.

It was, in fact, Cecelia's reputation which had motivated Uncle Luke to ask that Serena join her sister and Major Graham on their outing to Fort Totten and the ordnance yard on Craven Street.

"It's probably harmless, just two young people taking the Sunday air," Uncle Luke said, pausing to admire his handiwork with the pine boughs he'd wound over a frame to make an Advent wreath. "Still, it'd look better if you went along."

"If you think so." Serena sighed, wishing she hadn't sounded so ungracious. "I've seen the ordnance yard a million times, but I haven't been to Fort Totten."

"There's my girl," Uncle Luke said with a fond smile. "Now—which is it, three pink candles and one purple or the other way round?"

"No, it's three purple and a pink. You light the first two purple, then the pink for hope, and the third purple one the Sunday before Christmas."

Uncle Luke nodded. "I remember now. That's the day we put up the nativity set. You saw it last year, such beautiful figures from Italy. Your Grandpa Matthew brought it over when I was just a little nipper."

Serena vaguely recalled the set and felt a sudden sense of unease. She was looking puzzled as she went to fetch her merino shawl.

No, not *that* nativity set—another creche, not from Italy, but Mexico. Sent to Kirk and Peggy Parnell's children by Pembrose Stanhope while he was south of the border on government business. Serena shook her head with repugnance. How could the man who bought a nativity set for his distant relations also be such a sordid, violent maniac? Yet it fit Pembrose—that benign exterior which had masked an evil soul.

Major Graham wore another sort of mask as he came up the walk with Cecelia on his arm. The raffish charm concealed a far less appealing aspect of his nature, Serena thought as she gave him and her sister a weak smile of greeting. Resolutely, she marched to the carriage he had waiting in the street.

The late autumn weather was still quite mild. At Fort Totten, the earthworks built the previous August by the 3rd New York Artillery were sufficiently impressive, but after twenty minutes of wandering about the fortifications, Serena was bored to the point of irritability.

"You can't ever stop thinking about a counteroffensive," Major Graham intoned, snapping a smart salute at two privates who guarded a hulking Parrott rifle. "The Seven Days' campaign on the Peninsula showed the stuff Lee and his men are made of."

"I keep wondering if our brother, Matt, fought there," Serena said, looking longingly at the empty carriage and wishing her feet didn't hurt.

To Serena's relief, Graham was indicating that they should head back. "I don't like praising the enemy," the major said, taking Cecelia's gloved hand to help her over a piece of mortar, "but you have to give men like Lee and Stonewall Jackson their due."

"I hear Jackson is terribly prudish," Cecelia commented, gazing at Graham from under the brim of her huge beribboned hat. "And so pious! A regular hymn-hooter, I'm told."

Graham laughed in unbridled appreciation. Serena was glad they were a few steps ahead of her so that she could made a face at their backs.

"Naturally," Cecelia went on, "you'd expect him to look all sour and puckery, sucking on lemons all the time. I hope our generals don't do anything so odd."

"The oddest thing they could do about now is win," Serena declared, treading gingerly through a gravel bed.

"Now, now," Major Graham chuckled, solicitously helping Cecelia into the carriage, "let's not talk treason. McClellan is being given a second chance."

"The man's so slow he hasn't finished up his first one," Serena snapped. "Oh, he may have military and leadership abilities but," she added, ignoring Graham's proffered hand and hauling herself into the carriage while gesturing at the Parrott rifle, "you'd have to set one of those off under his rear end to get him moving."

"Serena!" Cecelia appeared shocked.

"Speaking of rear ends, move over, you're crowding me," Serena hissed. She had put up with enough from Cecelia and Major Graham for one day, and fervently wished they could head straight home instead of going on to the ordnance yard.

But no such alteration of plans was in store. As Major Graham flicked the whip at his two mares, he changed the subject to the flourishing black market in New Bern. Serena let her mind wander from the conversation, saying nothing at all until they reached the ordnance yard.

On Sunday afternoons, only a few soldiers drifted about, some of them draped against the split rail fence which enclosed the low-lying buildings and military supplies. Serena trudged along behind Cecelia and Major Graham while he droned on in dreary detail. Cecelia, who had a manner of looking as if she were giving her listener the most rapt attention, but actually wasn't hearing a word, bestowed frequent beguiling smiles on the fulsome Union major.

"Utterly fascinating," she declared as Graham excused himself to speak with a tow-headed corporal requesting advice about a recent delivery of materiel.

Cecelia untangled the mass of slim silver chains she wore draped over her jutting bosom. "Such a charming man," she sighed, glancing at Graham and the corporal across the yard. "A pity he's poor."

"What difference does it make?" Serena demanded, her temper still simmering. "You already have a husband. I shouldn't think," she said pointedly, "you'd look for another."

"I?" Cecelia's dark eyes were round with innocence. "Oh, what an idea!" The throaty laugh rippled on the balmy December air. "I was thinking of poor Abigail, with no man to call her own. How bored she'll be here in New Bern. I wonder why she came?" The lack of reply from Serena only goaded Cecelia into continuing: "But there, that was mean-minded of me, particularly since you are in reality, if not in truth, alone here, too. Except," she added quietly, "for Kirk, of course."

Serena was in no mood for a war of wits. "You *are* mean-minded. Kirk is not only the most noble man I've ever met, he's also my brother-in-law. And unlike some, I don't hold with making a play for my in-laws!"

The dark eyes grew even more round. "'Sakes alive, what do you mean?"

Serena took a step closer and spoke in low, angry tones. "You know what I mean, Cecelia Farrar Moncrief. You're just as 'alone' as Abigail and I are, but you've got half the bucks in the county running after you, including Major Aren't-I-the-Most-Dashing-Thing Graham. Not that you're satisfied with those minor conquests, you have to throw your skirts over your head and seduce my husband!"

Cecelia appeared genuinely flabbergasted. But her talent for play-acting had always been first-rate. "What a shocking thing to say!" Cecelia waved a gloved fist at Serena. "Listen here, you envious little snip, I've never tried to seduce a man in my whole life!" She squared her wide shoulders, the huge feathered hat swaying precariously. "Nor would I have to. They always prefer trying to seduce me first." Haughtily, she turned her back on Serena, facing the split rail fence with the long sash of her azure blue dress blowing in the breeze like a battle pennant.

Graham rejoined them just seconds later. By the time they were back in the carriage, Cecelia had resumed her flirtatious chatter and Graham was paying appropriate homage. Serena, however, sat glumly beside her sister. Had Cecelia denied intimacy with Brant? Upon reflection, Serena realized she had not—Cecelia had merely refuted Serena's charge of seducing Brant. There was no comfort for Serena in her sister's words; indeed, Serena wondered if there were any comfort for her anywhere.

"War is the last resort of civilized man. Only after every other avenue of rapprochement has been exhausted, is there justification for one people to take up arms against another. Even then, war must be waged with the goal of peace, not just victory, kept firmly in mind."

Serena nodded in approval at how the words looked on the printed page. Even as she handed the proof sheet, still sticky with printer's ink, over to Kirk, she could not suppress a smile of excitement. "It goes on for twenty column inches and I'm not sure it says much, but you have to admit it looks well."

Kirk scanned the page proof. He had already read it several times in draft form, making only a few minor changes and suggestions. "It's not so much pro-Union as pro-United States, which is what we intended. With so many Yankee families moving in, it's imperative that we do what we can to promote a peaceful occupation."

Their first edition, dated January 1, 1863, contained a recapitulation of war news during the previous six weeks. While only occasional sniper fire had disturbed the New Bern area, battles raged elsewhere, with the Federal forces mounting an offensive from the town in mid-December to raid Kingston and Goldsboro. But the fiercest fighting had taken place on the Peninsula, in northern Virginia. "Fredericksburg was a ghastly tragedy," Serena said, skimming through Kirk's account. "Over two thousand men killed from both sides! I hope Matt's all right—he must have been there."

"If anything terrible had happened, someone would have gotten word to you and your sister," Kirk said in reassurance as he put the proof down and took the inside pages from Herman, who had just emerged from the backshop.

Serena's eyes were still on the Fredericksburg story. Good-natured, fun-loving Matt, joined by so many other young men just like him— Serena could not imagine how war would temper his spirit, how changed she would find him when the battles were done. If, pray God, he lived through them. She had worried about him throughout the dismal Christmas season. Being on bad terms with Cecelia was difficult; Aunt Kathleen could speak of nothing else but her fears that the twins would sign up; even Uncle Luke appeared distracted and withdrawn. And Brant's image never let Serena rest for long. She was beginning to feel haunted by the man.

Tearing herself from such distressing thoughts, she looked up as Emaline Pigott came into the office, her bonnet askew and her three-quarter length coat missing a button. "Oh, my, are we going to have a newspaper today?"

"Here, Emaline, take a look," Kirk said with a broad smile, "we're about to go to press."

Hurriedly, Emaline pulled off her bonnet and removed her coat, then sat down to study the page proofs. Her taffy-colored curls bobbed up and down as she raced through the columns. Emaline was in her midtwenties, neither tall nor short, but with the same rangy body as her brother. Still, Serena thought, Emaline could have been pretty if she'd taken the time and trouble.

Emaline's cornflower-blue eyes were fixed on Kirk. "I think it's ever so fine! You've been very fair—there's nothing in here to rile me up. So far. Speaking of news, wouldn't it be helpful to have that— what is it called?—the telegraph lines that send news?"

"The wire service?" Kirk saw Emaline's curls bob. "Yes, but I think we'd have trouble getting it here since it comes out of Washington and New York."

"It sounds most magical," Emaline asserted, getting up and inspecting a small grease spot on her bodice. "Imagine, being able to know what's happening everywhere right away." She smiled brightly at both Serena and Kirk before hurrying to Herman in the backshop just as Caldwell Smith came in the front door with two young boys at his side.

"Here they are," he announced, giving each youngster a slight shove in Kirk's direction. "You got your newsboys, Major. The older one is Bill and the younger one is Phil. They've been living under a bridge on James Creek for the last six months."

Bill was no more than ten, his brother, Phil, a year or two younger. The boys were dirty, thin, and already too hardened by the vagaries of war to be frightened. "What happened to your parents?" Kirk asked in a kindly voice.

Bill tugged at one ear while Phil scratched himself with an almost frenzied motion. "They all run off," Bill said at last.

"All?" echoed Serena, though it was not the first time she'd heard of children—white and black—being abandoned since the war had started. She and Kirk thanked Caldwell before Emaline was summoned to take over the two young boys. Kirk handed his corrections to Caldwell and within a quarter of an hour, the *Carolina Leader*'s press was finally rolling.

It was midnight before Serena and Kirk left the newspaper office. One thousand copies of the *Leader* had been printed; fewer than five hundred had been sold. Serena was disappointed, but Kirk was not. "We're lucky we got that many the first time," he insisted as they walked down Craven Street, which was deserted except for the Union sentries posted on each block. "Since we're a weekly, we can still sell more before the next edition comes out. Caldwell can take them to the Union soldiers. They'll want to read something that isn't pro-Southern."

"So will their families," Serena said. "As more Northerners settle here, maybe we could expand on news of the home front. Actually, Emaline had a good idea about the wire service but the problems getting it here seem insurmountable."

"I'm afraid so," Kirk allowed, stifling a yawn. "I wonder if they've put it in at the *Mercury* yet."

Serena could not pass up this opportunity to ask Kirk a question which had nagged at her for some time. "Why did you leave the paper to join the army, Kirk?"

He didn't reply immediately and his step seemed suddenly to grow more brisk. "Oh—duty, I suppose. I saw all those boys signing up and decided they needed some men to lead them. Maybe I felt guilty, too."

"It must put Peggy at ease that you're not actually involved in the fighting these days," Serena remarked as they passed the Williams-Drew house and the carriage shop.

"She's pleased, yes." The answer seemed terse and ill-humored. Perhaps Kirk felt he was somehow shirking the duty he revered so much. Certainly his living arrangements were comfortable: At the end of November, he had received permission to move into the Union staff headquarters in the old Slover-Guion house on Johnson and East Front Streets. Kirk, however, was only one of many soldiers quartered in New Bern's finer homes, many now deserted by their owners.

Several of the houses they were passing seemed deserted as well. Serena shook her head sadly. "What a different sort of holiday this has been! Last year there were carolers out every night, bonfires in the town, garlands strung all over. You could see candles burning on the Christmas trees until Twelfth Night."

"People don't feel very festive these days," Kirk remarked as he paused in midstep, frowning at the empty street ahead of them. "That's strange, there's no sentry in sight. Where did we see the last one?"

Serena pulled her scarf more tightly around her head; the weather had turned much colder before Christmas. She glanced around, taking in the shuttered houses, the faint rustling sound of the wind in the elm trees, the chill of the night air, and the dim outline of the crescent moon which rode high in the winter sky. "Not that far," she said, wishing she'd brought her gloves. "He saluted you, I remember that."

"I remember it, too," Kirk said, but his frown grew deeper. "That was at least two blocks back, by the old palace." He turned, looking in every direction. "Well," he sighed, putting a hand on Serena's elbow and resuming their walk, "I suppose I'd better report the absent sentries to their company. It may be the night after New Year's Eve, but that's no excuse . . ."

The shot that rang out ripped through the night and sent Serena sprawling to the ground under Kirk's arm. "Don't move!" he barked as a second bullet exploded close by.

Serena lay pinioned on her stomach, her cheek resting on a patch of damp grass. She could have sworn she actually felt the third shot rending the very air they breathed. Then there were voices shouting and the sound of booted feet in the distance.

"Stay still," Kirk urged, removing his arm so that he could shift his body just enough to reach his pistol. Even in the faint moonlight, Serena could see the glint of steel out of the corner of her eye. Her heart was pounding heavily in her breast as she heard the footsteps come closer while Kirk cocked his gun. "It's all right," he breathed and lowered the weapon. "You!" he called to the sentry who slowed down just a few feet away from them. "Where were you?"

The Union sentry was no more than eighteen and looked almost as frightened as Serena felt. Kirk had gotten cautiously to his feet but motioned for Serena to stay where she was.

"I was just up by the Hutton house, Major," the young man replied with a gulp. "That's where I'm supposed to be."

"Then who's supposed to be here?" Kirk demanded, jabbing a long finger in the general vicinity of the empty street.

"Uhhh . . ." The sentry took off his cap and ran a hand through his unruly hair. "Brisker. He was here about ten minutes ago. I whistled to him. It's a sort of signal we got."

Kirk took another look in every direction before bending down to give Serena his hand and pull her up beside him. Two other sentries had appeared, both with rifles at the ready. Neither of them had seen Brisker—or the person who had fired at Serena and Kirk.

"Search the houses, especially the empty ones," Kirk ordered. "The gardens, too—and look for Brisker. He may have been attacked. If you find anybody suspicious, I want them held until I get back." He snapped a salute at the three men and grasped Serena firmly by the arm. "You don't have to run the rest of the way, but I don't think dawdling is a good idea."

"I don't intend to dawdle," Serena gasped, trying to keep up with Kirk's rapid strides. "Was somebody trying to kill us?"

"Probably." Kirk's angular features had turned grim. "Save your breath until we get to Uncle Luke's. And if anybody is still awake there, don't mention this tonight."

But only Leonard was up to greet them. The previous night, on New Year's Eve, Uncle Luke had become, as he quaintly put it, "pixilated." He had retired early, as had Aunt Kathleen. If Leonard perceived that Serena and Kirk were disturbed as well as rumpled, he gave no sign. Candle in hand, Leonard announced that if Major Parnell would lock up after leaving the house, he would bid them both good-night.

After Leonard was gone, Kirk followed Serena into the retiring room where he rummaged through Uncle Luke's liquor cabinet. "I don't think your uncle would begrudge me a dram or two," Kirk said, forcing his voice to sound light. "Or you either, Serena." He hoisted two glasses questioningly at her.

"Your brother taught me to drink brandy so you might as well do the honors with whiskey," Serena said, all but collapsing onto the settee. "Actually, I have drunk it before. I just don't much like it."

Kirk was smiling, his expression now genuine. "It's an acquired taste, I'm told. It didn't take me—or Brant—long to acquire it." He poured each tumbler half-full and handed Serena's to her before sitting down on the settee. After taking a big swallow, he turned to face her, his features now grave. "Do you know what that was all about just now?"

Serena was equally somber. "I can guess." She put the glass to her lips but didn't drink. "Someone doesn't approve of us publishing a newspaper."

"That's what I figure." Kirk leaned closer, resting his free hand on his knee. "I was afraid of that, but then we never expected to be popular. What really concerns me is that whoever that was tonight is only one person. You have to consider, Serena, there may be more. A lot more."

Serena finally sipped at her whiskey; it didn't taste any better than she remembered but it offered a comforting sense of warmth. "I know." She met Kirk's gaze head-on and forced a brave smile. "We can't give in. Once people get used to the idea, maybe they'll accept us. But Lord knows I don't want us—or anybody working for the *Leader*—to get killed."

Kirk took another pull on his drink before setting the tumbler on the carpet. Putting both hands on Serena's shoulders, he forced her to lean so close to him that their foreheads almost touched. "We're in this mess together, Serena. If I have to put an armed guard around you twenty-four hours a day, I'll do it to ensure your safety."

"Good heavens, I don't need an armed guard!" Serena spoke more adamantly than she'd meant to, but Kirk's nearness seemed to disconcert her almost as much as the rifle shots. She could sense his virility as if it were a tangible characteristic, like the warm brown eyes or the wavy dark hair. The Parnell men, Serena thought ruefully, seemed to exude the aura of the male animal. "Kirk, I'm very tired. I think I'd better go to bed while I can still get up the stairs."

Kirk took his hands from her shoulders, sat up straight, and cleared his throat. "I should get back to those sentries," he said, sounding quite stern. Taking a last drink from his glass, he rose, one hand at the pistol on his hip. "I'll come by tomorrow around nine to fetch you."

"Fine," said Serena, trying to smile in a natural manner. She started to lift the tumbler to her lips but discovered her hand was trembling and set the glass down on her lap.

"I'll see myself out," Kirk said quickly, and was gone before Serena could reply.

Private Brisker had been found under a hedge only a few yards from his sentry. He had a large bump on his skull and could recall nothing of what had happened until the other sentries discovered him just five minutes after Serena and Brant had hurried away. But a search of the neighborhood had uncovered no sign of a would-be assailant.

"Do you know any of those people who live there?" Abigail asked the next evening as she and Serena sat in the retiring room after Aunt Kathleen had gone up for the night and Uncle Luke visited in the gaming parlor with two of his cronies who had dropped by to lament the sad state of their plantations.

"Not really," Serena answered, sipping at a cup of hot chocolate. "They're just . . . people." She sighed and shook her head. "I didn't want to mention it to Uncle Luke or Aunt Kathleen."

"Of course not." Abigail scrutinized the row of needlework she'd just completed on a pianoforte stool cover Serena had abandoned. "Is Cecelia ready to move yet?"

"Almost." Serena knew Abigail was anxious for Cecelia to vacate the Moncrief house so that it could be used as a hospital. Abigail's plan had come as a surprise to Serena, but Cecelia's compliance had been even more astonishing. Somehow, Serena had expected her sister to balk at moving in with Uncle Luke and Aunt Kathleen. Cecelia, however, had accepted the plan readily enough, saying that she had grown tired of trying to supervise lazy, incompetent Negroes who had no respect for a Yankee mistress. As the family funds tightened, it was also impractical for Cecelia to maintain a separate establishment in Fitch's absence.

"Yancy is going to help with the project," Abigail said, holding up two skeins of silk thread to see if the dye lots matched. "He and Sergeant Davis are getting lumber to make the beds."

Curious as to Abigail and Yancy's future plans as husband and wife, Serena tried to phrase her question as delicately as possible: "Will he and Sergeant Davis move into town?"

Abigail put down the thread and frowned at her fingers. The one lingering childish habit she possessed was a penchant for biting her nails. "I don't know. Drew's Creek is close in."

Serena looked away, trying to conceal her impatience with Abigail's closely guarded private life. Not only was Serena naturally inquisitive, but she also felt reluctant to unburden herself to Abigail unless the confidences were mutual. Serena refused to regress to their former relationship, with Abigail being the dominant, omniscient personality. It seemed to Serena that if discretion wouldn't serve, shock tactics might.

"I assume Brant told you how Pembrose Stanhope died." Serena attempted to look every bit as composed as Abigail, but marred the portrait by banging her elbow on the corner of the side table.

"No." Abigail peered at the eye of her needle, then expertly slipped the thread through it. "Giles Stanhope told me."

"Giles! Damn all, Abby, when did you ever see Giles Stanhope?"

"Rena, dear, watch your language." Abigail managed to look amused and disapproving at the same time. "Let me think—it must have been just before Christmas a year ago. I know it was snowing because Giles had on the most hideous muffler and all I could see were his bulging little eyes. I would never have consented to see him at all, but the judge was visiting your father and I didn't want to cause a fuss by refusing. Giles said he'd been making inquiries about his wretched brother being missing in the New Bedford area and had come to the conclusion that he'd gone to see Brant." If Abigail noticed how Serena's mouth tightened at her husband's name, she gave no sign. "But Brant had left town so Giles surmised that perhaps Pembrose had paid you a call instead. Naturally, I knew nothing about it—only your very puzzling letter about abruptly departing for North Carolina. It occurred to me that Pembrose's disappearance and your leave-taking just might be connected. Of course I never said a word to Giles—or your parents."

Abigail was taking even, measured stitches, seemingly as calm as ever. "You're right," Serena said with a trace of defiance. "Pembrose attacked me. There was an accident and he died."

"Good." Abigail's needle took a sudden sharp plunge into the canvas. "It would be pointless—and hypocritical—for me to pretend I'm sorry."

They sat in silence for several minutes, Abigail coolly stitching, Serena forcing herself to keep still and staring down at the Persian carpet's perfect symmetry. But both young women started when Liberty banged open the door to hurtle into the room.

"Young Calvin gonna get me!" he howled, throwing himself against Serena's knees. "He say he gonna tar and feather me! Help!"

Serena patted the child's dark curls. "What did you do, Liberty?"

Slowly turning to make sure his persecutor hadn't followed him into the room, Liberty looked back up at Serena with round, innocent eyes. "Nothin', I just play with Young Calvin's cat."

Serena and Abigail exchanged glances. "Oh?" said Serena benignly. "What did you play?"

The innocence faded as Liberty's eyelids drooped. "Played cook. I put cat in a chamber pot."

Abigail's hand flew to her mouth as the slim shoulders shook with mirth. Serena started to laugh outright, but suddenly stopped. Liberty was still standing next to her, his eyes half-closed, his expression laconic. Abigail finally noticed Serena's frozen gaze and regained control. "What is it, Rena?"

Serena shook herself. "Nothing. I was just thinking about the poor cat. Is he all right?"

"He wet." Liberty opened his eyes wide once more and gave Serena an enchanting smile. "He fat, too, like Young Calvin."

"Never mind that," said Serena, tapping Liberty's nose with her finger. "You go back to Young Calvin and say you're sorry. And *be* sorry—you've been quite naughty."

It took a considerable amount of arguing until Liberty reluctantly scooted out of the room. Before Abigail could ask any untimely questions, Serena excused herself and went off to find Uncle Luke. The flash of intuition which had just struck Serena didn't seem quite so amazing as she made her way to the shed. Indeed, it had been strange that she hadn't realized the truth before. But Liberty's drooping

lids and laconic expression seemed almost positive proof that his father
was Yancy Clarke.

Serena never quite understood what Uncle Luke's latest invention
was but it had something to do with dispersing a poisonous substance
to kill the insects which plagued tobacco plants just before they reached
maturity. Judging from the scowl on Uncle Luke's face when Serena
entered the shed, the invention was not yet successful.

Still, he managed a smile when he saw Serena come to sit next
to him. "You look purposeful, Rena. A fox stalking its prey." He had
a peculiar-looking tool in one hand as he gazed inquiringly at his
niece. "Well?"

"As ever, you're observant," Serena said with an answering smile.
"Uncle Luke, I must know Liberty's origins. In fact, I think I do
know. It's time to tell me if I'm right."

Uncle Luke stopped fiddling with a valve and set it down on his
workbench. "I see." He rubbed at his temples and stared into space.
"If you think so. He came to us from old friends in New Orleans.
The Belvoirs, whose daughter, Marie-Diane, went to school in New
Bern with your Aunt Kathleen—we had one of the earliest schools
for young ladies at the time in the South. They became fast friends
and kept in touch over the years." Uncle Luke paused to take out a
cigarette, only to find his pocket empty. "Fine note, I own a tobacco
plantation and I've lost my cigarettes. Oh, well." He shook his head
at his own folly.

"About two years ago, we heard from Madame Belvoir who sadly
informed us that Marie-Diane had died of consumption, leaving a
husband and three grown children. There was also a mulatto baby
who had been sent to her by close friends named Beaulieu. Marie-
Diane had understood that the child would someday be claimed by
his parents, but Madame Belvoir said the facts of the matter were
very confusing and since she herself was in failing health and war
seemed imminent and the whole world was going to hell in a handcart—
or words to that effect—she thought it best to send the child to Marie-
Diane's old friend, Kathleen."

Uncle Luke again stopped, this time to reach down with a dipper
and scoop water from a metal bucket. He gestured to Serena with the
dipper but she shook her head.

"Well. What could we do? One more youngster around here wasn't
going to make much difference. Your aunt and I had been thinking
about a trip to New Orleans for some time and decided we'd better
not put it off because if we had a war, there was no telling how long
we might be marooned here." He smiled sympathetically at Serena.
"I'm quite the prophet, aren't I? So off we went and brought Liberty

home with us. He was very quiet and skittish for a long time. I think
Marie-Diane's family had been strict with him, or else he'd been ill-
treated previously. I suppose you're going to tell me those Beaulieus
are related to Abigail."

Serena twisted at the mother-of-pearl buttons on her dress. "Possibly. I wonder why Mrs. Belvoir didn't send the child back to them?"

"I don't know." Uncle Luke leaned forward on his stool. "He's
thrived here, with Leonard's guidance. Now tell me, Rena, why do
you ask?"

There was a point when secrecy no longer served a purpose. Serena
felt they had reached that moment in time. Slowly, she pieced together
the story as Uncle Luke listened in silent, rapt attention. Yancy's
marriage to a slave and the birth of their child, the probable encounter
in Mexico with Pembrose Stanhope, the death of Yancy's wife, the
marriage between Yancy and Abigail. Serena did not tell Uncle Luke
why Abigail had gone to New Orleans; as it turned out, she didn't
have to. Abigail was standing in the doorway of the shed, motionless
and intent.

"I don't mind letting Uncle Luke know what happened," she declared as they both turned to stare. "It's more important for Yancy to
find little Sam than for me to guard my past."

Abigail moved with quiet dignity to the workbench. Briskly and
virtually devoid of emotion, she recounted the assault by Pembrose
Stanhope and her subsequent flight to New Orleans. She had met
Yancy shortly after her arrival when a thief tried to take her purse
just off Bourbon Street.

"We fell in love, right there," Abigail said softly. "He asked to
call on me and I knew I should refuse. But I couldn't." She turned
away for just a moment, the green eyes bright. "I took my whole life
in my hands and told him the truth, that I was going to have a baby.
But I had no husband. He just . . . chuckled. And said he already had
a baby but no wife."

Abigail leaned toward Uncle Luke, her fingertips touching each
other under her chin. "It wasn't merely a case of Pembrose returning
Angelique to her owners. He had lusted after her when he saw her
with Yancy in Matamoros. That's where they were married, you see,
in Mexico. Pembrose followed them to New Orleans where he kid-
napped Angelique. She tried to escape and Pembrose killed her. When
Yancy learned she'd been murdered, he vowed to avenge himself on
Pembrose. But the horrible man had gone back North. It took Yancy
some time to find out where and it was an incredible coincidence that
I had been . . . victimized by Pembrose as well."

Uncle Luke looked thoughtful. "No, not really. I suspect you two
reticent souls turned loquacious with each other early on. It formed

a bond between you which grew into love. Oh, that 'first sight' business is well and good, did it myself, or thought I did, but it wasn't love. Not real love, at any rate, since that takes time."

Abigail reflected briefly on Uncle Luke's words. "I never thought of it quite that way. But you're right," she said with a sparkle in her eyes, "we did become candid very quickly. It was almost as if we knew each other's life history before we spoke."

"Soul mates," said Uncle Luke with a nod of approval. "I like that. Go on, my dear, it's quite a story."

"There isn't much more. My baby was born dead." Abigail squared her shoulders and determinedly plunged ahead. "Yancy and I were married just two weeks later but we agreed it was impossible for him to return to Brunswick with me. I'd have to go home and play out the farce Uncle Marcus had concocted to prevent a scandal. When enough time had passed—and Yancy had dealt with Pembrose—he could come to Brunswick, court me, and we'd go through another wedding ceremony to please the family. I'd planned on taking Liberty with me, though I hadn't figured out what I'd tell people. But I couldn't—it was too soon after losing my own child. Never mind that Pembrose was his father, the baby was still mine. And Liberty's presence was too sharp a reminder." For once, Abigail's composure broke. She bowed her head and wordlessly took Uncle Luke's proffered handkerchief.

"That was a mistake," she said, sniffing once and lifting her chin. "My Beaulieu relations were good people in their way, but very harsh with Negroes, even children. They were not well-off, having suffered serious losses in the sugar cane business. Yancy learned that they'd sent Sam—Liberty—to New Bern, to relatives of mine. As strange as it may seem, they didn't know your name. Mrs. Belvoir did, naturally, but she was dead by then. Yancy only figured it out when Serena showed up. But he still didn't know if Liberty were actually with the family."

Serena had grown stiff sitting so long. She stood up to stretch her legs. "I marvel that Yancy didn't start inquiring sooner. Goodness, I've been here over a year!"

"But he hasn't," Abigail replied, giving back Uncle Luke's handkerchief with a quiet thank-you. "He arrived after you did and then he was captured and there was so much turmoil. Besides," she added with a touch of defensiveness, "Yancy takes his time. Until very recently, the situation was too uncertain for him to accept responsibility for raising his son." Abigail stood up, too, and Uncle Luke was quick to join her.

"You're a gallant little lady," Uncle Luke asserted, putting a hand on Abigail's shoulder. "Bearing sorrows bravely is one thing. Bearing them in silence is quite another." He gave Abigail a warm, gentle smile. "Seems I ought to get to know Yancy better. It's a good thing Liberty's had me around—between Leonard and Yancy, he might get the idea men don't talk."

It was the perfect note on which to conclude the difficult conversation. In a rare impulsive gesture, Abigail threw her arms around Uncle Luke and hugged him tight. Serena smiled thoughtfully, aware that she remained in awe of Abigail but wise enough now to know why.

Chapter 16

THE FIRST WEEK of February, Kirk passed word along to Serena that Matt had apparently survived the Fredericksburg campaign. "His name wasn't on the list of casualties."

Serena was vastly relieved. The winter's fighting had been sporadic and inconclusive. Most of the war reports in the *Leader*'s January issues focused on the cavalry raids led by the devil-may-care Virginian, Jeb Stuart. Though Serena could not publicly praise the Confederate cavalry commander, she had great private admiration for his daring and flair.

Indeed, Serena and Kirk's lack of critical commentary in reporting the factual events of the war had helped increase their readership. The most recent issue of the paper, containing Leonard's lengthy article on emancipation, had actually sold out. It had been a timely story, since Lincoln had freed the slaves at the beginning of the year.

Leonard's views had thus far been reinforced by actual events: Many slaves had run off, some to join the Union army. Others stayed with their former masters out of timidity, fear, or, in Uncle Luke's case, genuine loyalty. Some, however, pillaged and harassed their former owners and their white neighbors. And then there were those who merely wandered off, to an unknown fate. The diverse reactions backed up Leonard's main point, however—that a race born into bondage could not easily embrace freedom.

"No human being," wrote Leonard, "regardless of color, can achieve this transition without a sense of dread. Despite whatever horrors lie in the past, what has gone before is always preferable because it is a known quantity. The future, no matter what its glorious promise, must always hold great terrors, because it is unknown."

"Did you ever ask Leonard how he learned to write so well?" Kirk inquired as they sifted through story ideas for their next edition.

"Uncle Luke told me Leonard studied in England for a time." Serena checked off a story idea Kirk had finished on the new Union commander, "Fighting" Joe Hooker. "But my uncle is very vague about Leonard's background. Even more vague than he usually is."

"I think your uncle is sweet," Emaline asserted, bringing them each a cup of hot coffee. "It's very courageous of him to stop by at least once a week to show everyone he's not afraid to be seen in the newspaper office."

"Neither are you," Kirk commented and winked at Emaline, who giggled with pleasure.

"Well now, that's so," Emaline said, placing the tips of her fingers together over her flat bosom. "But then I always did have a mind of my own. Isn't that the truth, Herman?"

Herman looked up from the bowl of soup he'd been eating for his noon meal. "That's right, Emaline, we always did say you had a mind of your own. And I didn't have none at all."

"Oh, Herman!" Emaline laughed and ruffled her brother's blond hair. "Now you finish your soup and work hard and I'll see you tonight. I must be off on my rounds." Emaline went to the tiny closet to get her tweed coat and the brown bonnet with its faded pink lilies. "I'll see you all later, you hear?"

Herman finished his soup on an effluent note and headed toward the backshop. Kirk turned to Serena: "I wonder where Emaline goes on her rounds."

Serena sampled her coffee before she responded: "She looks in on some of the families in the Rattle Hill area who've had hard times since the war started. I think Emaline is an angel of mercy for the local folk."

"She's very kind and such a hard worker," Kirk remarked, getting out half a dozen fresh sheets of foolscap. Outside, the February sun seemed wan and a cool breeze made spring seem far off, especially for the Carolinas. Serena frowned as she saw the four soldiers posted outside the office march past the window. She wished there was no need for their protection.

But then another uniformed man and a woman in red-and-white striped tafetta caught Serena's eye. "Kirk!" Serena called. "Look, it's Cecelia, with Major Graham fawning all over her!"

Kirk joined her at the window. "Unctuous devil," he remarked. "I don't much like him. I was always sorry I sent him in my place that time." He pulled a face at Serena. "What are they doing together?"

"Outraging half of New Bern." Serena peered at Cecelia and Graham, who disappeared into a haberdashery which received mysterious supplies of new clothing virtually every month.

Kirk turned away from the window to retrieve his coffee cup from the desk. "I'll tell you one thing, Serena, Graham is up to something. I don't mean your sister," he added with a chuckle and a shake of his head, "but he hasn't been in camp for some time now."

Serena also left her place by the window. "He's not a deserter, is he?"

"Obviously not, with four Union sentries watching him perambulate down Craven Street." Kirk rubbed the bridge of his long nose and looked thoughtful. "I wish I knew what he was up to."

"It won't bother Celia." Serena emitted a little laugh that was almost a snort. She grew serious as she started opening the mail. It seemed to be the usual notices they were beginning to receive in encouragingly larger numbers—engagements, weddings, birth and death announcements, religious services, requests for advertisements. But one piece of mail was alarmingly different. Printed on heavy paper in large type cut from the *Leader*'s own pages, it read: YOU WILL DIE, NIGGER LOVERS.

Serena glanced toward the backshop to make certain that Herman couldn't hear. Caldwell had taken Bill and Phil to the cobbler's to mend the shoes Kirk had bought for them. In six short weeks both boys had gone through their soles hawking the *Leader* on New Bern street corners.

"Kirk," Serena said in a low, controlled voice, "look." She handed him the piece of paper and watched his high forehead crease as the corners of his mouth turned down. His gaze seemed fixed on the bold, random typefaces. "Just some crazy bigot," he said, as determined as she to sound unconcerned. "It's a wonder we don't get one of those a day."

Serena sighed. "I suppose. Perhaps it's a reaction to Leonard's article." She saw Kirk tear up the threatening missive and toss it into the wire wastebasket. The act of dismissal should have reassured Serena. But for the rest of the day, she remained uneasy.

The clatter and whirring of five thousand spindles didn't seem to faze Marcus Farrar, but the incessant noise irritated Brant Parnell. "Would you mind," he shouted above the racketing spindles, "stepping outside, Mr. Farrar?"

Marcus didn't respond at once; he seemed to take pleasure watching the rhythmic movement of human and machine activity. At last he led the way from the airless spindle area, past a smaller room where some two hundred looms shuttled in grating cacophony, and finally reached the relative silence of the open air where he stopped by the mill's forging shop.

"We're doing all right, Captain Parnell," Marcus asserted, beaming at his son-in-law. "I gave my workers a penny an hour raise at the first of the year. A man's a fool not to pay a fair wage. I've even been thinking of cutting the workday back from sixteen to fifteen hours. So many of our folks seem to tire and aren't all that productive come nine o'clock."

"It's a long day, especially for women," Brant conceded, looking up at the gambrel-roofed, three-story structure built from undressed

granite. Marcus Farrar's number two mill stood opposite the adjoining
town of Harpswell, not far from Orr's Island Bridge. The Farrar empire
encompassed three mills for textiles and one for lumber and pulp.
After suffering severe initial losses, Marcus's fortunes had once again
begun to soar.

He had planted himself squarely on a patch of grass from which
the March snowfall had recently melted. "Thank God for wool! We
don't need to depend on Southern cotton and they don't have the
machines to use it. Have you heard about those shoddy paper uniforms?"

Brant had. It was a well-known scandal, bruited about in the North
not so much for its shocking disregard of the Confederate soldiers'
welfare, but for what it revealed about Southern industry.

"I hear the uniforms dissolve in the rain," Brant said. "Inspiration
and gallantry can only carry the South so far."

"True, true. You can't wage war without a manufacturing base."
Marcus shook his head at the folly of a people who thought a just
cause would bring easy victory. "Oh, the Union's had its setbacks,
but it's just a matter of time. Did you say you went to see Judge
Stanhope?"

"I was trying to bellow that in there," Brant said in mild irony,
gesturing at the factory. "He's failed a lot since Pembrose . . . disappeared." Indeed, Judge Stanhope had aged at least ten years. No
matter how vile Pembrose had been, he was still the judge's son.

"Poor old Stanhope." Marcus scanned the horizon in the direction
of Orr's Island. "The other son—Miles? Giles? Whatever he's called,
he let himself be conscripted."

Brant gazed down at the river which was still clogged with cakes
of ice. "I'd have expected Giles to pay someone to go in his place."

"Wants to be a hero, I expect. Like Matt. I can't understand it
myself—think of what Matt could learn about the business with a
war on!"

Brant rubbed at the cleft in his chin and gave Marcus a sidelong
glance. "Speaking of business, why don't we?"

For a moment, Marcus seemed taken off-guard. But he clapped
Brant on the shoulder and grinned. "Well, and why not? What are
business partners for, except to talk business? Especially when it's
prospering."

"It seems to be." Brant nodded pleasantly at several young girls
who had emerged from the mill to take their noontime constitutional
along the riverbank. Eying Brant from under their shawls, they giggled
and chattered among themselves. "As my pa used to say, 'A prophet
only sees the future. Profits ensure there'll be one,'" Brant quoted
after the girls had disappeared around the corner of the granite forge.

"Your pa sounds like a man after my own heart. But so are you, Captain, so are you." Marcus pulled out his pipe and began dismantling the stem. "Shall we go to my office?"

"Fine." Brant held his wide-brimmed hat in place as the wind picked up off the river. The two men wound their way down a stone path and indoors through a narrow corridor to the office. It was a Spartan room, with solid, plain furnishings and walls of granite which a quartet of English sporting prints did little to enhance.

"Mrs. Farrar and I finally got a letter from Serena last week," Marcus said as he sat down in a swivel chair and waved for Brant to seat himself across the desk. "She sent us a copy of her first edition. I have to admire the little girl—and your brother, too."

"It's better than twiddling their thumbs, I suppose." Brant's expression was bland.

Marcus scrutinized the bowl of his pipe. "Damned thing's broken. But then I haven't had any decent tobacco since my brother had to stop shipping it North." He paused to dump the pipe's pieces into a trashcan. "I must write to Serena, tell her I like her spunk. Mrs. Farrar isn't so pleased, of course, but then she thinks ladies should always be just ladies."

"Serena has a lot of ideas about what ladies should and shouldn't do," Brant said evenly. "I don't think being married to me is one of the things Serena wants."

Marcus's hazel eyes flickered. "Oh!" He chuckled and clapped his palms together once with a hollow, slapping noise. "Now, now, don't be too hasty. Sounds to me as if you two just haven't had much time to discover the boons of wedded bliss with this tomfool war going on."

"It's not that simple," Brant replied, making an effort to sound reasonable. His fingers rested carelessly on the desk's fine oak finish. "I don't think we're suited for each other. I'm willing to let her divorce me when the war is over. To prove I'm serious, I'm offering to resign from the business and take only my percentage of the profits to date."

Marcus was removing his handsomely tailored hacking jacket. "You don't seem to be making your usual good sense, Captain," he said with a touch of reproach. "Don't lose sight of the fact that we've only begun to make money. Why, I heard from Gideon Welles just last week. It seems our Secretary of the Navy thinks the world of you since you conjured up that idea of the bogus warship on the Mississippi." Originally, Marcus had considered Brant's plan to send a dummy ironclad into the Vicksburg area as lunacy. Secretary Welles and Rear Admiral Porter were highly enthusiastic.

"I've known Gideon for some time," Brant said equably. "Kirk considered going to work for the *Evening Press* in Hartford. Gideon founded it, you know."

"So he did. Smart fellow." Marcus draped his hacking jacket over the back of his chair. "So are you. Which is why we'll just forget this little chat about you and Serena." He chuckled indulgently. "The course of true love never runs smooth and all that, eh?"

Brant pushed back from the desk and regarded Marcus with unblinking sea-blue eyes. "Not quite. We're not discussing spindles and shipping tonnage. Serena and I are people, not parcels. She doesn't love me, doesn't want to be my wife, and is looking for every excuse woman ever found to get away from man."

Marcus cleared his throat noisily and compressed his lips. "Sorry, Captain, it all sounds vague and silly to me. We made a bargain," he went on, leaning forward so that his hands reached almost across the desk. "You and Serena formed your partnership, you and I formed ours. It wasn't capricious, not for any of us. The two of us do very well together in business. What you and Serena do—or don't do—in your marriage doesn't concern me. But I'll tell you one thing, if you think Mrs. Farrar—or I—would even whisper the word 'divorce,' you can row your boat right up the Androscoggin."

Shrewd gambler that he was, Brant knew when to fold and wait for the next hand. His eyes narrowed only slightly as he kept his level gaze on Marcus Farrar's set face. There were options, of course: He could just walk away and let Marcus take him to court—but that would mean he'd never see the rest of his profits, which were considerable, not just for himself, but for his crew. He could continue doing business with Marcus until after the war—and never live with Serena. Or he could tell himself he was wrong about Serena—women being more unpredictable than a deck of cards, it was possible that he had been mistaken. Unlikely, but possible.

Brant stood up and Marcus quickly followed suit, averse to being loomed over by his son-in-law. "We'll let it rest for now," Brant said quietly. "You've let me see your hole card." He picked up his hat and set it back further than usual on his head. "But you haven't seen mine." Pausing just long enough to watch his remark register on Marcus, Brant breezed out of the office. It didn't matter that his hole card might be useless; the other player could never quite be sure. But as Brant headed back up the stone path, it occurred to him that the game was far from lost. Somehow, Serena might prove to be his ace in the hole.

Serena and Kirk had gotten into their first serious managerial argument since founding the *Leader* two and a half months earlier. She was determined that they should go across the Trent River to the site of the Clermont Plantation where many of the freed slaves had fled to establish their own townsite under Union protection. Kirk insisted it was a foolish, even dangerous idea.

"Whether or not the Negroes side with us isn't the point," he countered. "It's no place for a white woman, regardless of political sympathies."

"I don't believe it's as chaotic as you say," Serena declared, fists on hips, facing Kirk squarely. "They're building cabins, even a church. If we take some of your men with us, what could happen?"

"We can't take any men with us, Serena, I told you that twice already." Kirk threw his pen on his desk where it bounced and rolled onto the floor. "You know damned well there are rumors of a Union naval invasion somewhere along the coast. All our forces are on the alert. I wouldn't feel right asking for an escort so that you can go chat with a suspicious horde of former slaves who may or may not care that you're tickled pink because they're free."

Serena clamped her mouth shut tight and glared at Kirk. "Oh," she finally said with great sarcasm, "I see how it is with you. It's well and good for me—as a woman—to stay in my place behind this desk and write stories off the top of my head. But it's quite different if I want to actively research new information. That's a man's work, I suppose!"

"That's right." Kirk appeared equally intractable. He seemed to tower over Serena, scarcely moving, his angular features set, with only the flicker of a nerve above his left eyebrow betraying his anger.

But Serena was undaunted. She drew herself up with as much dignity as possible and thrust her chin at Kirk. "Was it a woman's work to confront Fitch Moncrief or to save those children's lives?"

Kirk's stony gaze wavered ever so slightly. "No. Yes. Oh, hell," he exclaimed, throwing his hands over his head, "I'm just trying to keep you from getting yourself killed." He turned away for a moment to compose himself, apparently succeeded, and came to Serena's side. "Look, you're right about one thing, we're cooped up inside this place too much. It's a pleasant day, let's get a couple of horses and go for a ride."

Serena's eyes still snapped, but her voice softened. "Is this a bribe?" She started to pout, but felt Kirk's hand brush her cheek. "Damnation, I'll go," she muttered and tried in vain not to smile.

An hour later, Serena and Kirk were heading for Fox Hollow south of town. The March air had turned almost balmy and Serena had dared to ride with her head uncovered, the heavy, rich brown hair lifting slightly in the breeze.

"Do you know what day this is?" she called to Kirk as she guided her mount around a series of molehills.

"It's . . ." He paused and grinned. "It's March 13, just a year since the invasion. We'll have to make a story out of that for this week's issue."

"Yes, of course. We should have thought of it before." Serena nodded to herself as she drew up alongside Kirk. "I think it would be wise to emphasize how the Union soldiers helped put out the fires in the main part of the city and saved so many of the buildings."

"That's right. We can remind the locals how relatively peaceful New Bern has been . . ." Kirk stopped abruptly, reining up on his mount. "Listen, Serena—did you hear gunfire?"

Serena also brought her horse to a halt. "Gunfire? Don't tell me they're reenacting the invasion?" Her tone was humorous, but she felt a shiver of fear. Sure enough, the echoing sounds in the distance definitely were gunfire.

Kirk was sitting tensely in the saddle, his head cocked in the direction of the unsettling sounds. "I'd say it's coming from upriver." He squinted into the late morning sun, as if the gesture would somehow help him hear better. "It can't be the big Union invasion. We would have been told in advance." The dappled gray gelding stirred restlessly; Kirk absentmindedly patted its neck. "I think we'd better head back, Serena. But let's take a different route. The way we came might not be safe."

Serena jerked the reins in annoyance, causing her mare to startle. "It's not possible," she declared as both horses settled into a trot. "I can't believe that any serious fighting would take place exactly a year to the day of New Bern's capture."

"Armies don't pay much attention to dates," Kirk replied tersely. "Since this can't be a Union-initiated attack, we'll have to assume it's the Confederates. Damn," he said angrily, leading the way around a neglected hedge. "I hope those stubborn Southerners haven't got some wild idea to retake the town. It'll only cause a lot of bloodshed and more damage to property."

Up on a grassy knoll, Serena noticed the outline of an abandoned plantation. She could not remember who had owned it, but wondered if vagrants had taken it over, as had happened to several of the fine homes in the vicinity. "I can still hear the guns but they sound further away," she called out to Kirk, who was now some fifty feet ahead of her.

He didn't reply. They were skirting the west side of a lake which looked familiar to Serena. She thought she had gone boating on it that first autumn in New Bern when Uncle Luke and Aunt Kathleen had brought them to visit friends who were hosting a barbecue.

A small pine grove with scraggly branches was on their left. Kirk didn't see the half-dozen gray-clad men on horseback until it was too late to reach for his pistol. They emerged from the trees, rifles at the ready.

There was no hope of flight; the men were too close. Kirk pulled up on the reins and Serena followed his lead. Anxiously, she turned in the saddle as the Confederate soldiers cantered toward them.

Their leader was a lieutenant, young, fresh-faced, but sporting a bold, blond moustache. All except one of the others were privates, even more boyish in appearance than their lieutenant. Ruddy-cheeked, rawboned sorts, Serena thought, who had probably gone directly from their boyhood farms to find their manhood in the heat of battle. The sixth man, however, was quite different: A sergeant, at least thirty, with dark hair and small eyes the color of raisins. His muttonchop whiskers bristled like the spine of an angry porcupine when he saw Kirk's uniform with its major's insignia.

But it was the lieutenant who spoke, his rifle resting on the pommel of his saddle while his men kept Serena and Kirk within range. "Identify yourselves," he commanded in a soft, youthful drawl which sounded more suited to a plantation drawing room than a battlefield.

A surreptitious glance at Kirk confirmed her fears: The stiffening of his shoulders and the tight grip on the reins indicated his apprehension at revealing their names. If these Southerners knew anything about New Bern, they would not deal kindly with the editor and the publisher of a pro-Union newspaper. Southern gallantry aside, they might not treat Serena with the gentility due her sex and station if they knew she was unsympathetic to the Confederate cause.

"I'm Major Kirk Parnell, 21st Massachusetts Regiment." Serena held her breath as he turned in the saddle. "This is my wife, Margaret Stanhope Parnell, of New Bedford."

Serena wasn't certain if the lieutenant hesitated before sweeping off his wide-brimmed hat and bowing as deeply as he could while on horseback. "My pleasure, ma'am. Though war is not a pleasure for any of us." He shaded his face with his hat as the noonday sun struck him in the eyes. "I'm Julius Garnett of Wilmington, serving under General D. H. Hill who has assumed command of all Confederate troops in North Carolina. As much as it grieves me to do so, I must take your husband prisoner."

Serena's hands were resting lightly on her horse's neck. She sensed rather than heard Kirk's sigh of relief. Her initial reaction was to protest that wherever her husband went, she would go, too. Yet if she returned to New Bern, there was a good chance she could ask Yancy Clarke to press for Kirk's release.

These thoughts raced through her mind in split seconds. Yes, it was the sensible thing to do, certainly what Kirk's lie had intended. She gazed from the faintly apologetic face of Lieutenant Garnett to

the implacably set features of his sergeant, and finally to Kirk, who
surrendered his pistol before drawing up alongside Serena. Removing
his hat, Kirk leaned to kiss her cheek. "I don't think it's wise to ask
them to give you an escort," he whispered, apparently nuzzling her
ear in tender farewell. "Head straight for town as fast as you can."

Serena gave the faintest of nods. As Kirk was about to pull away,
she suddenly put her arms around him and clung so tightly that her
startled horse almost jostled her from the saddle. Surprised, Kirk
carefully extricated himself from her embrace and made certain she
was securely seated.

Embarrassed by such a display of domestic affection, the lieutenant
signaled for his men to surround Kirk as soon as Serena had edged
her mount out of the way. She sat very still as the little party cantered
toward the pine grove. Just before they disappeared among the trees,
Kirk swiveled in the saddle and waved to Serena. She thought he was
smiling.

Despite the midday sun, Serena suddenly felt cold. For some
moments she sat there, eyes unseeing, thoughts scattered and formless.
She was alone and afraid, though it was not the same feeling she had
experienced just a year ago when she had become separated from
Brant and Cecelia and the others during their futile attempt to escape.
Brant had saved her then; but now, he was far away.

The mare's ears pricked up and Serena glanced quickly in every
direction. Some yards off, lurking among the tall grasses, was a small
brown fox. The animal paused, gazing with suspicion at horse and
rider. Serena gazed back and smiled in spite of herself. She deliberately turned her horse around and rode away from the fox, hoping
it would be reassured by her retreat.

She hoped she would be, too. After all, it was less than two miles
back to the edge of town and the gunfire was now just a low, faint
rumble. Kirk would learn what was happening, Serena told herself,
as she would, too, when she inquired at Union headquarters.

A clump of daffodils nodded brazenly from under a stile. Their
golden bravado gave Serena a spurt of courage. She urged her horse
to a canter, but pulled up on the reins with a start; an unfamiliar voice
was calling her name: "Mrs. Parnell! Wait up!"

Serena pulled the heavy hair from her eyes as she turned around
quickly in the saddle. It was the Confederate sergeant, the sun glinting
off the gold buttons on his chest. "Lieutenant Garnett didn't feel right
about you riding back alone," the man said in a deep, thick voice.
"I can't take you into town, ma'am, but I can go as far as the outskirts."

"These *are* the outskirts," Serena said pointedly, noting that there
was no deference or gallantry in the raisin-colored eyes as they raked

her slim figure up and down. "You're very kind, but I can manage on my own."

He waved a beefy hand at her. "Sorry, but I've got orders. It wouldn't do none at all to have anything happen to a lady, Northern or not."

Serena sighed with resignation. It was useless to argue, and in any event, he was putting himself into more potential danger than she was. She flicked the reins and they began to trot along in unison, frightening a pair of chipmunks who fled to safety up the trunk of a young elm tree.

"You left your young'uns in Massachusetts, the major said." He spoke conversationally, making an attempt to be amiable.

"I have many relatives there to watch over them," Serena replied. She gave the soldier a curt, sidelong look. "I don't know your name, Sergeant."

"Nathaniel Brown," he replied, smiling to reveal at least three missing teeth. "From just outside Raleigh. Must be hard for you, being so far away. How old are they?"

Serena seemed intent on examining a frayed piece of her saddle. So Sergeant Brown—or perhaps Lieutenant Garnett—had been suspicious after all. Somehow, in the brief time since they'd led Kirk away, they had elicited the precise information which only a mother could know. Even if she could remember the Parnell children's ages, she didn't know their birthdays. And she was certain that would be the sergeant's next question.

"They're too young to understand the horrors of war, but old enough to know that their mother's place is with their father." She stared at Brown with fierce dark eyes. "I don't wish to discuss my personal life with you. I want to make this loathsome ride in peace. Please be quiet."

Brown uttered an exaggerated sigh. Anxiety mounting in her breast, Serena heard him fumbling for something in the pocket of his uniform. "I never did like being the quiet sort," he said in mock complaint, "so if I can't pass the time of day with you, guess I'll read instead." Brown reined up his horse and reached out to grasp the reins from Serena. The muttonchops seemed to flex as he held a letter in front of her face. "You're a mighty clever lady, Mrs. Parnell. You seem to be in two places at once. Now do tell how you managed to write your handsome husband from New Bedford on February 14 and be in New Bern one month later?"

Serena had forgotten that Kirk always carried Peggy's most recent letter with him. The one Sergeant Brown brandished had arrived only two days earlier. Kirk had read it aloud, even the more tender passages which had faintly embarrassed Serena. But Kirk apparently was proud of his wife's loving devotion.

Panic seemed to obliterate her rational thought processes. Kirk might have told a lie to protect her, but obviously it had not been convincing. And without knowing what he might have said, Serena was lost. She straightened her shoulders and glared at the sergeant. "I owe you no explanations. I told you, I don't wish to speak to you at all."

Brown stuffed the letter back into his pocket with a total lack of respect for either its writer or its recipient. He was still smiling as he put his hand on his pistol. "You don't have to say one little word to prove you're not a liar, Mrs. Parnell." He chuckled, a deep, heavy sound that held no mirth. "You and the major can just show me you're married. I'm the sort who believes what I see more than what I hear anyways. Let's move along."

Serena had no choice but to follow him. The slight chill she had felt after Kirk and the others had departed now became a tremor. Surely the odious man couldn't possibly mean what he implied. Nor was it likely that the well-mannered lieutenant would condone the indelicate treatment of a lady. Yet Brown had called her Mrs. Parnell even after stating that he knew she wasn't Kirk's wife. He must be aware that she had a right to the name, but as Serena Parnell, pro-Union editor, and not Peggy Parnell, New Bedford wife and mother of three.

Flight was her only chance. Surely he would not shoot her in the back. But he might shoot her horse out from under her. Even that was dubious; horses were hard to come by for the Confederate soldiers in the vicinity. They were almost at the grove of pine trees. To Serena's surprise, the fox still prowled among the long grass. She spotted the animal before Brown did and cried out: "Look out! He's vicious!"

As Brown pulled up to discover the source of Serena's alarm, she wheeled her horse around and urged the mare to a gallop. Over a low stone fence, past the stile, racing for the shelter of the elms she flew, hair whipping her face, not daring to look behind her, yet knowing that Brown was tearing along in pursuit.

Whether her horse stumbled in a rabbit hole or was knocked out from under her by a collision with Brown's own mount, Serena could not be certain. She only knew that the animal went down, mercifully unhurt, but that the sergeant had hauled her out of the saddle and dumped her across his thighs. He was swearing ferociously as he tried to calm the frightened mare and tie the reins to his own.

Serena felt as if there were no air in her body. It wasn't until they had begun to turn back once more at a walk that she finally was able to take in gulping gasps of breath. Her head hung down, the long

hair almost trailing to the ground, the saddle pressing against her
stomach, her arms and legs dangling awkwardly.

"That was just about the dumbest damned thing I've seen a woman
do," Brown observed in an irritable voice. "You got more nerve than
sense. No doubt about it, you must be the one who helps useless
slaves and loves that old baboon, Abe Lincoln."

The tone was more of one chastising a naughty child than of an
outraged patriot vilifying a political enemy. Yet its very lack of fervor
frightened Serena all the more. She did not, could not, reply; her
breathing was still considerably restricted by the painful position in
which she lay across the horse. All she could think of was how far
they had to go before reaching Kirk and the Confederate soldiers.

"I could be wrong," Brown was going on in his relentless manner,
"but I've heard stories about you and the major and your newspaper.
I wondered then what kind of gal would do such things. I figured
you'd be plumb ugly, all stringy and wrinkled, like some of them
snooty Raleigh spinsters. But that ain't so," he said, the heavy voice
deeper and thicker than ever. "Not at all, hey?"

Serena shuddered as she felt his hand on her buttocks. The horses
kept walking steadily, innocently indifferent to their human cargo.
"Yes, ma'am, nothing stringy about you. Nothing Southern, neither—
can't feel no hoopskirts or pantalets. A man doesn't have to dig so
far to get what he wants with you Northern gals, does he?" As if to
prove his point, he firmly squeezed the curving mounds and chuckled.
Serena screamed, a strangled, tortured cry that caused both horses to
startle. Brown soothed the animals but his hand remained in place.
"Now don't go making a lot of noise or you'll land right on your
pretty little Yankee head."

At last they had reached the shade of the pine grove. Dazedly,
Serena saw the cones scattered on the ground only inches from her
face. Brown was right—if his mount reared, she'd crash headfirst
onto the hardened earth. She closed her eyes and bit her lip to keep
from crying.

Then he withdrew his hand and she let out a great gasp of relief.
Perhaps he had suddenly realized that molesting her would bring a
sharp reprimand or even punishment from his lieutenant.

The brief spurt of hope was snuffed out like a lantern in the wind.
Brown was pulling up her skirt and petticoats with his free hand,
exposing her slim, white-stockinged legs and the dainty cotton undergarment. Serena felt the muslin skirts and ruffled petticoat tumble
over her head, almost smothering her. She was shrouded in a darkened
world, suffocating from fear and helplessness. It was difficult to hear
through the mounds of fabric, but Serena caught his exclamation that
Yankee meat looked as tasty as any Southern belle's buffet.

Serena thought she'd go mad with terror as Brown tugged at her undergarment, pulling it roughly over her hips. The memory of Pembrose Stanhope beat against her brain; the ecstasy of Brant's embrace seemed like a mockery.

Brown's voice suddenly sounded all too piercingly clear: "I declare, I just got to have all of this New England picnic. Let's spread you out on the ground like a regular feast."

He slapped her buttocks and started to dismount as Serena felt the tears stream down her cheeks to mingle with her hair. Her only consolation was that unlike Pembrose, Brown wouldn't dare kill her after he'd raped her. Though, she thought miserably, perhaps she'd wish he had.

The sound of the bullet was dulled by the pile of clothing which covered Serena's head. But at least the skirts and petticoats cushioned her fall as the horse whinnied in fright and hurled her to the ground. Struggling for breath once more, she grappled with her garments and finally emerged to see Sergeant Brown lying facedown just a scant two feet away. Standing only a few yards further was Abigail, attired in a dusky blue riding habit with a small revolver in her gloved hand.

"Good God almighty!" Serena breathed, digging into the ground to get enough leverage to raise herself to her knees. "What in heaven's name are you doing here?"

"I'll explain later." Abigail tucked the revolver into her petit-point needlework bag and whistled. A big roan which Serena recognized as belonging to Uncle Luke's stable trotted between the trees and stopped next to Abigail. "Ride that dreadful man's horse and lead your own. We don't have time to switch round." She already was in the stirrups, heading the roan out of the pine grove.

Serena, still rearranging her clothes, glanced with revulsion at the motionless form of Sergeant Brown. But her cousin was already almost out of sight; Serena clambered up on the soldier's horse, hitched her skirts to her knees and followed Abigail.

They rode for a mile without exchanging a word. At last, Abigail reined up outside an abandoned woodshed. Nearby, Serena could see the burned timbers of a farmhouse which apparently had been laid waste by marauding soldiers.

Both young women dismounted and led their horses to a sluggish stream in back of the woodshed. Serena collapsed on what had apparently been the chopping block while Abigail leaned against a hollow tree trunk.

"Are you all right?" Abigail's tone was calm but the green eyes betrayed deep concern.

Serena put both hands to her face, rubbing her cheeks in a desperate circular motion, as if she could wipe away the humiliation she still felt. "Oh—yes, I'm just stunned." She let her hands fall to her lap and stared at the lazy motion of the horses' tails as the animals quenched their thirst in the creek. At last she turned to her cousin: "Did you kill him?"

The veiled crown of Abigail's riding hat moved just once in negative response. "That little revolver couldn't kill anyone."

Serena's shoulders slumped in relief. "He was hateful. But I hope he isn't dead." The faintest smile tugged at her mouth. "Very well, Abby, now tell me how you came to be out riding with a gun in your needlework bag."

"I always take my revolver with me," her cousin answered matter-of-factly. "It was a necessary precaution in Washington. But finding you was no accident. Yancy and I had come to the *Leader* office to see if you and Kirk might write an article about our plans for the hospital. Just as we arrived, Caldwell told us that General Hill's forces were attacking Union positions on both sides of the Neuse. And Emaline said that you and Kirk had gone for a ride, probably in the Fox Hollow area. Where is Kirk—or dare I ask?"

It was with a tremendous surge of guilt that Serena realized she had not thought about his plight since the odious Sergeant Brown had begun his loathsome assault on her body. In a dazed voice, Serena told Abigail that Kirk had been taken prisoner by the men who had been with the sergeant.

It was Abigail's turn to look relieved. "I was afraid he'd been shot," she said bluntly. "Perhaps Yancy can help him."

"I hope so. And where is Yancy?"

Abigail involuntarily scanned the horizon. "We took separate paths to look for you. He could come this way, though I doubt it." Her features were composed, but Serena noted the tension in her cousin's voice.

Serena also realized she was in pain: There didn't seem to be any part of her body that didn't ache and the shock of what had happened to her—and Kirk—finally began to set in. Abigail's nursing experience alerted her to Serena's condition. Without a word, she walked over to Serena's horse and removed the saddle blanket.

"Here," Abigail said in a low, calm voice. "Wrap this around you. The sun is clouding over a bit."

It was true; heavy banks of white clouds were blowing in from the east. Serena huddled inside the coarse blanket and wanted to cry. But that was a childish reaction. Tears would do no good, nor would feeling sorry for herself. She was in the middle of a war and there were worse things happening to people than being groped by a vulgar Confederate sergeant. Still, her emotions had to have an outlet. Serena chose anger: "I'm fed up with men who act like animals! For almost twenty years, I grew up without any man so much as making an improper remark—and now I seem to find a bunch of raving beasts every time I turn around!"

Abigail was biting at the insides of her mouth to keep from smiling at her cousin, who had gotten to her feet and was waving a finger almost under her nose. "Well, there was a time when I detected you might secretly want men to find you desirable."

For once, Serena did not find her cousin's fey humor amusing. "Don't you dare make inane comparisons, Abigail Beaulieu! First Kirk finds me half-naked with Pembrose Stanhope, then you come along while I'm in a most humiliating position! How would you enjoy almost being raped twice?"

Abigail's fine lips tightened. Whether it was the rising note of hysteria in Serena's tone or the indignant outrage of the question, not even Abigail could be certain. She drew back a pace and gazed without blinking at Serena. "I did not enjoy being raped—even once." Abigail didn't pause for Serena's apology: Slowly, and with grave dignity, she walked away to stand downstream of the horses, her booted feet just out of reach of the creek's creeping waters.

Serena had stopped trembling by the time Abigail began moving back upriver. "I just didn't think," Serena asserted as her cousin sat down next to her. "I'm terribly sorry to have been so tactless."

Abigail looked strangely bleak. "I don't talk about it, but that doesn't mean it wasn't horrible. I always marvel," she went on, appearing genuinely mystified, "that so many people equate the amount of verbiage with the depth of despair on the part of others." Abigail nibbled on a fingernail and sighed. "You may have accidentally killed Pembrose, but I was the one who shot him on purpose."

"What?" Serena gasped. "*You* shot Pembrose?"

"That's right." Abigail stared out over the river. "I told Brant. I didn't tell you because, until recently, you didn't know Yancy's history. It seems," she went on with a tight, bitter little smile, "you or I was destined to do Pembrose in."

Briefly, Serena meditated on her cousin's words. The Stanhopes seemed to have played a strange, sometimes sinister role in the lives of the Farrar family and their relations. The judge, using and being used by Marcus Farrar; Pembrose assaulting both daughter and niece, then finally dying by Serena's unwitting hand; Kirk taking a Stanhope wife; Yancy's first wife victimized and murdered by Pembrose; and somewhere Giles lurking in the background, an unknown yet malignant shadow.

"Did we really leave New England behind us?" Serena asked in a hollow voice.

Abigail turned a bittersweet gaze on her cousin. "Did we want to?"

Serena couldn't repress a rueful little laugh. "All the same, we left." She got to her feet, shaking out the saddle blanket. "We'd better head back to town and find Yancy."

"He said if he didn't find you and Kirk, he'd go back to Drew's Creek. I wonder if there's any fighting there."

Serena moved stiffly toward her horse. She had momentarily forgotten about the alleged counteroffensive which might complicate their efforts to rescue Kirk. For the first time, it occurred to Serena that it might not be possible to rescue him at all. Climbing into the sidesaddle, Serena felt a hollow sensation in her chest and grimly urged her horse to a canter.

Chapter 17

IT WAS LATE afternoon by the time they reached Drew's Creek. Though the sound of gunfire kept up, no skirmishes were actually sighted. Serena had considered letting Abigail go alone to Yancy's farmhouse. The urgency of getting Kirk out of Confederate hands and the duty of publishing a special edition of the newspaper pulled Serena in different directions.

"I'm not sure what I'll write for the paper since I don't know what's happening," Serena confessed to Abigail as they trotted along the dirt road outside of town. "I suspect the men who know are all out fighting."

"A sensible conclusion," Abigail remarked as they came within view of Yancy's wood frame house. "My, it seems Yancy has company."

Several horses were tied to the hitching post at Yancy's gate. Men wearing the blue of the Union army were gathered in the front yard where only a few clumps of long grass grew out of the drab gray earth. Yancy and Sergeant Davis were in their midst, talking to a man who appeared to be their leader. As Serena dismounted, she recognized Major Graham. He and Yancy both turned toward the gate as Serena and Abigail hurried up to the little group.

"Greetings, ladies," Major Graham said with one of his sweeping, unctuous bows. "My comrades and I were just discussing loyalty with Captain Clarke and Sergeant Davis."

"In a pig's eye, we were," murmured Yancy with a lift of one eyebrow. "Now that we have ladies present, why don't you just mosey along?"

Graham stared at Yancy in feigned surprise. "But we haven't finished—you still didn't explain why you aren't compelled to go back to your regiment now that the gallant Confederates are trying to retake New Bern."

"I told you, I don't owe you no explanation, Graham. The only person I ever explain anything to is me." Yancy drew himself up to his full, shambling height and frowned. "Now head on out before I lose my patience."

Graham glanced at his four subordinates and shrugged. "I had such an attractive offer for you, Clarke. I thought that you, like so many of the less affluent citizenry, might want to join my little war on the wealthy."

"Buffaloes," Yancy rumbled. "Mostly white trash. You're welcome to them."

Graham's eyes narrowed almost imperceptibly. "Mostly local lads, like these," he said, gesturing at the quartet of youthful faces who had turned hostile gazes on Yancy, "and even a few who have money to burn." The smile Graham bestowed on Serena and Abigail looked malicious. "Such as Mr. and Mrs. Farrar's twins."

"What?" Serena would have flown at Graham but Abigail restrained her with a touch on the arm. "They're not yet seventeen! And they'd never fight for Yankees!"

Graham shook his head. "They're half-Yankee, as you well know. It seems your aunt made them swear not to sign up with the Confederates until they were eighteen. But she didn't make the same demand concerning the Union army."

Serena looked at Abigail, who was watching Yancy. The Texan stood deceptively still, as if he were posing for a tintype. Graham actually yelped when Yancy grabbed him by the lapels and hauled him off his feet. "You underhanded, no-good snake! Snatching boys away from their ma! I should shake you until you're spitting teeth!"

Graham lunged at Yancy but missed. "Get him, men!" Graham shouted as Yancy continued to hold him almost six inches off the ground.

The four young men hesitated only a moment before rushing at Yancy, fists flying, feet kicking. Yancy dumped Graham unceremoniously onto a patch of grass, then struck out at his attackers as if he were warding off a swarm of pesky flies. Two of the youths were on their knees; the other pair were grappling with Yancy, trying to pull him off his feet. Graham's hand had gone to his pistol. Serena screamed to Yancy as the major raised his weapon.

No one except Abigail had noticed Sergeant Davis slip away. Serena jumped as the rifle shot tore through the air and sent Graham's pistol spinning out of his hand to thud in the dirt just out of reach.

"The party's over," Davis said firmly. "Run along now before Captain Clarke really gets mad."

The four young men all backed away, their faces a mixed study in anger, humiliation, fear, and hostility. Graham, however, had gotten to his feet and was brushing the dirt from his uniform with studied nonchalance. He avoided looking at Davis or the women, but stared hard at Yancy. "That was a damned stupid stunt, Clarke. You got the wrong man riled up this time." Deliberately, he walked over to retrieve his pistol and stuck it back in his holster, still ignoring Sergeant Davis and the rifle which remained ready to fire. As Serena, Abigail, Yancy, and Davis closed ranks in the front yard, Graham and his men mounted their horses, then rode off up the road at a gallop.

It had taken little inducement on Yancy's part to convince Serena and Abigail they ought to stay on for supper. Sergeant Davis went to work in the kitchen where a kettle of chicken soup boiled and a ham was waiting to be carved.

Serena collapsed on one of the rickety chairs, suddenly aware that she was hungry and exhausted. It had been a frightening, disturbing day in more ways than one.

"Kirk said Graham was up to something besides just squiring Cecelia about," Serena said peevishly as Abigail sat down next to her. "But enticing the twins to fight for the Union is an outrage!"

"Enticing them to fight at all is the outrage," Abigail remarked, gratefully accepting a cup of hot coffee from Yancy.

"Hell's fire," Yancy put in, "those boys aren't fighting for the Union, they're going to glory for nobody but Graham."

Serena wrinkled her nose and set the coffee mug down on the table. "You mean his command isn't sanctioned by the Federal forces?"

Yancy nodded vehemently. "I'd bet my last cent on it. He's getting all those poor buffaloes to sign on just to make himself rich."

"No sense of honor, let alone duty," Sergeant Davis grumbled, piling slices of ham onto everyone's plates. "War isn't anything but the main chance for an opportunist like Graham."

Or Brant, thought Serena, attacking her ham with unusual aggression. Brant was no better than Graham, using other people to turn a profit.

"War's a strange kind of heifer," Yancy declared, spooning out soup into battered tin bowls. "I was all for defending Southern sovereignty, seeing as how everybody has a right to their own ideas. But," he went on at such length that Serena was drawn out of her angry reverie to listen, "I won't fight to keep slaves. Hell's fire and damnation, every living creature has a right to live free as a great Texas Northern."

Serena scrutinized the big shambling man with his unruly beard and tired gray eyes which looked as if they'd seen too many sunsets. She wondered how long it would take before Yancy and Abigail acknowledged their union and took Liberty to live with them. Perhaps it would not be possible until they could move out of New Bern. The townspeople would no doubt find it difficult to accept Yancy's mulatto child. Certainly they would look upon his first marriage to a slave with shock. Even Abigail, with her New Englander's abolitionist background, must have been stunned when she learned about Yancy's previous wife. But Yancy had ignored the scandal of Abigail's illegitimate baby. However different they might seem on the surface, Abigail and Yancy were, in a sense, both outside society. It didn't seem to bother them; since they had found each other, the rest of the world could go its own way.

Except that it didn't work quite that way, Serena mused as Abigail helped Yancy pass the soup around. The world had a way of imposing itself on the strongest, most wayward wills. Even Brant's, she thought with some self-satisfaction; sooner or later, the world was bound to catch up with that scheming, greedy, self-centered scoundrel.

Serena hadn't heard much of Sergeant Davis's recital of the crops he and Yancy had planted for summer harvest. It was the sudden silence inside the kitchen which drew her back into the circle at the supper table. The other three sat motionless, ears alert to something that was going on outdoors. The old hound had let out a doleful howl and the chickens were making a cacophonous noise.

"What's that all about?" Yancy murmured, getting up from the table. Before he could reach the door, a flaming missile hurtled through the kitchen window above the sink, shattering glass and landing just short of Abigail's hem. Sergeant Davis yanked her by the wrist, pulling her away while the sound of more broken glass came from the little parlor. Outside, the harsh hoots of hostile men could be heard tearing apart the soft Southern night.

A third fireball had crashed into the little bedroom. Though Sergeant Davis had managed to stomp out most of the kitchen blaze, Yancy's efforts to beat out the fire in the parlor were in vain. He came back into the kitchen, a scorched pillow in his big hands. "It's hopeless," he said in that low, rumbling voice. "Let's get out."

"But you can't!" Abigail protested, going to him and putting her hands on his arms. "This is your home!"

Yancy shrugged. "Home's just a word." He shook free and put an arm around her shoulders. "Come on, Abby, this place is getting full of smoke. I think the bed's afire."

"Our bed!" Abigail gasped, with more emotion than Serena had ever seen before. But Yancy only smiled ruefully and hustled his wife toward the back door.

Sergeant Davis was peering through the one window in the kitchen which hadn't been broken. "They're gone," he announced and crashed a fist into his palm. "Damn! It was Graham, I'll swear to it in six courts!"

"Won't do any good, Charlie." Yancy kicked open the door. "There's a war on, remember?"

"Damn the war! The Union command doesn't hold with arson and pillage!" Davis glared wrathfully toward the parlor, its aged furnishings already consumed by flames.

Serena, who had gathered up the ham in her arms, coughed twice before following Yancy and Abigail through the door. She gave Sergeant Davis a sad smile as the timbers in the parlor began to crackle and the bed collapsed in the room next door. With a glance over her shoulder, she bade good-bye to Yancy's dream of a small farm on the edge of Drew's Creek.

The burning of Yancy's farmhouse gave Serena the opportunity to write a searing indictment of the renegade Major Graham and won her considerable admiration for defending a former Confederate officer. Serena felt as if she had finally justified herself as a journalist.

"Major Graham was not, in any way, following orders given by his Union commanders," the provost marshal had said in his formal statement to Serena. "From this moment on, Major Graham and his followers are considered deserters from the Army of the Potomac."

Serena had nodded with approval—until she realized that the twins were numbered among Graham's men. No wonder Aunt Kathleen was so subdued and vaporous these days, with her sons not only wearing Yankee uniforms, but now vilified as deserters. Not only was Serena's triumph tarnished by the twins' defection, but no word of Kirk had yet reached New Bern.

Aunt Kathleen was abed when Serena returned home that evening. Since the twins' departure, their mother had spent a great deal of time in seclusion. Uncle Luke did his best to cheer her, but failed, and in the process, had grown uncharacteristically glum.

"I blame myself," he declared over his second snifter of brandy that evening. "If I'd kept my Yankee ideas to myself, they wouldn't have joined up with what their mama considers the enemy."

"Major Graham is everybody's enemy," Serena said. "Maybe they'll realize that and leave him."

Uncle Luke waved a hand at his niece. "They're too wet behind the ears to realize anything except the adventure of it all. Those other youngsters, the poor ones, are out for money and revenge. But Nathan and Jason just want excitement." He stood up and stretched; it was well after ten. "Damned fool war, making people half-crazy, with some of them that way to begin with. I wish to God President Lincoln would find a commander who wasn't a nincompoop."

"I have to admit, when it comes to officers, the South has the cream of West Point and . . ." Serena broke off as Leonard coughed discreetly from the doorway of the sitting room.

"A Miss Pigott to see you, Mrs. Parnell." Leonard tilted his head, indicating the hallway.

"Emaline, from the newspaper," Serena said to Uncle Luke as she hurried past him. A sense of alarm hovered over her; Emaline wouldn't go out after curfew unless something was very wrong. Serena breezed by Leonard to see Emaline's rangy figure bobbing at the far end of the hall.

"I found him!" Emaline asserted with an air of triumph, "Rattle Hill is where they took our Mr. Major Publisher."

Serena grasped Emaline's thin shoulders. "Did you see him? Is he all right?"

"I didn't see him, but one of the Confederate soldiers swore six ways to Sunday that he was finer than frog hair." Emaline fumbled inside her coat, extracting a lumpy drawstring purse. "They're interested in an exchange," she went on, loosening the strings and pulling out a piece of crumpled paper. "You know somebody named Harold Saile?"

"Saile!" Serena's hand flew to her cheek. "Good grief! Of all people!"

Emaline's pale brows went up. "You do know him, then. Sergeant Brown said as how you would."

"Not that . . . loathsome man!" Serena involuntarily took a step backward. "Oh, ugh, I should have guessed he and Saile crawled out from under the same log!"

"You've met Sergeant Brown, too? I thought he was kind of sweet." Emaline saw Serena blanch. "Excuse me, Mrs. Parnell, I keep forgetting you're a Yankee. Anyway, that's their offer, Harold Saile for Major Parnell."

Serena was pacing the hallway, wondering if Emaline had such good sense after all. Any woman who found Sergeant Brown "sweet" was either a poor judge of human nature or woefully naive. "I don't know where Saile is," Serena admitted, turning to look at Emaline, "but Yancy Clarke might. I'll find out first thing in the morning."

Serena agreed to meet Emaline in the newspaper office before ten o'clock. A few moments later, the front door closed as Leonard glided into the hallway to lock up for the night.

"Good night, Leonard," Serena said, her voice weary.

"Good night." There was a pause as the latch was slipped into place. "Mrs. Parnell?" Serena turned to see Leonard's calm gaze. "I understand Liberty's father has come to claim him."

Serena stepped back down to the bottom of the stairs. "I . . . I didn't know he'd talked to you yet." She tried to scrutinize Leonard's face, to see if the impenetrable mask were cracking. "Does Liberty know?"

"No. I only learned about the situation this evening." Leonard's features remained very still, the dark brown eyes clear and steady. Yancy had moved into the Farrar house with Abigail two days earlier. Cecelia had evinced shock, Aunt Kathleen seemed determined to ignore the marriage, and the others found the couple's unspoken acknowledgment no more unusual than other misfortunes of war. "It will be difficult, of course."

"Certainly, the child is as fond of you as you are of him," Serena said in reassurance.

But Leonard shook his head. "I didn't mean that, though naturally you're correct. I meant for Mr. and Mrs. Clarke. Many people will spurn them for raising a child of mixed heritage. It will be far more burdensome for Liberty—that is, Sam—to be raised by white parents than black parents."

Serena frowned into the parquet floor. She knew he was right. "Mr. and Mrs. Clarke are both strong, sensible people. They'll manage better than most, I would guess."

"I hope so." Leonard's lips pursed in the familiar look of faint disapproval, but his forehead was creased and he finally looked away from Serena into the shadowy corners of the hallway. "I would like to think times could change after the war is over. I would not want Liberty—Sam—to grow up as I did, belonging to neither world, and in consequence, to no one."

Serena did her best to keep from letting her jaw drop. Leonard's candor bewildered her. His experience was completely outside her understanding.

Leonard was aware of her dilemma. To Serena's surprise, a faint smile tugged at his mouth. "I belong *here*," he said quietly, "I know that. But a place is not a person. What, for example, would you do if I asked permission to court you, Mrs. Parnell?"

"I . . . you mean if I weren't married?" Serena stopped abruptly, searching Leonard's intense features. No man had ever asked to court her except Brant and all he'd ever wanted was her father's money. Clarence Prendergast's tentative overtures had been pitiful. And men like Pembrose Stanhope and Sergeant Brown weren't men at all, but vicious creatures who preyed on women. "I'd say yes, by heavens, you're more of a man than most of them, Leonard! I don't care if you're green!" Serena had taken a step closer, fists now on hips, defying Leonard to dispute her.

It was his turn to look astonished. He also seemed incredulous and yet pleased. "You're extremely generous," he allowed at last. "And kind."

Serena emitted a nervous little laugh. "Well, when you get to know someone, you don't think of them as a certain color, you think of them as people. I suppose this sounds crazy, but I wouldn't feel the same way about Big Jed or Roscoe because they aren't educated and they're . . . different. Maybe it's because they've always been slaves."

Serena seized the opportunity to pose a delicate question: "But one thing I don't know, Leonard, is your last name. What is it?"

The V-shaped eyebrows rose just a fraction. "Why, I assumed you knew by now. It's Prendergast. I'm your aunt's half-brother."

Incredibly, the only thing that seemed to register in Serena's brain at first was that Leonard was related to Clarence. Two more unlikely kinfolk she couldn't imagine, unless it could be Peggy Parnell and Pembrose Stanhope. "Your father was . . . Thomas Prendergast?" she finally asked.

Leonard nodded, relaxing slightly. "After his first wife—your Aunt Kathleen's mother—died, he went to the Caribbean for a time. He met my mother in Jamaica and married her. Unfortunately, she died in childbirth. My father brought me back here and later sent me abroad to study since there were no suitable schools which would accept me as a student. When your uncle assumed ownership of the plantation and the townhouse, he insisted I live as I pleased since I had also inherited a most satisfactory share of the estate. But I didn't want to be idle and preferred to earn my keep in an honest way. I have considered striking out on my own, but the times haven't seemed very propitious."

"Maybe that will change. After the war, as you say." Serena gave her head a little shake. "Good heavens, I had no idea . . . But of course you're managing the plantation now. That's quite fitting, isn't it?"

Leonard shrugged. "It's appropriate, at least your uncle thinks so. I'm sure there are many people in the county who don't agree with him."

"Obviously, they're all backing the wrong side in this war," Serena declared with some asperity. She turned as she heard Uncle Luke move slowly toward the backstairs, heading to his bedroom without disturbing their conversation. "Poor man," she murmured, "I think I hate this war mostly because of people like him. They don't deserve to be hurt." She turned back to Leonard who still wore a faint smile. "It's time for me to retire, too."

"Rest well, Mrs. Parnell," Leonard said, moving to turn down the lamps in the hallway. He cleared his throat in his discreet manner. "I've appreciated our conversation. I should hope," he added, lowering his voice, "that you are not the only white woman with such heroic sentiments about mixed blood."

Serena paused, her hand on the balustrade. Leonard's cryptic words puzzled her. Was he referring to women in general? To those who might encounter Liberty as he grew up with white parents? Or to someone in particular? But Leonard was already closing down the lamps, shrouding the hallway in darkness.

*   *   *

Neither Leonard nor Roscoe had been eager to accompany Serena to the Trent settlement, but she had persisted. Serena felt duty-bound to take advantage of Kirk's absence to see for herself the community which was abuilding on the old Clermont Plantation site.

So far, it wasn't much more than a handful of shanties. Serena was frankly disappointed, but realized that a newly freed people could hardly be expected to construct what her New England-bred mind had envisioned as an orderly, well-appointed village.

In general, the former field hands were reluctant to talk to Serena at all and regarded her with suspicion. They were only somewhat less reticent with Leonard, whose light skin, tailored clothing, and well-schooled speech marked him as a stranger, too. For the first time, Serena understood clearly what Leonard had meant by not belonging to either the white or the black worlds. Only Roscoe could elicit information freely from the former slaves.

Two hours after returning to the newspaper office, she had finished her story and taken it to the backshop where Herman was setting advertising type and sneezing incessantly.

"I think you have a cold, Herman," Serena told him as he blew his nose with a trumpeting sound. "Why don't you go home and let Emaline make you a hot toddy?"

Herman stuffed the red-patterned handkerchief into his back pocket and sniffed loudly. "Don't you want this story set?"

"It can wait until tomorrow. Or I can do some of it myself." She paused as Herman sneezed again, recalling the handkerchief to duty. "I've learned a bit about composition, you know. Woman or not, I'm no jinx in the backshop."

As a novice printer, Herman wasn't inclined to adhere to newspaper folklore, and in any event, he wasn't feeling well enough to argue. But as Herman loped through the back door, he almost collided with Brant Parnell. Serena dropped the font with a crash, spilling type all over the floor.

"My God!" she gasped as Herman kept on going and Brant lounged in the doorway. "What are you doing here?"

"A good question." Brant tipped back his cap and regarded her with appraising eyes. "I thought you might be able to tell me."

Unable to look at her husband, Serena bent down to scoop up the pieces of type and dump them into a tray. "Kirk's a prisoner," she blurted, wondering if that was the reason Brant had suddenly appeared in New Bern.

"I just heard that. I understand he's to be exchanged shortly." His voice was disconcertingly flat, even remote.

Serena continued fiddling with the type, pretending to rearrange it but actually not even recognizing the letters. "Are you here to help him?"

"It sounds as if he has help aplenty." Brant finally pulled the door closed and walked slowly but deliberately toward Serena. "You and Yancy seem to have matters under control."

"We do, it's just a matter of days." Serena spoke sharply, aware that she sounded defensive. Brant was almost at her elbow; she finally stopped fidgeting with the type and clenched her hands together so that he could not see she had begun to tremble. "Is your ship here?"

"We're bound for Cuba. Sugar's hard to come by these days with the Louisiana supply cut off." He brushed her arm with his, though by accident or design, Serena couldn't be sure. The contact made her edge away, but Brant reached out to grab her firmly by the wrist. "Are you coming with me, Serena?"

At last she was forced to meet his gaze. The question rendered her speechless. Certainly Brant wasn't serious—after his callous, brutal behavior the last time he'd visited New Bern, he couldn't possibly wander into port and expect her to rush off to Cuba with him. The suggestion was incredible.

"Of course not!" Serena tested his grip on her arm but found it unbreakable. "How could I, how could you think of such a thing?"

Brant pulled her closer so that her bosom touched his chest. "Is it pride or is it perversity?" Brant's face was so close that Serena could feel his breath.

"It's neither," she whispered, wishing her breasts didn't feel a compelling urge to press even harder against Brant's body. "I have the newspaper to publish. I have a duty to this town as long as there's a war on." Her voice had risen, even grown a bit shrill. "You may feel no responsibility for doing your part in this conflict, but I do!"

Brant's eyes flickered dangerously for just an instant before he put his other hand under Serena's buttocks, lifting her just enough so that when he pressed closer she could feel the brute strength of him against her thighs. He held Serena in a wordless, tantalizing challenge for what seemed like a very long time. She felt as if she couldn't breathe, but knew that if she struggled she'd risk a nasty fall on the cement floor. For once, Serena wished she had adopted the Southern custom of hoops and petticoats; Brant's maleness was all too vivid against the thin cotton of her dress.

Serena opened her mouth to order Brant to set her down. But pride held her back. Or was it something else? Against her will, she sensed that flame of desire which Brant's touch could ignite like a bolt of summer lightning in a tinder-dry forest.

The hand which held her arm let go to grip her chin. "My God, you're stubborn!" Brant's expression held no irony, only incredulity.

"I have purpose," Serena said, though the words were stiff and jerky, with Brant's hand all but immobilizing her jaw.

The sea-blue eyes now held purpose, too, a cool yet commanding gaze that dared Serena to surrender—though whether it was her body or her will he challenged, she could not be sure. Through the thin dress, she could feel his manhood swell and throb against her thigh.

Serena was the first to look away, hoping that Brant would not see the gesture as a concession to defeat but as concern for discretion. "The back door is unlocked . . . Herman might come in the other way." She nodded in the direction of the editorial office. "And the windows . . ."

Slowly, Brant edged her backward toward the long, flat composing table. "I locked the door to the front office when I came in." Brant spoke without inflection. "The back doors and windows face an alley. I suspect no one ever uses it but you and your *Leader* staff."

That was an accurate surmise, but Serena wouldn't admit it. Nor did it seem so very important at the moment. She felt her back press against the composing table's edge, and then Brant lifted her onto the cold, flat surface with such deft swiftness that she had no opportunity to resist. And though he was no longer pressing himself against her, she could still feel the throb of his flesh—or was it her own, kindled into pulsating response?

"Are you crazy?" she demanded in a low, rattled voice. The table was hard and unyielding, not unlike the expression on Brant's face.

"I don't think so." Again, he sounded deceptively bland. Brant stood next to the table, one arm holding Serena down across her abdomen. His free hand began to undo the buttons of her honey-colored dress as Serena watched with a mixture of shock and excitement.

From the editorial office, a loud thump carried into the backshop. Brant's hand paused at the neckline of Serena's camisole while she froze in place. "Good God!" she gasped, grabbing at Brant's wrist, "stop! It's Herman! Or Caldwell!"

Brant shook off her grasping fingers, but waited a few seconds, ears keened toward the backshop door. But no one tried to come in. With the same cool determination, he started to pull the camisole down over Serena's breasts.

The noise had brought Serena to her senses. She attempted to sit up, tried to shove Brant's hand away, made an effort to wriggle out from under the arm which pinned her down. But Brant was heedless of her resistance and had bared her breasts, which pushed up and out from between the folds of her parted garments like twin white roses tipped with pink.

The craggy features softened for just an instant and despite her own best intentions, Serena anxiously awaited Brant's caress. Instead, he continued unbuttoning her dress, moving his arm so that he could open the skirt and pull down her undergarment to bare the rich brown curls which hid the burning core of her desire.

The wary, yet unnaturally cool gaze rested on that secret, aching place. No longer touching Serena at all, Brant folded his arms across his chest and shifted his stare to her eager face. "Legally," he said with a nod toward her naked torso, "that is all mine. I can do as I please, when I please, with you." He paused to let his declaration sink in. "But I don't want you that way. The question is, do you want me?"

Serena had listened with lips parted, palms sweating, and that incessant ache racking her entire body. Disconcerted by his lack of demonstrable ardor, she pulled herself up on her elbows, aware that her bared breasts had sharpened with longing. "I never said I didn't want you!" Serena swallowed hard, and realized she was breathless.

Almost indolently, Brant brushed the tips of her nipples with one hand. "Can you say the words, Serena?"

Words, words, words, thought Serena, which words? She knew a million of them, her life's work was words. But her only coherent thought was not a word, but a name—*Brant*. She uttered the single syllable through taut lips, watching his stony expression alter just a fraction.

"'Brant'? It that all you can say to me?" He glowered in a mockery of disapproval, as if she were an obtuse pupil stumbling over her primer and he was the stern, demanding schoolmaster. Brant moved his hand down to the magic mound, covering it lightly with his palm. "Try again, Serena. Do you want me or not?"

"Yes!" The reply blazed out of her throat like a flying ember. Brant's shoulders relaxed slightly and the sea-blue eyes began to thaw. His hand pressed more firmly, the fingers searching, seeking the already moist, throbbing flesh. Through her haze of desire, Serena marveled at how different a man's touch could be: Sergeant Brown had evoked only loathing and revulsion; Brant made her ache for consummation.

Her arms wrapped around his neck, pulling him down on top of her. "Take me Brant, please!" she gasped, moving her hips in a frantic motion to further free her body from the garments which still covered her legs. Heedless of the hard, cold composing table beneath her, anxious for release from her all-consuming need, enveloped by passion's disorienting delirium, Serena was aware of nothing more until she felt Brant drive deep inside her body, turning the drab, gray backshop into their own private Eden.

Even as he lay on top of her, his chin resting in her hair, their bodies still united in mutual triumph, Serena ignored the discomforts of reality. She loved the feel of him inside her; she loved the melding of their flesh into one. It was only when Brant slipped away from her and stood up to adjust his clothes that Serena felt the world pry open the door to her happiness and make its unwanted intrusion.

Brant fastened his belt buckle and offered Serena a bemused little smile. "I've heard the expression about putting a newspaper to bed in the backshop—I never realized you could do the same thing with the editor."

Making a haphazard effort to pull her dress around her, Serena grabbed Brant's hand and rubbed it against her cheek. "You're impossible, you know. Think of it, Brant," she said, her eyes widening up at him, "you could stay here in New Bern and we could be wildly happy."

The dark brows drew together. "In New Bern? Why not the Gobi Desert or an Amazon jungle or Hades?" He traced her profile from forehead to nose to chin with his index finger. "Not New Bern, Rena. Cuba."

With some effort, Serena struggled to a sitting position. Brant gave her a boost with his arm and sat down next to her on the hard slab. "But Brant, I don't see why it matters. Somebody else can go fetch sugar from Cuba. What if Kirk doesn't come back? You could help me with the paper. It would be perfect!" Her eyes were very bright, her smile wide and winsome. "You said yourself we might enjoy it very much if we ever lived together. You were right, we can do just that, now!"

Brant kept his arm around her waist, idly caressing the firm underside of one breast. But he looked at his other hand which rested on his knee, and his face had darkened. "I can't do that, Rena. I've undertaken an assignment to bring that cargo back to Maine. Captains who jump ship don't get offered a lot of jobs." He turned back to her, wearing his most ingenuous smile and appealing to her reason. "You can understand that, Rena. Now think instead about those balmy nights at sea with the two of us tussling in my bunk."

It was Serena's turn to look away. In agitation, she rubbed at her left eye and bit her lower lip. "I can't. I've finally made some progress with the paper. People are beginning to see that I'm not just a Yankee rabblerouser, that I'm fair-minded and objective and more than a propagandist. We've got so many Union families here now and I can help ease the strain between them and the local . . ." Her voice trailed off as she saw Brant's jaw set. "Besides," she went on in a far fiercer tone, "your brother isn't here to help." Somehow she made it sound as if Kirk's capture were Brant's fault. "Who'll put out the paper if I leave?"

"Homer or Hiram or whoever the hell that lanky lamebrain is," Brant snapped, and stood up abruptly. "Good God, Serena," he all but bellowed, whirling around to face her, "a hundred years from now, who'll give a damn if the *Leader* never came out again? It all goes in the bottom of the birdcage anyway!"

"Brant!" Serena slid off the composing table, paying no heed to the bare breasts which protruded between the open bodice. "That's not true! This newspaper," she asserted, waving a hand to take in the entire backshop, "is as important as a bunch of sacks of sugar!"

With enormous self-restraint, Brant kept his eyes on Serena's angry face. He fingered his creased forehead and silently counted to three. "See here," he said in a controlled voice, "let's stop this stupid argument. The solution is simple—will you go to Cuba with me?"

As Serena took a deep breath, she finally realized that her thrust-out bosom was uncovered. Flushing, she clutched her bodice closed and fought to keep her limbs from trembling. More than anything in the world, Serena wanted to say yes. She would go to Cuba—or the Gobi Desert or the Amazon or even Hades if Brant wanted it. But she had made a vow to stay in New Bern until the war was over. She had a promise to keep, to all the people of this alien city, white and black, Union and Confederate. And though Brant might desire her, did he love her? He hadn't said so, not ever.

Brant hadn't moved. "Well?"

"I told you!" Serena cried out in anguish, "I can't!"

Brant's dark eyebrows lifted slightly. "I sail at dawn," he said. When she didn't respond he shrugged and turned away toward the back door. With his hand on the knob, he paused to look back at Serena. "That's an enticing body you've got, Serena. What a pity to waste it on mankind instead of a man."

Serena struggled to come up with a retort, but words failed her once more. It didn't matter; Brant had already disappeared into the alley.

Her dress still undone and her hair tumbling into her eyes, Serena picked up the nearest form of type and smashed it onto the floor of the backshop.

It took Yancy Clarke three days to find out where Harold Saile was being held prisoner. "I'm plumb surprised they still had him, since he never was a soldier," Yancy remarked over cups of coffee in the *Leader*'s office that first week of April. He glanced down at the headlines of the newspaper. "Looks like the Confederate offensive fizzled out."

"It was foolish," Serena responded with impatience. She was far more concerned about Kirk than the futile effort to retake New Bern.

"The Federal forces outnumbered them overwhelmingly. Is Saile willing to be exchanged?"

The sleepy eyes hovered above the newspaper. "Sure is. But," Yancy went on, setting the *Leader* aside with a crackle of fresh newsprint, "are you willing to have him released?"

Serena had not considered the consequences. "You mean he might seek revenge because of what I did to him at Wexford?" She saw Yancy nod. "Oh, hell's fire, Yancy, half of Craven County probably wants to see me strung up by my thumbs!"

"I hear the provost marshal does that to soldiers who rough up the locals," Yancy remarked. "He sure knows how to keep order."

"He sure does," Serena echoed, wishing that the usually silent Texan hadn't chosen this particular time to try out new conversational gambits. "How soon can you get Saile out?"

Yancy scratched at his beard. "Oh—tomorrow, the next day. Just a matter of paperwork." He rose from his chair, tugging at his leather vest, then ambled to the door, and signaled what passed for a wave of farewell. Watching him go, Serena let her shoulders slump. A day, maybe two—then Kirk would be back with her in the *Leader*'s office. Armed with renewed confidence, Serena headed for the backshop to see if the press run was finished on her latest edition.

It took another three days to gain Harold Saile's release. Aunt Kathleen, who had finally ventured out of bed, suffered a relapse when she heard the news. She was certain the former overseer would return and murder the entire household.

It was close to midnight and everyone had gone to bed except Serena. The birds had long since ceased their litany of the day's activities. Even the crickets were silent. As always, Serena found the total quiet of a New Bern night vaguely unnerving. If Yancy's mission were a failure, surely he would let Serena know before morning. Or at least that's what she kept telling herself as she leafed through a sketchbook one of the twins had assembled before joining Major Graham's raiders. "Nathan Farrar," it said on the cover. The sketches were mostly of people, family members, slaves, even a neighbor or two. They verged on caricature, but there was also kindness in them. Uncle Luke's inventive creativity apparently had shown up as artistic talent in at least one of his sons.

Jason, Serena had learned, was the more practical of the twins. A throwback to Thomas Prendergast, perhaps, since Aunt Kathleen had struck Serena as no more earthbound than Uncle Luke. Yet both young men had heeded the siren call of Major Graham, who, like a Pied Piper wearing Union blue, had lured them away from their home to ravage the East Carolina countryside.

Serena looked up as the clock on the mantel struck twelve. Abigail had kept the vigil with her until a half-hour ago, but had started to doze. Serena had insisted her cousin go to bed. "You look peaked, Abby. You've been working too hard getting your hospital ready."

Abigail hadn't argued. She'd been putting in long hours to meet her own opening date of April 20. There was already a waiting list of eighteen men who were now occupying overcrowded quarters in some of the city's other makeshift hospitals.

Turning her attention back to the sketchbook, Serena studied a drawing of Leonard. The high forehead, the V-shaped brows, the pursed lips were all exaggerated, as was the supercilious look in his eyes. Still, it was an affectionate likeness and Serena wondered if the twins regarded Leonard as their uncle.

Young Calvin was depicted in grotesque obesity, and Fitch Moncrief looked almost effeminate. Serena realized how little she had thought about Fitch in recent months—and how equally seldom anyone in the Farrar household mentioned him—including Cecelia. Someone had brought news only a few days ago that Fitch was serving under General Mouton, who had successfully repulsed a Union assault in the direction of Bayou Teche. The battle for control of the Mississippi appeared to be far from over.

Serena gazed at the last drawing in the sketchbook, a soldier in Federal garb. He looked vaguely familiar—perhaps one of the sentries who patrolled Pollock Street. It wasn't the face which reminded her of someone, however, but the eyes, which Nathan had made to look protuberant. Her young cousin had also drawn the beard in a ruffled, cloudlike manner, obscuring the man's mouth. He seemed to be peering from under his visor in a menacing, almost venomous manner. The longer Serena stared at the sketch, the more unsettling she found it. At last she closed the book and set it back on the pianoforte, telling herself that the soldier probably looked so strange because he had not wanted to be sketched by a member of a Confederate household.

The clock chimed the quarter-hour. Serena touched the keyboard of the pianoforte, then quickly drew her hand away, lest she wake the rest of the family. Restless and anxious, she paced the room, painfully reminded of the night she had waited so eagerly for Brant to make love to her. But Brant had preferred to dally with Cecelia, blatantly showing callous indifference to his wife's feelings.

If, she thought, I love him, I'll get over it. First love, in particular, was said to be an illusion. Once the war was ended and she was out of New Bern, she could escape the memories of their too-brief encounters. She would never go back to New Bedford so she needn't see reminders of him there. As for Brunswick, she had a lifetime behind her; surely the days she had spent with Brant would not overshadow that.

Yet, when she closed her eyes and envisioned the house on Pleasant Street where she had grown up, all she could see was Brant, casually sitting in the parlor, with a trayful of empty teacups in front of him. Or the stable, where he had kissed her that first, surprising time. Or the dining room where he had sat in pleasant conversation with her family.

Annoyed at the tricks her memory was playing on her, Serena slammed a hand against the red bricks of the fireplace. The venting of her anger hurt; she rubbed the stinging fingers and cursed under her breath just as a noise sounded from the hallway. Picking up her delaine skirts, Serena flew out of the sitting room and down the hall to the front door. Yancy, Emaline, and Herman stood on the porch with Kirk Parnell.

"Oh, thank God!" Without thinking, Serena threw herself against Kirk's chest.

Kirk hugged her tightly, lifting her off the slate tiles. "I'm dirty and bedraggled, Serena," he said in a low voice above her head. "You may want to reconsider your enthusiasm when you get a closer look."

"You *are* pretty grimy," Serena said with a big smile as he set her back on her feet. She glanced at the others, still beaming. "Emaline, Herman—won't you come in?"

"No, no," answered Emaline, whose bonnet was more askew than usual, "we must hustle off home. It's been a long day." She motioned to Herman, who bobbed his head before making a gawky wave of farewell. The Pigotts were heading down the walk as Yancy closed the door.

"Lot of wrangling," he said, taking off his big hat and rubbing his forehead. "Garnett lets himself be cowed by his sergeant."

"Brown," Serena said with distaste, but her attention was directed to Kirk, who indeed looked disheveled. He had not shaved for at least a couple of days and his hair had grown down over the collar of his tunic. The blue of his uniform was patched with dirt and there was a tear at the shoulder.

Yancy moved with a noiseless tread toward the staircase. "I'll set up a tub and get some clothes," he said to Kirk. "Mine may be kind of big, but not a lot."

Kirk nodded, giving Serena a grin before following the other man up the stairs. "I could eat something," he whispered over the gargoyle decor of the balustrade.

"I'll fix eggs. And ham." Serena hurried toward the kitchen, hoping she could start the fire. Yancy would need it to heat the bathwater as well.

Half an hour later, Serena and Kirk were sitting in the family dining room. Yancy had declined Serena's offer of food, saying he was afraid Abigail might have awakened and wondered where he was. For the last week, he and his wife had been occupying the twins' old room. They had considered moving into quarters at the hospital but decided not to take up any space which could be used by the patients. Sergeant Davis, however, had set up housekeeping next door in his capacity as caretaker.

"Did they mistreat you?" Serena asked with some reluctance.

Kirk chuckled as he buttered a piece of cornbread. "Garnett is a gallant soldier. The only hardship was the so-called prison itself—an old henhouse I had to share with half a dozen other men. I wish we could have exchanged them, too."

"Did you see Harold Saile?" Serena asked, pouring hot tea into Kirk's cup.

"Only from a distance. Yancy said he wasn't very pleasant company on the trip to Rattle Hill." Kirk paused to finish the first of four fried eggs Serena had cooked for him. He was wearing a flannel shirt of Yancy's which had been carefully mended by Abigail. The stubble of beard was gone, his hair was combed, and except for a weariness about his eyes, he showed no remnant of his captivity.

"I've been worried," Serena confessed, averting her eyes as she stabbed at a piece of ham. "Some of the stories about prisoners of war have been . . . frightening."

The hazel eyes scanned her face. "More the exception than the rule," Kirk said. "Only Sergeant Brown was a troublemaker." Kirk paused in the middle of peppering another egg. "The day I was captured he came back with a flesh wound. What happened, Serena?"

She felt her cheeks turn pink. "He . . . he made odious advances." Serena kept her eyes riveted on the everyday stoneware plate before her. "Abigail happened to come along, she and Yancy had gone looking for us, and she had a small pistol . . ."

Kirk reached across the table and clasped Serena's hand. "Damn," he breathed, the angular features suddenly taut. "I was afraid he'd harm you. He'd found out from Peggy's letter that you were the wrong Mrs. Parnell."

Serena couldn't control a bitter laugh. "In more ways than one, it seems." At last she looked directly at Kirk and felt her color deepen to crimson. "I mean . . . your brother never loved me," she said in a lame voice.

His grasp on her fingers had grown painfully tight. "I don't know if he does or doesn't." Kirk swallowed hard, his face stripped of pretense. "I only know that I love you. Very much."

"Oh!" It was a low sort of gasp as Serena drew back, her fingers still entwined with Kirk's. "Oh, no!"

His half-smile was not without irony. "Do I offend you?" There was alarm in the hazel eyes.

With her free hand, Serena nervously pushed at the tendrils of hair which cascaded over her forehead. "No . . . no. Never. You're so kind, so good, you couldn't offend me." She looked up at him tentatively from under quivering lashes. "It's just that you mustn't love me. You have Peggy. And I . . ." She faltered, feeling his grip on her hand loosen as he stood up and came to stand by her chair. She should tell him Brant had been in New Bern, but the words wouldn't come out.

"You what?" he asked in a low, faintly unsteady voice. Kirk dropped down on his knees beside her. "You just said that my brother doesn't love you."

"But there's still Peggy!" Serena protested in a frantic tone.

For a brief moment, Kirk turned away. "I know. And," he continued, facing Serena again and putting his hands on her shoulders, "I love her, too. Am I crazy?"

"I think so." Serena nodded her head vigorously, then saw the forlorn look in Kirk's eyes. "I mean, not really, just . . . confused. It's this damnable war, Kirk. It makes us all crazy."

"Maybe." Kirk leaned slowly toward her, pulling her face to his. Briefly, Serena strained backward but neither her will nor her strength seemed able to resist him. His mouth found hers in a probing, hungry kiss which robbed Serena of everything but the need to be loved. Right or wrong did not exist in that mystical moment. Serena wanted only to be a woman cherished by a man.

At last, Kirk released her, giving his head a little sharp shake, as if to clear his senses. "God almighty, I've wanted to do that for so long." He spoke as if to himself while Serena rested in the circle of his arm. Laying his cheek against the top of her head, he continued in a low, uncertain voice. "Are you angry?"

"No." To prove her sincerity, Serena rubbed her chin against his shoulder. "But we mustn't do this again."

Kirk didn't answer right away. Finally he sighed and gently moved her away from him back onto the chair. "That's going to be difficult to remember," he said with a hint of his familiar boyish grin.

"We'll try," Serena asserted, attempting to look resolute, but discovering that her voice was oddly breathless.

The three-pronged candelabrum Serena had lighted on the dining room table had begun to drip wax onto the lace cloth. Hastily getting up to blow out two of the candles and take the other in her hand, Serena smiled apprehensively at Kirk. "It's very late. You must be exhausted. I'm tired, too. I'll say good-night." She grimaced slightly at the staccato note in her voice.

Kirk offered her a twisted half-grin. "Yancy told me I could stay in that small bedroom under the eaves. The cubbyhole, he called it."

"That's all the space we have left these days," Serena replied, hoping she sounded more like herself. "Even with the twins gone, we're a bit cramped. Cecelia, Yancy, Abigail, little Mark—it's quite a houseful," she rattled on, leading the way from the dining room. "Liberty has a room of his own, too, a converted closet, next to Yancy and Abigail." She sighed in exasperation as she started up the staircase. "I still can't get used to calling Liberty Sam. He seems to like Yancy, but still favors Leonard."

They had reached the head of the stairs. Serena's room was at the far end of the hallway from the cubbyhole. Kirk stopped, putting a hand on Serena's arm. "You don't have to play games with me, Serena," he said in a hushed voice. "I realize I've put you in an awkward position."

Her face was bathed in a circle of light from the candle. Her eyes were clouded. "I can't help jabbering so," she whispered. "It makes me think nothing has changed."

"Everything changes. It's part of life." Kirk was silent for a moment, scanning the hallway to make sure it was empty. He looked back at Serena, a plaintive expression on his angular face. "Just for once, would you dream of me, instead of Brant?"

Serena opened her mouth, about to deny that she ever dreamed of her husband. But that would be a lie; Brant prowled through her unconscious mind like a riverboat gambler seeking an easy mark. Licking her lips, Serena met Kirk's pleading stare. "I can't control my dreams. But I'll think of you before I sleep."

He gave her arm a tender squeeze. "Fair enough." Kirk's face eased into its familiar, comfortable look. "Good night, Serena."

She echoed his farewell as he turned to move down the hallway with his usual brisk step. Shielding the candle with her hand, Serena moved at a much slower pace in the opposite direction.

It was impossible not to think of Kirk. Lying in the canopied bed, Serena stared into the darkness and cursed a fate which had ordained that the wrong Parnell brother should fall in love with her. She was fond of Kirk, she found him attractive, she could even admit that the idea of letting him make love to her was exciting. Yet it was also impossible. Given her strict upbringing, she couldn't surrender to him in an adulterous liaison which would only bring them both to grief.

She should never have let him kiss her. That had been an unforgivable—and dangerous—lapse on her part. Lydia Farrar would reel at the mere idea. But repelling Kirk's tender ardor would have crushed him. The man had spent three weeks in a Confederate prison camp, he had been separated far too long from his wife and family, and his past kindnesses to Serena should not be repaid in stinging rebuke.

It must go no further, Serena promised herself, pulling at the pillow and trying to make herself comfortable. Once they were back in their old routine, Kirk would recognize his folly.

To her shock, Serena didn't find that idea of much consolation. It couldn't be that she was in love with Kirk. Or was she in love with the part of him that reminded her of Brant? Could she succumb to Kirk because he was all she had left of her husband? Then why had she not sailed to Cuba with Brant? Was it pride—or principle?

Serena burrowed into the pillow and tried to make her mind go blank. At last she fell into an uneasy sleep. In her dreams, she was with a tall dark man who was neither Brant nor Kirk. Or was he both? The splendid song of the mockingbird awoke her before she could find out and Serena discovered that her face was damp with tears.

PART THREE
North Carolina
1863 – 1864

Chapter 18

"FEELS LIKE tornado weather," Emaline asserted, running a feather duster over the bookcase behind Serena's desk. "You folks don't have twisters in New England, do you?"

"We get blizzards instead," Serena answered absently, trying to unravel the latest military dispatch from a place called Chancellorsville, not far from the Rappahannock River. "I'm confused," Serena admitted, handing the sheaf of papers to Kirk who had just come in from the backshop. "The battle is taking place near Fredericksburg. I wonder if Matt is there."

Kirk gazed down at a poorly drawn map. "It's possible. Have you heard any more about Stonewall Jackson?"

Serena shook her head. "That's all mixed up, too. It appears he was shot by his own men."

Emaline stopped dead in her tracks, the duster held at an angle in midair. "Not Stonewall! He's been hurt?"

Kirk gave her a commiserating smile. "I'm afraid so. There was some terrible mistake. He's been taken to a field hospital."

"Oh, lordy, that's plain stupefying!" Emaline flipped the duster onto a wooden cabinet and dashed to get her coat. "Please excuse me, but Stonewall Jackson is just about the finest fighting man alive—except for Robert E. Lee." She stuffed her arms into her coat, clapped the bonnet on her corn-colored hair, and hurtled through the front door.

At that precise moment, Herman ambled into the editorial office, a smudge of ink on his left cheek. "Where's Emaline going in such an all-fired hurry? Her beau come round?"

"Her beau?" Serena was wide-eyed. "I didn't know your sister had a beau."

Herman rubbed at his nose with a long index finger. "She don't talk about him much. Never met him myself, but he comes a-courtin' pretty regular these days."

Serena and Kirk exchanged bemused glances. Herman collected Kirk's story about the Union's perseverance on the Mississippi and disappeared into the backshop.

Kirk sat down on the edge of Serena's desk. "I'm overdue for my leave," he began, folding his arms across his chest so that Serena would realize he had no intention of touching her. "You've already proved you can handle the paper without me. I've asked permission to go home for a month, beginning May 10."

It had been over three weeks since Kirk had stated his feelings to Serena. Since then, neither had alluded to the brief romantic interlude in the Farrar dining room. It might never have happened, if it hadn't been for the unwelcome hint of tension which existed between them as they worked side by side on the *Leader*. There was nothing tangible in their new attitude, yet their customary banter and the relaxed atmosphere they'd shared for so long was suddenly strained.

Serena forced her features to remain composed. She set down her pen, tilting her head to one side. "You should have gone months ago. Peggy and the children must be pining with loneliness." When Kirk made no rejoinder, Serena cleared her throat and frowned. "I'll manage just fine," she went on briskly, "as long as I can sort out garbled reports such as this one." She forced a smile and tapped at the dispatch in front of her.

The tension seemed to ease in Kirk's angular face. As he stood up and stretched, Serena directed her attention back to Chancellorsville. Hard work was a wonderful remedy for a troubled mind.

It had seemed like a less than reckless idea for Serena to stay late at the newspaper on the longest day of the year. It was still light at nine o'clock and, as ever, a Union sentry guarded each street corner. Indeed, on this first day of summer, Serena noted that one of the soldiers had been paralleling her walk along Craven Street for at least two blocks.

The sweet evening air erased the memory of the humid afternoon. Serena, as usual, had found it difficult to work in hot weather. But she had much to write for this week's edition of the *Leader*. Not only had activity along the Mississippi stepped up in recent weeks, but there were still reports coming in from Chancellorsville. To Serena's great relief, she had finally received a letter from Matt, who had fought with General Hooker.

"It was a vexing campaign," he wrote in his sprawling style, "seeing that we had the Confederates outnumbered. But General Hooker deemed it wise to halt at Chancellorsville, allowing the enemy to use the cover of the wilderness to attack. It's not up to me to criticize the Union command, but only another hour's march would have gotten us well beyond the danger point. So here we are, on the wrong side of the Rappahannock. We hear that Longstreet's three divisions are being brought up for a possible offensive on Union soil. I'm afraid this will be a perilous summer."

Serena reflected on her brother's ominous words as she turned toward Pollock Street. Somewhat to her surprise, the Union sentry turned, too. She wondered if Kirk had given orders to make certain she never walked home alone during his absence. Typical of his concern, Serena thought, but unnecessary.

She dismissed the sentry from her mind and resumed ruminating about the current Confederate mood.

Certainly the South was imbued with new confidence since Chancellorsville. Even the news of Stonewall Jackson succumbing to pneumonia could not stifle Confederate enthusiasm. Matt was right about Longstreet's divisions moving north. All but a skeleton Confederate force had marched into Virginia from North Carolina, while rumors were rampant that Lee was assembling every available man except for the forces needed to fend off the Union along the Mississippi.

Two blocks from the Farrar townhouse, Serena noticed that the sentry had crossed in the middle of the street, heading toward her. As he came closer with a dogged kind of step, she gave him a brief, polite nod. When he didn't acknowledge her greeting, she looked at him more carefully. He appeared young, with a curly blond beard and overround eyes.

Serena faltered, staring at the sentry's face. It was familiar, yet somehow not quite real. He was within ten feet of her, never varying his pace. The sketchbook, she thought with a shock; Nathan had drawn this man's picture.

Immobilized, Serena opened her mouth to speak but no words came out. The sentry was directly in front of her, his hand outstretched. From behind him, a figure appeared in a trap. Serena found her voice to call out to Leonard. "You needn't have troubled, I'm almost home."

"No bother," Leonard said smoothly, bringing the horse to a halt and alighting from the pinewood platform. "Mr. Farrar had begun to fret."

The sentry's hand dropped to his side. He hadn't paused when Leonard appeared but kept walking straight ahead, past Serena, as if he had never seen her.

Allowing Leonard to help her into the trap, Serena stared at the soldier's retreating figure. "Good Lord, how strange! Or did I imagine something sinister about that man?"

Leonard peered into the gathering dusk. "There's something strange, all right." He nodded at the intersection of streets. "No other sentries are on duty for at least a block or more."

In spite of the warm evening air, Serena shivered. "I don't like it. And to make matters more bizarre, I could swear that man's picture is in Nathan's sketchbook."

"Oh?" One of the V-shaped brows lifted as Leonard flicked at the reins. "But that's not so strange. Nathan sketches a great many people."

"Yes, that's so." Serena arranged her skirts, which had gotten bunched up when she climbed into the trap. Folding her hands in her lap in an effort to compose herself, she tried to smile. "I'm being silly, I imagine."

Yet, she reminded herself, the drawing had evoked some fragment of memory. In itself, she argued, her reaction was hardly unusual. The occupation had gone on for so long that it was a wonder half the union soldiers weren't known to her by name. "I'm just tired," she said, noting with comfort that the brick chimneys of the Farrar townhouse could be seen outlined against the setting sun. "Fatigue makes me jumpy."

"Of course." Leonard's always calm voice was especially soothing. "The *Leader* must be a great responsibility. Naturally, you'll be pleased when Major Parnell returns."

"I will," Serena responded almost too swiftly. She bit her lip, turning from Leonard as he directed the horse up the carriage drive. But *why?* Serena wasn't sure of the answer.

Kirk Parnell returned to New Bern on July 8, as news of the crucial Union triumph at Vicksburg began to seep through the South. Not only had the Confederacy lost its hold on the Mississippi, but the name of a forceful, competent Union commander was suddenly on everyone's lips: Ulysses S. Grant.

"His background sounds very unimpressive," Serena asserted, going over some notes she had made in an interview with the provost marshal, who had known Grant in Ohio.

Emaline hovered at Serena's shoulder. "Demon rum plagued him, I see. And faced with a court-martial! Now do tell how he ever got to be a general!"

Serena moved away from Emaline; it made her nervous to have the other woman read over her shoulder. "I understand the war gave him a second chance in life. He'd resigned from the army and was working in his father's store."

"You Yankees do have the oddest commanders!" Emaline giggled, then her face split into a huge smile as Kirk came through the backshop door with Caldwell Smith. "Oh, isn't it just nicer than kitten's mittens to have our Major Publisher Parnell back?"

Serena couldn't help roll her eyes at Kirk who gave Emaline a kindly smile. He had called on the Farrar family the previous evening, just a few hours after his arrival in New Bern. Since then, he and Serena had had no time to talk except about matters related strictly to the newspaper.

"The important thing about Grant is that he wins battles," Kirk said in gentle reprimand.

"It's about time, too," Caldwell put in, picking up some sheets of foolscap. A prematurely balding man in his thirties, Caldwell was of medium height and spare build. He had been a printer well over half his life, and was eternally grateful to Kirk for pulling him from the army ranks to work on the *Leader*. "It sounds as if we made Lee look like a fool at Gettysburg."

"Oh!" Emaline bristled with indignation. Despite the ongoing arguments over the war, real rancor was not evident among the *Leader*'s staff. But a personal affront to Robert E. Lee destroyed Emaline's good humor. "General Lee is too dependent on General Longstreet. And Jeb Stuart, God love his debonair ways, dawdled in bringing back the scouting reports."

Kirk and Serena exchanged swift glances. "My, Emaline," said Serena with forced affability, "perhaps we ought to let you write a piece on Southern military strategy. You know more than our field sources do."

Emaline flushed, nervously patting at her huge hoopskirted gingham dress. "I manage to pick up bits and pieces on my rounds in the country. These days, folks got nothing to do except mess around and wag their chins. What crops they got left get stolen by the armies."

"I know," Kirk said in a placating tone. "Even here in town, rations are getting thin." He turned to Caldwell, who was wiping beads of perspiration from his bald pate. "I don't think Caldwell meant his comment as an insult. If the North and the South could agree on only one thing, it would be the brilliance and gallantry of that exemplary soldier."

Emaline's eyelids drooped with chagrin, but her spirit wasn't cowed. "Then why don't you say so in print, Major Publisher Parnell?" She gave Kirk a coy yet challenging smile.

"Maybe I should." Kirk stopped as Yancy Clarke shambled in, hat in hand, boots tracking patches of dust on the hardwood floor. He went directly to Serena and bowed his head.

"Ma'am," he said on a formal note in deference to the presence of the others, "I've got sad news."

Serena gripped the arms of her chair as visions of the carnage at Gettysburg thundered in her brain. This time she had known for certain that Matt had been involved in the battle. She closed her eyes shut tight, waiting for the grim words.

"Mr. Moncrief has been reported as killed at Vicksburg. The body'll be sent home by steam car, soon as possible." Yancy took a deep breath, but the sleepy eyes rested speculatively on Serena.

To her horror, she laughed, a high, piercing hoot like an owl gone mad. Kirk came to her side, a hand on her shoulder. It took Serena only a few seconds to control herself and put her hands over her eyes. "I'm sorry, I was just so sure it was Matt . . ."

Having discharged his duty, Yancy had regained his usual indolent demeanor. "I'm plumb surprised. I never thought he'd get mixed up in fighting." Yancy thoughtfully fingered the big silver buckle he wore at his waist. "I have to admit, I respect him for it."

Serena sat up straight. "I'm quite sure," she said in her normal voice, "that we'll all discover Fitch is far more admirable dead than alive." She saw the shocked expressions on the faces of the others, including Herman, who had come loping into the editorial office when he heard Serena's shrieks of bizarre laughter. For a brief instant, Serena considered another apology, but kept silent. What she had said was true. Fitch had earned himself a hero's mantle. If war could turn men into savages, perhaps it could also redeem them. The thought, however, did not offer Serena much consolation.

Widowhood suited Cecelia in more ways than one. Not only was she liberated from a man she didn't love, but, as she noted with great satisfaction, black set off her raven hair and subdued the unfashionable olive tone of her skin.

While Cecelia made a public show of mourning, Serena had to give her sister credit for not carrying the hypocrisy too far within the family circle. Indeed, the news of Fitch's death had eased the strain between the two sisters. Needing someone to confide in, and never at ease with Abigail, Cecelia had turned to Serena.

"Will I lie to little Mark and tell him how wonderful his father was?" Cecelia mused after the guests had departed from the cold collation served following the funeral.

Serena fanned herself with her hand as Cecelia sat down on a bench in the small brick courtyard at the back of the house. The August day had been too hot to hold the wake indoors. Out on the lawn, the house servants were clearing away the trestle tables and plates. Aunt Kathleen, still suffering from ill health, had gone to lie down even before the last mourners had departed. Abigail, who had only recently announced that she was expecting a baby in September, also took to her bed. Aware that knowledge of her delicate condition would bring genteel pressure from Aunt Kathleen to desist from her hospital activities, Abigail had kept her secret as long as possible. She had acceded to etiquette's demands by not attending the funeral, though more from acute discomfort than from any desire to please New Bern society.

"Maybe Fitch was a hero," Serena said, fingering the metal clasps on the family Bible. She watched Cecelia's classic profile, outlined against the flawless blue sky. Perhaps nothing had happened between

Cecelia and Brant. After all these months, it didn't seem as important as the more obvious fact that Brant had abandoned his wife. He was off to Europe at her father's bidding, trading Pennsylvania oil for leather and wool. Or so Kirk had told her, in a too-casual aside. Serena had been almost as angry with Kirk as she was at Brant. Now she could forgive Cecelia's flighty, flirtatious nature far more easily than Brant's decision to make an extended voyage without so much as a word to his wife.

"The letter from Fitch's commanding officer was ambiguous," said Cecelia, flicking at the tiny pleats in her black mourning gown and recapturing Serena's wandering attention. "During the Union siege, the people of Vicksburg fled to caves in the hills. It's unclear if Fitch was helping the inhabitants seek safety—or trying to hide himself."

Serena opened the Bible to the place where a snippet of Fitch's golden hair lay coiled on a Gustave Doré woodcut. The sun caught the gilded glints, giving the strands a life of their own in startling contrast to the gruesome drawing of the earth after the flood, with corpses strewn grotesquely across the page. Had Vicksburg resembled that Old Testament horror? With a thud, Serena shut the Bible.

"Since Abby isn't feeling well, have you considered helping at the hospital?" Serena asked to take her mind off death amd damnation.

Cecelia lifted her dark browns. "I? My word, no!" She couldn't have sounded more indignant if Serena had asked her to work in a New Bern bawdy house. Indeed, Serena thought uncharitably, that suggestion would probably have elicited a mere throaty chuckle.

"It was just a thought," Serena murmured, as Young Calvin stumbled and almost dropped a large glass pitcher. "I suppose you could go home to Brunswick."

"I could. So could you." Cecelia stared at her sister with inquisitive black eyes. "Why don't you? Surely the newspaper wouldn't keep you?"

"But it does." Serena spoke calmly, watching Leonard as he emerged from the side of the house to make certain the servants had completed their tasks.

"Does it." The lack of a question in Cecelia's tone annoyed Serena. Cecelia shook out her taffeta skirts and frowned. "I must have more black dresses made. It's so hard to get good quality fabric. With so many men dying, do you suppose they'll run out of mourning cloth before this damnable war is over?"

"They're more likely to run out of men." Serena bit her lip as she saw Cecelia bristle. But before her sister could speak, Uncle Luke came hurrying through the courtyard door.

"God be praised, there's good news after all this day!" He paused, catching his breath and leaning against one of the pillars. "Jason's come home!"

It would have been unseemly to have termed the family gathering that night a celebration, yet Fitch's burial seemed forgotten as Jason was welcomed back into the Farrar fold. Aunt Kathleen's cheeks were pink, her eyes bright, and she readily accepted each refill of her rum punch cup. Still, the excitement was tempered by Jason's statement that his twin, Nathan, seemed to have no intention of returning.

"We argued and argued," he explained, basking in the fond hovering of his mother, "but Nathan thinks Major Graham is some kind of hero, out wreaking vengeance on the wealthy for the sake of the poor. It took me a long time to realize the truth about Graham, and what a grasping, thieving scoundrel he really is, but Nathan won't see it. He thinks I'm a cynic."

"He's always been a dreamer," Uncle Luke said with a sigh. He glanced at Aunt Kathleen, who had stopped doting on Jason just long enough to give her husband a reproachful look. "Yes, yes," allowed Uncle Luke with a touch of impatience, "I know where he gets that from. Let's just pray that Nathan comes to his senses before . . . anything terrible happens. God forbid."

Chapter 19

ABIGAIL GAVE BIRTH to a robust son in early September. Her petite size made the delivery terrifyingly long and difficult, but a week later she was chafing at her confinement.

"I simply cannot lie abed and watch those poor little servant girls fan me," she complained to Serena, who was walking about the bedroom with the baby in her arms. To everyone's confusion, the child had been named Sam. Abigail, however, found it all quite simple—Liberty had never grown used to being called by his real name and had obstinately insisted he hated it. Loath to abandon the honor due Sam Houston, Yancy had decided that what didn't suit his first son might sit well with his second. Abigail agreed.

"Abby," Serena said in a firm voice, "you scared the wadding out of us with this baby. Poor Yancy almost cried, he was so frightened. You simply must take your time recuperating."

"I'll get blisters." Abigail glared at Serena. "If that lazy sister of yours would help at the hospital, it would ease my mind at least a bit. As for Aunt Kathleen, now that she's vertical more than she's horizontal, you'd think she'd put aside petty politics and do her share."

"She does, for Preacher Roth and his church." Serena allowed Elvira, the wet nurse, to take the baby away for his feeding.

"Preacher Roth! The man positively bellows!" Abigail turned fretfully against the pillows. "Speaking of bellowing, what is that commotion outside? If it weren't so hot in here, I'd have you close the windows."

Curious, Serena looked down into the drive. Kirk, Herman, and Sergeant Davis were talking in a highly agitated manner as Leonard came out of the house.

"I thought I was good as dead," Herman wailed, his long arms waving like a windmill. "Talk about hell's fire!"

Serena tried to call out to the men but they couldn't hear her over their own voices. Abigail insisted on silence; she felt a headache coming on.

Giving her cousin an unsympathetic look, Serena rushed out of the bedroom and down the stairs, all but tripping over Liberty and Mark who were riding hobbyhorses in the entrance hall.

"Serena!" Kirk cried as she flew through the front door, black skirts billowing in her wake. "The newspaper's been bombed!"

"God, no!" Serena clutched at Kirk's upper arms, all but shaking him. "Who? Is it destroyed? Was anyone hurt?"

"Caldwell was singed," Kirk answered rapidly, lowering his voice to calm Serena. "He's next door, at your cousin's hospital with Yancy. Emaline wasn't there, neither was I, I'd just left to go see the provost marshal." He took a deep breath, his forehead furrowing. "The press may be all right, but most of our paper is gone."

Serena clamped her lips together to prevent the escape of a foul oath. She rocked on her heels, still hanging onto Kirk's arms. "Let's go look," she said at last, her face grim.

Kirk carefully extricated himself from her grasp. "Why don't you wait until Herman and I have had time to clean up?"

"Nonsense," Serena said briskly, starting to walk toward the horses which were tethered at the hitching post on Pollock Street. "I can face it. I have to, if I'm to write about this outrageous act."

Kirk didn't argue further, but signaled farewell to Leonard and Sergeant Davis. Herman loped along, shaking his head. "I should've gone with Emaline to Rattle Hill," he lamented. "She asked me specially to help her take some bedding to the Clancys and didn't we get into a big to-do about it. Now she'll say it served me right for turning her down."

"It was your day off," Kirk said, helping Serena mount Caldwell's horse.

"I know, I know," replied Herman, shaking his head. "But Caldwell was going to show me the new font of type we got last week. He's been mighty kind about helping me learn the trade."

"I'm the one who should have been there," Serena declared in self-reproach, awkwardly trying to ride astride in her voluminous skirts and deciding to ignore the fact that her black-stockinged legs were exposed almost to the knee. "If it hadn't been for wanting to keep Abigail company, I would have been at the *Leader*."

"Just as well you weren't," Kirk said, spurring his horse to a canter as a sentry saluted. "We're very lucky no one was hurt except for Caldwell's minor injuries."

Serena didn't comment. Their horses picked up the pace as curious onlookers paused to stare. Past Beers and Company, with its window full of books and magazines, beyond the government bakery where the smell of fresh-baked bread mingled with the late summer air, by W. G. White's stationery store, and finally, just before the newspaper office, the brick building which housed S. Blagge and Company, with its new shipment of flour, pork, butter, cheese, and ham recently arrived from the North.

On the outside, the *Leader* looked much as usual, except for a dozen or more townspeople and soldiers who had gathered to hear the details of the explosion and fire. Without waiting for Kirk's assistance, Serena dismounted. She held her head high, marching straight into the editorial office where four Union soldiers stood on guard, rifles at the ready.

Acrid smoke clouded the room, making Serena cough. A thick layer of ash and soot covered every object, including the bust of Benjamin Franklin. Serena's step faltered before she headed into the backshop. The smell of paper turned to pulp mingled with charred wood and melted metal, the floor was covered with water, the press was blackened by smoke, and even the brick walls were seared on two sides.

Feeling herself slump, Serena fought back the tears. "Damn the soul of whoever did this!" she whispered as Kirk slipped an arm around her waist. "Was it Graham?"

Kirk's long, lean mouth turned down at both corners. "I don't think so. He wouldn't dare come into town for fear of being arrested as a deserter."

Serena made as if to go further into the backshop, but quickly discovered that the water on the floor would cover her shoes. "How did it happen?" she asked in a resigned voice.

"Herman said somebody hurled a big ball of fire through that rear window." He pointed with his finger at the jagged glass. "I'm not sure if his report is accurate, and Caldwell had his back turned, which is how he got hurt. The fire or explosion or whatever it was landed just a couple of feet from him, setting off a stack of yesterday's newspapers." Kirk went on to explain that the two printers had fled the backshop, with Caldwell insisting that he'd be all right while Herman went next door to Blagge's for help. Buckets of water were passed along by a hastily formed brigade of Union soldiers and the fire was put out before it could harm the editorial office or destroy the press.

"It needs repairs, of course, but Caldwell says he can manage when his hands heal. I'll help him. So will Herman." Kirk looked down to see Serena's lower lip thrust out in a full-blown pout of frustration. "It's not as bad as it looks," he soothed. "If we can get more newsprint, we'll be back in business in a couple of weeks."

"We'd better be." Serena all but growled. Angrily, she whirled away, slapping her hand against the smoke-stained wall. "If not Graham, who?"

Kirk lifted his palms face up in a helpless gesture. "I don't know. Maybe whoever sent us that threatening note a while back. Or took a shot at us last winter."

Serena reflected for a moment. "You had just left?" She saw Kirk
nod. "And I should have been here." Suddenly she recalled her previous encounter with the Union soldier. Kirk's return, Fitch's death,
and Jason's escape from Graham's clutches had combined to blot out
the unsettling incident.

Kirk was thoughtful when she had finished. "A pity Nathan hasn't
come home too. He could at least tell you where he sketched that
man."

"Oh, maybe I'm being fanciful." Serena looked vexedly at her
soot-covered hand. "For all I know, he may have wanted to tell me
I wrote like a second Mrs. Stowe." She gave the chaos of the backshop
a long, hard look. "If we ever find out who did this, I'll personally
pistol-whip him senseless!"

"Serena . . ." Kirk put a restraining hand on her arm.

"Don't try to stop me being mad! I'm going back home and write
an editorial that'll be ten times hotter than this fire ever was! And
when the press gets rolling again, don't you dare let me change a
word of it!"

Kirk decided that Serena's testy mood dictated agreement. He and
Serena went back into the editorial office, where Herman stood chat-
ting with the soldiers. Pausing to relay orders about the cleanup
operation to the men, Kirk told Herman he might as well head home.

"I am tuckered out," Herman admitted. "I hope Emaline and her
beau aren't late. She said she'd fix ham and bean soup tonight."

"Her beau?" Serena stared at Herman. "I thought she was deliv-
ering bedding to Rattle Hill."

"That was early on." Herman paused to scratch behind his right
ear. "Her gentleman friend was taking her on a picnic to Contentnea
Creek."

"I see." Serena gave Herman an agreeable smile, then nodded at
the soldiers and took Kirk's arm as they went out through the front
door.

Only a few citizens remained outside, most of them children. Smile
still in place, Serena acknowledged the onlookers. As Kirk handed
her into the saddle, a redheaded boy of about fourteen called out in
a voice that vacillated between octaves:

"You done telling Yankee tales now?"

Serena fingered the reins and tilted back her head. "I never started.
The *Leader* deals in truth, not tales." Ignoring the stares of the little
group as well as a stocky woman's comment about "riding bareheaded
and barelegged like a common hussy," Serena guided her horse down
Craven Street.

"Idiots," Serena muttered as Kirk drew up alongside her. "I suspect half of them don't even know about the separate peace movement in North Carolina."

"It's mainly in the hill country but the state legislature—" Kirk interrupted himself as Serena turned away from Pollock Street in the opposite direction. "Hold up, are you lost?"

"Of course not," Serena said evenly. "Did you really think I'd go home after what Herman said?"

"Herman?" Kirk guided his horse next to Serena's. "What do you mean?"

"I mean Emaline and her gentleman friend sound just a trifle odd to me. I'm going to Contentnea Creek and find out." Seeing Kirk's face furrow, Serena doggedly pursued her path of reason. "I'm not saying Emaline is too homely to have a suitor—heaven knows the world has just as many ugly men as women. But she's been too secretive about it, she's the sort who at least would make a lot of giggling girlish allusions to having finally ensnared some poor male. She also seems to know a great deal about Southern military moves— and too much about the North, though we can't hide information from her. And," Serena concluded, "today's events strike me as too co-incidental. Emaline had gone, trying to get Herman out, you'd just left, and at the last minute I stayed home with Abby. It all smacks of Emaline up to no good."

Kirk still looked skeptical. "Even if I could see Emaline ferreting out military news we suppress for strategic purposes and handing it over to her ardent Confederate suitor, I don't see how that implicates her in setting fire to the *Leader*."

But Serena's mind was made up. They rode in silence the last quarter-hour until they reached a bluff above Contentnea Creek. The September breeze had shifted and the air had turned heavy. Dark clouds gathered on the horizon in the west as Serena and Kirk tethered their horses to a young cedar and began walking along the bank above the creek.

They had gone about a mile when Serena began to feel a sense of chagrin. "They couldn't have turned back already, we would have met them," she said in an irritable tone.

"They might have gone another way," Kirk suggested. "We'd better head back, Serena, it's going to rain." He waved a hand skyward, indicating the heavy gray clouds which were settling in over the countryside.

Serena stood still, looking glum. She had been so certain she was right about Emaline. The rain clouds seemed to weigh down on her, the atmosphere had turned so close that she felt stifled. Just as she was about to give in and head back to their horses, Kirk pointed in the direction of a sharp bend in the creek. Two figures were walking hurriedly toward a path which led up the bank. From the gawky gait and billowing skirts of the smaller figure, Serena was sure it was Emaline. But to Serena's astonishment, Emaline's companion wore the garb of a Union soldier.

"Emaline, consorting with the enemy?" Serena gaped at the pair as they scurried up the steep path.

Kirk wore a look of bemusement. "Maybe she's a spy, stealing secrets from a smitten Yankee. If so, he couldn't be her accomplice in setting fire to the newspaper."

Serena was still staring as Emaline and her companion disappeared among some old box hedges. "Damnation," she murmured. "I wonder if we should follow them?"

"I'd feel like a fool if we did," Kirk said, holding out his hand. "Besides, it's raining."

"Double damnation," said Serena as a drop splattered her nose and thunder rolled nearby. "I suppose we'll end up dying of pneumonia because I completely misjudged Emaline's romantic interlude."

"Writers have to be imaginative," Kirk said with a smile that faded fast as lightning crackled only about a hundred yards up ahead. The jagged flash seemed to herald a deluge as the rain pelted down in stinging drops.

"Good God! Is there any shelter around here?" Serena twisted her head in every direction. "Wait—the old Murphy house, I think it's just up the hill." She started to run against the wind, rain-soaked skirts impeding her pace, the driving torrent obscuring her vision. But the untended carriage drive suddenly appeared directly in front of them, and beyond old japonica and lilac bushes stood a once-proud house now slowly being reclaimed by nature.

Serena and Kirk were both out of breath when they reached the wide, creaking veranda. "They were kin of the Prendergasts," she gasped as Kirk pushed open the unresisting front door. "We drove out here a couple of times to see what damage the soldiers had done."

They had accomplished less than time and weather: The decaying smell reminded Serena of Tryon Palace. The house was virtually empty except for a few dilapidated pieces of furniture. Some of the floorboards had been ripped up, mute evidence of marauding armies searching for hidden treasure.

"It all looks so sad," said Serena, surveying the sagging walls and encroaching moss and mold. "But at least it's dry in here."

"It must have been a fine place at one time." Kirk walked over to the fireplace with its bricks covered in cobwebs. "A handsome setting too, on the little hill above the creek."

The thunder rumbled again, but this time further away. "I think it was built before the Revolution. There were some wonderful stories connected with the family, but I can't remember..." She paused, noting that Kirk had moved away from the fireplace to stand directly in front of her.

"I tried to make my feelings change. I can't." He looked distressed, even miserable. "I thought going back to New Bedford would cure me."

"You should have stayed," Serena replied and bit her lip. The words sounded too harsh. She was suddenly angry with herself for uttering them, angry with Kirk for giving her cause. "You ought to be more like Brant—he has no trouble staying away!" To her horror, Serena discovered there were tears in her eyes and her voice shook. Kirk took her in his arms and held her close.

"I don't understand Brant, maybe I don't want to. Good God, Serena," he said in a choked voice, "I don't understand myself!"

Serena tried to stop crying. She felt Kirk's hands move in caressing motions across her back. She dug her fingers into the wet fabric of his tunic and cursed herself for taking so much comfort from his embrace.

His mouth sought her temple, her ear, the curve of her neck above the high collar of the calico mourning dress. Serena closed her eyes and surrendered her lips to his.

If ever Serena had thought Kirk the private, self-contained, dispassionate Parnell, that illusion was shattered by the unleashed urgency of his desire. His tongue thrust deep into her mouth, his hands grasped the curve of her buttocks, the weight of him seemed to crush her in an overpowering onslaught of passion. Serena knew it was useless to resist him; to her horror, she didn't even want to try.

With one arm supporting her, Kirk's other hand worked at unfastening the black cloth-covered buttons of her dress. The tears now drying on her cheeks, Serena put her fingers in Kirk's brown hair, entangling the damp strands against her palms.

The stamping of feet and shouts of masculine voices froze them both in place. Kirk raised his head, ears suddenly as alert as any terrier's though he still wore a dazed expression on his long, angular face. "Goddamn," he breathed as Serena craned her neck in stunned surprise.

"Who is it?" she whispered, heart racing, senses quivering.

"Soldiers, from the sound of it." He got to his knees and gave Serena a hand to help her up. "Maybe they won't find us," he said as two of the soldiers appeared in the doorway. They were Union men who saluted Kirk smartly.

"It looks as if you were caught in the storm, too," Kirk said with an effort at nonchalance. "Is it passing over yet?"

"Yes, sir," answered a corporal who wore the insignia of a New

York artillery regiment. "We must have ridden a mile or more to find this house."

"Our own horses are that far away," Kirk said, taking Serena's arm. He introduced her and himself to the men who had now been joined by the others. Two of them were distinguished as New York volunteers by their Garibaldi garb. Kirk acknowledged the colorful blue and red uniforms modeled after the Italian patriot's followers.

"*Grazie,*" beamed a short, square-shouldered sergeant. He prodded the volunteer with a blunt finger. "Pietro and me, we only in America for three years. We want to help save great country."

"Very gallant of you both," said Kirk as Pietro nodded vigorously. Serena shifted from one foot to the other, aware of Kirk's conversational gambit to divert the soldiers' suspicions, but anxious to escape their watchful eyes.

But the men were headed for New Bern. They generously offered to share their mounts with Serena and Kirk partway back to town. After another ten minutes of casual talk, the corporal announced that the rain had stopped. Serena felt a sense of relief as they trooped from the decrepit house, but as she rode down the hill on a chestnut mare she shared with the Italian sergeant, she glanced back over her shoulder. The old house looked forlorn, it was true; but for a few moments its ramshackle shelter had offered not just comfort, but pleasure. Relief was swept away by regret—until Serena realized that even if she had kept her honor, she seemed to have lost her shame.

Serena did not see Kirk again for the next two weeks. Along with Herman and Caldwell, he spent his days repairing the damage to the backshop and trying to find more newsprint. Somewhat to his surprise, Mr. White, of W. G. White, dealer in books, periodicals, and stationery, conveyed the information that several reams were to be found in Chapel Hill. Caldwell, his burns healing satisfactorily, was dispatched to fetch the paper.

Telling herself that the commotion caused by the men making repairs would disturb her concentration, Serena composed her stories and editorials in the Farrar townhouse. The effort at self-delusion failed, but at least it provided an explanation for the rest of the family. Or so Serena thought until Abigail revealed otherwise.

"As long as you are remaining at home these days," her cousin said one September afternoon that held the first soft touch of a Carolina autumn, "I'd expect you to cheer me in my convalescence. If I may be candid, I find you glum, Rena dear."

"Glum?" Serena stared at Abigail, who was sitting in the shoofly chair, stitching her son's baptismal gown. "And why not—our newspaper was almost destroyed."

Abigail's fine features wore the familiar innocently bland look that Serena had come to recognize as dangerously deceptive. "But it wasn't destroyed and you will be publishing in another week or two. So," she went on, apparently much absorbed in the skillful plying of her needle along the edge of a tiny cuff, "I must conjecture that something else troubles you. You're being very foxlike, as Uncle Luke would say, only like a fox who has espied a henhouse but finds no way to creep inside." She looked up briefly to see Serena blink several times. "You've been very restless, you know. And your conversation is quite disjointed."

"Having a baby seems to have drained your wits," Serena huffed. "I'm still upset about the fire. We don't know when he—or she, or they—will try again. It's like living in a minefield."

Abigail's eyebrow lifted almost imperceptibly. "Oh." She turned slightly in the shoofly chair as Liberty hurtled into the room with Young Calvin puffing close behind him. Liberty clutched Nathan's sketchbook to his small chest and all but dove at Abigail's feet.

"Mamagail!" he cried, half-giggling and half-wailing, "Young Calvin gonna murder me for sure!"

Abigail composed her startled features. "Please don't be so loud, Liberty." She looked calmly at Young Calvin who stood a few feet away, a study in frustrated vengeance. "Why are you two quarreling?"

From his fetal position next to Abigail's skirts, Liberty started to reply, but Young Calvin's adolescent voice overrode the younger child. "He show everybody my picture! And they all laughin' at me, 'cause Massa Nathan draw me so fat!"

"You *be* fat, Young Calvin," Liberty retorted from the sanctuary of his stepmother's chair. He had scrambled to his feet, still holding the sketchbook tightly. "You be fat as two pigs and a great big cow."

"Liberty!" Abigail didn't raise her voice, but she sounded quite cross. Serena put a hand to her mouth, stifling a spontaneous urge to laugh. "You're being very rude, as well as ungrammatical. Apologize at once to Young Calvin. And give me that sketchbook. Please."

The huge brown eyes darted from Abigail to Young Calvin and back again. Serena noted the defiance and watched with curiosity to see how her cousin would handle Liberty's insouciance. "It's not your sketchbook," Liberty finally said, with a toss of his head. "It be Nathan's."

Abigail's green eyes narrowed slightly. "Oh? Why did you steal Nathan's property?"

Liberty's little face puckered in confusion. "I didn't steal it." He paused, pulling at one ear, then brightened with inspiration. "I borrowed it."

"I see." Abigail nodded once. "Then give it to me so I may return it to Uncle Luke to keep for Nathan."

Liberty had salvaged enough honor to permit capitulation. He handed the sketchbook to his stepmother, but leaned closer and whispered loudly, "Look at Young Calvin's picture. You'll about bust laughing!"

A little strangled cry of protest erupted from Young Calvin but he remained in place. Abigail gazed at Liberty's eager expression, started to put the sketchbook down, and then changed her mind. "Very well. Let's see how well—or how poorly—Nathan has drawn Young Calvin." She flipped through the pages quickly, then stopped to study the allegedly hilarious drawing of the older boy. "Hmmm," murmured Abigail, looking very serious. "It is recognizable, but much too exaggerated." She ignored the disappointment etched on Liberty's face and turned to Young Calvin. "Nathan has some artistic talent, but he's not mature enough to capture character. When he is, he'll be able to show your honesty and compassion. He'll also be more accurate in depicting how you really look."

If Young Calvin didn't quite understand what Abigail was saying, he was well aware of her kindly intentions. "I wasn't but 'leven when he drew that. I be different now."

Abigail smiled. "Of course. You're growing up. And part of growing up," she added, with a meaningful glance at Liberty, "is not making fun of other people." Her smile widened as Yancy entered the room, directing Young Calvin to attend Leonard in the smokehouse.

As Young Calvin, his shoulders squared a bit more than usual, started out the door, Liberty charged after him. "Me too! I'll help Leonard!"

"I don't think so," Yancy countered in his soft, drawling voice. He grasped Liberty by the shirttail. "I hear you've been raising cain with Young Calvin again."

"Liberty owes Young Calvin an apology," Abigail said. "Will you tell him you're sorry the next time you see him?"

Liberty shifted from one foot to the other, almost stepping on Yancy's boot. "Does Leonard say so?" He turned questioning eyes first to Abigail, then to his father.

Serena noted the quick exchange of glances between Yancy and Abigail. "Leonard is not your father," Abigail stated firmly. "Though I'm sure he'd agree that you must apologize."

Liberty suddenly seemed absorbed with his fingers. "Oooh . . . Mamagail . . . you sure?" He turned to stare up at Yancy, who nodded twice. The child emitted a huge sigh, then clapped his hands together. "I know, I'll draw him a picture! I'll make him skinny, like a bean!" He bolted toward Abigail, reaching for the sketchbook.

"Say please," commanded Abigail. Liberty obeyed with alacrity, but as Abigail handed him the book, he dropped it. Serena gasped as she saw the pages fall open to the drawing of the Union sentry.

Yancy and Abigail stared at her with curiosity. "What's wrong?" asked Abigail, the fine brows drawn together.

"Oh—nothing, I suppose." Serena bent down to indicate the sketch. "That man, I saw him on duty last June and he acted strangely. It was probably my imagination."

Yancy picked up the book, one hand signaling for Liberty to be patient. "I've seen him." He frowned in concentration. "On duty, I reckon. Or..." He rubbed at his bearded chin. "Funny, that doesn't seem right. But it must be."

Abigail had stood up to scrutinize the picture. "I've seen him, too. At least those eyes are familiar. Rena, do you remember if he was from a New England regiment?"

"I don't think so." She closed her eyes briefly, trying to recall details of the man's uniform. "I don't remember. But if he had been, I might have noticed." Annoyed with herself for piquing Yancy and Abigail's curiosity to no purpose, Serena waved the sketchbook away. "We've probably seen him a dozen times. As I said before, the Union soldiers all look familiar. Yet in uniform, they're also indistinguishable. They've been here so long, they're just part of the landscape."

"Heaven knows, that's true enough." Abigail noted that Liberty's patience was wearing thin; he was all but jumping up and down. "Here," she said, taking the sketchbook from Yancy. "Go make your picture now, Liberty."

The child started to turn away, saw his stepmother raise one finger, and halted. "Thank you, Mamagail," he said with a saucy little smile. But before he could get out of the room, Yancy called after him:

"You need some help, son?"

Liberty turned in the doorway, looking momentarily puzzled. Then he gave Yancy an enthusiastic grin. "Yep." He nodded vigorously. "Yep, Pa, I do."

Serena and Abigail both smiled at the retreating figures of the tall, shambling man and the exuberant, curly haired child.

Serena's reluctance to face Kirk was mitigated by her elation over having the *Leader* back in business. Emaline surprised everyone by declaring that they should have a party in the editorial offices with rum punch and cookies and coffee. Serena agreed and felt guilty about thinking Emaline had anything to do with the attack on the *Leader*. At least thirty New Bern citizens crowded into the newspaper office for the celebration, leaving scarcely any room to move about. Emaline had made four different kinds of cookies, Caldwell had requisitioned the rum, Herman had found some old bunting in an attic, and Bill and Phil helped serve the guests. Caldwell, who seemed to have taken the boys on as his private charity, told Serena he would probably end up moving them back with him to Rhode Island when the war was over.

In the genial party atmosphere, Serena could talk to Kirk with only a minimum of awkwardness. It seemed almost as if they had never touched or aroused each other's passions.

"Emaline and I will clean up," she told Kirk as the guests began to drift out into the dusky evening. "You and Herman have worn yourselves to the bone these past couple of weeks, and Caldwell has to take Bill and Phil home. Look, they're half-asleep now."

"They each ate a dozen cookies," Kirk commented, grinning at the boys who had roused themselves sufficiently to quarrel over the last few peanuts from a large bag brought by the obliging Mr. White.

"Caldwell will learn to be a father before he ever has a wife," Serena laughed. She motioned to Emaline, who was just closing the door behind the last of the partygoers. "Let's tidy up while the menfolk go home. I've arranged to have Young Calvin come for us later in the trap."

Emaline's cornflower eyes widened. "Oh, Mrs. Parnell, I never thought . . . I'm to meet a . . . special friend right away. Indeed, I'm tardy now. But I'll do my share first thing tomorrow morning." She offered Serena an engaging smile that displayed almost as much gum as teeth.

"I'll help Mrs. Parnell," Kirk volunteered, patting Emaline's bony shoulder. "I wouldn't want to detain you from meeting your . . . special friend." He gave Emaline a conspiratorial wink, which set off a rather unnerving giggle.

"You are the kindest man, Major Publisher Parnell. I tell just everybody how gracious you are, Yankee or not." After an admonition to Herman concerning the consumption of any more rum punch, Emaline snatched up her coat and hat and sailed out into the night. Five minutes later, Caldwell left with the still querulous Bill and Phil. Herman departed in their wake.

"I can't stand facing a mess in the morning," Serena declared, busying herself with cookie trays and punch cups. "If we want to have the *Leader* start publishing again on Friday, there won't be time to spend on washing up dishes tomorrow."

"I'll get some water and start a fire in the potbelly stove," Kirk said, already heading toward the backshop. When he returned with a pail in one hand and firewood under the other arm, Serena had finished gathering up the serving pieces.

"We haven't had a fire in this stove since last March," Kirk said, checking the draught and the woodbox.

"No, but we certainly had one in the backshop," Serena said lightly, stuffing a bundle of soiled napkins into a hamper. "I'll have these laundered at home. Now did I empty the coffeepot or not?"

Kirk lighted a match, dropping it among the paper and kindling in the stove. He closed the little cast-iron door and put the pail of water over the fledgling fire. "That newsprint isn't very good quality," he said, opening the draft just a fraction more. "We should get better out of Raleigh by early October."

"Good. We can make do meanwhile." Serena glanced around the office, looking for additional chores. "Maybe I should sweep," she said, heading for the broom closet.

Serena heard Kirk sigh deeply behind her and she paused in mid-step. "It isn't any good, Serena," he said in a voice that was touched with anger. "We can't go back. Not now."

She turned very slowly. "We have to. It's wrong. We're both married. And my . . ." She seemed to stumble over the word. "My husband is your brother. That makes it even worse."

Kirk was silent for a long time, his hazel eyes riveted on the pail of water, as if he could see answers floating there. He did not look up when he finally spoke: "Do you love me, Serena?"

She had moved closer but kept at least four feet of distance between them. It was a valid, honorable question. She had asked it of herself many times these past weeks, always certain that the answer was no. But now, seeing Kirk with his angular features touched by pain, watching the merest hint of defeat in the broad shoulders, knowing the hazel eyes were no longer private and aloof, but pleading and vulnerable, Serena wasn't sure. Did she love Kirk—or just that part of him which reminded her of his brother?

He lifted his head and met her gaze. Something inside Serena winced, but she took a deep breath and smiled sadly. "I love you. I love you more than any man." She felt the tears well up but willed them not to fall. "Except your brother. God help me!" she cried as Kirk's lips tightened, "I still love that miserable bastard!"

They stood without moving for what seemed like a very long time. It was Kirk who broke the taut tableau. "I hope you understand yourself, Serena," he said in almost formal tones, folding his arms across his chest. "I have great admiration and respect for Brant, though I may have led you to believe otherwise. You're not the first woman who has told me she loves him. But Brant has never loved any of them in return."

For just a moment, Serena let the long lashes droop, as if they could conceal her feelings from Kirk. "It doesn't seem to matter whether Brant loves me or not," she confessed, twisting her hands together in obvious distress. "I wish it did, I wish I'd never married him, I wish I'd never even met him!" Kirk started to speak, but Serena had whipped herself into a small frenzy of candid self-reproach: "I dreamed of beaux and suitors and a small cottage overlooking the sea. When that didn't happen, I built my hopes on my writing. And then I suddenly got both—and yet nothing."

Serena's hands had fallen to her sides; she stood trembling, desolate, drained. Kirk's folded arms seemed to tighten in an involuntary effort to maintain his self-control. "None of it seems quite fair," he said in a strangely detached voice that might have been analyzing General Pickett's strategic errors at Gettysburg. "You fell in love with a man who may not return your feelings, but who wanted to marry you anyway. I married a woman I loved very much, I still do, despite everything, and she loves me. But," he added with a sudden, sharp touch of irony, "she doesn't love me as a man—only as part of mankind. And Brant thinks he loves women—without ever having loved a woman." Kirk shook his head, finally unfolding his arms and rubbing one hand harshly across his brow. "You say it's the war that makes us all a little crazy. I wonder if we weren't born that way."

"Maybe." Serena dragged herself to her desk and sat down. She stared for a long time at the wood grain of the desktop, noting with fleeting disapproval that punch and coffee cups had left stains on the surface. "If I were noble," she said into the unsettling quiet of the office, "I'd insist you go home to New Bedford. But I don't want you to." She emitted a strangled little laugh. "That *is* crazy."

Kirk was opening the door of the potbelly stove to stoke up the fire. The water in the pail had long since boiled away by half. "What's even more crazy is that I won't go." He set the poker down just as Young Calvin's shadow appeared at the front door. "We're due for heavy seas, Serena. There's a chance we'll never make it to port."

Young Calvin was tentatively opening the door, his rotund form sidling into the office. Serena composed her features and nodded at the youth, then turned to Kirk. "It's up to each of us to make sure we never lose sight of land. Remember that, Kirk." She stood up, motioning to Young Calvin, whose perennial vagueness had not been ruffled by the exchange between his elders. Serena took her shawl from the cupboard, bade Kirk a pleasant if somewhat stilted goodnight, and left the *Leader*'s editorial office.

There had never been such a bleak Christmas in New Bern. Though many shops advertised shipments of meat and clothing and butter and cheese, prices were prohibitive. Even a man of means such as Lucas Farrar could not splurge his dwindling fortune on an elaborate celebration. While Wexford still sold tobacco to a few local buyers and the Union troops, the profits of the past had all but disappeared. Uncle Luke's loyal Negroes had turned into a burden. Since they were now free, Uncle Luke felt obliged to pay them wages. Aunt Kathleen might rail until the lace on her cap wilted, but her Yankee husband insisted upon a fair salary for his devoted people.

For Aunt Kathleen and all the rest who heartily endorsed the Confederate cause, the winter of 1863–1864 was demoralizing. It had become clear that King Cotton had been defeated in European markets by King Wheat. The trump card the South had thought to play in an attempt to gain English intervention had turned into a joker. Queen Victoria's government had deemed it more prudent to maintain the balance of power and the status quo. Support for a rebellious pack of pro-slavery Southern states was considered impolitic in London. Nor could the English ignore the resiliency of the North's economy. While the South was being drained, the North flourished.

But the tide at home was also turning away from the Confederacy. The zenith of Fredericksburg and Chancellorsville had faded into the nadir of Vicksburg and Gettysburg. By the New Year, Southern sympathizers had little to cheer—and less with which to make merry.

"They're not just eating crow," Uncle Luke said with compassion as he rose to shutter a window against the January drafts, "but Missionary Ridge. U. S. Grant—my, I *love* that name—seems to have emerged victorious from the Chattanooga campaign."

Serena looked up from the editorial she had been outlining on Jefferson Davis. "The South has become so disheartened. I've just been putting a piece together about how secretive Davis is, how he's put loyal Confederates off with his blatant favoritism."

"The man's a bit of a fool, I'm afraid." Uncle Luke sat back down in his favorite armchair. Since Aunt Kathleen retired so early in recent months, Uncle Luke had taken to spending his evenings in Serena's company. Jason often joined them, and occasionally Abigail and Yancy, but on this chilly night in late January, only uncle and niece were settled in the parlor by a flickering fire. "I only met Jeff once, back in '60, when he was still serving in the Federal . . ." Uncle Luke turned as Leonard came into the room. "Ah, Leonard, won't you join us? Maybe we can find a dram of whiskey hidden away, eh?"

Leonard's eyebrows twitched slightly. "If you do, you may wish to share it with Major Parnell. He has come bearing gifts." Leonard stood aside as Kirk entered the room, a duffel bag in each hand.

"My soul," exclaimed Uncle Luke, "aren't you a bit late for Epiphany?"

"I was hoping to make it by Christmas." Kirk grinned and let Leonard help him start unloading the bags. Sacks of flour and sugar and salt, canned meats and fruit, onions, spices, butter, and cheese tumbled out onto the worn Persian carpet.

"I'll be," breathed Uncle Luke, tugging at his ear. "How did you manage that?"

"A sea captain out of Boston I used to know quite well," replied Kirk, glancing at Serena and looking very pleased with himself. "I did a favor for him once years ago when he fell among some rowdies on the wharf. He hadn't forgotten."

"Ham," said Serena clapping her hands. "I thought I was tired of it until last October when we ran out."

"And claret!" Uncle Luke beamed at Kirk. "Young man, you're a credit to New England! Let's have a toast."

Leonard could not suppress a smile as he went to fetch the glasses. Uncle Luke was chortling over a tin of coffee as Kirk turned to Serena. "I even managed to wheedle this out of Captain Hardesty," he said, digging into his tunic and extracting a tiny, amber-colored vial. "From Paris." With a flourish, he handed the perfume to Serena.

"Oh, my!" She clasped the tiny bottle in her hand and smiled delightedly at Kirk. For one brief instant, she started toward him, but halted in midstep. "How very thoughtful! Thank you so much, Kirk."

The sudden awkwardness of her words went unnoticed as Aunt Kathleen entered the room in mountainous folds of black delaine. Her inactivity of the past year had increased her girth and the once matronly figure had grown to commanding proportions.

"Such a commotion," she declared in reproach. "I thought we had been invaded." She took a few halting steps forward and stared down at the pile of foodstuffs. "What is all this, may I ask?"

"You may indeed, and have a swift reply," Uncle Luke said cheerfully as Leonard handed him a glass of claret. "Major Parnell has lavished the wealth of the Indies upon us in a gesture befitting Caspar, Balthazar, and Melchior."

Aunt Kathleen frowned, then pursed her lips. "This is not Bethlehem. Nor are these gifts worthy of the Wise Men of old." She turned to Kirk, her small, squat figure looking much like a black storm cloud. "It would be more appropriate, sir, if you had brought us gold, frankincense, and myrrh. You Yankees may bury us, but we will indeed rise again as did Jesus Christ."

Uncle Luke paused with his glass to his lips; Leonard froze in front of Serena whose jaw dropped in astonishment; Kirk drew himself up to his full military posture, jawline set. "Am I to assume that my gifts aren't welcome, Mrs. Farrar?"

The black lace cap bobbed in slow but firm assent. "Nor," Aunt Kathleen added in that soft, Southern voice which had turned to frost, "are you. For all that my husband is a Yankee, this is still a Confederate house." With a chilling look that would have withered a lesser man, Aunt Kathleen stared at her husband, picked up her voluminuous skirts, and glided from the room like a deadly black beetle.

Uncle Luke had made the most profound apologies to Kirk, explaining that his wife's ill health and concern for their son, Nathan, had apparently taken a grave toll on her mind, as well as her manners. And while he and Kirk and Leonard and Serena sipped at the claret, Uncle Luke regretfully informed their benefactor that they would have to refuse the generous gifts. Kirk was understanding, but suggested he take them next door to Abigail and Yancy's hospital instead. Uncle Luke nodded in agreement, and appearing still somewhat bewildered, retired with Leonard to the study.

"I'll help you with all this," Serena said angrily, getting down on her hands and knees. "I wonder why Uncle Luke married that woman. She has all the brains of a turnip!"

"She's facing loss," Kirk replied, stuffing lard and starch and soda into one of the duffel bags. "The loss of everything she grew up with, the loss of principle, perhaps the loss of a son."

"There are times when you're just too good-hearted," Serena said in a heated tone. "How could she be so rude when you've been under this roof so many times! It's a wonder she doesn't send me packing."

"She won't. You're kin." Kirk finished filling the second bag and offered Serena his hand to pull her to her feet. She hesitated for just an instant; it was the first time they had touched since their encounter in the old house at Contentnea Creek.

"I'll get my cloak and go over to the hospital with you," Serena said, moving away from Kirk as swiftly as possible. "I think Yancy is still there."

He was, but the unusually startled look he wore upon seeing Serena and Kirk made them pause in the doorway.

"I'm plumb surprised," he said in greeting, but his voice was overly jocular. "I was about to bid Sergeant Davis good-night."

"We brought some donations," Kirk said, indicating the duffel bags which he set down next to a trestle table in the hallway. "They just arrived from Boston."

"Mighty nice." Yancy's beard dipped in approval. "I'm beholden to you. Mind if I walk back to the house with you?"

Kirk started to speak, but Serena interrupted. "What's wrong, Yancy? You're being very odd."

Yancy grimaced, pulled off his hat, and fretted the wide brim with his big hands. "I thought maybe it should wait 'til morning. But I reckon not. It's your brother, Serena. He's here and he's pretty bad off."

"Matt!" Serena gasped, reeling against the trestle table. "Where is he? What's wrong?"

Yancy passed his hand over his face, buying time to find the right words. But it was Sergeant Davis who came forward to take Serena by the arm. "Your brother lost a leg at Missionary Ridge, ma'am. He was heading home, via ship out of Hampton Roads. They were blown off course, foundered off Cape Hatteras, and somehow reached New Bern as a safe port under the occupation." He halted for a moment and took a deep breath. "Infection has set in. He's delirious, I'm afraid."

All three men gathered around Serena, as if to shield her from the dreadful news. She covered her face with her hands but did not cry. At last, she looked up at the circle of faces. "I must see him." Her voice was a whisper.

Yancy and Davis exchanged glances; the Texan inclined his head. "This way," said Sergeant Davis, starting down the hall past two exhausted orderlies. Serena's feet felt like lead as she followed Davis with Kirk and Yancy close behind.

When Abigail and Yancy first opened the former Moncrief house as a hospital, they had decided that no one should be turned away, regardless of political allegiance. If Northern soldier and Southern citizen could live side by side under the occupation, then they could be nursed under the same roof. With so little military action taking place near the city, most of the patients were not combat victims, but suffered instead from more ordinary illnesses. Indeed, half of the second story was reserved for women and children. And despite an outcry from local residents, the third floor was used to treat Negroes.

The room in which Matt lay had been the library. There was space for only a half-dozen beds, all of which were occupied with men from the ill-fated Union ship. A faltering fire burned in the grate, mingling wood smoke with the smell of chloroform.

Serena looked apprehensively around the dimly lighted room, unable to tell which of the men was Matt. Yancy prodded her gently toward the far wall where a mound of blankets writhed in the shadows.

"Oh, God!" she breathed. Edging closer, she could make out the bearded face, the twisted mouth, the sunken eyes, and the matted auburn hair. She fell to her knees beside the cot, and remained as if in a trance. Hearing Matt's occasional incoherent cries, she forced herself not to look toward the foot of the bed, lest he kick away the covers and she would see the ghastly stump.

Attempting to control her wild thoughts, she tried to pray. Oh, dear God, let him live! Why, God, why Matt, so happy and vigorous and full of life! Why her brother, of all the young men, why Matthew Farrar?

Yet he was but one of thousands, equally young and eager for the future. For almost three long, tragic years the ferocious war had claimed life after life, mocking the future for a generation of men.

Serena tried to get to her feet without aid, but Yancy put a hand under her arm. As Matt shuddered violently, she flinched and turned away. "Can you save him?" she whispered.

"I don't know." Yancy's voice was flat. "A day or two, we'll be able to tell more."

Serena nodded, letting herself be led from the little room. The brightly lighted hallway assaulted her eyes and she stopped for a moment. "I must tell Cecelia," she murmured. "And the others. At least he's with us," she went on, forcing her voice to sound more normal. "I would have thought the ship might have made it back to the Potomac."

"It wasn't possible," Yancy said. "And once headed South, there was no other choice."

"That's true," Kirk put in. "In winter, Cape Hatteras is a sailor's graveyard." He saw Serena blanch at the words and tried to smile but failed. "I'm sorry, Serena, but just be thankful they must have had an experienced captain. Your family owes him a debt of gratitude."

For once, Serena forgot about her resolution to avoid touching Kirk. She put both hands against his chest and sighed. "How true. If Matt . . . gets better, I must send a note to the captain." She glanced at Yancy. "Do you know his name?"

Once again, Yancy seemed absorbed in rearranging his hat brim. "It's . . . He was here for a bit . . . uh . . ."

Serena gave Yancy an impatient look. It seemed to her that Yancy Clarke was belaboring his usual reticence this evening. "If you can't remember, tell me in the morning." She ignored the pained expression on Yancy's face and put her arm through Kirk's. As she started to bid Sergeant Davis good-night, a voice from the doorway paralyzed her entire body.

"Yancy hasn't forgotten, but maybe you have, Serena."

Brant Parnell stood before her, outlined against the night.

Chapter 20

DR. HOOPER was an optimist by nature. Thirty-five years of medical practice hadn't daunted his belief that his patients would recover, even if it took a miracle. When such miracles didn't always occur, he seemed quite astounded, as if each death were the first defeat he had ever encountered.

"Now that's a basically healthy young man," he stated to Serena and Cecelia in his rumbling Carolina accent. "Oh, I know, the rigors of war and the loss of the leg take their toll, but that's no reason for despair. Pluck up your courage, dear ladies, your brother will be well again before you know it."

Serena and Cecelia watched the chubby figure bounce from the sitting room before looking doubtfully at each other. Serena was pale and drawn; Cecelia's olive skin had taken on a jaundiced hue. Although Cecelia had not been unduly disturbed over Fitch's death, Matt's alarming condition had stunned her. When Serena delivered the news to Cecelia and Uncle Luke that morning, the elder Farrar sister had fainted dead away. Leonard had fetched Aunt Kathleen's smelling salts, Jason arrived in time to help his father carry the statuesque Cecelia to the settee in the sitting room, and Serena had plied her with a fan. Luckily, Dr. Hooper had arrived only a few minutes later.

Cecelia was now sitting up among the cushions, twisting at a black-edged handkerchief. "You should have told us last night," she chided Serena peevishly.

"You were all abed when Yancy and I got home." It was true, though not the entire story as far as Serena's postponement of the bad news was concerned. The shock of discovering her maimed brother writhing in an agony of delirium had been shattering enough; but the unexpected arrival of Brant Parnell had rendered Serena incapable of coping with any more emotional traumas in one night.

Not that she had had an opportunity to speak with Brant: After the initial exchange, which Serena could not even recall, Yancy had whisked her home, and Kirk had left with Brant. Yancy's prescription of a large dose of bourbon had relaxed Serena's taut nerves, and Abigail, who already knew about Matt, put her cousin to bed.

Serena awoke to a bleak, chilly morning which seemed to match

279

her mood. As sleep melted away, fear crept over her, and with it, the knowledge that she would have to tell Cecelia and the others about Matt. Aunt Kathleen did not come down to breakfast, however, and in the ensuing distress over Matt, no one thought to mention her rude behavior of the previous evening.

Nor did Serena allude to Brant Parnell's return. Yancy referred to it in passing, telling Uncle Luke that *The Irish Rover*'s master might have tried making for another port, but because Matt was on board, a decision was made to take him to his relatives in New Bern. Uncle Luke's eyes rested briefly on Serena, but he made no comment.

And now Serena and Cecelia were alone in the sitting room. Uncle Luke and Jason had gone with Yancy to see Matt, whose condition remained virtually the same.

"I don't know if I could bear seeing Matt . . . like that," Cecelia said, all semblance of artifice gone. "It's strange, but I feel the most awful pain in my own leg, as if what happened to him somehow happened to me, too." Her ghostly laugh was but an echo of its usual throaty sound. "Good God, how bizarre!"

"He wouldn't recognize you if you went," Serena said, tucking a stray lock of hair into her net snood. She had not bothered to put up her hair this morning and only now realized she had missed a button on her mourning dress and the collar had come out uneven. As she adjusted the buttons, one hand froze against her breast. This was the same dress she had worn when Kirk had unleashed his hungry kisses and caresses. And she had returned his ardor with no sense of shame. Now Brant was back, and those moments in the old house above Contentnea Creek suddenly took on a tainted memory.

Serena all but leaped to her feet. "I've got to get outside," she said with a rising note of panic. "Will you be all right?"

Cecelia looked at her sister. "I'll have Chloe rub my back," she replied absently, her strong features pinched and oversharp. "Or Leonard drive me to Wexford. Or . . ." The black brows drew together. "What's this I hear about Aunt Kathleen refusing Kirk's victuals?"

"It's true." A flickering smile touched Serena's lips as she noted a spark of life returning to Cecelia's black eyes. "Ham, sugar, cheese, wine—Aunt Kathleen would have none of it from a Yankee."

"Ohhh!" Cecelia pounded the carved mahogany arm of the settee. "The woman's a cretin! And from the looks of her, it's no wonder we're short of food, she's eating all of it herself!"

Serena was about to reply when Liberty and Mark bounded into the room. "Is it true I got another uncle?" Liberty asked wide-eyed as he tugged at Serena's skirts. "Is he dying or can he play?"

"He's doing neither at the moment." Serena couldn't help but smile now. Liberty's ever-expanding world of relatives seemed to thrill as much as confuse him. He was like a small but avid collector, acquiring a father, a stepmother, a half-brother, and an ever-growing circle of family members.

At two and a half, Mark was not as impressed. Instead, he appeared more frightened and had buried his head in Cecelia's lap. Seldom maternal unless for effect, Cecelia surprised Serena—and possibly Mark—by pulling him up into her arms. "When Uncle Matt is well, we'll all go on a picnic." She hugged the child close, gazing over his blond head at Serena. "We used to have the most wonderful picnics at the shore, didn't we, Rena?" The husky voice was wistful with remembrance.

Finding herself unable to speak, Serena nodded. Her sister was right—the Farrar family picnics hadn't been just a frolic by the sea, but an event staged by Marcus. Lobster, crab, scallops, shrimp, French champagne, blackberries, strawberries, huckleberries, bread and biscuits and Danish cheese, with Lydia overseeing the elaborate fare with only slightly less elegance than she would have expended on a formal dinner party in the house on Pleasant Street. And now Serena Parnell and Cecelia Moncrief were living on cornbread and salt pork and beans in New Bern.

Serena hugged Liberty and went to get her cape.

The logical place for Serena to go was the newspaper office. The next edition was due out in two days and as usual, there was much to be done, including an article on the defense of St. Louis. But Serena found herself going in the opposite direction from Craven Street and acknowledged that she didn't want to see Kirk. Not just now, with her mind in such a turmoil over Matt—and Brant.

There was, of course, nothing she could do about Matt except pray. Brant was another matter, however. Unless he sailed *The Irish Rover* immediately out of New Bern, she would have to confront him. But the ship had weathered severe storms and it was probable that Brant and his crew would be in port for some time.

Serena slowed her pace as she passed one of the city's finer homes, now sheltering Union soldiers. Several were outdoors, daring the wintry weather to hang out their Monday morning wash. Across Middle Street, Serena noted the Presbyterian Church where the Reverend Horace James delivered his uplifting sermons. She admired James not so much for his oratory, however, as for the help he was giving the freedmen in the Trent River colony.

He was worthy of a story in the *Leader*, Serena mused as she turned off onto King Street. The wind had picked up, making Serena shiver. It was unusually cold, with ominous gray clouds hanging low over the Neuse River. Perhaps, she thought, burrowing her bare hands inside her cape and cursing herself for forgetting her gloves, New Bern might be in for one of its rare snowfalls.

At the corner, where King met Front Street, Serena stopped. While there were still Union sentries posted within view, she had thoughtlessly ventured into a part of town where ladies usually did not go. Her aimless walk had taken her almost to the river's edge and the docks of New Bern.

"Damnation," she breathed at a little mongrel who seemed excited at having someone pay attention to him. "I don't know about you, but I'm going back the other way."

The dog scampered beside her, then began jumping up on her skirts. Serena waved a hand at him. "No, no, I only have two black dresses. Behave yourself."

But the eager little animal would not desist. Hungry, no doubt, thought Serena, and wished she had some scrap of food with her. She did not see the large retriever which raced up from behind, leaping so high his paws struck her shoulders. Serena would have fallen had she not been a scant six inches from a lamp post. She caught herself and swore one of her father's favorite oaths as the two dogs began to fight.

"Stop it!" she cried as the retriever mauled the mongrel. The smaller dog howled pitifully while the larger animal let out a deep growl. Serena whirled to search out the nearest sentry, but his back was turned and he was apparently accustomed to the quarreling dogs along the riverfront.

The mongrel's howls had diminished to a whimper; Serena snatched up a rock and hurled it at the retriever. It struck the dog in the flanks, but only caused him to pause momentarily in his vicious assault. Scrambling in the dirt, Serena found a splintered board, seized it firmly, and advanced on the animals. Before she could swing, the retriever reared back and leaped at Serena. She toppled onto the ground, the board flying out of her hand, the enraged dog snapping dangerously close to her throat. Serena screamed and shut her eyes as a sharp paw dug into one shoulder. A bullet whined through the air, instantly killing the dog, which collapsed at Serena's side.

Slowly, Serena pushed herself up on her elbows. The sentry stood about ten feet away, his pistol still smoking. But directly in front of her was Brant Parnell, his captain's hat pushed back on his forehead, one hand reaching out to help pull Serena to her feet.

"You do the damnedest things, Serena," he said, yanking her to an upright position. "What in hell are you doing down here inciting animals to riot?"

"I went for a walk!" Serena all but bellowed. "A long, restorative walk!" She grabbed at her cape and tried to straighten it. The net snood had fallen from her hair and the thick brown strands tumbled over her shoulders and into her eyes. With the back of her hand, she brushed the errant locks away. "Don't you ask me questions! You're nothing but a self-seeking son-of-a-bitch!"

The sentry actually gulped as he bent down to minister to the little mongrel. Serena and Brant both ignored the soldier who gathered the panting animal in his arms and moved away down Front Street.

"Oh, shut up, Serena!" Brant's blue eyes snapped, his square chin thrust out. "If we weren't out in the middle of the street, I'd swat your rear end until it looked like pork loin!"

Fists on hips, Serena glared furiously at her husband. "You rotten cad! Gone for over a year, and you dare talk to me like that! I marvel you dare talk to me at all, you shabby swine!"

That was sufficient to ignite Brant's temper past all reason. Wordlessly, he grabbed Serena around the waist and dumped her over his shoulder. Black skirts billowing in the brisk wind, cape flying like the sails of a storm-tossed ship, hair whipping about her stunned face, Serena felt herself being carried at a fierce pace along a short stretch of street, down a flight of rickety wooden stairs, and across uneven planks where she could glimpse the dark waters of the Neuse River. Seconds later they were aboard a ship and Serena heard someone call out: "Brant—what's happening?"

"Not much, Press," she heard him reply in a startlingly casual voice. "I just met up with my wife. We're going to have a little domestic discussion." Serena's hip bumped against the side of the hatch as Brant carried her below deck. She heard him kick open a cabin door and the next thing she knew, he had thrown her unceremoniously onto what she assumed was his bunk. Dazed and somewhat dizzy, Serena tried to sit up, but miscalculated and fell back upon the heavy comforter. From out of the corner of her eye, she could see Brant looming over her, his hands hanging deceptively at his sides.

Serena felt her heartbeat quicken. There could be only one reason why Brant had dragged her here onto his ship—to still her anger with the fury of his passion. Even as her cheeks grew flushed, Serena's lips parted, and she took in a short, sharp little breath. Perhaps it was time to admit her longing, to give voice to the desire which surged up from the depths of her body and soul. She was certain that Brant's yearning matched her own—yet, Serena wondered with a sudden stab of fear, did it? Why was the infernal man standing there with that strange, intense expression on his face?

He wasn't acting at all the way Serena wished he would and his sudden lack of ardor was highly unsettling. Meeting his gaze head on, Serena willed Brant to respond. He could right it all by making love to her, here, now, in the cozy confines of *The Irish Rover*'s bunk.

In that moment, Serena knew she had never wanted Kirk, she had only succumbed to his embrace because he reminded her of Brant. True, she might love Kirk in her way, but as a brother or a friend. It was Brant that she wanted to plunder her body and make the world spin round like a dervish.

But Serena didn't know how to tell him. The boat rocked gently as she inwardly cursed the warm, throbbing ache between her thighs and watched Brant's impassive face.

"Aren't you going to sit down?" she finally demanded in a high-pitched, arch voice.

Brant sighed, his broad shoulders slumping. "I don't think so, Rena. Not now." He saw the uncontrollable look of rejection which made her features fall. "Now pay attention," he urged in a calm voice. "I brought you here so we could talk. You and I have a lot of sorting out to do. And let's be honest, our last impassioned interlude didn't turn out too well." He saw her start to interrupt but went right on speaking. "Right now, the whole world seems out of control, even more than it usually does. I know you're upset about Matt—believe it or not, I am, too. Damned upset." He leaned closer so that she could almost feel as well as see the spark of outrage that kindled in the sea-blue eyes. "Over and over, I've said this war's a waste. Your brother is more proof of that than I ever wanted to see—but at least he's still alive. But it doesn't put me in the mood to sort out all our differences and feelings and whatever else we're both packing around with us like Silas Marner's albatross. Most of all," Brant asserted in a flat, quiet voice, "it doesn't make me want to romp around the *Rover* with you just now."

If Brant had figured he was playing a losing hand, he was right. Serena could translate his words in only one way: Not only didn't he love her, he didn't even find her desirable. The very notion that Brant could be so upset over Matt that he didn't want to make love to her was incredible. Serena would have found the physical closeness a great comfort.

Hastily, she stood up and glanced around the cabin, taking it in for the first time. It was sparsely furnished, the only concession to decor being a collection of exotic shells hanging on one wall. The bunk itself sported a worn but colorful red-and-white quilt. In deference to the gloomy day, two whale oil lanterns burned on opposite sides of the cabin.

"I'm going now," she announced, not looking at Brant.

But he had seen the pain in the pinched, foxlike features and once again touched her shoulder. "Goddamn, Rena," he sighed and shook his head with regret, "I'd hoped you might be more open-minded for once." Pulling her closer and forcing Serena to look up at him, he all but gritted his teeth in an effort to penetrate the closed doors of her mind. "Don't you realize I think you're the most enchanting—if pigheaded—creature who ever lived? That you've got more intriguing ways in your left thumb than a dozen other women have in their whole bodies? That I've already proved how great a hold you have over me just by being here?"

It took Serena less than two seconds to consider his heated words. "No," she snapped, then saw the craggy face sag. "Oh—hell! You get me so mixed up!" To the consternation of them both, she began to cry.

Brant gathered her into his arms, letting her sob soundlessly against his chest and wondering if maybe he shouldn't change his mind and make love to her after all. But while it might make them both fleetingly happy, once it was done with, they would still face the same confusion and uncertainties.

Serena managed to pull herself together rather quickly. "I'm all right," she announced in a muffled, shaky voice and eased away from Brant. But before she could move toward the hatch, he leaned down to kiss gently the hollow under one eye. Serena swayed, felt him hold her firmly in place, and gave his upper arm a little squeeze. "I'm so mixed up," she said again and wiped at her eyes with her hand.

"I know." Brant sounded resigned as he let her go. Serena tried to smile as she moved across the deck, but succeeded only in looking pathetically unsure. It was little comfort to realize that Brant appeared equally rudderless, like a ship heading for the shoals.

As she emerged on the upper deck, she glanced furtively around her. Several seamen were absorbed in their duties, though one paused to nod in her direction. Brant had called him Press, she thought, and nodded back with as much dignity as possible. Serena held her head high and walked briskly onto the dock.

Back at the newspaper office, she would reflect upon the unsettling scene with Brant. In her present mood, she could almost believe what he'd said about finding her attractive, but Serena believed in facts— and the only one she could grasp was that Brant hadn't wanted to make love to her. Serena began to walk faster, back to King Street, turning directly onto Craven Street, and hurrying past the ordnance yard. A snowflake flitted against her cheek as the footing grew slick. Slowing her pace to prevent a fall, Serena saw Kirk coming toward her from the opposite direction.

"Serena!" He waved, halting until she could join him on the corner.

The snow was falling in earnest now, obscuring her view of Kirk until she was almost in front of him. With a sudden fear, she noted the agonized look on his face.

He knew what she was thinking and shook his head, the raven's feathers in his officer's hat defying the snowflakes. "It's not Matt." He cleared his throat and took her arm, steering her back toward the doorway of a small cafe. "It's Peggy. The baby was born over a month early. She was able to reach Brant by telegraph while he was still in Washington."

Serena leaned against the doorway embrasure, slanted eyes staring up at Kirk. "Baby? What baby?" she whispered and knew she sounded extremely stupid.

Kirk's skin darkened. "Peggy conceived a child during my leave last summer." He was trying hard to speak in a brisk, impersonal way, but his voice broke. "I got a letter last November, I think, around Thanksgiving. She was fine then. I heard again from her at Christmas but she wasn't feeling quite so well. Still, it's like that, with women and babies, and . . ."

Kirk's words seemed to become lost in the sound of the wind and the swirl of the snow. His concealment of Peggy's pregnancy hurt her, especially since Kirk had always quoted freely from his wife's letters. "Well?" Serena demanded, not knowing or caring if she had interrupted Kirk. "How are they?"

"They were alive two weeks ago," he replied in a barely controlled voice. "That was when Brant sailed out of Hampton Roads."

Serena moved aside as two Union officers came out of the cafe and exchanged salutes with Kirk. "I suppose you'll be going back home." Serena lowered her gaze, seeing yet not seeing the snow begin to stick on the single wooden step of the cafe entrance.

"If I can." Kirk appeared half-angry, half-forlorn. Serena wondered if the boy were fighting with the man, and which would emerge as the real Kirk Parnell. "Brant won't be able to leave for at least ten days. He doubts if any other ships would sail north this time of year."

Serena nodded rather absently. She had a sudden, urgent need to escape from Kirk, to forget about Brant, to be with her own kind— Uncle Luke, Abigail, even her desperately ill brother and her mercurial, exasperating sister.

"Everyone has troubles, it seems," she said, aware that her bare hands were growing stiff from the cold. "I'm sorry about Peggy and the baby, of course." She looked up to meet Kirk's eyes and hoped she sounded sincere. "But now I must get back to Matt. I'll probably see you tomorrow." Without waiting for his response, she moved out of the doorway, walking as quickly as she dared through the white world of New Bern.

To Serena's great relief, Dr. Hooper's optimism had not been unfounded. That evening, Matt rallied, recognized Uncle Luke who was at his beside, and drifted off into a peaceful sleep. Only Aunt

Kathleen did not join in the prayers of thanksgiving offered by the family at supper. To everyone's amazement, she announced that she would remain in her bedroom until the Yankees left New Bern.

How far off that day might be, no one could be sure, though Aunt Kathleen's heroic—if muleheaded—gesture indicated her personal surrender. Strange, Serena thought as she prepared for bed, how people could delude themselves about even the most obvious matters. She was shaking her head and adjusting the chintz curtains at the window when the moonlight caught the gold of her wedding ring. Had Brant spoken the truth? Serena still couldn't guess. It seemed to her that both Brant and Kirk Parnell had brought her nothing but empty promises. Serena climbed into bed and thought about Matt. For the first time in months, she remembered to say her prayers.

The following day, Serena visited her brother, making her way through the slush which was all that remained from the previous day's snowfall. Matt was lucid, but very weak. He managed a smile when he saw Serena.

"Damn, Rena," he said in a low, rasping voice, "where are we?"

"New Bern. In North Carolina." She tried to adjust the pillow behind his head. "Uncle Luke owns this house. Cecelia used to live here with Fitch and their son."

Matt frowned. "You sure? Aren't we in Brunswick?"

"No. Your ship ran into a storm. My . . . the captain had to turn south." Serena smiled feebly, eyes intent on Matt's ravaged face. She was still terrified at the idea of seeing the useless stump.

Matt sighed, then coughed, a deep, racking sound that alarmed Serena. "Maybe it's better I'm here." He gave Serena an ironic look. "What's Pa going to say when he sees me like this?"

"He'll be so glad you're alive, he'll pay all his workers a bonus," Serena said heatedly.

But Matt remained unconvinced. After a few minutes of uneasy, yet loving silence, Serena left him to drift back to sleep. She understood Matt's concern, knowing how their father might react to his son and heir's handicap. Marcus despised imperfection; he wanted his world to be splendid and unflawed. Unless, as with the rustic cabin in the Maine woods, his whims carried him into the realm of perverse whimsy.

Yet, Serena thought, climbing into the trap where Young Calvin awaited her in the driver's seat, the world had caught up with Marcus Farrar. No matter how much he had scoffed at the war or turned it to his own profit, even Marcus could not escape the consequences of a nation set upon bleeding itself to death.

As the horse's hooves clip-clopped through the slushy streets,

Serena's mind turned to Kirk. Having admitted to herself that she didn't want to give him her body, Serena was puzzled over the nagging sense of aggrievement she felt. It was only natural that Kirk would make love to his wife while he was at home in New Bedford. But Kirk's secrecy somehow smacked of betrayal. It was as if he were living in two separate worlds—one in which he was a respectable married man, the head of a large family, and an officer engaged in defending his country. It was a world in which Serena played no part, except to be hazily recalled by its inhabitants as the young lady from the newspaper who had married Kirk's brother and left town.

In the other world, Kirk was on his own, publishing a newspaper for a sometimes hostile readership, wearing his uniform as a reminder of the authority it gave him, and falling in love with a woman he could only have in the most illicit of relationships.

As the trap drew up in front of the *Leader*'s office where Emaline was vigorously sweeping the slush off the sidewalk, Serena realized that Kirk was indeed half-man, half-boy, unable to commit himself wholly to either of his worlds. Or, perhaps, she realized with sudden insight, he had never really left his cozy home in New Bedford; Serena was only a passing fancy.

It might not be a fair assessment, but it armed Serena well. Giving Emaline a vague wave, Serena pushed open the newspaper office door and prepared to greet Kirk.

But only Herman was in the office, fumbling with some sheets of copy. "I'm missing a story," he said, one hand rubbing at his temple in anxiety. "Major Parnell went to see his brother and he told me to make sure I set the article about General Grant's new command. But," he went on, looking stricken, "it's nowhere to be seen."

Serena hung up her cape and came over to Kirk's desk. A quick rifling through papers told her the Grant story was not there. She checked her own desk, then asked Herman if he was absolutely sure it wasn't already in the backshop. Herman had been known to lose things, yet they invariably turned up, often right under his nose. But Caldwell, who strolled in with Bill and Phil, asserted that Kirk's article had never showed up in the backshop.

Serena stood thoughtfully in the middle of the office, tapping her chin with one finger. "Hmmm. He wouldn't have taken it with him by mistake." No doubt Brant and Kirk were aboard *The Irish Rover*, gulping whiskey and figuring out how Kirk could get home to his wife and baby.

Emaline breezed in the door, waving her broom at the others. "It's colder than a penguin's leg out there! Why, last night my hoops froze to my petticoats!"

A vaguely coarse remark flitted through Serena's mind, but she retained her dignity and kept silent. Then she remembered that some-times Kirk locked up one of the drawers overnight, particularly if they had received privileged dispatches on military plans that were not for publication until the orders had officially been given.

Sure enough, the story on General Grant was lying atop the other papers. She produced it for Herman, who looked immensely relieved and loped off to the backshop, with Caldwell and Bill and Phil following close behind.

"Poor Major Publisher!" exclaimed Emaline when the menfolk had left. She edged closer to Serena, looking extremely confidential. "He told me yesterday about his dear wife and the tiny baby. I was so moved. Why, the dear man was almost in tears!"

"That's a shame," remarked Serena and hoped she didn't sound as grudging as she felt. She bit her lip and decided to think not of Kirk or Brant, but of her story about the provost marshal's stringent punishment of deserters. It was hardly a pleasant subject, since he had ordered their execution no matter what the excuse, but at least it temporarily kept her mind off the men in her confusing, unsettled life.

Chapter 21

BY THE TIME Kirk returned from the harbor, Serena was immersed in wrapping up her interview with the provost marshal. The sole allusion to personal matters was Kirk's fleeting comment that Brant was investigating ship movement to find out if there were any captains who would risk sailing North while the weather remained so unstable.

That was the only word concerning Brant which Serena heard until the following Saturday, when he appeared at the Farrar townhouse to visit Uncle Luke. Indeed, Serena was unaware of his presence until Cecelia glided into her sister's bedroom, wearing a black dressing gown with an early white camellia in her hair.

"Whatever are Brant and Uncle Luke talking about in the study?" Cecelia asked, glancing at her image in the mirror.

Serena darted a surprised, puzzled look at her sister. "I've no idea," she replied, waiting for the inevitable prying questions from Cecelia about Brant.

Cecelia, however, seemed indifferent to her own inquiry. She opened a jar of Serena's face cream and patted a dab on one cheek. "I used to dislike having olive skin," she said. "But I'm beginning to think it's quite alluring."

"You put everything but house paint on your face over the years," Serena remarked dryly, and waited for Cecelia's sharp retort.

But Cecelia was scrutinizing the symmetry of her eyebrows. "I used lard once," she said good-naturedly. "Matt's going to get up today."

"I know, Abby told me." Serena had visited Matt the previous evening, finding him much stronger, though still dispirited. She fervently wished there was some way to make her brother realize that the loss of his leg didn't condemn him to a futile existence.

Cecelia moved away from the mirror. "Someone—Leonard, I think—saw Harold Saile in Dobbs County, married to a woman who'd been widowed by the war." She flung her long dark hair over her shoulders. "The poor thing must have been desperate for a man."

"You don't seem to be," Serena commented, realizing with some surprise that her sister's conduct since Fitch's death had been above reproach.

"I?" Again Cecelia seemed unruffled by her sister's gibes. "All in

290

good time." The black eyes slid away from Serena to rest on a jack-in-the-box Liberty had left in the bedroom. "Mark and Liberty leave their toys all over the house. I all but fell over one of Mark's warhorses this morning." She darted a long finger almost under Serena's nose. "You're the literary one, Rena—tell me, why are future husbands always referred to as 'white knights'?"

The unlikely query made Serena's slanted brows rise. "Purity of intentions, I suppose. Not that I'd know much about that," she added with asperity.

"Now, now," rebuked Cecelia, sounding uncomfortably like Abigail, "all men aren't alike. Thank God." She fastened the camellia more securely in her hair and announced that she must get dressed. "Ugh, I'm sick of black," she asserted, gazing down at her dressing gown. "If Matt had died, I would never have forgiven him."

That, at least, sounded more like Cecelia. Serena couldn't repress a smile as her sister closed the door behind her. But the smile faded as she contemplated the proximity of Brant Parnell. She had no desire to confront either Parnell brother in her present mood.

Moving to the dresser, Serena replaced the cover on the face cream jar Cecelia had left open. In the mirror, Serena's image gazed back with empty eyes. How different the face was from the one which had so eagerly, if naively, stared out from above her dressing table on Pleasant Street. But that was before she met Brant Parnell.

When Brant left the house without calling on Serena, she told herself she was relieved. And then reluctantly acknowledged that she was disturbed as well. She yearned for him, yet feared to face him. It would, she told herself, be much better if Brant stayed away permanently.

Uncle Luke, however, was grateful for Brant's presence. Two days later at Wexford, he explained to Serena that her husband had expressed concern about the Farrar properties. Serena listened with curiosity, wondering if Uncle Luke was too discreet to inquire as to why Brant didn't seem to exhibit the same concern for his wife.

"Your papa is a mite bit nervous that my part of the family holdings could be lost." Uncle Luke paused to shake his head at Roscoe, who was showing off one of the few stud horses left at Wexford. "That's Rooney, Roscoe. He's about twenty years old. I don't think he'd know a mare from a calliope." Uncle Luke turned to Serena as Roscoe led the aged stallion away. "As I was saying, Marcus has visions of Northern speculators or even the freedmen swooping down on the land after the war and gobbling up the losing side's acreage." He tapped his pipe against the barn door. It was a mild February day and the sandy gray earth smelled fresh. "You know your papa," Uncle Luke went on with a touch of irony, 'he never leaves much to chance."

"How well I know that," Serena remarked with bite as Roscoe came forward once more, this time with a dispirited-looking gray.

"That one has spells," called Uncle Luke. "Fits, too, as I recall. Where's Lord Fielding?"

"He done died." Roscoe's big brown eyes offered Uncle Luke sympathy. "The soldiers come and took all the rest, 'cept for Silver Dust."

"Silver Dust is almost as old as Rooney." Uncle Luke scraped at the bowl of his pipe with a tiny tool and sighed. "All right, take Silver Dust out to pasture with the mares. He'll probably go to sleep before the first one nuzzles him." As he turned away from the barn, Uncle Luke's face puckered. "Brant tells me that if we deed the plantation over to him or to Marcus, it'll be safely registered with Yankee owners. If Aunt Kathleen heard that, she'd have a stroke."

Serena gave her uncle a sidelong glance, thinking that for once she had to agree with Aunt Kathleen. "What is Leonard's opinion of all this?" she asked.

There was no chance to find out. From the direction of the barn came Roscoe, legs pumping; around the curve in the dusty road cantered a lone horse and rider. Serena could tell from the set of the broad shoulders and the rakish angle of the brimmed hat that it was Brant.

"Silver Dust be sick, Mister Luke," panted Roscoe. "You come?"

"Certainly, certainly," sighed Uncle Luke, hailing Brant with a wave. Asking Serena to have Brant wait in the plantation office, Uncle Luke headed off with Roscoe.

The horse Brant rode was coal-black and sleek, a far cry from the pitiful nags in Uncle Luke's stable. Brant dismounted, tied the animal to the hitching post, and walked swiftly to where Serena was standing motionless by the buggy.

"I see I have my usual devastating effect on your relatives," Brant remarked by way of greeting. If he had intended to be amusing, the effort was lost on Serena.

"Uncle Luke has a sick horse." Serena flipped the black veil on her riding hat off her forehead and tried to keep her gaze level. Brant had exchanged his sea captain's garb for a well-cut if plain black frock coat and trousers, with a black vest and white shirt. He was very tan, the craggy features seemed harder than ever, and, if possible, the blue eyes more wary. But though he tried to maintain his easygoing air of authority and confidence, Serena detected a new tension in his attitude.

"Your uncle is lucky he has any horses left at all," Brant said, casting a glance toward the barn. "He'll be even luckier to have a roof over his head when this war is over, unless we take some precautions."

" 'We'?" The word sliced through the air like a sabre.

The blue eyes snapped at Serena. "Luke Farrar's one hell of a man, Serena, but he's got all the practical sense of a beet. He's damned lucky to have a brother with enough money and influence to secure the future for him here in New Bern."

"To secure the future for whom? Uncle Luke or Papa? Or," she demanded archly, "you?"

The muscle's along Brant's jawline tightened. "Your father has a commercial interest in Wexford, of course," Brant replied, forcing his voice to stay calm. "But he's even more concerned about what happens to Luke and his family. It would appear that one-half of the twins is at least half-baked, and, at best, the other is still a boy. Aunt Kathleen, I gather, is playing with a short suit these days, and for reasons known only to herself, Cecelia has a sudden lack of interest in returning to Brunswick."

"She has?" Serena's curiosity momentarily overcame her indignation at the high-handed manner exhibited by both her husband and her father. "How would you know?"

"Uncle Luke says so." Brant paused as his horse whinnied at a pesky dragonfly. "As for Matt, you can see what kind of problems his sorry situation will create, if only because he'll let it."

"You're forgetting Abigail and Yancy," said Serena in a tone which implied she'd scored a point over Brant.

Brant stared at her for a jarring second. It occurred to him that it was useless to be candid or reasonable with Serena. To Brant, it seemed that she was utterly incapable of seeing things any way but her own. "Oh, no," he replied, his voice dropping several notches. "I could never forget Abigail and Yancy. If it hadn't been for those two ill-mated free spirits, I'd have had time to get my brains out of my pants and think twice about marrying you."

"Oh!" Serena's hand flew to her mouth and the tall riding hat swayed precariously. "You're hateful! And mean!"

There would be neither an explanation nor a riposte from Brant, however, as Uncle Luke had emerged from the barn. "Good morning," he called to Brant. "I'm afraid old Silver Dust is about to bite the dust, if you'll excuse the expression." He took Brant's hand and smiled at Serena. "I thought you'd be having a hot toddy in the plantation office by now."

Brant answered for Serena: "We were just taking the air," he said, rocking slightly on the balls of his feet and clasping his hands behind his back. "If there's one thing Serena and I have enjoyed since we've been married, it's a lot of air."

Uncle Luke raised one eyebrow. "Oh? That so?" He didn't seem to notice that Serena was glaring at Brant. "I like it myself—when it's clear." There was the merest hint of reproach in his voice.

Brant stopped rocking while Serena ceased glaring. Uncle Luke invited them both into the plantation office. Serena went with reluctance, but the visit was short. Brant explained that he had come to the townhouse to tell Serena that Kirk would be leaving the next day aboard a British ship bound for Boston. Upon learning she had gone to Wexford with her uncle, Brant had made the short ride to meet them there.

"His duty is at home," asserted Uncle Luke, who had had to withdraw his offer of hot toddies because there was no fire in the grate. "Why don't you have him join us for supper this evening?"

"I'll ask." Brant stood up, his hat in one hand. "I'd better head back. I want Kirk to take a letter North to your brother."

"Of course, I'll write one myself." Uncle Luke suddenly looked wistful. "It's been a long time since I've seen Marcus. And the lovely Lydia." He took a deep breath. "Well. Someday, perhaps."

Brant rested a hand on Uncle Luke's shoulder. "Someday." He smiled with at least a show of confidence. "We'll all go home someday."

Serena watched the two men and wondered why she felt so empty.

It was probably the way it should have been, Serena thought as she moved restlessly in the canopied bed. Supper had been a more relaxed, pleasant meal than she had hoped, with Cecelia vivacious, Abigail charming, Uncle Luke philosophical, Yancy droll, and the Parnell brothers the most faultless of guests. Matt had joined them, a haggard, quiet presence who seemed to relax a bit as the evening spun out. Serena had been encouraged by the improvement. At least Matt had enough will to make an effort at sociability.

For her own part, Serena had remained quiet, if polite. She and Kirk had spent a busy afternoon in the office, going over all the projects she would have to assume during his absence.

But while Kirk had talked of his trip home in terms of another visit, Serena was certain he would never come back to New Bern. She was grateful that there had been no chance to speak with him alone. The farewells with the others were trying enough, particularly Emaline's, who was profuse with sentiment and tinged with tears.

After supper, Brant and Kirk left together. Kirk had expressed his appreciation for Uncle Luke's generous hospitality over the years and only a slight pause evoked the image of Aunt Kathleen's rude chauvinism.

When Kirk took Serena's hand, the hazel eyes seemed to look beyond her. He thanked her for the pleasant hours they had spent on the newspaper and for being so kind. She wished him good luck, said good-bye, and then he was gone. The scene had been played out with a sense of unreality, as if taking place behind the gauzy chintz curtains which fluttered in the night breeze at Serena's window.

Did I really love him? Serena stared up into the dark vault of the canopy. Yes, if love was comfort and desire and laughter and pain. Yet Serena didn't feel wounded, so much as hollow. Kirk had confused her, but he hadn't hurt her.

Serena admitted that she had not gotten off so lightly with his brother.

It would be just another day at the *Leader*, Serena had decided. After all, she had put the newspaper out by herself before. It might even be possible to find another publisher. Certainly Kirk Parnell wasn't the only competent newspaperman who'd joined the Union army. Idly, she glanced up at the old clock which Herman had recently hung on the wall. From a home abandoned by its owners, he said. It was precisely nine o'clock. Kirk had been scheduled to sail at eight-thirty. He was probably well on his way down the Neuse River headed toward Pamlico Sound.

"Off to a busy start, I see," said Emaline from the doorway, making Serena jump. "But won't it be dull around here without Major Publisher Parnell?"

"It's been dull before," Serena answered noncommittally. "Where's Herman? He hasn't come in yet."

Emaline took off her hat and examined the frayed grosgrain ribbons around the crown. "He's taking his monthly bath. I make sure he does, whether he needs it or not." She burst into high-pitched laughter while Serena forced a smile.

Both the laughter and the smile died abruptly as Brant Parnell burst into the office, the chiseled features frighteningly grim. He covered the space between the door and Serena's desk in just six long, quick strides.

"Kirk's dead." His mouth clamped shut, his eyes riveted on Serena's thunderstruck face.

"My God!" Serena had remained seated, clinging to the edge of the desk as if she feared falling out of the chair. "Oh, God," she said again, in a small, shattered voice. "How?" The single word seemed to cost her dearly.

Brant started to pull up a chair, apparently thought better of it, and began pacing the width of the room. "Some rotten, cowardly bastard shot him as he was boarding the ship." He stopped for a moment, his hand to his head. Angrily, he snatched off his wide-brimmed hat as if cursing a world that demanded good manners but devalued human life. "A sniper, it seems," he said, coming back to Serena whose mouth was still agape with shock. "The sentries couldn't find whoever it was, though I swear if I ever do, I'll kill him with my bare hands!"

As if to prove his point, Brant thrust clenching hands at Serena in a vivid gesture of blood lust. She shrank back, but tried desperately to say something which would soothe him. The words seemed to suffocate in her throat, while Emaline clutched at the bookcase, her face dead white. The old clock ticked loudly in the silence until Emaline emitted a shuddering howl and fled the office, leaving the door open behind her.

Serena's eyes darted after the other woman but Brant hadn't seemed to notice. His hands finally fell to his sides. He kept the ice-blue eyes on Serena. "Do you know who it was?" The question was raspingly harsh.

"I?" Serena put her head in her hands, elbows on the desk. She could no longer bear Brant's chilling, anguished gaze. "No, no, no." The rifle shots fired at Serena and Kirk had happened so long ago she couldn't even remember when except that it was Christmastime. Her brain was too numb to recall how many Christmases she'd spent in New Bern. Sometimes it seemed as if she'd been there forever, doomed to live out her life in this alien city, surrounded by strangers.

At last she looked up, but avoided Brant's eyes. "Someone who resented our opinions, our sentiments about the Negroes, I suppose. We've had letters, the backshop was set afire, there were other incidents . . . Still, it's been so long. I don't think we . . . took them seriously."

Brant retrieved his hat from where he'd flung it on the floor. "Incredible," he breathed, with a sharp shake of his head. "Only you and Kirk could have been so damned naive."

"Brave, I call it," Serena retorted, realizing that she had started to cry. "Kirk died for the Union just as if he'd been in battle."

"Damn it, Rena!" Brant glowered at Serena, the heavy dark brows quivering. "Why do fools like you think dying for a cause is so admirable?"

With Kirk dead and Matt maimed Serena had no reply. Clumsily, she wiped at her tears as a draft banged the front door shut. "Maybe I could answer if I knew what was worth living for." She leaned forward on the desk, her body limp, her tear-filled eyes vacant, dull.

Brant started to speak, slapped his hat against his thigh, turned on his heel, and left the *Leader*'s office.

Serena was hardly aware of his departure. She seemed to be shrouded in a thick fog, as if cut off from the world as she had been the night New Bern was invaded. But Brant had rescued her then and taken her to Kirk. Now Kirk was dead and Brant was gone. Serena felt the fog close in and put her head down on the desk. It was Herman who found her there a half-hour later and took her home to Uncle Luke.

Brant Parnell had not been so drunk since he was seventeen and on his first voyage to Europe. In his youthful inexperience, he had not intended to drink himself insensate. At thirty-two, he had downed the Irish whiskey with a fierce determination to obliterate the world.

Brant had started drinking just fifteen minutes after the British merchant ship carrying his brother's body sailed down the Neuse River to meet the evening tide. Five hours later, he realized that there wasn't enough whiskey in North Carolina to assuage his sense of loss. He needed a woman. In years gone by, he would have sought out the most expensive whore in whichever port he was visiting. While New Bern had its share of brothels, it occurred to Brant that he had no need to patronize any of them. After all, he had a wife who lived within walking distance of the dockside tavern.

He also had a pass which got him by the sentries. If they noted he was somewhat uncertain of his footing, they made no comment. Brant Parnell did not look like the sort of man to challenge on that moonless, silent spring night.

Brant had no idea what time it was though he knew it was very late since the Farrar townhouse was in total darkness. It took him several minutes to figure out which room was Serena's. His first efforts to strike her window with pebbles failed. But at last, on the fifth attempt, he heard the pane rattle and in a few moments, Serena warily looked down into the garden.

"Let me in," Brant whispered up at her. "I need to see you." The fresh air had cleared the slur from his speech.

Serena hesitated. She could hardly refuse to see Brant when he had suffered the loss of his only brother earlier that day. Perhaps talking to Brant would ease her own pain. Without bothering to put on her slippers, she threw a cotton wrapper over her shoulders and went downstairs to let Brant in.

She could smell the whiskey as soon as she opened the door. That didn't surprise her, however, and she stepped aside as Brant entered the hallway. He headed straight for the stairs but Serena called out in a low voice: "Everyone's asleep. We can talk in the sitting room."

With the candle she was carrying, she gestured to the door directly behind her.

Brant retraced his footsteps. Only the slightest waver betrayed his intoxicated state. "I don't want to talk," he muttered, standing in front of Serena.

"Do you want coffee?" she asked, beginning to realize the extent of her husband's drunkenness.

"No." Brant put a hand on her shoulder. "I want you."

Serena's chin shot up. "Nonsense!" she exclaimed, then lowered her voice. "Why don't you come into the sitting room? You can sleep on the settee." She carefully extricated herself from his grasp, shielded the candle with her hand, and led the way through the double doors. "I can get you a blanket and a pillow," she said, pointing to the settee. "We're short of rooms upstairs with Matt here and Jason back."

"What's wrong with your room?" The blue eyes sharpened into focus as Brant stared down at Serena.

Serena took a deep breath. "Very well. Then I'll sleep on the settee."

Brant waved his big hand over the candle, plunging the room into darkness. "For once, I'm not going to let you be obtuse."

It occurred to Serena that for a man so steeped in drink, he seemed to be in disturbing command of his faculties. Tentatively she backed toward the settee, trying to feel its outline with her leg. When Brant grabbed her around the waist, she was so startled she dropped the candle, let out a little shriek, and sprawled backward onto the settee.

He put a hand behind her head, clutching at the thick hair. "You may not love me, but you love what I can do to you," Brant said into her ear. "You wanted me on the *Rover*, now I want you."

The cotton wrapper had already slipped onto the carpet. It took only one wrenching tear of the nightgown to bare Serena's body. She put one hand over her bosom and the other against her thighs. Yet the room was so dark that she could see only Brant's outline.

But she could feel his fingers digging into her upper arms, pinning her against the rigid back of the settee. Serena wanted to scream but didn't dare rouse the others. Brant *was* her husband. And she was stark naked, with Brant kissing her neck and the hollow between her breasts.

Serena's primary response was confusion: Brant didn't love her, he was merely using her, as he would use any trollop to vent his drunken grief. Even if he did love her, this was hardly the time to seek pleasure in each other's bodies. Serena wanted kindly words, a comforting arm around her shoulders, a tender hand to wipe away the tears.

"I realize you're upset," she began, but her words were obliterated by a smothering kiss. He knelt before Serena, his mouth holding hers captive, while his hands lifted her so he could knead her buttocks. Then his hands moved to her breasts, caressing and molding them with a savage intensity which swept away Serena's hesitation and made her shudder with an unexpected yearning that took her breath away.

Instinct, rather than recognition, told Brant that he no longer needed to silence Serena with his kiss. His lips traveled purposefully to the fullness of her breasts, goading the eager pink tips to aching tautness. With a soft moan, Serena tried to wriggle off the settee. She wanted to feel Brant pressed against her, to be sheltered by his hard, virile strength, to savor the tenderness of his embrace. But his grasp was tight, even fierce, pushing her back onto the settee, exposing the most vulnerable secret part of her to his suddenly focussed, probing gaze.

He clutched at her hips while his mouth began a searing, sensuous journey down the length of her trembling body, edging ever closer to the core of her desire. "Brant, no . . . no," she gasped, in confusion and denial. But he didn't stop. In that intimate invasion of her flesh, the ferocity of his lips set Serena afire, obliterating shame and grief and resistance.

At last he released her to undo his trousers. Clumsily, Serena struggled into a sitting position, breathing with difficulty and shoving the heavy hair away from her face.

Before she could move off the settee, Brant silently raised himself up to plunge into the core of her being again and again, as his hands clutched at her breasts. Her reluctance and confusion ebbed away; Serena knew only the urgent need for completion. It came in a blinding, searing crescendo of light, as if the room had been illuminated by a dazzling comet.

By the time Serena was able to speak, Brant was completely clothed and standing a few feet from the settee. "If it saves your foolish pride," he said in a low, tightly controlled voice, "you can pretend this never happened. I think it would be best for both of us if we considered it merely a drunken dream."

From somewhere in the bewildered maze of her mind, Serena tried to protest. For once, Brant didn't need to apologize; he had healed her spirit, at least for now, and all she wanted was to be cradled in his arms and feel his rough cheek against hers.

She started to speak, but he was already heading for the double doors. Drunk or not, Brant seemed to have no trouble finding his way out, and a few seconds later, she heard the front door click shut. If the day had been a nightmare, had the last few minutes been a dream? Serena put a hand to her head, which was suddenly throbbing. Had Brant truly believed that she wouldn't want to remember this night? As harsh and tempestuous as he had been, he had still sought her out as the source of his comfort—and given her the opiate of his body in return.

Yet it seemed that his loveless possession had meant nothing to him except the expiation of his own sorrow. Serena staggered slightly as she stood up, then bent to search for her nightclothes. Securing the wrapper around her body, she carried the torn nightgown over one arm. As she moved across the sitting room, she felt the damp remnants of Brant and fervently wished that he were still with her instead of pouring out his lonely, drunken rage into the empty night.

Shortly before nine o'clock, Brant awoke to a violent pounding in his ears and a racking headache. It took him a full minute to realize the someone was knocking outside his cabin aboard *The Irish Rover*.

He had collapsed fully clothed on his bunk in the small hours of the morning. Struggling to his feet, Brant swore at the incessant pounding and walked unsteadily to the door. The ferocious scowl with which he greeted his visitor would have cowed a lesser man than John A. Winslow, U.S. navy captain and honored veteran of the war with Mexico.

"Captain Parnell." Winslow bowed, a gesture more Confederate than Yankee. But Winslow was a native of North Carolina who had put his country before his state.

Those fleeting facts tugged at Brant's unwilling memory as he stared with curiosity. His visitor was balding, of middle age, squinting with one eye as if he were unable to see without his telescope. The naval uniform was sharply pressed but strained over a considerable paunch, while a scraggly gray beard did little to hide a weak jaw. Yet Brant discerned dignity and intelligence beneath the unprepossessing facade. Unfortunately, he was in no mood to appreciate either quality.

"Sir," Winslow said, shifting from one foot to the other under Brant's bleary-eyed scrutiny, "may I come in?"

Brant sighed. "If you like. Just leave the little pink men outside. I'm feeling a bit rocky this morning." He moved slowly to a pitcher and basin which stood on a shelf next to the bunk. Splashing his face with water, Brant wondered if Press Prescott had any beer in his cabin. "I'm thirsty," Brant announced, then toweled off his face and stared as his guest came into focus. "Damn," Brant breathed, "I'm sorry, Captain Winslow." He put a hand on the other man's shoulder. "My brother was killed yesterday, right here in the harbor."

Winslow nodded gravely. "I know. My condolences, sir. It was most tragic."

"It was worse than that, it was a coward's act." Brant's rage was starting to return. He motioned to a chair. "I drank myself about an ounce short of suicide last night. I almost wished I'd taken that last gulp."

Winslow sat down, carefully adjusting the crease in his trousers. "Not a wise plan. Losing one Parnell is sad enough."

Brant went to the door and called for a cabin boy to bring coffee. "It's the waste," he said, dropping onto the bunk and rubbing at the stubble along his jaw. "This whole damned war's a waste."

Winslow was thoughtful. "That depends, sir, on your view of human progress. Sometimes it appears we have to sacrifice a great deal—even sanity—to change our world."

"The world never changes," Brant scoffed. "Oh, it shifts about and ideas differ, but it's still the same rotten, ugly place it was when so-called civilization first sprang out of the Tigres and Euphrates."

A cabin boy appeared with a coffeepot and two mugs, eyed his captain with alarm, and scampered away. Brant poured the coffee and handed a mug to Winslow.

"I gather you and Major Parnell disagreed over the war," Winslow said, calmly blowing into his mug.

"Only on taking part," Brant replied, wishing his head would stop throbbing. "I've no quarrel with the Union's stand, just with getting myself killed to defend it."

Winslow's good eye gazed questioningly at Brant. "Oh? But you'd use your wits to help the Union win. Or so Gideon Welles told me."

"Welles?" At the mention of the Secretary of the Navy's name, Brant straightened slightly.

"Yes, I saw him last week in Washington. He was most impressed, sir, by your innovative ideas concerning warfare on the Mississippi. It occurred to me you might have some equally creative notions regarding another vexing problem at sea."

"Such as what?" Brant wondered if he really wanted to know, but didn't have the energy to fend off his guest.

Resting the mug on his paunch, Winslow settled into the chair. "You know of the Confederate commerce raiders, of course." He saw Brant nod and continued. "As a seaman, I'm sure your own insurance rates have become almost prohibitive—though I'm told your backers are more fortunate than most in having a great deal of wealth."

The familiar wry look stole over Brant's face. "I have a rich father-in-law, yes."

Winslow looked apologetic. "I beg your pardon, sir, I meant no indiscreet references. However, only the most affluent shippers and captains have been able to keep their vessels under American registry since the commerce raiders began wreaking havoc. I daresay, if this were a war fought only at sea, the Union might find itself hard-pressed."

"Not militarily," Brant countered, pouring more coffee. "The Confederate navy is a joke."

"Perhaps. But its raiding ships are not. There is no sea lane, no foreign port in the entire world where our merchant ships are safe." Winslow paused, the good eye fixed on Brant's face with a mesmerizing stare. "I give you one word, sir—*Alabama.*"

A spark of life appeared in Brant's blue eyes. "Ah, the elusive, destructive Raphael Semmes. Didn't you serve with him in the Mexican War?"

"That I did, and respect him for his daring. If I were a wiser man, I'd fear him as well." Winslow fingered his scraggly beard. "Maybe I do, which is why I'm here. Will you sail to Europe with me on the *Kearsarge?*"

Brant uttered a hollow laugh. "I spent the better part of last summer eluding commerce raiders such as Semmes and his *Alabama.* I don't go looking for trouble I can avoid."

Winslow gazed into his coffee mug, ruminating. "Sinking the *Alabama* would mean a great deal to American seamen. Or have you forgotten the capture and destruction of eight Yankee whaling vessels in the Azores?"

In his whiskey-induced mental paralysis, Brant had indeed forgotten. But at the time he'd heard the news, he'd vowed to throttle the wretched Semmes if he ever had the chance. The whaling trade was dying on its own; men such as Semmes were attempting to deal the fatal blow. Born into a whaling dynasty, Brant had taken the destruction as a personal affront.

"I swore I'd kill the bastard," Brant recalled, shaking his head which seemed to be throbbing just a trifle less painfully. Abruptly, he leaned forward on the bunk. The words he had just uttered jarred him. Only the previous day he had made a similar vow, to avenge himself on his brother's murderer. But the man who had fired the shot which killed Kirk might never be found. And Brant was in a mood for vengeance. "When do you sail?"

Winslow took a deep breath, as if to control his exultation. "No later than the end of February. But the *Kearsarge* is at Hampton Roads."

"This ship is almost ready," Brant said, more to himself than to Winslow, as he gazed around the cabin. "My crew could take her back to New Bedford." He turned to Winslow once more. "All right. How soon do we leave New Bern?"

Winslow set his mug on the deck. "A day, maybe two. Will that give you enough time to complete your business here, sir?"

Brant nodded. "I think so." Whatever else needed to be done about

Wexford could be handled by Leonard; Press would see to *The Irish Rover*.

Winslow stood up. "I'm most grateful, sir." He put out a hand as Brant got to his feet. "I was afraid you might refuse me, despite Secretary Welles's insistence that your shrewd and agile mind would be at our disposal."

"Not the word I'd have chosen," Brant replied with a wry smile. "My mind isn't for disposal, but it is for hire. However, we'll worry about those little niceties later." For once, he was serious. Sinking the *Alabama* would almost be sufficient recompense—for Kirk, for all Yankee sea captains, for himself.

Winslow paused at the cabin door. "We're not sure where Semmes is at present. But we'll find him." The one good eye was unblinking. "I hope you're not in a great rush to come back?"

Brant's gaze was equally unwavering. "No. No," he repeated in a firm yet flat voice, "I'm not sure I have anything to come back to."

Serena's hand tightened on the candlestick atop the pianoforte. "It's unthinkable!" she gasped, the slanted eyes bright with anger. "Having lost your own brother, do you want to take mine as well?"

Brant leaned against the mantelpiece, trying to keep his temper in check. "For once, try to be reasonable. Matt needs to prove he's still a man. Sailing on the *Kearsarge* will give him that chance. For God's sake, do you think I'd let anything happen to him?"

Serena loosened her grasp on the candlestick and began pacing the sitting room. "You can't ensure his safety," she asserted, lower lip thrust out and fists clenched at her sides. "It's imbecilic even to pretend! Not to mention that he's still a very sick man."

"Bored and disheartened, mostly." Brant looked dispassionately at Serena. "He wants to go. Don't create obstacles, Serena."

It was true: While Matt had at first stated that he'd only be a burden, he'd let Brant convince him that was not the case: As the only civilian aboard the *Kearsarge*, Brant would feel ill-at-ease. He needed the support of another nonnaval man. Despite Gideon Welles's enthusiastic endorsement, when it came to actually applying methods which didn't conform to regulations, Brant was afraid he'd be outnumbered. Matt succumbed to the entreaties, unable or unwilling to see through Brant's well-intentioned ruse.

Serena, however, had found the idea appalling. She had tried to marshal Cecelia and Abigail to come to her aid, but without success. Cecelia was indifferent; Abigail refused to meddle. And Serena hadn't yet confronted Matt. Time was running out—they were due to sail in just over an hour. Even now, Brant had taken out his watch to check the time.

"Almost seven. Are Matt's belongings ready?"

Serena threw up her hands. "Yes. No. I have no idea." She hurtled across the sitting room, grabbing Brant by the thick wool of his seaman's jacket. "You can't do this! It's crazy!"

"Leave off, Serena," said Brant, sounding more bored than angry. "I'm damned sick of arguing."

Serena let go of his jacket, rage mingling with pain on her face. "All right. Maybe," she said in a quavering voice, "I find it strange that you seem so much more concerned over the rest of my family's problems than you ever have over mine."

Brant shrugged. "You appear hellbent on solving your problems without my help. At best, I've been a convenience to you."

Serena all but jumped up and down. "Oh! You—a convenience! If that's true, I've been a bankroll! Except," she rasped, "for the other night! I was just another slut to you! I don't care what my parents or anybody else thinks, when this damned war is over, I want a divorce!" The words spilled out in a reckless torrent, astonishing Serena as much as Brant.

The muscles tightened along Brant's jawline, the blue eyes turned steely. "Of course. I never thought you wanted anything else." He took a deep breath, his face darkening. " 'The other night' never happened. Bury it, Serena, with the rest of the dead."

"I . . . I spoke in haste . . ." She wrung her hands, feeling the wedding band dig into her finger. "I meant that I . . . that we . . ." Serena wound down helplessly, and grew very still as Brant's chilling gaze rendered her speechless.

"You've never known what you meant, Serena. Maybe someday you'll figure it all out. But now, for me, I need to go away, to help Matt, to try to blunt the pain of Kirk's death. *All* the pain," he added and suddenly looked haggard, weary, yet resolute.

The silence wedged between them like a shaft of ice. It was broken by Leonard, who appeared in the doorway dressed for travel. "The luggage is in the hall," he announced, seemingly oblivious to the room's tangible tension. "There is rather a lot of it. Passage has been booked for four additional passengers."

Serena and Brant stared at Leonard. His usually unruffled exterior exuded a sense of unease. "I suppose I could ask who," said Brant, his brow creased.

"Certainly." Leonard cleared his throat and seemed to look beyond some vague point between Serena and Brant. "Mrs. Moncrief, her son, his mammy and . . . uh, me."

"What?" exploded Serena, finding her voice again. "Cecelia is going home?"

Leonard gave a slight shake of his head. "No. To Europe." He paused, his mouth puckering in consternation. "If not on the *Kear-sarge,* then another ship."

"Hold on, Leonard." Serena wagged a finger at him. *"Why* are you all going to . . . to Europe?" She asked the question as if she couldn't quite believe what she was saying.

Amid a rustle of black tafetta, Cecelia glided into the room. "To live there, ninny," she announced in a cross tone. Cecelia put her arm through Leonard's. "We're going to be married aboard ship."

"Oh, no!" Serena all but reeled against the pianoforte as Cecelia bestowed an adoring smile on Leonard's set features. Brant still stood by the mantel, his hand on his head.

"All things—and people—being equal, which I might point out, they are not," said Brant with a weary sigh, "the *Kearsarge* isn't a honeymoon ship. She's going to war, for God's sake."

"But not until she gets to Europe." Cecelia playfully tickled Leonard's cheek. "Any ship crossing the Atlantic could fall prey to raiders. Why not sail on one that's armed?"

"I give up." Brant turned his back on the room, elbows rigid on the mantel.

"It's quite true what you say about people not being equal," Cecelia said airily, "which is why we're going to Europe. Foreigners are so much more broadminded. They'll just think Leonard is Portuguese."

"With a name like Prendergast?" Serena was still clinging to the pianoforte.

"Oh, pooh, as I said, they're all foreigners, how will they know the difference?" Cecelia gave her sister a disparaging smile. "My skin is almost as dark as Leonard's and Mark isn't his son anyway. Thank heavens." She looked at Leonard through her lashes. "But won't we have the most marvelous black-eyed babies?"

"According to the law of dominance with regard to heredity, yes," agreed Leonard, giving Cecelia's hand an affectionate pat. He turned to Serena. "Your uncle has given his consent. It's a most gracious gesture, since I disliked leaving the management of Wexford. However, Mr. Clarke should do well in my stead."

The idea of the shambling Texan supervising a North Carolina tobacco plantation struck Serena as incongruous. But then, so did the marriage of Cecelia and Leonard. Even if there had been no difference of color, it was hard to imagine a more unlikely couple. Unless, of course, it was Abigail and Yancy. With a sharp pang, it occurred to Serena that love seemed to thrive in the rockiest soil. Except where she and Brant were concerned.

Serena stood up straight, gazing from Leonard to Cecelia and back again. She remembered her conversation with Leonard about interracial courtships and shook her head in dismay at her own obtuseness.

No wonder Cecelia had seemed so unconcerned about pursuing another husband. No wonder her sister had not been interested in going
back to Brunswick. And even less wonder that she had ceased trying
to whiten her olive skin and asked strange questions about "white
knights" and seemed so difficult to rile. Serena marveled that she had
been so blind.

Still, it was an outrageous plan. Marcus Farrar would explode with
wrath; Lydia would reel from the scandal. It was very possible that
the Farrars would disinherit their elder daughter outright.

Which meant they were left with a crippled son and a daughter
who had impulsively stated that she wanted a divorce. Serena eyed
Cecelia and Leonard critically. They made an imposing pair, really—
the flamboyant, Junoesque woman and the restrained, dignified man.
If ever anyone could rein in Cecelia, it would be Leonard with his
limitless self-control. And Cecelia would bring zest and flair into
Leonard's regimented life. On second thought, they made an excellent
match.

"I am not penniless," Leonard said, as if reading Serena's mind.
"While there is little cash here in New Bern these days, I have a
portion coming to me from the plantation when times get better. I
have also made investments abroad, particularly in London."

Resignedly, Brant turned around. "Knowing you, Leonard, you
own London. Or at least London Bridge." He started to laugh as he
reached out his hands to the other couple. "Get Mark and his mammy,
we'd better go meet Captain Winslow." He kissed Cecelia's cheek
and wrung Leonard's hand. Serena watched in disbelief, suddenly
aware that a great part of her world was about to slip away, perhaps
forever.

"Wait!" The word came out in a strangled, frantic wail. The others
turned, regarding her with curiosity.

For one brief moment, Serena was about to insist that she join
them. Uncle Luke still had Abigail and Yancy, the *Leader* would
survive under Kirk's command . . . Except that Kirk was dead. During
the last quarter hour of tumult, she had forgotten that ghastly fact. It
still seemed impossible—kind, boyish, charming Kirk, now nothing
more than a corpse bound for burial in New Bedford among the other
dead Parnells. And only Serena could keep the *Leader* alive.

"Well?" It was Cecelia who broke the awkward silence. Apparently
Serena had stood mute for some time.

"I . . ." Serena caught Brant staring at her and looked away. "I
wish I had a wedding present. And I must see Matt before you go."
She licked her lips and shook her head. "It's such a shock . . . where's
Uncle Luke?"

"You know he hates farewells," Cecelia replied. "He's in the study, reading the 'The Tempest.' Not a good choice before a voyage, I'd say."

Serena struggled with her composure. "I'll join him, after I've seen Matt. And little Mark. I'm not keen on farewells myself," she added with a lame little laugh.

At least there was no time to linger. Supported by a crutch, Matt refused to let Young Calvin help him into the carriage. He still looked very drawn, but there was a faint sparkle in his eyes as Serena reached up to hug him tightly.

"I'll bring you French perfume and Belgian lace," he said with bravado. "Maybe I'll bring back a French coquette. As long as she isn't much for dancing." He chuckled in a self-deprecating manner which made Serena wince.

"You never could dance worth beans," Cecelia declared, but her voice was affectionate. She proffered her cheek to Serena. "He'll be fine," she whispered into her sister's ear. "A not-quite-whole Farrar is still ten times better than anybody else. He just needs reminding."

Serena's eyes opened wide in her sister's embrace. Leonard—or life—seemed to be working wonders with Cecelia.

After hugging an excited if bewildered Mark who seemed to think he was going to Raleigh, Serena took Leonard's hand. "I think you got your wish," she said, low.

One V-shaped eyebrow lifted, then the stern face softened into a smile. "Oh, yes, our discussion that night in the hallway. I should have known that any blood relation of Lucas Farrar would see the world through unhampered eyes." He paused, his eyes flickering toward Brant, who was making sure the baggage was secured. "Allow me one impertinent word, Serena."

The use of her given name underscored the kinship between them. "Yes?" she asked.

"Even the clearest view is sometimes obscured by storm clouds. But the winds shift and the seasons change. Remember that, Serena." He brushed her cheek with his lips and climbed into the carriage.

The moment Serena had dreaded most was at hand. Brant stood next to her, gazing at his watch. "We're behind schedule. Let's go," he called to the others as Young Calvin hauled himself into the driver's seat. "Good-bye, Serena."

"Good-bye." She held her breath, waiting for him to speak again. But he did not. Brant took one great leap into the carriage, slammed the door shut, and settled back into the seat next to Matt. As the wheels began to grind over the driveway, Serena discovered she barely had the strength to lift her arm in a wave. The carriage had disappeared into the darkness for several minutes before Serena made her lonely, lead-footed way back to the house.

PART FOUR

FRANCE AND NORTH CAROLINA
1864–1865

Chapter 22

"THE VARIOUS plantations and lands abandoned will be leased for a suitable term to loyal and responsible parties who will stipulate to cultivate and manage the same . . ." Serena stopped reading aloud and looked at Emaline, who was washing the windows. The sharp tang of vinegar hung in the office as Emaline wrung out a cloth in a bucket.

"Excuse me for saying so, but it's just not right," Emaline declared, scrubbing mightily at some greasy fingerprints on the glass. "How many Yankees know how to make tar and turpentine or grow cotton and tobacco?"

"Most of them probably aren't Yankees," Serena said, marking the notice for Herman who was loitering behind the desk. "I've heard most of the people taking over such properties are local Union supporters."

Emaline snorted. "So they say. Turncoats, I call them." She stood back to admire her efforts. "Hardly know there was glass in those casements, if I do say so myself. And I do." She beamed at Serena, picked up the bucket, and followed Herman into the backshop.

It was pointless to argue, Serena decided, nor was Emaline entirely wrong. At least it appeared that Wexford was secure. Brant and Uncle Luke had made the necessary arrangements, deeding the New Bern property in its entirety to Marcus Farrar. If Uncle Luke had any misgivings, he never let them show.

The press started up in the backshop, causing Serena's desk and chair to vibrate slightly. She was used to the noisy distraction, but this afternoon it made her edgy. Three editions had been published since Kirk's death; she ought to have adjusted by now to being alone. The press groaned to a halt, then started up again.

But then she wanted to be alone, Serena reminded herself sharply. Why else had she made that bold demand for a divorce? The press wound down again. Serena made a face in the direction of the backshop, but it expressed her irritation more with herself than with the wayward printing equipment.

Why, she asked silently for the hundredth time, did I ever say such a thing? To force Brant's hand? To let him talk me out of it? To free myself forever from his domination? The press started to rumble again.

With great resolve, Serena shoved Brant out of her mind and tried to concentrate on her work.

Serena looked at the proof of an ad from J. Hume and Company. They had a new shipment of shoes. Glancing down at her own worn footwear, Serena wondered if perhaps she should take advantage of her foreknowledge and go to Hume's right away while the selection was good.

Just as Serena was pulling her cape away from Emaline's coat in the wardrobe she felt, rather than heard, something crash not three feet from her hem. Whirling around, she saw with horror that the clean pane Emaline had just finished washing was shattered in a thousand pieces. A large stone with a piece of paper wrapped around it lay in the middle of the glass.

Serena looked through the gaping hole in the window. Though several onlookers stood outside with puzzled expressions, she saw no one fleeing nor anyone in pursuit. Baffled, Serena carefully picked up the stone, flicking away tiny shards of glass with her fingernails.

The paper was attached to the stone with a piece of string. Impatiently, Serena tugged at the knot. With a growing sense of dread, she unfolded the paper. Printed in big handwritten block letters were the words: YOU ARE NEXT.

Serena crumpled the paper in her hand and let out a small, sharp cry. Was it possible that Kirk's assassin had not been a vengeful Confederate as she had concluded—or at least had hoped? Was she still to be dogged quite literally to death by that relentless presence which seemed to haunt her days in New Bern?

She called out to Herman and Emaline but the roar of the press drowned out her voice. Starting for the backshop, Serena noted that she had knocked down both her cape and Emaline's coat from the wardrobe. She picked the garments up cautiously and shook them out. A few splinters of glass fell to the floor. So did an envelope which apparently had come out of Emaline's coat. Serena started to find a pocket but the name on the envelope made her waver: It was her own, written in Kirk's unmistakable scrawl.

If the rock hurled and the threat had shaken Serena, the discovery of Kirk's letter in Emaline's coat was shattering. There must be a logical explanation. Serena stuffed the letter and the note into the bosom of her calico dress and was cleaning up the glass when Emaline returned to the office and shrieked.

"Just a prank," said Serena, feigning a calm she didn't feel. "It's a shame they didn't break the window before you washed it."

"Boys up to no good," Emaline grumbled, fetching the dustpan. "Did you see them?"

"No. They must have run off." But where? Surely, Serena thought as she swept up the last of the particles, it was impossible to hurl a rock through a window on the main street of New Bern in the middle of the day and remain undetected. "Why don't you ask around, Emaline? If anyone has anything to say, they'll tell you before they would me."

"Maybe and maybe not. But I'll ask just the same." She dumped the contents of the dustpan into a wastebasket. "Dear me, Herman will have to replace that window right away. Spring's too far off for this much fresh air."

"I could use some just the same," Serena declared, retrieving her cape. "I'm going to Hume's for a bit."

"I see they got needles and hooks and eyes. Please, would you get me some? I'll pay you when you come back."

Serena nodded. "Fine. How many?"

Emaline tapped her forehead with her finger. "Oh—twelve dozen of each, I figure."

Serena paused with her hands on the clasp of her cape. "Twelve *dozen?*"

Emaline lifted her bony shoulders. "My poor farm families on Rattle Hill. And pins, too, as many as you can manage."

Serena nodded again, then all but bolted through the front door. She looked defiantly in every direction, but the residents had resumed their normal pace. Moving quickly down Craven Street with a sharp wind at her back, Serena passed the Bank of North Carolina and entered J. Hume and Company's double doors. A somewhat seedy chair was provided for customers trying on shoes. Serena sat down and told the whey-faced clerk she wanted to see every pair they had on hand which might fit.

"We hardly got them unpacked," the clerk said in a nasal voice.

"Take your time. I'll wait." Serena watched him start to balk. "Or would you like to be blamed by Mr. Hume for having his advertisement run upside down in the *Leader?*"

The clerk bounded away like a frightened sheep. Serena looked around to make sure no one was nearby, then delved discreetly under her cape and inside her dress for the letter.

"My dear Serena," it began and the familiar handwriting jarred her so badly she had to stop and take a deep breath. "Had our lives been different, I think we may have found great happiness together. But we met too late, and reality is my wife and our children, your marriage with Brant. In New Bern, you and I existed as if we were suspended in time. All things seemed possible here. But when I faced the reality of losing Peggy, I knew our dream world was done. No matter how much I love you or how little Peggy loves me, I have been given her as my charge under the laws of holy matrimony. The hovering of angel wings over her has been a warning from God. A most blessed, special woman has been entrusted to my care. If I fail to honor that commitment, I fail in my life's mission. It is not for me to be happy, but to do right. I beg you not to fault me for putting honor above love."

Serena's sad eyes looked up just in time to see the clerk staggering out under a three-foot stack of boxes. Hastily, she removed her shoes before turning her attention back to the letter.

"As for Brant, I would probably come to despise myself for betraying him. Even now, I am guilt-ridden for coveting his wife. I must confess, I have never fully understood my brother, but I admire and respect him. And I know, too, that no matter what you and I might have been to each other, he would remain first in your heart. Perhaps the greatest pleasure I could have, short of making you my own, would be that you and Brant might be happy together some day. Farewell, my love——K."

"Bad news?" twanged the clerk, seeing Serena's tear-filled eyes.

She nodded dumbly. A woman weeping over a letter was scarcely a rare sight in New Bern these days. The clerk wrinkled his brow and shook his head. "Too tight. How about brown?"

"No," Serena whispered. "Black. I'm still . . . in mourning."

"So's most of the town. We're short on black. You could dye these." He held up a plain pair of cordovan leather.

"Perhaps." Serena sat woodenly as the clerk rummaged through the boxes. Kirk had not tried to deceive her, he had only wanted to spare her, to keep their private world intact for as long as possible. She fervently wished there had been an opportunity to tell him she understood.

She refolded the letter, noting there was a postscript on the back of the last page. "I want to be far away when you read this so I'm putting it inside my locked drawer as I know eventually you'll need to go through the privileged military dispatches."

Serena moved so abruptly that her foot struck the clerk in the shin. "Oh! I'm sorry!" Standing up on unsteady legs, she nodded jerkily. "These feel wonderful, I'll take them."

"But they're red," the clerk protested. "It's hard to dye."

"Never mind, just have them sent to the Farrar house on Pollock Street." She shoved the letter back inside her cape and raced from the store, the whey-faced clerk staring after her.

It was all Serena could do to keep from running the length of Craven Street. When she entered the *Leader* office, Emaline was polishing the brass spittoon and humming. She looked up with a smile at Serena. "Got my pins and needles and such?"

"No." Serena advanced on the kneeling Emaline, the breeze through the open window fluttering her cape behind her. "What do you really do at Rattle Hill, Emaline?"

"What?" The cornflower eyes were round. "Why—I cook and tend the sick and clean a bit and sometimes I just visit. It's a hard life for those poor folks," she explained, her face growing sad. "Wasn't easy before the war, now it's plain pitiful."

Serena was unmoved. "You searched Kirk's private drawer. You took my key. Why?"

Emaline's mouth flew open but no words came out. Her eyes darted around the office, as if seeking an ally. The press had stopped running; presumably Herman had gone to get a new windowpane. "Someone . . . a Union officer . . . came by a few days ago and needed some important information. You were out so I helped him." Emaline twitched a smile at Serena.

"I don't think," asserted Serena, pulling the letter out from her cape, "the information he wanted was a letter from Kirk to me. Why did you take this, Emaline Pigott?"

The long face seemed to fall almost to Emaline's flat bosom. She made as if to snatch at the letter, but Serena battered her arm away. "You didn't deserve him!" Emaline screeched, her features contorted. "You, married to his brother, the major so good and kind with a wife and children! But you made him fall in love with you and be miserable and watch you with those big brown spaniel eyes of his! You're nothing but a Yankee whore, Mrs. Editor Parnell!"

Emaline flew at Serena, nails clawing, feet kicking. Impeded by the folds of her cape, Serena went down under the onslaught. Emaline had one thin but tenacious hand on Serena's throat, cutting off her breath. With a desperate jab of her elbow, Serena caught her adversary in the ribs. Emaline's grip loosened as her voluminous hoop skirts rolled her off-balance. Serena, gasping for breath, sat up, leaning on one arm, and stared as a hammer, a small bolt of cloth, several spools of thread, and a bottle of whiskey rolled out from under Emaline's skirts.

"Good God!" cried Serena, momentarily stupefied. "You're not just a spy, you're a smuggler!" She reached out to grab the hammer as Emaline struggled to sit up.

"I'm a loyal daughter of North Carolina!" Emaline screamed. "I do what I can for our poor soldiers, while sluts like you use them!"

Serena wielded the hammer menacingly. "Oh, shut up, Emaline! You talk of Kirk so adoringly and yet you hoodwinked him into thinking you were just a good-hearted country girl! And all the time passing information and material to our enemy. No wonder you wanted twelve dozen needles! You could have stitched up half the Army of Northern Virginia!"

Emaline sat huddled with her arms wrapped around her knees.

More items had fallen from her hoops—medicine bottles, bandages, a pound of lard. She threw Serena a proud yet antagonistic look. "I can get a whole bushel load in these hoops. And walk for miles."

Serena sighed wearily. "I'm sure you can. What about your Union beau? Did you use him, too?"

Emaline clamped her mouth into a tight, straight line. Apparently Serena had gone too far. "All right," sighed Serena, getting to her feet with an effort and keeping a firm grasp on the hammer. "I guess you and I will have to go see the provost marshal."

"Oh, no!" Emaline shook her head in panic. "He'll shoot me! That man has no mercy!"

The provost marshal's strict enforcement of discipline and harsh punishment of criminals was legendary. It was also responsible for the usually flawless behavior of the Union soldiers and the rarity of reprisals on the part of Confederate supporters. If one man deserved credit for the relatively peaceful years of the occupation in New Bern, it was Henry T. Lawson of the 2nd Massachusetts Heavy Artillery.

"I don't think even the provost marshal will shoot a woman," Serena said with impatience. "But I'm more than willing to crack your silly head open with this hammer. Get up, Emaline, before I lose my temper."

Emaline had witnessed enough of Serena's anger to know that the words were no bluff. Clumsily she got to her feet, her cheeks flushed, the wheat-colored hair hanging over her shoulders. Serena ordered her to get her coat.

"We're going to walk right down Craven Street as if we were taking a stroll," Serena said, hiding the hammer under her cape. "But one squeak out of you, Emaline, and I'll have the sentries haul you away. They'll be considerably less kind than I will."

Doggedly, Emaline walked out of the office, Serena just behind her, making innocuous small talk. Except for some casual greetings and a few nods, no one paid much attention to the two women. The sentries on duty at each corner blended into the landscape, looking bored.

Major Lawson was a man of average height, in his forties, with a distinguished yet brusque air. His usual aplomb faltered, however, when Serena announced the reason for her visit.

"A spy?" he repeated, looking skeptically at Emaline. "Mrs. Parnell, are you quite certain?"

"Ask her," replied Serena. "And if some female is present, have her look under Miss Piggot's hoops. She'll find enough supplies to outfit a regiment."

Emaline gave Serena a malevolent stare. "I still say I only did my duty."

"Well, I'm doing mine," Serena retorted. For a fleeting moment, she felt guilty. Emaline was right, after all. She had only acted in a manner befitting any loyal Confederate. But she had also done something else far less forgivable—she had tried to prevent Serena from reading Kirk's last message. If fate hadn't intervened, Serena would never have known Kirk's true feelings.

Major Lawson summoned two guards who led a still defiant Emaline out of the office. Serena finally laid the hammer down on the provost marshal's desk. "You won't really shoot her, will you?"

Major Lawson sighed. "Probably not, though we don't yet know the extent of her crimes. Was there actually much of vital importance in your dispatches?"

"Not really, I suppose." Serena tried to repin her disheveled hair but gave up and let it tumble over her shoulders. "She was seeing a Yankee soldier, though. No doubt she wheedled information from him."

Major Lawson was making a few notes on a large pad of paper. "Do you know who he is?"

Serena shook her head. "No, I only saw him once, from a distance. And she never told me his name." Strange, Serena thought, how hazy was the memory of Emaline and her beau on the banks of Contentnea Creek—and how vivid the recollection of Kirk and his ardor in the old house nearby. "Captain," she began, trying to dispel the distressing imagery, "have you learned anything about who shot Major Parnell?"

The corners of Lawson's mouth turned down. "I'm afraid not. It's most baffling, especially since the major had no personal enemies here in New Bern."

"But there had been threats because of the newspaper. Someone threw a rock into the office just this afternoon saying 'You are next.'"

"My word." Lawson stroked his graying muttonchop whiskers. "Today? Did no one see him?"

"Apparently not. It's enough to make me believe in ghosts." Serena attempted a laugh but shivered instead.

Major Lawson looked solemn. "Mrs. Parnell, you must have protection. I understand Miss Pigott's brother works for you, but possibly not for long, considering. However, there is only one other man at the newspaper, correct?" He saw Serena nod. "So I must insist you let me assign someone to help you." He furrowed his brow in concentration. "Quenette, I think, from Pennsylvania. Artillery commander wounded at Gettysburg and a former newspaperman from Philadelphia. Yes, he'll do nicely."

"Do what?" Serena queried in a waspish tone and saw Major Lawson straighten his already military posture. "I'm sorry, I've had a tiring day. Threats and spies and all." She gave Lawson a forced but engaging smile. "I'm not accustomed to having other people choose my employees for me."

Lawson was clearly not accustomed to having a twenty-two-year-old woman question his decisions. Serena, however, had to give him his due when he recovered gallantly: "Most understandable," he said, with a little bow from the waist. "I should never argue with a lady who carries a hammer. Why don't you meet Major Quenette and see if you find him acceptable?"

"That sounds reasonable," agreed Serena, rising from the finely crafted Duncan Phyfe chair. The house where the provost marshal resided had belonged to a Mr. Jones and contained several excellent pieces. "If Major Quenette turns out to be an illiterate boor, perhaps I can pound some wit and courtesy into his head with this." She brandished the hammer and gave Major Lawson another charming smile.

The strain had finally taken its toll on Serena by nightfall. While she had hoped the disposition of Emaline into the custody of the provost marshal would be the last trying episode of the day, her wishes were dashed when a bewildered Herman hailed her outside the *Leader* office. Serena had taken the distressed young man inside, trying to explain as tactfully and kindly as possible what had become of his sister. He seemed to have no idea what Emaline had been doing all these months and was highly agitated over her arrest.

"I'm not blaming you exactly," he had told Serena earnestly. "I'm just mighty afraid those Yankees'll do something terrible to poor Emaline."

"I doubt that very much," Serena had soothed. "Emaline will probably end up a local heroine and a legend to boot. Meanwhile I'll do everything I can to see to your well-being." Serena winced inwardly at the pompous words, though she sensed that Herman wasn't quite sure what she meant. In truth, neither was she. It just seemed clear that Herman wasn't used to coping with the world on its own terms.

When she finally climbed the stairs to the townhouse, Serena wasn't sure she could cope much longer, either. For the first time in her life, she requested a drink of whiskey to bolster her deflated spirits.

"I could stand a bit of that myself," Uncle Luke confessed, getting out the decanter and glasses. "By God in heaven, I don't know who I miss more, your Aunt Kathleen or Leonard."

"Won't she even talk to you any more?" Serena asked as she gratefully accepted a half-filled tumbler from her uncle.

"She won't talk to anybody but Jason and her maid, Bathsheba. And poor Jason hates going to her room because she acts so queer." He gave Serena a pathetic little smile. "I wish you'd known Aunt Kathleen better when she was young. So lively and pretty and full of fun. Half the bucks in the county were in hot pursuit but she fell in love with a Yankee dreamer. Oh my, we were happy then." Uncle

Luke's eyes were very far away, looking into the past and an era that seemed to have vanished along with his wife's spirit.

He rallied after a few moments, focusing his attention on Serena's problems which she had revealed during supper. She had even told him about Kirk's letter, and, with some hesitation, their unfulfilled romantic interlude. Uncle Luke had not appeared at all surprised.

"A fine man, Kirk," he asserted, setting down his tumbler and pulling out a cigarette from his pocket. "Just a shame that he and his brother both should have fallen in love with you."

Serena's hand tightened around her glass. "Brant doesn't love me. He never did. You know that." Her words were crisp.

"No, can't say that I do." Uncle Luke spoke matter-of-factly. "Kirk didn't think that, either. If he had, he'd have made love to you." Uncle Luke paused to flick a speck of tobacco from his lip. "Excuse your old uncle's bold tongue, Rena, but it sounds to me as if you were only offering token resistance. I kind of suspect that if Kirk thought his brother didn't love you, he'd have been more determined. Brothers are funny people, you know, they trust each other."

Serena took a large swallow of whiskey which made her eyes water. "I'm sorry, I'm sure you're wrong. Brant's agreed to give me a divorce."

"He'd agree to give you Vermont about now, I imagine." Uncle Luke's tone was deceptively mild, his gaze unsettlingly shrewd. He reached out and put a gentle finger on Serena's nose. "What's that, little fox?" She opened her mouth to reply, but he shook his head. "Plain as the nose on your face, Rena. Not *that* kind of mirror," he said, gesturing to a Venetian oval in a heavy gilt frame on the opposite wall, "but the one inside."

They sat looking at each other for a long time. But when Serena finally spoke, it was of other things.

Cecelia Farrar Moncrief Prendergast, her husband, her son, and the child's mammy had disembarked at Rotterdam June 10. The bride was radiant, the groom benign. They would honeymoon in Amsterdam, Brussels, Paris, and the Côte d'Azur.

Two days later, as the *Kearsarge* lay at anchor off the Dutch coast, Captain Winslow received word that the *Alabama* had put into port at Cherbourg. He fired a gun signaling his crew on shore to return immediately to the ship. Within forty-eight hours, the men of the *Kearsarge* sighted the legendary, elusive *Alabama*.

"At last," sighed Winslow, taking a deep breath as he stood on the bridge with Brant. "I thought she'd never leave Capetown."

Brant stood in silent homage to a valiant fighting ship. No matter how dire the devastation she had wreaked among Yankee vessels, the

Alabama's proud lines and bold enterprise could not help but evoke the respect of any seagoing man.

"Semmes has had a long voyage," Brant remarked at last. "He'll be making repairs."

"We shall let him continue," Winslow said, with a smile of anticipation. "He foiled me once at Gibraltar on the *Sumter,* but he'll not do so again. And no one will say it was because I didn't give him a fighting chance."

Matt, however, found Winslow's gallantry foolish. "Damn it," he exclaimed to Brant two days later, "we've sailed thousands of miles, waited for weeks, and now Winslow just sits here! Why don't we blow the bastard out of the water?"

"This is the navy, not the army," Brant replied, studying a bottle of Dutch beer he'd picked up in Rotterdam. "They play by different rules."

"Stupid ones, if you ask me," Matt grumbled. He grasped his crutch and got up from the bunk. The long voyage and the camaraderie of the seamen had done much to divert Matt's attention from his handicap. Yet, as Brant observed the younger man out of the corner of his eye, he noted the youthful, cocky air of self-confidence had not resurfaced. Considering that Matt had long since passed from boyhood and had witnessed the cruel face of war, that was hardly surprising. However, the assurance of the mature man was not apparent, nor was there any joy evident in the once-brash, ebullient Matt. Sometimes it seemed to Brant that his brother-in-law had gone from youth to old age overnight at Missionary Ridge.

As far as Matt's opinion of Captain Winslow's gallant approach to naval warfare was concerned, Brant was inclined to agree but wouldn't say so out loud. Being a captain himself, he was too steeped in the ways of the sea to question his commanding officer. And, as always, there were other resources available when it came to changing a man's mind. A shame, thought Brant ruefully, it didn't work that way with women. At least not with Serena.

But Brant refused to dwell on his wife. Or at least he tried not to. It wasn't always easy to forget Serena when her relatives were his shipmates.

The thunder of a few broadsides ought to put Serena out of mind for a while, Brant thought grimly. He peered through the cabin porthole. The *Alabama* rode higher in the water. No doubt they had cast off nonessential spars and rigging to lighten the ship and make it more maneuverable.

A tap at the cabin hatch was answered by Matt, swaying slightly on his crutch as the tide shifted the deck beneath him. Winslow smiled faintly as he entered, the sparse beard looking more scraggly than ever.

"It shouldn't be long now," Winslow said. "They're holystoning the deck, I see."

"I hear Semmes is in Cherbourg this afternoon." Brant nodded in the direction of the city. "I also hear the *Alabama* has collected quite a contingent of French admirers. It makes me feel as if we're part of a circus sideshow."

"We shan't let that distract us, sir," Winslow asserted. "As soon as the *Alabama* lifts anchor we shall proceed directly to the confrontation and ignore all foreign sentiment."

"I've never had any trouble ignoring sentiment, whatever the source," Brant said, deliberately sitting down so that Matt would not feel compelled to remain leaning on his crutch. "But I'd suggest we sail further out, beyond the three-mile limit. After all this trouble, I'd hate to have the battle end in a deadlock because one of the ships could seek sanctuary in neutral waters."

Winslow fingered the sparse beard while Matt finally sat down on the bunk. "An excellent point, sir. While I would never consider such a move myself, Semmes might." He reflected for a moment and nodded. "It's unlikely, but possible." The one good eye gazed at Brant. "Your advice is well-taken, sir. I trust we shall be able to act upon it in the morning."

Winslow's prediction was fulfilled. The *Alabama* began heading out toward the Channel shortly before ten o'clock that Sunday morning. There was a carnival air both on land and at sea: A huge crowd lined the shore, fortified with picnic hampers and bottles of wine. Many small pleasure boats bobbed in the wake of the *Alabama*. One of the larger private crafts sported a band which played "Dixie."

Even the sun had come out to watch the spectacle. Brant stood between Matt and Captain Winslow, whose reading of the Sunday service had been interrupted by news of the enemy's approach. The *Kearsarge* was heading in a northeasterly direction, appearing to move away from her adversary, but actually in accord with Brant's advice to avoid neutral waters. At last, the Union vessel began turning about. Brant peered through his spyglass, noting the Confederate ensign hoisted aloft. At that moment, the *Alabama* opened fire.

Matt wore an impatient look. "What's Winslow waiting for now?" he asked Brant in a low voice. "For somebody to play 'The Battle Hymn of the Republic'?"

Brant didn't seem to hear Matt at first, but then shook his head. "No, we're not quite close enough." He spoke without inflection, his mind obviously elsewhere. "Captain," he called to Winslow, who was talking to one of his officers, "if we follow the current and steer a parallel course to the *Alabama*, we can move in closer. She's not as

fast and her broadsides aren't as heavy. And I'll give you better than
even odds that after all this time at sea, their ammunition is unreliable."

"I'm not a gambling man," Winslow replied. He paused to give the
order to commence firing. The starboard battery opened up, making the
deck tremble underfoot. "However, your point is well-taken," he went
on, raising his voice to a shout. "We'll start the circular maneuvers."

Brant headed for the stern, Matt trailing awkwardly on his crutch.
It had become a habit with Brant to pay no overt attention to Matt's
difficulties. But he rarely let the younger man out of sight.

Close to the stern, shells exploded in the water, sending big plumes
skyward and splashing down on the deck. Clouds of acrid smoke
hung in the air as the Union sailors passed along crisp orders. A well-
drilled lot, Brant noted as he moved closer to one of the *Kearsarge*'s
two eleven-inch Dahlgren guns. It was mounted on a pivot and well-
suited to close range combat.

The two ships moved in their circular rhythm as if engaged in a
stately dance to the cadence of the ear-shattering broadsides. Brant
gave the sailors manning the Dahlgren a sign of approval by doffing
his cap, then turned back to Matt who was watching with obvious
envy. Brant started to make a flippant remark but before he could get
the words out, Matt shouted in warning, and thrust out his crutch in
a slashing motion. It caught Brant at the knees, sending him sprawling
onto the deck just as a shell exploded next to the Dahlgren.

Matt had also crashed to the deck. With great difficulty, he crawled
on his stomach toward the three sailors who lay motionless next to
the big gun.

The thick smoke made Brant cough. Cautiously, he raised himself
on his elbows and turned his head. "Are they alive?" he called to Matt,
who was testing the pulse of an inert man in a blood-soaked uniform.

"Barely." Matt got a handhold on the pivot of the gun and hauled
himself to his feet. The ship's surgeon and two seamen came racing
across the deck to tend the wounded. Brant had stood up, but stepped
aside as the first of the injured soldiers was carried below. Except for a
bruised shoulder from hitting the deck too hard, Brant was unharmed.
He joined Matt at the Dahlgren just as a cannonball exploded off the
port side.

"Can you fire one of these?" Brant asked.

"The question is, can I aim it," Matt replied, grappling with the
big gun to pull it into position. "Take hold of that other rope."

Brant took the thick coil in his hands as three seamen arrived to
replace their fallen comrades. From amidships, the voice of Captain
Winslow called out over his speaking trumpet: "Aim low for the
waterline! Load and fire as rapidly as possible!"

Matt complied, the shell ripping through the air to tear into one of the *Alabama*'s gunports. The Union men cheered loudly, some waving their dark blue caps.

"It seems to me your aim is pretty good," Brant said mildly. "Do you want to quit while you're ahead?"

"Hell, no!" Matt grinned, signaling the other men to help him keep up the barrage. Brant watched with a wry smile as Matt and his compatriots cried out with glee each time a shot hit home. Two more shells had torn through the *Alabama*'s gunport. The Confederate ship's deck was littered with dead and wounded men.

Brant retrieved Matt's crutch and wordlessly placed it not far from the gun implacement. The Dahlgren was wreaking havoc with the *Alabama*, which had begun to list to starboard as her own guns grew increasingly erratic. Brant observed the exultation on Matt's face and walked away to join Captain Winslow.

Winslow's excitement was less obvious but just as genuine. "She's turning," he said to Brant, folding his hands over his paunch as if offering an act of thanksgiving. "I trust it's not a trick."

"They're throwing the dead overboard," Brant noted grimly. "Damn, but war's a wasteful business."

"If men must fight, some must die." Winslow spoke without inflection. "The realities of the world are often very unpleasant."

Fleetingly, Brant thought of Kirk and turned away. The *Alabama*, the scourge of Yankee sea captains, would sail no more. Brant did not savor the taste of victory.

The two ships were very close, no more than five hundred yards apart. Captain Winslow peered with his good eye and pointed. "See there, the Confederate ensign is being lowered. Their guns are silent."

But the *Kearsarge*'s were not. Through the clouds of smoke and clusters of men, Brant could still see Matt and the others firing the Dahlgren. Questioningly, he looked at Winslow. "Don't tell me you still suspect a trick?"

"Semmes is most ingenious," Winslow replied, looking through his spyglass. "Ah. The white flag is going up. Praise the Lord!"

"And the Dahlgrens," murmured Brant as Winslow finally gave the order to cease fire. "By God, they're abandoning ship! And the poor bastards did most of their damage to our lifeboats so we can't rescue them."

Dozens of Confederate seamen floundered in the water. Many were wounded and some of the French pleasure craft were hauling them aboard. A dinghy from the *Alabama* had been let down; soon it was filled with men. Winslow ordered that his own two remaining boats be lowered.

"You're right, sir," he frowned at Brant, then gazed back into the Channel waters, "we need help."

Brant pointed to a steam yacht flying the Union Jack. "That's the *Deerhound*. Ask her to pick up survivors."

Winslow called out through his speaking trumpet just as the *Alabama*'s stern dipped inexorably beneath the gray-green waters. Matt, who had joined Brant and Winslow, jubilantly urged the enemy ship to sink even faster. But the two captains watched with heavy hearts. A naval victory was not the same as the loss of a ship. No matter what colors a vessel flew, the ultimate triumph of the sea over men struck some primeval, frightening chord.

Even as the *Kearsarge*'s crew began bringing the prisoners aboard, Brant remained silent. It was Matt who interrupted his reverie of respect by clapping his brother-in-law on the shoulder. "God almighty, this is the first time since I got shot that I wanted to get drunk because I feel good!"

Brant forced a grin at the other man. "Why don't we do that tonight in Cherbourg? Then we can go to Paris and I'll introduce you to the Montreux sisters."

The elation ebbed slightly from Matt's features. He glanced down at the severed leg. "I don't know..."

Brant's eyes flickered at the crutch to make sure that Matt was balanced firmly, then slapped him on the arm. "Hell, you aren't going to pleasure the mam'selles with your feet! Come on, let's see if we can help with the wounded." Brant started to lead the way to the starboard side where more men were being brought on deck. He paused, looking at Matt over his shoulder. "Good work with the Dahlgren. You blew the hell out of that gunport."

Matt looked self-deprecating, but his hazel eyes were happy. "Lucky shot, that's all."

"I'm a great believer in luck." Brant scanned the faces of the Confederate crewmen, many of whom were lying bloodied. "By the way," Brant said casually, "thanks for saving me from ending up like these poor devils."

"That was luck, too." Matt shrugged diffidently. "You had your back turned to the shell."

"A dumb stunt," Brant remarked as he knelt to care for one of the wounded. "I rarely turn my back on anything. It's a good thing you were there."

Matt watched Brant make a tourniquet from the man's shirt. Leaning against the rigging of the mainmast, Matt turned seaward so that Brant could not see the wide smile which spread across his face.

Chapter 23

SERENA HAD to force herself to read the letter from Peggy Parnell. It had arrived in late September, along with a lengthy epistle from Lydia Farrar. Duty demanded that Serena open her mother's letter first, though it also turned out to be burdensome reading. Lydia spent three pages bemoaning Matt's fate while at the same time trying to come to philosophical grips with the tragedy.

"If such a terrible disaster had to be visited upon a young man as fine as your brother, at least he will have the courage to overcome his handicap. Your father has vowed that every measure will be taken within the business to ensure that when Matthew assumes his rightful place, no one shall ever treat him any differently than if he were a whole man."

Serena shook her head over her mother's peculiar naiveté. Or was it snobbishness, she wondered, and decided that must be so when Lydia went on to discuss Cecelia's second marriage.

"We were always led to believe that Leonard was colored. However, there must be some confusion in Lucas's accounts over the years regarding Leonard's connection to Kathleen's family. Cecelia's description of him as half-Irish and half-West Indian is extremely vague. Your father and I hope that he is at least as much of a gentleman as Mr. Moncrief."

Having already dismissed Abigail's marriage to Yancy Clarke in a previous letter as "a grave social lapse," Lydia tersely stated that she hoped little Sam was thriving.

As for Serena, the prodding voice of Marcus Farrar reverberated behind Lydia's words: "We hear that this abominable war will not last much longer. Your father and I look forward to the day we are reunited with you and Captain Parnell."

Perhaps, Serena thought bitterly, it was time to resume correspondence with Josiah Holland and the *Springfield Republican*. She certainly had no intention of going back to the house on Pleasant Street and living there as the divorced black sheep of the family. Cecelia would cause even greater scandal when she arrived with a mulatto husband in tow. Matt's crippled state began to take on an aura of honor, as well it should, Serena told herself. For all the lamentations, Matt would go home a hero while Serena and Cecelia were both in disgrace and Abigail would no doubt suffer snubs. It appeared to Serena that in the Farrar family at least, the women had been more victimized by war than the men.

But not among the Stanhope-Parnells. Lydia devoted a paragraph to Judge Stanhope's demise, which she attributed to a combination of grief and drink. "Neither Pembrose nor Giles has ever been seen again. However, the late judge believed Giles had gone off to war."

Serena's hand tightened on the letter, crumpling the fragile notepaper. Over the years, she had succeeded in suppressing the memory of Pembrose Stanhope, though an occasional nightmare would bring him vividly back to mind. Abigail never talked about him, but Serena wondered if she, too, sometimes awoke in the middle of the night to find his tainted shadow haunting her.

As for Giles, Serena wasn't sure she'd ever met him, unless it had been when they were children. A wedding, perhaps—she seemed to recall a particularly nasty blond boy of about ten with chocolate-covered fingers threatening to stain her snow-white frock.

At last, she opened the letter from Peggy. She recognized the careful, girlish penmanship from Kirk's correspondence. Somewhat to Serena's surprise, the letter was remarkably brief.

"My dear Serena," Peggy began. "Please forgive me for the delay in writing to you but I have been so busy with the new baby (the Lord be praised, he is prospering at last and is named for his late and much beloved father) and the shelter here in New Bedford that I have had little time for anything else. Now that I have joined that sad state of widowhood, I have even more compassion for these brave, noble ladies and their precious children. I have vowed to devote my poor, humble efforts to a lifelong work of caring for the bereaved and the lonely so that I may offer them some small sense of consolation and comfort. As for my husband of loving memory, on his behalf I wish to thank you and your family in New Bern for being so kind to him. Yours devotedly, Margaret Stanhope Parnell (Peggy)."

Serena clenched her teeth and stared at the pristine stationery. "Ever the afterthought," she said aloud. "I wonder if Peggy put that on Kirk's tombstone."

"You're talking to yourself," Abigail said from the doorway. "How has your mother managed to rile you this time?"

Serena jammed Peggy's letter back into its envelope. "Mama isn't the only one who can do that." She put both letters on the dresser and pounded on them with her fist for emphasis. "The widow Parnell makes my flesh creep."

Abigail raised one elegant eyebrow. "Oh? You do seem to have problems with the Parnells and your . . . flesh."

"Damnation, Abby, that's not funny! I wish I'd never even heard

of that wretched family! Old do-good Peggy is up there in New
Bedford wallowing in widowhood while poor Kirk is dead and buried.
Assuming she remembered to bury him. But then I suppose he'd take
up too much room underfoot in the kitchen."

It was Abigail's turn to be put off. "Serena, dear! Don't be tasteless!" But though the tone was reproachful, the green-flecked eyes
sparkled with amusement.

"As for Brant," Serena ranted on, prowling the bedroom's length,
"I'd hope he sank except that Matt is aboard, too. On top of everything
else, it's too warm here for September! I'm tired of summer!"

"So am I," Abigail admitted, going to the window in search of a
breeze but finding the air outside as still as it was inside. "I'm also
tired of New Bern." She leaned against the wall, hands behind her
back, facing Serena. "As soon as peace comes, Yancy and I and the
boys are going to Montana."

"Montana!" Serena uttered the unfamiliar name as if it were an
obscure African village. "But I thought Yancy was going to stay on
and run the plantation! What's in Montana? Gold?"

Abigail shook her head. "No, though everyone else is heading
there for that reason. Gold is too ephemeral. But miners have to eat.
And now that Montana has just been named a territory, there will be
settlers. Yancy has heard that the land is perfect for cattle. He'd like
to bring a large herd up from Texas."

Serena tried to conjure up a mental map of North America. All
she really knew about Montana was that it was vast and somewhere
far to the west. "Is it near Texas?" she inquired, feeling woefully
ignorant.

"No. Quite the opposite. It borders on Canada to the north. It's
said to be very beautiful."

The full impact of Abigail's announcement was just beginning to
sink in on Serena. "But they must have Indians! And it's so far away.
You can't go, Abby, I'll never see you again."

Abigail's eyes flickered, with just a hint of mist in her quiet gaze.
"People have been known to travel between Montana and the East.
Someday there may even be a railroad. But," she went on more
seriously, "Yancy would never fit in back here. He's not the sort to
settle down much and if we're to have any kind of stable life together,
it must be one where he has a total sense of freedom. Montana sounds
like that sort of place."

To Serena, it sounded like the most raw, primitive expanse of
wilderness. As for Abigail, picturing her in a makeshift ranch house
with one eye on the cook stove and another on the horizon watching
for encroaching savages was an incongruous idea.

Yet Abigail would manage, Serena admitted. She could shoot a would-be scalphunter with as much aplomb as she'd fired at Sergeant Brown or Pembrose Stanhope. She'd care for the ranch hands or cowboys or whatever they were called with the same skill she'd displayed in Washington and New Bern. She'd probably even bring a sense of grace and taste to the untamed frontier. If Abigail couldn't find civilization in Montana, she'd bring it with her.

For the moment, however, Abigail and Yancy's dreams of herding cattle in the West were just that—dreams. Reality was joining Uncle Luke and Yancy and Jason for supper. It was a meager meal of hominy and biscuits. No one had much appetite, however, since the endless humid days had taken their toll.

Jason was particularly interested in Abigail and Yancy's proposed Montana venture. "I've thought about Oregon myself," he said, suddenly looking much older than his eighteen years. "It's on the ocean, too. Or maybe California."

For once, Uncle Luke permitted practicality to take the upper hand. "And who is to run Wexford if you go west and Nathan doesn't come back?"

Jason shrugged his ever-widening shoulders. "He'll be back. But this part of the country is dead as a doornail. Out in Oregon, everything is new and alive."

Uncle Luke suppressed a sigh. There was some truth in his son's words. Certainly the old way of Southern life was dead, trampled into the ground just as the Confederacy's last hopes had been buried when General Sherman took Atlanta three weeks earlier.

"I'm a Yankee by birth," Uncle Luke said at last, "but it seems to me that if a man's looking for a challenge, there's just as big a one rebuilding our world here as there is out in the jungle fighting off savages and wild animals."

"It's not a jungle," Yancy drawled, "it's just a heap of trees. You can always cut them down if they get in your way."

"Maybe." Uncle Luke stared at his empty plate.

Serena decided to change the subject. "Judge Stanhope died," she said, overbright.

Everyone turned to stare except Jason, who hadn't the foggiest notion as to Judge Stanhope's identity. He asked to excuse himself and was given permission by his father.

"Poor devil," sighed Uncle Luke and Serena wasn't sure if he meant his son or the judge. "I used to know him well enough," he went on, clarifying the matter. "He and his brother came from dirt-poor potato farming stock and made their way up in the world through law and medicine. Dr. Stanhope died young, I'm afraid."

"Was he Peggy's father?" Serena asked.

"Peggy?" Uncle Luke's brow furrowed. "Oh, little Margaret, yes,

one of eight children. I'd forgotten that, poor Kirk's wife." He stopped
to turn in his chair and then shook his head. "My, my, I can't get
used to not having Leonard here."

Young Calvin appeared, more slow of foot than usual. Uncle Luke
ordered a raid on the diminishing liquor cabinet. "Yes, yes," he said
as their glasses were filled with cognac, "the Stanhopes. A poor but
proud family. Judge Aaron and Dr. Celleous. Did you know they both
courted your mothers?" He gave Serena and Abigail a fey smile.

"Heavens, no," replied Serena, leaning toward her uncle. "Which
courted whom?"

"Ah, let me think—Aaron sought the hand of your mother, Sarah."
He gazed at Abigail. "She was the prettiest little thing, all curls and
dimples and grace. But shrewd and stubborn, too. I don't think she
cared much for Aaron but she did lead him on. Sarah was like that,
if only to make your father jealous and spur him on to matrimony.
Your father, dear Abby, gave Frenchmen a bad name when it came
to ardent romance. If I knew it weren't out of the question, I'd say
Sarah did the proposing herself." He chuckled over his cognac, lost
momentarily in the follies of youth.

"Then there was Celleous," he continued, turning to Serena. "He
dared seek out the lovely Lydia. Oh, my, can you imagine your mother
being courted by the son of an Aroostock potato farmer? As if in
revenge for such an affront, she announced to her parents that she
would marry no one but the first son of the wealthiest man in Brunswick. I suspect she had no idea who that might be, but Mr. and Mrs.
Holland took her at her word and goaded your Farrar grandparents
into a match with Marcus."

Serena and Abigail exchanged apprehensive glances. Deep inside
her stomach, Serena felt her simple supper turn over. In some convoluted, malevolent way, their mothers' rejection had been visited
upon their daughters. Pembrose Stanhope had avenged the intentions
of his father and his uncle by preying upon both Abigail and Serena.
It was incredible—and yet it made a perverted kind of sense.

Yancy, however, had another point of view. "Folks coming from
poor stock always seem to have a need to be better than somebody
else. And richer. Maybe that's why Pembrose and Giles went into the
slave recovering trade."

Uncle Luke tilted his head to one side. "Yes, perhaps so. Strange,
isn't it, how those two seem to have become totally evil while their
cousin, Peggy, chose to be flawlessly virtuous."

"Very strange," murmured Serena over the lip of her cognac glass.
Everything seemed strange this evening, she thought absently, noting
that Uncle Luke's color had risen. The liquor, of course. Now he was
talking about Aunt Kathleen and how she would no doubt he her old

self after the war was over and the Yankees had left. Wishful thinking, it seemed to Serena, and she poured herself another glass of
cognac.

It turned out that Uncle Luke's high color had nothing to do with
drinking. He became quite ill the following day, as did Young Calvin.
Serena had hesitated to leave the townhouse in the morning but Abigail
dismissed her concern out of hand. "It's probably this dreadful weather.
And our unfortunate diet. I'll see to them while you go on to the
newspaper office."

Serena did, though she knew that Major James L. Quenette could
manage without her. He had worked on three daily papers in Philadelphia during his career and found the *Leader* no particular challenge.
An easygoing man with a wife and six children back home, Quenette
had proved himself a treasure. He had even made the effort of be-
friending a bewildered Herman, who still couldn't quite figure out
why his sister was being held a prisoner in the old Jones-Lipman
house.

"Sherman's moving east," Quenette noted, looking up from the
military dispatches he'd received that morning. He was in his mid-
thirties, with a handsome moustache and merry brown eyes. He wore
a perpetually self-deprecating air but Serena had found him extremely
shrewd and a fast, competent writer. If Kirk's presence during the
last year or so of their professional association had made her nervous,
Quenette put her at ease.

"How long, I wonder," Serena mused, scanning the latest reports
on the devastation of Atlanta. "Heavens, it seems as if this country's
troubles may finally be over. I can hardly believe it."

"The country's, yes." Quenette put the dispatches down on his
desk and eyed Serena quizzically. "Mrs. Parnell, I'm hearing the
damnedest rumors in town."

Serena frowned. "Such as, Major?" She had decided it was best
to keep their relationship on the most formal basis possible.

Quenette held both hands out in a perplexed gesture. "I'm told
people are dying around town. It's some sort of fever."

Serena sat back in her chair. "Oh! My uncle is ill this morning,
and so is one of the servants. But it doesn't seem serious."

"I hate to hang crepe before it's due, but have you ever heard of
yellow fever?" Quenette looked apologetic, as if he were solely ac-
countable for the dread disease.

"Not in Maine." Serena turned grim. "Oh, my God, do you really
think so?"

Quenette lifted his shoulders. "I talked to Dr. Hooper this morning.

He's an optimistic sort of fellow, but even he is afraid that we're in the beginning phase of an epidemic."

If Dr. Hooper had prophesied the worst, it might be true, Serena realized with numbing apprehension. "Can we do anything about it?"

"We can talk to the provost marshal and get him to have the soldiers take care of any stagnant water." Quenette gave another shrug. "I'm told there's some connection and it won't hurt to have it done."

"No. Of course not." Serena's voice sounded far away. It didn't seem possible that after New Bern had survived the war, the city should be visited by pestilence. Perhaps Quenette was overreacting. But not Dr. Hooper, surely. Serena turned her attention to the news of Farragut's victory over the Confederates at Mobile Bay, the last Southern seaport left on the Gulf of Mexico. The reports of naval activity made her think of Brant. It occurred to Serena that she'd prefer to think about yellow fever.

Neither Uncle Luke nor Young Calvin appeared to be in any danger that evening, and Serena wondered if Dr. Hooper had suddenly fallen victim to a counterattack of pessimism. After all, Serena reasoned, a medical man who professed such a perpetually sunny outlook was bound to turn gloomy eventually.

There was gloom enough to write about in the newspaper. Serena had put off composing her editorial on the execution of six deserters from the Union army. They had been ordered by Major Lawson to be shot to death while seated on their coffins. Serena had admitted to herself that she didn't know what to say—certainly the provost marshal's heavy-handed justice was necessary in wartime. But since she had been unable to witness such brutal carnage, it ran through her mind that it could not be morally justified.

"I must be wrong," she told Quenette, who was handing a set of page proofs to Caldwell Smith. "Lawson is a moral man. Why am I so squeamish about how he treats deserters?"

"Probably because womenfolk in general aren't keen with regards to killing." Quenette gave Serena a dour smile. "You ladies wouldn't go to war if somebody set your hair on fire."

"Well, you'd put it out first. And then ask why they did such a stupid stunt." Serena couldn't help but smile back. "By the time you were done talking, you'd be too sleepy to fight."

Quenette nodded. "That's what I mean." He fingered his trim moustache and made a face. "Six more people died in the last two days, all of fever."

"My aunt wasn't well today," Serena remarked, putting aside the official account of the executions. She simply could not confront the moral dilemma when the lingering autumn heat was so oppressive. "But my uncle is better."

"Good. And here's some happy news—North Carolina's native Union naval hero, Captain John A. Winslow, is coming home next week." Quenette brandished the announcement at Serena and was surprised when she blanched.

"I was thrilled to hear the *Kearsarge* had defeated the *Alabama*," Serena said primly, "but I had no idea the ship's crew would come *here*." Surely Brant wasn't returning to New Bern. But if Brant came, so would Matt. Serena told herself she ought to be happy about that, at least.

"This information just mentions Winslow, not the crew. They've all been in Washington, having President Lincoln pat them on the back." Quenette paused, his eyes going down the page. "They only lost one man. That's amazing."

"Who?" Serena demanded, tensing in her chair.

"Let me see . . ." Quenette looked up sharply. There's a Farrar and a Parnell listed as nonnaval personnel. Anyone you know?"

"Yes," Serena breathed. "Are they . . . all right?"

Quenette nodded. "Apparently. But who are they?" It seemed to Serena that his cheerful brown-eyed gaze was much more probing than usual.

"My brother and my husband." She spoke tersely, then picked up her pen and began to write swiftly, if disjointedly, across a sheet of foolscap. Quenette stared at Serena for just a moment too long, then resumed his own work. Serena pretended she had not noticed. Major Quenette was the kindest of men, but he did not need to delve into her private, painful world.

Three days later, Young Calvin appeared fully recovered while Uncle Luke seemed on the mend. Aunt Kathleen, however, had grown worse. She hadn't eaten since falling ill and her maid, Bathsheba, was very concerned.

"I've spoken with both Dr. Hooper and the occupational medical director, Dr. Hand," said Abigail that evening. "Dr. Hooper insists it's yellow fever and Dr. Hand says it's malaria. Either way, we face a most dire dilemma."

Serena nodded solemnly. She already knew that the hospital next door was filled to capacity. Indeed, some of the other large homes in town were being converted virtually overnight to accommodate the increasing number of fever victims.

The following day, Dr. Hand and Major Lawson supervised the burning of an old warehouse next to the dock at the foot of Craven Street. The cellar was full of stagnant water which bred the mosquitoes thought to cause the dread disease. Serena and Quenette watched from a distance, at one point worried that some of the adjacent structures would catch fire. Providence intervened, however, with a drenching rain that lasted an hour and soaked the nearby roofs.

The destruction of the warehouse did not stop the spread of the fever. Day after day, the list of dead grew to the point that Serena printed the names each morning and had them posted in different parts of town.

At the end of the third week, Aunt Kathleen's name was added to the roll of victims. She had died at dawn on a Sunday, refusing to see Uncle Luke one last time.

"I'm sorry, Uncle Luke," Abigail said, trying to console him as he sat hollow-eyed in his small study. "In her delirium, she had no idea what she was saying."

"She hasn't known that for a long time," Serena persisted gently. "I truly doubt she would ever have gotten well. Here, I mean," she added, tapping her temple.

"Maybe not." Uncle Luke sounded empty. He seemed healthy but had lost a considerable amount of weight. "My God," he suddenly exclaimed, "if only Nathan had come back!"

"He has," said a soft, drawling voice from the doorway. Uncle Luke stared at Yancy Clarke as Serena and Abigail turned around in their chairs. But it was Brant Parnell, not Nathan, who stood directly behind the Texan.

Both women stood up, Abigail going to Yancy, Serena remaining uncertainly by her chair. Yancy was dressed in his work clothes, Brant more formally in dark trousers, a cream-colored shirt, and a dark jacket with the wide-brimmed hat in his hand. He was very tan, almost as dark as Leonard, Serena noted, as she asked about Matt.

"He went on from Washington to Maine," Brant replied without inflection. Although his glance raked Serena from head to foot, he appeared indifferent to her presence.

Meanwhile, Uncle Luke was interrogating Yancy. In his usual slow, careful manner, Yancy explained that Nathan had been captured not far from Wexford. Nathan had asserted that his destination was home, but the men who placed him under arrest had rejected his story. Nathan had been taken to the provost marshal's headquarters and charged with desertion.

Uncle Luke leaned against the desk for support. "Good God almighty," he whispered, his face ashen, "they'll shoot him, just as they did those poor others last summer!"

"But he never really joined the Union army," Serena countered. "He joined Graham, after that horrid man had already deserted."

"The fine points of law may be overlooked in wartime," Brant said as Abigail rummaged in the liquor cabinet for a restorative. "We'd better take matters into our own hands."

Yancy shrugged. "Suits me."

Abigail proffered bourbon to Uncle Luke. She turned to Brant, speaking in a calm, quiet voice. "Did Yancy tell you Mrs. Farrar passed away this morning?"

Brant bowed his head in Uncle Luke's direction. "Yes. My condolences, sir. It's been a year of loss for us all."

Yancy accepted a shotglass of bourbon from Abigail. To her horror, Serena noticed that the big, shambling Texan's hand shook. And she realized that Brant was not just deeply tanned but flushed. Suddenly Serena wanted to scream, to vent her fears and terrors of what seemed to be a nightmare without end. Instead, she took a large swallow of bourbon and shut her eyes. Brant and Yancy couldn't possibly both be ill. Nor could Major Lawson parade Nathan Farrar down Craven Street on top of a coffin with a cross marked on his naked chest. Serena drained her glass and sank back into her chair just as Yancy Clarke slumped to the floor at Abigail's feet.

Abigail dropped down beside her husband, the color drained from her face. Beseechingly, she looked up at Brant. "We must move him upstairs."

Brant set his shotglass down on the desk. Uncle Luke had risen, making a gallant effort to compose himself. "I'll help you, Captain. He's a very big man."

"I've hauled him around before, I can do it again." But Brant didn't protest when Uncle Luke came to his assistance. Abigail followed the men out of the study but Serena remained alone, the empty glass clutched in her hands. Five minutes later, Uncle Luke returned. He seemed to have aged ten years in the last twenty-four hours.

"Rena, dear," he said softly, putting a hand on her shoulder. "I'm afraid your husband is ill, too. He's in your room. Perhaps you'd better go to him."

Serena hadn't moved since the others had left her. She continued to stare woodenly in the direction of the marble-fronted fireplace until her uncle nudged her. Slowly, she looked up at him. "And what of you?"

He put a hand to his neck to straighten his cravat, apparently forgetting that he had not bothered to put one on during this day of grief. "What? Oh, I'll go see the provost marshal, of course. I can't believe that any man from Massachusetts is totally without mercy. Or reason." The hint of a smile trembled on his lips as he headed toward the door.

"Wait." Serena rose and ran to catch up with him. "I'll go with you."

A spark of life returned to Uncle Luke's eyes. "Didn't you hear me, Rena?" His voice held an unfamiliar note of anger. "I told you Captain Parnell is ill. I can take care of my son. Your duty is with your husband."

In deference to her uncle, Serena hung her head. But she refused to surrender totally. "I'll stay if you promise to take Jason with you."

Uncle Luke wagged a finger in her face. "See here, Serena, I am not a doddering old fool. Until this war came along, I was the third wealthiest plantation owner in East Carolina. Despite my Yankee upbringing, I've held a position of respect in this town for nigh on twenty years. In Brunswick, Maine, I may be Marcus Farrar's younger brother, but in New Bern, North Carolina, I'm Lucas Farrar. Period. I'm going by myself to see the provost marshal and you're going to march up those stairs and act like a wife!"

Serena was so shocked that she did precisely that. She had reached the second landing before Uncle Luke was out the front door. Moments later, she was inside the bedroom, one hand on her breast as she surveyed the outline of Brant Parnell lying on his side under the chintz canopy.

"Brant?" Her voice sounded strangely shrill. "What can I do for you?"

He moved his head slightly. "Shoot me," he muttered, and made an attempt to roll over. She came to the bed, startled by the look of pain on his face. He lifted his arm and let it fall back on the counterpane. "Go away, Serena, you'll only end up getting sick, too."

"Nonsense," retorted Serena, summoning up her composure. "If this fever is all over town, I can hardly avoid it. Would you like some water?"

Brant gave a slight nod of his head. The ice in the pitcher by Serena's bed had long since melted but the water was still cool. She poured a mug half full and sat down next to Brant. "Can you raise your head?" He tried, but without success. Serena grasped one of the extra pillows and attempted to support him with it. He sipped tentatively at the water but finally fell back in apparent exhaustion.

Anxiously, she watched the craggy features slacken. At least he wasn't sweating yet so the fever couldn't be terribly high. It was a deceptive disease, however; Serena already knew that its victims often recovered sufficiently to get up for a day or two—and then suffered a relapse which frequently proved fatal.

Setting the mug down, she went to the bureau and got out a large linen handkerchief which she dipped in water. Gently, she began wiping Brant's forehead. He seemed to be asleep. Serena paused and bit her lip. Even in this ill and helpless state, Brant seemed to possess more vitality than other men. How unfair of fate to have brought them together only to tear them apart before they even got to know each other, Serena thought bitterly. If she had been able to fall in love with him under such unfortunate circumstances, perhaps, given time and opportunity, he might have grown to love her, at least a little. Hesitantly, she ran her finger down the side of his cheek to the hard jawline. The skin was peeling just by his ear, she noted, and tried to remember at what stage of the disease that happened. Her mind didn't seem to be working properly; she couldn't recall.

Brant groaned deep in his throat and shifted his broad shoulders in misery. Serena decided to remove his jacket to make him more comfortable. It was an awkward task but she managed without rousing him. After loosening his shirt, she tried to take off his boots. At first, it seemed impossible, but she finally succeeded. Then she pulled up a chair and sat back down next to the bed.

Serena must have dozed, for it was dusk when she sat up with a jerk and rubbed her eyes. Brant was still asleep, but his breathing seemed even. She touched his forehead and was relieved to find it relatively cool. The skin was also peeling next to the dark hairline, however, and she frowned just as Brant murmured something unintelligible. In spite of herself, Serena smiled. He looked so guileless, so lacking in arrogance, and most of all, so handsome. Surely Providence would spare him. But many such as Brant had been laid to earth in the prime of their vigor and virility. How often she'd heard about young ladies who had sent young gentlemen off to war with a meaningless promise of devotion or a false whisper of undying love. Serena had looked askance at such well-meant hypocrisy. Still, she realized that the exchanges were intended to help armor the fighting man, to give him some comfort should he fall wounded or lay dying.

And here was Brant who had never truly gone to war, but who might be just as near to death, and who had never heard one loving word from his own wife. The irony, Serena told herself fiercely, was that she actually loved this man. Brant might die and never know how much she had cared. Serena felt the tears sting her eyes and laid her head down next to Brant's shoulder.

The shock of hearing him speak practically made her fall off the bed. "If you'd taken off the rest of my clothes, you could have saved one of us a lot of trouble, Serena."

Open-mouthed, she stared directly up into the sea-blue eyes. Was he delirious? Or was she? Serena started to sit up but Brant had pinned her next to him with one arm. He reached over with his free hand to wipe a tear from the corner of her eye. "You're crying, Serena. I'll bet you five to two, you're crying for me."

"You ghoul!" Serena wailed, making a fruitless effort to pull away. "You aren't sick!"

"No. Just sunburned. I went to sleep on deck just out of Hampton Roads. A dumb thing to do. But useful." He put both hands behind her head and brought his mouth down hard on hers before she could shriek at him again. Serena stiffened, then felt his tongue thrusting and his lips savaging and his big, hard body pressed against hers. She went limp for a moment, then wrapped her arms around his waist, giddy with desire and relief.

"I hate you, I just hate you," she breathed when he finally released her mouth to kiss her throat and the curve of her neck. "You're the most devious, horrible man I ever met!"

"And damned near as stubborn as you," Brant murmured into her ear and gave it a sharp little nip. "Only the most stubborn—or stupid—man would ever have come back to New Bern."

"I don't know why you did," Serena retorted. "You never loved me!"

Brant responded by taking the collar of her mourning dress in both hands and shearing it right down to her waist. "I probably should have mentioned that," he admitted, unfastening her skirt band and ripping the rest of her dress to the hem. "But I kept having the feeling you didn't want to hear it."

"You are stupid! When did a wife not want to hear her husband say he loves her?" Serena pushed the ruined gown from the bed and kicked off her shoes, then grabbed the front of his shirt and ripped it across one shoulder.

"When she's trying to convince her husband she hates him." Brant pulled off the rest of his shirt and sailed it past Serena to land atop her crumpled dress. "And you were convincing, you obstinate little brat." He hesitated just an instant, his hand at the top of her chemise. "Well?"

"Say it." Slanted foxlike eyes met the wary sea-blue gaze. "Say it, so I can stop telling you I hate you."

Brant lifted one bare shoulder. "I love you. I always have. You should have known I'd never leave a poker game for a woman I didn't love. At least not when I was winning."

Serena's mind leaped back to that long-ago night in the Tontine Hotel. "You knew then?" The question came out in an incredulous whisper.

"Of course." Brant fingered the cotton fabric of the chemise. "Well, maybe not then exactly." He pulled the chemise down to her hips, grinning at the full, pointed breasts. "I've got a wonderful memory, but it hasn't done you justice. Now are you going to say you love me or shall I ignore your charms and leave town?"

"You beast!" But Serena was smiling, a wide, delighted smile that softened as she took Brant's hand and placed it over one breast. "I love you. I love you more than anything in the world."

Brant's slow, triumphant smile held no hint of irony. He caressed her breast and bent to kiss the flat of her stomach, then slipped the chemise down to her knees. His lips trailed lingeringly toward the rich brown curling hair between her thighs and Serena felt the aching need for him throb throughout her entire body. Moments later they had removed the rest of each other's clothing and Brant had eased Serena over him so that her knees rested against his shoulders. She gasped as his fingers slid into the cleft of her buttocks, then began to tantalize the tender, intimate flesh. Serena leaned down so that her breasts brushed Brant's belly, then, with uncertain fingers, she touched the firmness of his manhood and heard his murmur of appreciation. Her hands stroked him with increasing assurance but she paused as his lips began to work their incredible magic. A gasp of exquisite pleasure escaped her lips before she shyly moved to pleasure him in equal measure.

When Brant finally pulled her onto her back, their hearts were pounding so hard she thought she could hear their shared rhythm. Brant entered her so quickly that Serena did not even have time to think about how desperately she needed to be released from the pent-up desires which racked her to the very core. He exploded within her just as she cried out in astonished joy—and then they both lay still, bereft of any emotion except for their mutual victory.

At last, Brant withdrew from her and rolled over. They didn't speak or move again for at least a full minute. It was Brant who finally broke the silence, putting a hand on Serena's thigh in a gesture of intimate, compatible possession. "Just think, if we'd both had yellow fever, we would have died happy."

"Happy!" exclaimed Serena. "I'd forgotten about being happy." She nuzzled Brant's shoulder with her nose. "How can we be happy when Aunt Kathleen is dead and Nathan may get himself shot and Yancy really is sick?"

"I guess we're just callous," Brant said in his familiar breezy manner. But he held Serena close and kissed her left ear. "I've waited three goddamned years for this and they can blow New Bern clear to Cape Hatteras before I stop enjoying it."

Serena tried to nod in agreement but felt too enervated to make the effort. "When did you decide to trick me?" she asked in a drowsy voice.

"When I brought Yancy upstairs and Uncle Luke told me you loved me."

Serena was suddenly wide awake. "Uncle Luke! But he didn't know!"

"Of course he knew," Brant replied equably, patting Serena's naked bottom. "He's a wise bird. I'd come here knowing I'd have to get you to finally show your hand, but I wasn't certain how to do it. Yancy's illness gave me a brilliant idea. So did the sunburn."

Serena shook her head, the tangle of brown hair sprawling across Brant's chest. "It was a cheap trick, you mean. I should have walked out."

"But you didn't." Brant let go of Serena and sat up. "It's dark. And I'm hungry. Do you suppose the rest of them have eaten?"

"Uncle Luke went to see the provost marshal but I suppose he's back." She noticed Brant's raised eyebrow, but continued. "I don't know about the others. Though we aren't precisely foundering in foodstuffs these days."

"I'll have some of the victuals sent from the ship," Brant declared, standing up and stretching. "If you've got another dress, let's see if I can make my shirt presentable and we'll go downstairs to announce my miraculous recovery."

Serena couldn't suppress a giggle, but suddenly turned wistful. "It's strange—I've waited so long for this, yet I thought it would never happen. Am I dreaming?"

Brant had his trousers flung over one arm. He came back to where Serena lay on the bed and sat down. "You wouldn't let it happen, Serena. What scares the hell out of me is that tomorrow morning, you'll be sorry you did."

Serena shook her head in vigorous denial, one hand touching Brant's broad chest. "It's just that I can't believe it. Even when you told me Papa had lost most of his money, I thought you were tricking me somehow."

He picked up a thick strand of her hair and wound it around his fingers. "I was trying to tell you then that I loved you. But you wouldn't listen."

She moved one leg so that her knee pressed against his side. "It might have been easier if you'd said so, straight out."

Brant entwined the thick coils around her breasts, then brushed some of the strands across her bosom so that only the nipples peeked through. He didn't appear to be listening to Serena anymore. "You say the larder's pretty low?" he asked, his voice sounding deeper than usual.

"All but empty." Serena smiled delightedly, as if announcing the happiest of news.

Brant encircled her waist with his hands and fell on top of her. "I guess I'm not as hungry as I thought I was." He tickled her ear with his tongue. "At least not for hominy."

Serena made a purring noise in her throat as she reached out to clasp Brant's hard buttocks. "We can always say you had a relapse," she breathed, as his lips moved down the curve of her shoulder.

"I'm under quarantine," he murmured. "We'll have to stay here for weeks."

Serena laughed and wound her legs around Brant's as his mouth continued tracing a path of pleasure down the length of her eager, joy-filled body.

They made love again that night and then talked for hours by the light of the gas lamp. There seemed to be so much each had to say to the other: Brant, telling her about the battle between the *Kearsarge* and the *Alabama;* Matt's rebirth of self-confidence; the glowing happiness evinced by Cecelia and Leonard en route to their honeymoon tour of the Continent; the details not mentioned in her mother's letters concerning Marcus Farrar's ever-expanding empire and post-war plans. Serena's accounts were not nearly as sanguine: the sad saga of Aunt Kathleen, the persistence of yellow fever, the new fears for Nathan, the arrest of Emaline Pigott, the plans Yancy and Abigail had made for Montana, the letter from Peggy Parnell.

"Poor Kirk," Brant said with a shake of his head against the pillow. "I'm not one to regret things that happen, but he's an exception. I look back on that day and wonder if I'd not taken so long to say good-bye—or taken longer—or gone aboard with him or . . ." He put a hand to his head, his eyes in shadow, his craggy face pensive.

"You never had a chance to see who shot him?" Serena touched Brant's upper arm, rubbing it in tender consolation.

"No. I went to him first. Whoever it was stood above the docks on the bank. But the sentries on duty swore they hadn't seen anybody with a rifle. The shot must have come from one of the tenements close by, but it would take incredible marksmanship." He shifted his body so that he could turn down the lamp beside the bed. "It must be long after midnight." He flashed her a grin in the darkness. "You're a very exhausting woman, Serena Parnell."

She snuggled against his chest. "Better than being tiresome." Serena heard him grunt in agreement and closed her eyes. She was still afraid she'd awake in the morning alone. After three years of struggle with herself and yearning for Brant, the reality of his love overwhelmed her. At least, she told herself sleepily, she'd have a lifetime to learn.

Chapter 24

THE ONLY GOOD NEWS that morning in the Farrar household was Brant's miraculous recovery. Dismissing his sudden collapse as a consequence of eating bad pork, Brant, along with Serena, joined Jason and Uncle Luke at a breakfast of cornbread and coffee.

If Uncle Luke had any suspicions about Brant's alleged illness, they were submerged under his concern for Nathan and Yancy. Abigail was with her husband, who had suffered from violent black vomiting and a raging fever since dawn. She, better than anyone, knew there was little to do except wait. And pray.

Nathan's fate appeared equally uncertain. Uncle Luke's visit to the provost marshal's office had proved fruitless. Major Lawson had also fallen ill with the fever. All Uncle Luke could find out from a confused and decimated band of subordinates was that Nathan had been charged with desertion and would be executed within the week.

"Can he have visitors?" Brant asked as Young Calvin poured more coffee.

Uncle Luke shook his head. He looked very drawn and haggard. "No. Even I'm not allowed to see him."

Brant drummed his fingers on the table. "There's no such thing as hopeless," he remarked while Serena looked at him questioningly. "I'll think of something."

"I'll help," Jason asserted.

Brant gave the youth a smile. "Good. We'll talk about it tonight, after supper."

Uncle Luke continued to stare at the place where Aunt Kathleen used to sit. He seemed quite unaware that the others were in the room.

Serena was not at supper that night, however. She had spent the better part of the day at the *Leader* while Brant had supplies hauled from *The Irish Rover* to the townhouse. When she returned in the late afternoon, she discovered that Abigail was ill, suffering from chills and fever in the same bed with her agony-racked husband.

"Are Pa and Mamagail gonna die?" Liberty demanded, tugging at Serena's hand. His small face was wizened with fear, making him look like an aging midget.

The terrible question was one which Serena had not dared ask

340

herself. Forcing a thin smile, she squeezed Liberty's fingers. "Young Calvin didn't die," she pointed out and derived at least a meager portion of reassurance from uttering the statement.

Liberty brightened, but still clutched Serena's hand. "You be right. Young Calvin be better. He not so fat now, neither." The child gnawed thoughtfully at his lower lip. "But Missus Kathleen, she died."

"That's so," Serena admitted. "But she was ... older." She watched Liberty nod slowly, but he still wore a worried expression. Freeing her hand, Serena bent down to cup his chin. "Liberty, you like your Pa and Mamagail a lot, don't you?"

The round brown eyes glistened with tears. Again, Liberty nodded. "They be nice folks. Like Leonard." He cleared his throat and passed a too-casual hand over his eyes. "They won't go away—like Leonard did—will they?"

With far more conviction than she felt, Serena shook her head. "No. No, Liberty, they won't go anywhere without you. And Sam."

Liberty sniffed once as Serena stood up. "Guess I'll go bounce Sam around some. He be lonesome, I'll bet, being so small." With a brave smile, Liberty hopped away, though Serena noted that his usual exuberance was subdued. Feeling as heavy of heart as she was of foot, she went upstairs to wash for dinner. And hoped that she hadn't made Liberty a promise that Yancy and Abigail could not possibly keep.

"Good God," she exclaimed to Brant when she met him at the top of the stairs after he came up from the evening meal, "where will it all end? Herman is sick, Quenette didn't feel well, and somebody told me Dr. Hooper took to his bed today."

Brant was unusually tight-lipped. "Uncle Luke learned that Aunt Kathleen can't have a private funeral and will have to be buried with all the others in the cemetery at Forest Grove. And," he went on, taking a deep breath and resting one hand on the newel post, "Nathan is to be executed tomorrow morning."

Serena leaned against Brant, almost toppling them down the stairs. He gripped the newel post tightly and steadied them both. "You said you'd think of something!" she wailed.

"I'm not a wizard, Serena," Brant answered grimly, taking her arm and leading her away from the landing. "Security is especially tight at the prison right now because of the fever. Some of the prisoners have it and they don't want them escaping outside of the town and spreading the disease any further. And a loyal local named Poor is in charge. He's hellbent on making sure there are no lapses while Lawson is ill."

"Damn." Serena leaned against the wall, knocking a scenic watercolor askew. "Does Uncle Luke know?"

"Yes." Brant frowned, the image of Uncle Luke's stricken face still before him. "We have one chance," he said after a pause, reaching inside his jacket and pulling out an official-looking document. Carefully, he unfurled it beneath the gaslight which perched atop a cherub-shaped wall sconce.

"What is it?" Serena demanded, her eyes unable to focus.

"It's Nathan's order of execution." Brant pointed to a blank space at the bottom of the page. "Lawson didn't sign it before he got sick."

"How did you get that?" Serena asked in amazement.

Brant shrugged. "Never mind. The important thing is that I have it and the army doesn't. Not that Lawson can't sign another one. But Colonel Poor can't unless Lawson dies. And if that happens, Poor will have too much on his plate to worry about as far as Nathan is concerned. I hope."

"Oh, my heavens," Serena breathed, "I can't wish for Lawson to die, he's a very decent sort, really, but . . ."

"I know, blood's thicker than water and Lawson's sick as hell anyway." He gave her an ironic smile. "I've always admired your practical approach, Serena. It suits my own so well."

Serena looked pleased, but her step was unsteady as she headed back to Yancy and Abigail's bedroom. How long did any of them have to live, she wondered, if the rampaging fever didn't soon abate? Perhaps only Uncle Luke, who had already overcome the disease—and who suddenly had so little to live for.

The toll was already into the hundreds. The city seemed like a ghostly hull, with most of its businesses shut down and the streets all but empty. On Serena's way home she had witnessed a fearful sight as a tall, rangy man stood on the street corner, convulsed with fever and already turning a bright saffron. Not far away, she had seen half a dozen men from the self-styled "Dead Corps" bringing bodies out of houses on Broad Street.

That memory hovered over Serena as she opened the door to her cousin's bedroom. Yancy and Abigail seemed very still—too still, Serena thought with alarm, and hurried to the bed. But Yancy's breathing was deep and even; Abigail turned in her sleep, the faintly jaundiced skin free of perspiration.

Serena left them, aware that she was famished. In the kitchen, Young Calvin and Bathsheba piled a plate with ham and cheese and boiled potatoes, bounty from *The Irish Rover*. Serena mentally blessed her husband, greedily shoved a piece of ham into her mouth, and suddenly realized she was no longer alone. She nearly choked on the meat as she started to cry, the tears of joyous relief coursing down her cheeks.

While Abigail and Yancy were both able to sit up and take broth the next morning, the pall of imminent death had not yet lifted from the Farrar house. Nathan was due to die at ten o'clock. Uncle Luke was up at dawn, wandering about like a wraith. Serena, coming out of a deep sleep in her husband's arms, seemed to sense more than hear that her uncle was already up. Wrapped in her emerald-green peignoir, Serena found him in the pantry, trying to make coffee.

"What's he going to do?" Uncle Luke asked tonelessly, as his usually sure hands found great difficulty making the lid fit onto the coffeepot.

Serena didn't need to ask who "he" was. For Uncle Luke—indeed, for Serena—Brant had become their unofficial commander-in-chief. Her response was terse. "Wait." Serena knew the answer wasn't completely satisfactory, but she had nothing else to offer. "They can't do anything to Nathan until the order is signed. It may be days before . . . anything happens."

"God forbid." Uncle Luke walked disconsolately from the pantry, leaving the coffeepot on the counter. Serena picked it up and took it to the stove. She swore under her breath as she noticed that Uncle Luke had not remembered to start a fire. At least it had been laid by the servants; she struck a match and watched the kindling begin to glow. By the time the pot had started to perk, Uncle Luke had returned to the sanctuary of his bedroom.

That day and the next were like living in a suspension of time. Lawson was still very ill, Nathan remained in his prison cell, Yancy and Abigail veered between bouts of fever and periods of lucidity, and Brant quietly assumed the running of the hospital next door. When Serena expressed her surprise at his decision, Brant gave his familiar shrug.

"Yancy and Abigail are sick and Sergeant Davis is at Wexford. Who would you have run it—Young Calvin?"

Serena looked at her husband with rueful eyes. "Did I misjudge you all these years? I always had the feeling you weren't keen on endangering your hide."

Brant looked genuinely astonished. "God, I'm not! My hide is my most precious commodity. And yours." He gave her a quick, hard kiss. "Now I'm off to take pulses and relate my favorite bedside stories. I wonder how they'd like to hear about Gloria St. George?"

"Who?" asked Serena. But Brant was already gone.

* * *

With both Herman and Major Quenette confined to bed, Serena and Caldwell Smith were hard-pressed to put out that week's edition of the *Leader* by themselves. Serena had considered halting publication, but realized that New Bern residents needed more than ever to learn what was happening in their city, no matter how grim the news, and that retaining a sense of normalcy was imperative to local morale.

By Thursday, the last full week of October, Bill and Phil were hawking the latest edition, while Yancy was finally back on his feet. Abigail remained in bed but was apparently on the road to recovery. The next day, Major Lawson died.

As soon as Brant heard the news, he rode straight to the new provost marshal's office. "It's a violation of the U.S. Constitution to take orders from a dead man," Brant told Lieutenant Colonel Walter Poor. "I wouldn't know that if the Secretary of the Navy, Gideon Welles, hadn't mentioned it the last time we got drunk as skunks together, but he *does* tend to run at the mouth when he's in his cups." Brant flourished Nathan's order for execution. "Not that the Union army ever had adequate grounds to condemn this poor deluded lad."

Colonel Poor's salt-and-pepper moustache seemed to droop. "I must confess, sir, I wasn't involved. As a North Carolina man myself, I should hate seeing a local boy shot."

Brant gripped the execution order between his thumbs and forefingers, shredding it in two. "I knew you'd see it that way. Now why don't you release Nathan and I'll take him home. He's needed at the hospital on Pollock Street."

Poor made a wry face. "He—and fifty like him—are needed everywhere. The occupational forces are literally dying by the hundreds." Poor's hand slapped down on the latest long list of victims. "My God, what an irony! We've already lost more men in this past month than in all the fighting put together around the New Bern district."

"The soldiers have no immunity, I'm afraid." Brant folded his arms across his chest and waited for Poor to respond to his request. But the other man seemed absorbed in his own problems. Brant tilted his head to one side, the blue eyes glinting. "Colonel . . ."

"Oh—young Farrar! Sorry, my mind was elsewhere." Poor pulled open a drawer and got out a piece of official paper. "Here," he said, scrawling his name at the bottom, "take this to the Jones-Lipman house. That's where your kinsman is being detained."

Brant tipped his hat to the colonel and smiled winningly. But as he left the provost marshal's headquarters, his thoughts were already galloping in another direction. Serena had mentioned that Emaline Pigott was also a prisoner in the Jones-Lipman residence. As soon as he secured Nathan's release, he'd pay a call on the partisan Miss Pigott.

Securing the compliance of the guards proved simple enough. It was Nathan who offered the obstacles.

He was being held in the condemned prisoner's cell which was part of the root cellar. Brant found him huddled on the floor in a darkened corner. Suspicious gray eyes peered out of the gloom as a soldier opened the cell door for Brant.

At first, Nathan didn't recognize his savior. Then he refused to believe that Brant had come to rescue him. It was a trick, he insisted, a means of getting him to leave the haven of his prison without a struggle. Only when Brant showed him the torn execution order did Nathan begin to lose his air of disbelief. But it took Brant the better part of a half-hour to coax Nathan out into the fresh, cool air of a late October morning."

"It can't be. It can't be," Nathan muttered over and over, looking around warily as if to make certain no Union soldiers were ready to pounce and drag him to the place of execution at the end of Craven Street.

"It can and it is," Brant asserted with a trace of impatience. "Why don't you run on home before your poor pa perishes from anxiety?"

"My ma already did," Nathan said bitterly. "Did I break her heart?" His youthful gaze was forlorn.

Brant sighed and put a hand on Nathan's too-thin shoulder. "No. The war did that. Go home, Nathan. Go home and let your father teach you how to be a man."

Nathan started to open his mouth in apparent protest, but slowly averted his eyes and turned from Brant. With a dogged step, he passed the soldiers guarding the Jones-Lipman house and walked on his way to freedom.

Emaline Pigott occupied what had probably been the master bedroom. Most of the handsome furnishings were still in place, including a huge dark oak four-poster bed and a matching bureau with at least two dozen commodious drawers. The floor was covered with a deep red Oriental carpet and dark blue brocade drapes hung at the windows. Emaline sat in a rocking chair with a petit-point covered back. Her worn dress was in sharp contrast to the appointments of the room and Brant realized that never had a gilded cage held such a plainly plumed bird.

Emaline didn't move when he entered nor did she speak. She maintained her rigid posture as he approached and Brant saw that she had been crying.

"Do you remember me, Miss Pigott? I'm Brant Parnell." He took off his hat and waited for her to indicate that he should sit.

But Emaline only nodded. Brant stood for a moment, fingering his hat brim, and then pulled up a cane-backed chair next to Emaline. "Is something wrong?" he asked quietly.

Again she nodded, but this time she spoke: "Herman is dead."

Brant started to touch her arm in sympathy but drew back. "I'm sorry. I hadn't heard."

"He died an hour ago." Emaline began to rock in the chair, very slowly, very deliberately.

Brant suppressed a sigh. He was saddened by the news, sorry for Emaline, sympathetic, too, for Serena, who had suffered more than her share of loss in recent months.

"I know how you feel more than most people would," he said quietly. "I still mourn Kirk."

Emaline rocked just a little faster. "Major Publisher Parnell was a good man. I liked him."

Brant rubbed at the cleft in his chin. "It doesn't seem fair, some-how—here you are locked up for taking thread and flour and a few bits of information to your Confederate friends—and Kirk's murderer goes free." Brant shook his head. "No, it just doesn't seem fair."

"Not much in life is fair." Emaline's lower lip thrust out. "Look at Herman, he never harmed a june bug."

"Neither did Kirk." Brant turned silent, eyeing Emaline from the periphery of his vision. The rocker creaked faster and faster until Brant wondered if Emaline would eventually hurl herself headlong across the room. At last he put out a strong hand and gripped the arm of the rocker, bringing Emaline to a standstill. "If you thought so much of my brother, why would you allow his killer to go unpunished?"

The cornflower eyes riveted on Brant's face. "Maybe I think more of who killed him." The thin mouth clamped shut as Emaline turned away.

"Oh." Brant let go of the rocker and stood up. "I can understand that. Good-bye, Emaline." He put his hat back on and headed for the door as Emaline began to rock again, in a quick, almost frenzied cadence.

Serena was reminded of the parable about the Prodigal Son. A dinner of baked ham, hushpuppies, candied yams, squash casserole, and blueberry cobbler was served to celebrate Nathan's return. Uncle Luke's spirits were restored, though his grief over Aunt Kathleen lingered like the last leaves of autumn. Yancy joined the others, though Abigail still wasn't sufficiently recovered to leave her bed.

A few days later, however, she was back at the hospital working side by side with Yancy. A week after that, the yellow fever epidemic waned.

The death toll had risen to over thirteen hundred men, women, and children, the majority of the victims members of the occupational army.

"I suppose it's safe now to ask how you and I were so lucky not to get sick," Serena said to Brant one crisp November evening as she took down her hair in front of the dressing table mirror.

"As I've said, I'm a great believer in luck." Brant was pulling off his boots after having spent a long day with Uncle Luke at Wexford, making a thorough survey of the planatation lands and studying possibilities for the future.

Brant captured Serena's neck in the crook of his arm as he stood behind her. "Since you're not so wrapped up in calamities now, I thought I might tell you about Emaline."

"Emaline!" Serena gave a guilty little laugh. "I'd almost forgotten about her. When Herman died, it was rather as if Emaline ceased to exist, too."

"Maybe she has," Brant said absently, watching their reflection in the mirror as he caressed her temples, "but she knows who killed Kirk. Did you tell me she had a beau?"

Serena leaned back to rest her head against Brant's mid-section. "That she did, but he was a Union soldier, not a Confederate. Kirk and I saw him the day we . . ." Serena lowered her eyes and felt her cheeks grow warm. "We followed them, actually," she went on quickly, "much as I hate to admit it. But we never got close enough to see who he was."

Brant's hands paused at the nape of her neck. "That doesn't make sense. A Union soldier wouldn't want to shoot Kirk, nor would he try to vandalize the *Leader*." He stared into the mirror, apparently trying to unravel the puzzle, but Serena felt uneasy. The brief romantic interludes she had shared with Kirk were tucked away at the back of her mind, all but erased by the fulfillment she found in Brant's arms. The two of them had been through too much, waited too long, endured too many hardships to let anything—even a memory—cloud their happiness.

She felt a surge of relief when Brant leaned down to kiss her shoulder. "I asked Nathan who the soldier was that he'd sketched," she said. "He didn't remember, just said it was a sentry on Middle Street."

"I should look at the drawing," Brant said, lifting her from the chintz-covered stool and into his arms. "Not that I'd know him, but maybe I've seen him around town." He buried his face against her throat and when he spoke again, she went rigid in his embrace: "I know about Kirk—and you. Don't fuss over it, all right?"

"How?" she breathed as he laid her on the bed. The big eyes were wide as she stared up at him. "How could you know?"

Brant shrugged, pulling off his shirt. "Kirk could never keep a secret from me. He might as well have painted 'I want Serena' on his forehead."

"It . . . it was all quite innocent," Serena asserted, one hand pressed against the opening of her peignoir. "Kirk was an honorable man."

"I know," Brant replied cheerfully. He took off the rest of his clothes and stretched out beside Serena. "I'm not about to play the role of jealous husband. I know you almost as well as I know Kirk." He yawned and put an arm around her, his hand searching through the peignoir for the mound between her thighs.

Serena, however, was not so easily diverted. Brant seemed to be taking her feelings for Kirk—and his for her—far too cavalierly. "It was a most awkward situation," she said, trying to ignore the fingers which taunted her flesh. "I had been deserted by you, and Kirk was separated for such a long time from Peggy."

"You two had some problems," Brant remarked airily. "All that time together on the newspaper, too. It was just plain natural you'd want to console each other. Who could blame you?"

"Brant!" Serena bolted out of his arms and almost fell off the bed. "You're making fun of me! And your poor dead brother! That's horrible!" Serena scrambled back across the comforter, rising up on her elbows to glare down at her husband.

"No." He gave her his ingenuous look, tinged as always by irony. "I just want you to know I realize what went on—and why. Then we can forget about it. Even," he went on in a more serious vein, "if you and Kirk had acted like hares in heat, I wouldn't get wildly outraged. What matters is that you love me. And because of that, you managed to put Kirk off. By accident or design, nothing happened. Or maybe," he added, with a wry little smile as he slipped his hands inside her peignoir, "it was just plain dumb luck."

Serena wriggled herself free of the peignoir and covered his face with her breasts. "You're so damned smug, Brant Parnell. I think you could have let me cool my heels for ten years in New Bern and still expected me to fall into your arms." She pulled away just enough so that her nipples brushed his nose.

Brant frowned in feigned skepticism. "I don't know, ten years is a long time. Six or seven, maybe." He flicked at one rosy tip with his tongue.

Serena pulled just out of reach. "If you think I knew I loved you all that time, I didn't. It took me quite a while to realize how I felt."

Brant grasped her breasts in his hands, grinning at their full firmness. "Most people don't see what they're looking at. Fortunately, I do." He started to press his mouth against the underside of her bosom, then froze, let go of her, and sat up straight. "My God! That's it!"

Atingle with anticipation, Serena was annoyed by Brant's abrupt cessation of their lovemaking. "What's what?" she asked, sounding cross.

"What people don't see." Brant leaned against the carved headboard, gesturing at Serena with his forefinger. "You recall that the sentries said they saw no one above the docks with a rifle. But that's obviously not true—the sentries had rifles. They always have rifles, that's the problem. You said the day somebody threw a rock through the *Leader*'s window that the sentry on duty told Emaline he hadn't seen anybody do anything unusual. That's because it *was* the sentry— the same one who shot poor Kirk. No doubt the same one who approached you that night you were going home alone. Didn't you say there were no other sentries around?"

"Why, so I did. In fact, I remember saying something to Abigail and Yancy about the soldiers being so familiar they were part of the landscape." Serena settled back next to him, turning just enough so that she could see his face. "But who, Brant?"

"Why and who," Brant muttered. "That's what I can't figure out." He inclined his head toward Serena. "Wait—the sentry who shot the dog—he was on duty in the vicinity where Kirk was gunned down. Do you remember what he looked like?"

But Serena's face was blank. "No. But I'm sure it was a different man."

"Damn!" exclaimed Brant in frustration, "I know there's got to be a solution!"

Serena was frowning up at him. "Somebody might recognize Nathan's sketch," Serena said hopefully.

"Maybe." Brant stroked his craggy chin. "Considering all the soldiers who died from fever, it's likely that the poor bastard is already dead."

"Nothing has happened—nothing menacing, at least—for some time. But it's always been like that, as if whoever has been after us has temporary fits of derangement."

"It would have to be that way, or else he'd never maintain his position in the army." Brant looked thoughtful for several moments, then shook his head. "The sketch is our best bet. I'll show it around town. Discreetly, of course."

Serena flung a leg across Brant's thigh. "And what do you intend to do until morning?"

Brant looked at her with pretended indifference. "Oh, I don't know—do you play cribbage?"

"Oh!" Serena started to pound on his chest with her fists, but Brant laughed aloud and pulled her up to straddle his hips. She felt the male strength of him move and grow under her tender flesh, making her forget everything but the powerful need to be his.

* * *

It was impossible for Brant to query more than a couple of dozen soldiers a day. At the end of two weeks, he had no success in finding anyone who could identify the sketch, but that wasn't surprising, considering the drastic changes of personnel in recent weeks.

Major Quenette, returned to health though a bit gaunt around the cheekbones, was no more helpful than the rest. "Except for those strange eyes, he looks like any one of a hundred Union soldiers."

"It's the eyes that bother me," Brant said, fingering the sketch which was beginning to tatter around the edges. "Nathan has either captured some elusive quality or else I've seen that face before." He shook his head vexedly. "I know him; I'm sure of it."

"I had the same feeling," Serena agreed. "So did Yancy and Abigail. Perhaps we want to remember."

Brant didn't reply. He tucked the drawing inside his seaman's coat. It was a raw December day, with the wind blowing from the sea. Just an hour earlier, he had said farewell to *The Irish Rover* and her crew, bound for New Bedford. While only two of his men had come down with mild bouts of fever, the sole surviving physician in New Bern, Dr. Chambers, had ordered the ship—and all other vessels—to remain under quarantine. He would not risk the possibility of carrying such pestilence to other ports.

When the quarantine was lifted in late November, Brant had made a desultory effort to convince Serena she should sail home with him. She, in turn, reiterated her commitment to see the *Leader* through the end of the war, but had stated that if Brant felt an obligation to his crewmen, he should join them. He rejected the suggestion, telling Serena that he owed it to her father and her uncle to remain in New Bern to secure the family property. Neither had taken the other's urging seriously. Somehow, it seemed only fitting that having waited so long, they should stay until peace came and go home together.

It appeared that their departure would not be delayed for more than a few months. Even as Brant made ready to leave the newspaper office, Quenette read from the latest reports, citing the loss of twelve Southern generals outside of Nashville. Sherman was marching relentlessly toward Savannah. Only Robert E. Lee stood between the Union army and the Confederate capital at Richmond.

"Hood's done for," Quenette declared. "He may have forced a strategic retreat by the Federal troops into Nashville, but he lost all those officers and over six thousand men."

Brant stood with his hand on the doorknob. "I wonder if the survivors will figure it was all worth it," he mused with a touch of bitterness.

Quenette looked up from his dispatches. "I've got a lung that doesn't work quite like it used to as a souvenir from Gettysburg. But if that helped save this country and abolish slavery, I'd say the price came cheap."

Brant lifted one dark eyebrow. "Would you say the same if you were lying under the dirt in some farmer's field in Virginia?"

Quenette's gaze was unflinching. "Yes. For me, this was a war about what's right and what isn't. I felt I had to help fight it."

Serena tensed as she watched the exchange between the two men. She had come to learn that her husband was no coward. If nothing else, his voyage on the *Kearsarge* had proved that. But she still found his attitude toward letting other men do battle in his place incomprehensible.

"I could be wrong," Brant said from the doorway, "but I always felt that if the Federal government had let the Confederate states secede, within ten, twenty years they'd have come running back to Mother. Their way of life was dying, slavery was dying. I know sometimes people have to be kicked in the backside to change their minds, but I never yet saw anybody take better to a new idea than when they thought it was their own. And you save one hell of a lot of lives in the process."

Quenette looked impressed in spite of himself. "I've wondered why you weren't in uniform. I guess now I know."

Serena offered Brant a warm smile which faded as she saw the door being pushed in behind him. It was Bill and Phil, each clutching a handful of mail.

"Lots of letters now that the port's open," cried Bill, plunking a packet down in front of Serena. "You, too, Major," he said, racing to Quenette.

With pleasure, Serena noted a postmark from Vienna and Cecelia's florid handwriting. With a frown, she also saw a letter from her mother. Brant came over to her desk. "Anything important?" he inquired.

Serena sorted through the rest of the correspondence. "Yes. Here's something from Papa for you." Resignedly, she slit open Lydia Farrar's envelope which smelled faintly of sachet. The first two pages spoke generally about the mild fall Brunswick had enjoyed, the increase in shipbuilding, and the general elation over President Lincoln's reelection. The most important news was reserved for the last page:

"Despite our most affectionate and diligent exhortations, Matthew is determined to move out West. He has spoken with a man who helps run a sawmill in the town of Seattle and who insists that there are fortunes to be made there in timber. Your father has reminded Matthew that we already have a fortune in timber right here, but that fact in no way daunts him from his purpose of making a name for himself in the West. How he can entertain such foolish notions in his condition

I am unable to say, but the more we try to dissuade him, the more intent he is on going to this primitive place."

Serena couldn't help but laugh aloud. If Matt had been there, she would have hugged him and hailed his audacity. Impatiently, she waited for Brant to finish the letter from Marcus.

But Brant had also been told about Matt's plan. Before she could say anything at all, Brant went to the little wardrobe to get her cape. "Let's take a walk, Serena."

Quenette, engrossed in his mail from home, gave them an absent-minded wave. They stepped out into the chilling wind, heading briskly toward the water. Neither spoke until they reached the Gaston House, a large brick mansion which had been converted into a hotel. Brant greeted the proprietor, Edward McAlpin, and steered Serena into the comfortable dining room.

"You know what Matt's decision means," Brant said after they were seated and had ordered coffee and biscuits.

"I know it means that Matt has faith in himself." She paused as the waiter set two cups on the table. "I also know what you did for him and I'm grateful."

Brant shook his head. "No, he did it for himself. I just gave him a little nudge. But if Matt goes to Seattle, your father will have no one—no relatives, that is—to take over the business. Except you. And me."

Serena sat very still as the coffee was poured and the biscuits were served. "I see." For just a fleeting moment, she wondered if Brant had somehow orchestrated all this. But that wasn't fair; it wasn't even possible. Serena sighed and felt her shoulders slump. "I've waited so long to go back to Brunswick. Then I thought we'd be heading for New Bedford and I realized I didn't want to live in Brunswick any-more. I've missed Mama and Papa a great deal, but being under their thumb again . . . I can't do it, Brant."

He buttered a biscuit for her and put it in her hand. It was warm to the touch and light as a breeze. But Serena had no appetite. Brant regarded her with his wry expression. "It won't be the way it was," he said quietly. "You have me now. You're not just a daughter any-more, you're a wife."

Serena remained unconvinced. "Why not Cecelia and Leonard?" she demanded in annoyance.

"Let's be realistic, Rena. I don't think Brunswick is ready for miscegenation. If Cecelia wasn't so brazen and Leonard so strong, Europe might not be ready, either. But they'll manage over there, I suspect. They couldn't do that in Maine."

Serena watched her husband devour a biscuit. "I'll have to think about it," she said at last. "You should, too. Do you really want to be my father's minion?"

"Minion?" Brant gave her an ironic look as he reached for another biscuit. "Hell, for the kind of money your father's offering, I'd be a bunion!" He saw her shocked stare and grinned. "Stop worrying. Do I strike you as the kind of man who'd let Marcus Farrar walk all over me?"

Brant didn't, of course. Yet she knew her father well, knew how he'd walked over every other man he'd ever encountered. He'd even walked over her.

"I still say we should think about it." Serena gave Brant a pleading look.

"If you like." He lifted one shoulder, then peered into the jam pot. "Marmalade—a great favorite of mine."

Serena watched him pick up a third biscuit which he covered with what seemed to be half the contents of the jam pot. She sipped at her coffee thoughtfully and wondered if life in a brawling frontier town such as Seattle would be any more difficult than living under Marcus and Lydia Farrar's noses in Brunswick.

Brant had headed back to the docks after they left the Gaston House. He wanted to see if any of his seagoing cronies were on the ships which had come into New Bern that afternoon. Serena returned to the newspaper for an hour, but felt restless and accomplished little. Just after four o'clock, she told Quenette she was going home. It was still broad daylight but would soon get dark this time of year.

The wind had died down when Serena went outside again. It was still cold, however, and she tucked her gloved hands inside her cape as she walked up Craven Street. After hurrying along for two blocks, she had warmed up considerably and decided to slow her pace in order to think.

Certainly she had changed in the past three years. She was no longer the naive, immature girl who had run away from home and eloped with a man she hardly knew. She had proved herself a journalist, she had endured severe hardships, she had suffered through the deaths of people close to her, and—most miraculous of all—she had found love with a man who loved her. If the war had purchased freedom for the slaves, it had done no less for Serena Farrar Parnell.

The insight was almost overpowering. Serena stopped in midstep, suddenly aware that she had gone a block out of her way and was standing directly in front of Tryon Palace's sagging shell. With a faint smile, she recalled the meeting there with Brant so long ago and how nervous she had been in his presence. Now she found only the greatest comfort when he was with her, and was as eager for his touch as he was for hers. Surely that was an indelible mark in the change that had transformed her from girl to woman. Her smile grew wider; she felt like waving at the broken windowpanes, as if they could see what time had wrought in her turbulent life.

She jumped when the soldier spoke to her. Serena had not heard him approach and was startled to find the man almost at her elbow. She was actually terrified when she recognized him as the man in Nathan's sketch.

"It's getting dark, ma'am," he said in a polite New England accent. "May I see you home?"

"I'm almost there," Serena answered, hearing her voice sound high and thin. She started to turn away, but he put a firm hand on her arm.

"You're Mrs. Parnell and I know you live several blocks away. Please let me have the honor." The bearded face was bland, the eyes too intense and piercing.

"Who are you?" Serena demanded, trying in vain to pull away.

"An old family friend," the man replied, pulling Serena toward the palace's gravel drive. "Yes, indeed, our families go way back."

Serena tried to dig her feet into the gravel but he propelled her toward the front entrance. She screamed, but knew there was no one close enough to hear. The man cuffed her alongside the head. Something glinted in his free hand. Serena gasped as she saw it was a knife. He was dragging her now, up the steps, her feet stumbling, her arm aching.

The door was already ajar. He hurled Serena inside where she crashed face forward among a heap of rubble. Struggling to get to her feet, she felt his boot come down on her thigh, pressing hard.

"Think, Mrs. Parnell. Who am I? Who did you and your brother-in-law murder in New Bedford?" The protuberant eyes seemed to bulge from their sockets. "Who did you kill?"

Serena knew the answer, though the accusation was false. Pembrose Stanhope had died by accident. Yet, as she struggled to escape the heavy boot, she could not remember his brother's name.

"Giles!" he cried, as if able to divine her dilemma. "Giles Stanhope! Your mother, your aunt found my father and my uncle unworthy! And you can't even remember my name!" His boot pressed harder and Serena gasped in pain and fear, knowing he was as demented as Pembrose. "You hid my brother's body! I could never claim my money from the niggers we sent back! Oh, high and mighty Farrars and Hollands and Beaulieus! Too good for the rest of us!"

The knife flashed in his hand; Giles spread out his arms, as if imploring some primitive god of vengeance. Serena clambered to her knees, but he dove down beside her, his arm catching her around the neck. Giles's mouth was at her ear. He held the knife a scant inch from her face.

"I'm going to carve you up so fine," he breathed, his voice now raspy. "Your face for your mother, your tits for your aunt, your belly for your father who turned mine into a sot so that he could control him! And your heart for what you did to Pembrose—and me." He pressed the knife flat against her cheek. Serena felt the sharp steel prick her flesh and watched with horror as Giles Stanhope died with that ghastly smile still on his face.

"Jesus Christ." Brant's grim expression didn't quite retrieve Serena from her state of frozen terror. She remained kneeling next to Giles's body, her ears still reverberating from the pistol shot.

Brant didn't try to move her but knelt in the rubble by her side. He put an arm around her shoulders, which were trembling uncontrollably. Two Union soldiers entered the hallway to take command of Giles's body.

Slowly, Serena touched the place where Giles had pricked her with the knife. A small drop of blood stained her fingers but she didn't feel any pain. Brant tossed the pistol at one of the soldiers. "You can have it back," he said in an unusually harsh voice. "I've never shot anybody before. I wouldn't want it to become a habit."

The soldier who apparently owned the gun gave Brant an uncertain smile. "For a first time, that was pretty impressive shooting, even at close range."

"I didn't have any choice." Brant carefully lifted Serena to her feet, letting her lean against him. He looked down into her pale face and shut his eyes for just a second. "I was afraid I'd hit you instead of that lunatic."

Serena finally found her voice. "You almost shot Abby once instead of a deer." She uttered a little laugh that bordered on hysteria.

"I know." He guided her toward the door. "Let's get the hell out of here."

Serena clung to Brant as they went down the stairs and out onto the gravel path. She didn't turn back to look at Tryon Palace with its ravaged facade and crumbling interior. It occurred to her that the palace was like the Stanhope men—permeated with ruin and decay, eventually doomed to destruction.

Brant reserved the story of how he had rescued Serena until she was lying on the settee at Uncle Luke's house and had a snifter of brandy in her hands. The others had gathered by then, evincing various reactions of shock, outrage, and relief. Serena was physically exhausted but emotionally revived.

Brant's account was actually quite simple: He had returned to the newspaper office to meet Serena and learned from Quenette that she had left about five minutes earlier. Knowing that his long stride would overtake her before she got home, he had been puzzled when he couldn't see her up ahead of him after a few blocks. Since he was aware of her contemplative mood, he decided that perhaps she had taken a stroll, though the encroaching darkness made that seem unlikely. Still, he retraced his steps, asking each sentry he met if Mrs. Parnell's familiar figure had been observed. Finally, at the corner by Tryon Palace, he found no sentry.

"I remembered what you said about the time the man you recognized from the sketchbook accosted you," Brant said from his chair next to the settee. "There had been no sentry in sight then, either. I went past the palace to the next corner and found two sentries, changing the four o'clock guard duty a bit late. I asked them to come with me, although I wasn't sure where I was going. Then I realized that the only place you could have been taken was where no one would see you. It had to be the palace. And," he added, putting a hand in Serena's, "it was."

"Thank God." Serena gazed with loving gratitude at her husband. "Did you recognize him?"

"Yes. I'd met him, but he didn't have his beard. Between that and the military cap, I didn't recognize Nathan's sketch." He nodded at the twins, who sat together in rapt attention.

"I never knew him as an adult," Abigail put in, her voice wispy. "The one time I saw him close up in recent years, he was muffled to the eyes. The other time"—she exchanged a swift glance with Yancy— "it was too dark to see him at all."

Serena looked away from both Brant and Yancy. That other occasion had, of course, been the night that Abigail shot Pembrose. She had, Serena thought, no doubt relived her own hour of infamy with Pembrose Stanhope.

Uncle Luke fingered his pipe, then laid it aside on an end table. "It must have been like fits. Otherwise Giles would have done both you and Kirk in right away."

"You're probably right," Brant said. "Certainly he seemed to cause no trouble in his regiment. Who knows, maybe he only acted queer when the moon was full."

Yancy pulled himself up in his armchair. His big body almost seemed to overlap the elegant French lines of cherrywood and brocade. "I don't know—for some men, the chase is more to their liking than the kill. It keeps the victims scared longer."

Brant regarded Yancy, then nodded. "There's some truth to that."

"The insane can't judge the sane," Abigail asserted. "Nor, alas, does it work very well the other way round."

"I wonder if Emaline ever guessed he was crazy," mused Serena, tightening her grip on Brant's hand. "I told myself he used her but perhaps she used him as well."

"Perhaps." Brant tugged at Serena. "You look as if you could sleep for a week. Upstairs, before I have to carry you."

Serena stood up, taking Brant's arm. She started to smile up at him, then suddenly looked alarmed. "You won't be charged...or anything, will you?"

Brant shrugged. "I suppose they'll have to conduct an inquiry. A civilian shooting a soldier isn't to be ignored."

Serena's foxlike eyes narrowed. "But you shot a Yankee. The local population should cheer you."

Brant grinned as he propelled her across the room. "You can write me up on page one. 'Son of a Sea Captain Saves *Leader*'s Lovely Leader'. Then, if you could figure out where Pembrose stashed all that money from the slave business..."

Serena moved awkwardly back to her desk and collapsed in the chair. It was warm for April, more like June. At least, she consoled herself, the baby would be born before the hottest weather arrived. In the seventh month of pregnancy, she found the walk to the newspaper tiring, and in the past week, had allowed Brant or Young Calvin or Sergeant Davis to fetch her each afternoon in the trap. And as the time dragged by, she stopped working just a bit earlier each day.

Today, however, was an exception. Word had come through the previous evening that Joe Johnston had surrendered to Sherman at Durham. Almost three weeks earlier, General Lee had handed over his sword to Ulysses S. Grant. The long, bloody war was over. The soldiers could return home. So could Serena and Brant.

But Serena still wasn't sure that was what she wanted to do. When she discovered that she was going to have a baby, she realized she could postpone the decision until after her delivery. The days were passing, however, and Brant was more than a little impatient for her to make up her mind.

She had remained steadfast in one important matter: Now that the guns were silent and the cannon stilled, she would close down the *Leader*. The issue of April 27, 1865, was the last. The newspaper had been put to bed—and laid to rest.

For a few moments, Serena sat staring around the office, her eyes scanning the bookcases, the cast-iron stove, the bust of Benjamin Franklin. She could still picture Emaline twittering in the doorway, Herman loping in from the backshop, and, most of all, Kirk standing by her desk with his boyish grin, eager to read something amusing aloud to her.

Caldwell Smith was already making plans to go home to Rhode Island and take Bill and Phil with him. To everyone's delight, Caldwell was also taking the widow of a Confederate captain to wife.

Major Quenette knew his discharge would come through before

too long. When the press had started up for the last time that afternoon, he had surprised Serena by hastily wiping at a tear.

"Damn," he had said sheepishly, "I just hate to see a good newspaper stop publication. And this has been a good newspaper, Mrs. Parnell. You've got a lot to be proud of."

Serena was. She had started out on her road to becoming an adult by wanting to work for a newspaper. She had ended up running one instead. In her final editorial, she had written, "Let no one say that peace drove the *Leader* out of business. Let them proclaim instead that the *Leader*'s business was peace, and having now attained it, this voice will go silent. Let men and women who struggled in war now raise their own voices in a clamor for perpetual peace."

It would not be easy, Serena reflected. New Bern was still beset by shortages, the town's ranks thinned first by those who had fled the invasion, and more recently, by yellow fever. Commerce, except for the Yankee ventures, was all but nonexistent. The black market still existed and no doubt there would be ruthless speculators who would prey on local property and residents. As for the freedmen, the Trent settlement was prospering, but many blacks, especially those who had served in the Union army, would find their new lives frustrating and futile.

The months ahead would present hardship and deprivation, change and adjustment, toil and trial. Upon occasion, Serena would consider that the *Leader* still might be needed in the immediate postwar period. But she would not change her mind; she had the child to think about. Most of all, she had Brant. So many others were gone from her life, or soon would be. But with Brant's love to envelop her, Serena felt that her world was complete.

So when she saw Sergeant Davis arrive outside the office, she rose from the desk, gathered up the canvas bag which held her personal belongings, walked slowly if resolutely across the office, and closed the door on the *Leader* for the last time.

Roscoe and Josepha had asked permission to leave Wexford with their two children. Uncle Luke had parted from them with a pang, but understood why they wanted to make a new life for themselves in the Trent settlement. They had been there now for two months and during that time, Brant had made several trips to the burgeoning townsite to help organize supplies and give advice on commercial ventures. The Reverend James was fulsome in his gratitude, which Brant passed off as "preacher babble" but which made Serena quite proud. If any of the local citizenry, particularly those connected with the occupational forces, had found the half-hour inquest into Giles Stanhope's death too cursory, the untrammeled support of the reverend stilled errant tongues.

Brant, in fact, had become something of a legend in New Bern. The

breathtaking rescue of his wife from the clutches of a murderous madman evoked the spirit of gallantry which seemed to have all but disappeared with the antebellum way of life. A Yankee he might be, but
never one who wore a uniform, and certainly his wife and his brother
had both demonstrated a temperate view of the war in their newspaper.
And while Brant might dispense advice to the freedmen in the Trent
settlement, he had been equally generous in his counsel to white businessmen. For a Yankee sea captain, Brant Parnell was almost a gentleman.

Not that local opinion made much difference to Brant, one way
or the other. What pleased him most was that he had assembled a
cadre of expert poker players, including Yancy and Sergeant Davis.
A game was planned for that evening in the gentlemen's parlor. Uncle
Luke occasionally joined in, but demurred upon this occasion.

"You're all a cut above my old cronies," he asserted as the supper
table was cleared away by Young Calvin. "Maybe when Yancy treks
off for Montana, I'll sit in for him. And Davis, if he goes, too."

"He's not coming along," said Yancy, pushing back from the table
and stretching his long legs. "Abby and I tried like Billy-be-damned
to talk him into it, but he says this is home."

"That it is, for some of us." Uncle Luke glanced apprehensively
at his twins.

"I'd like to see some of the world," Nathan put in, catching his
father's eye. "But not for a while. I'm still thinking about going to
the university at Chapel Hill come fall."

Uncle Luke nodded in approval. "Then maybe a year abroad,
studying art, eh? You can visit Cecelia and Leonard."

Serena gazed down at the napkin she had refolded and felt the child
move in her womb. The latest letter from Cecelia had reported that they
were staying at a spa in Bavaria and would go to Italy in early summer.
Serena wondered if the hardships Abigail and Yancy would face in Montana could actually be any more burdensome than the social dilemmas
Cecelia and Leonard must endure even in Europe. She could almost hear
Cecelia's husky laugh in answering such a question: "Certainly it's tiresome—but the food and wine are much better, and where could Abby
show off the latest couturier gown in Montana?"

Yancy had turned to Jason. "If you're serious about Oregon, you
could go with us when we leave in July." He lifted those sleepy eyes
to Uncle Luke. "If you're willing, that is, Mr. Farrar."

Before Uncle Luke could respond, Jason made a funny face, as if
mocking his own folly. "I don't know—I've thought about it, and maybe
Oregon—or California—aren't right for me." He leaned forward,
looking very young and very earnest. "I want to make money, that's for
sure. But I don't know that I want to do it from the ground up."

Serena only half-heard Luke's comment that eventually there would still be money to be made from Wexford. She thought instead about Jason's change of heart, aware that he had been courting the winsome daughter of a Union colonel stationed in New Bern. From Portland, Maine, Serena remembered, and perhaps the city of the same name in Oregon no longer held the charm of its Eastern counterpart. The baby gave a vigorous kick and Serena jumped. Brant tried to look sympathetic but was unable to suppress a proud grin.

"Rugged little nipper, isn't he?" Brant whispered.

"Ornery little she-cat, just as likely," Serena hissed back. The baby's movements had increased considerably in the past few days, reminding Serena that time was running out on her decision to return to Brunswick. She tried to concentrate on the conversation, but Abigail and Yancy were already excusing themselves.

"Maybe it's my Yankee blood from you, Pa," Jason was saying as Serena resumed listening more closely. "But I just don't think I want to spend my whole life down South. It's too slow for me, too old-fashioned."

"That may change," Uncle Luke countered. "The world we knew before the war has been left behind us. In another five, maybe ten years..."

For once, Serena forgot her manners and interrupted Uncle Luke. "Jason, have you ever considered working for my father?"

Obviously, he had not. He gave Serena a questioning look, then shook his head. "It never occurred to me. He has Matt and he hardly even knows who I am."

"Matt's going to Seattle," Serena replied, ignoring Brant's hand on her arm. "Papa certainly knows who you are, he and Mama have kept close track of you over the years. He needs someone to learn the business, his own kin, someone he can trust. If you want to make a fortune, my father is just the man who can show you how. And," she added with a sly little smile, "Brunswick isn't all that far from Portland."

Jason flushed slightly. "Well, I suppose I could think about it..."

"I can write to Papa," Serena raced on, a hint of triumph in her voice. She still resisted the pressure of her husband's grasp. "You're not so much younger than Matt and you've got many of the same qualities. It seems to me like an ideal situation for everyone."

"Everyone?" Brant spoke the word on a deep, ironic note.

Serena wouldn't look at him. Instead, she started to rise from the table and smiled at Uncle Luke. "If Jason is to leave New Bern, wouldn't you rather have him stay in the East?" She saw her uncle give a faint, bemused nod. "If he were to some day assume control of Papa's empire, you could be assured that the ties with your own commercial ventures would be even stronger. For Nathan's sake, eventually."

Nathan appeared as if that were the least of his concerns, but Uncle Luke nodded again, this time more firmly. "It's best to keep such things in the family, if possible. I'll allow that much anyway."

"Of course. It all makes such good sense!" Serena fumbled at her voluminous skirts and made her way from the table. Brant started to follow her, but the arrival of his first poker guest deterred him. As she grasped the balustrade tightly, she heard Brant mutter from the hallway: "Later, Serena. Later."

It turned out to be much later, well past one o'clock, when Brant finally came to bed. Serena had been asleep, but as she grew more uncomfortable with the baby, even the slightest noise seemed to wake her. Muddled with sleep and unable to see more than Brant's outline in the darkness, Serena realized that the bravado she'd displayed after supper had evaporated.

"Did you win?" she murmured, hoping to divert him.

She heard him taking off his clothes. "I did not. I lost everything but my eyebrows." One boot, then the other, fell to the floor.

"But you don't play for high stakes," she mumbled, trying without success to make herself more comfortable.

"No, not here." He pulled back the comforter and climbed in beside her. "But you do, Serena."

She yawned. "I rarely play at all, you know that. Good night, my love."

"Good night, my foot!" Brant ignored the curve of her backside as she attempted to nestle against him. "Were you really trying to throw our future away into the callow hands of your cousin?"

"I'm tired, please let's go to sleep, Brant." She sounded querulous and he knew her lower lip was thrust out against her pillow.

"I can't go to sleep, damn it. How could I when I seem to be married to a pigheaded woman who doesn't even trouble to ask my opinion about what we plan to do with the rest of our lives but who makes a public announcement instead? Hell, the local Yankee haters have more respect for my advice than you do!"

Brant was actually shouting and Serena cringed. No doubt he'd probably awakened Abigail. If Yancy hadn't already. "I never said *we* weren't going to Brunswick, I just said Jason ought to think about it," Serena whispered furiously, now wide awake. "Do keep your voice down! Other people are trying to sleep, even if you aren't!"

Brant lowered his voice, but not his temper. "Oh, no, you won't get away with that kind of side-stepping chicanery. I know what you meant—that Jason should take my place. Has it ever occurred to that solid oak head of yours that I *want* to work for your father?"

Serena clumsily rolled over onto her back. "No. Not since you told me you loved me."

Brant was silent for a long moment. Finally he grunted. "You're right. I never intended to work for him after the war was over. How in hell did you know?"

Serena emitted a low little laugh and put her head against Brant's shoulder. "Maybe I've learned to recognize a bluff when I see one. Maybe I could never see you taking orders from anybody, even Marcus Farrar. Money or not, it all sounded wrong to me."

Brant sighed as he put his hand on the mound of her stomach. "Is he asleep?"

"She can sleep through your noise even if I can't." Serena yawned again. "Oh, my, I can't really say I'm sorry I don't have to trudge off to the newspaper office tomorrow. Some day maybe I'll regret closing down the *Leader,* but not now."

"You've already outraged most of New Bern's ladies by appearing up and down Craven Street in your delicate condition. They probably expected you to have the baby in the backshop." Brant gave her belly a gentle pat and put his arm just under her heavy breasts. "So you prefer New Bedford to Brunswick after all?"

"Hmmm." Serena was feeling drowsy again. "No, not necessarily. Have you thought about New Bern?"

"Staying *here?*" Brant sounded incredulous.

"Well, it *is* a port."

"True." Brant tickled Serena just enough to make sure she stayed awake. "I thought you hated this town."

"So did I. But I've been happier here than anywhere else. Our baby will be born here. We could buy some land, build a house, raise our family . . ." Serena's voice trailed off against his shoulder.

Brant, however, still wasn't sleepy. He lay staring up into the darkness of the canopy for some time, while Serena's breathing grew deep and rhythmic. His hand slid back to the fruitful curve of her body. "What do you think, son?" This time Brant felt the tiny being flutter under his touch. "All right, we'll try New Bern. I've a feeling you're going to be a gambler like your pa." He could just make out Serena's profile, the lower lip seeming to pout even in sleep, the thick, rich hair flung out over the pillow, the heavy lashes dipping against her cheeks. "Or maybe," he murmured into the night, "you'll be a stubborn, willful minx like your ma who'll make a man realize that love is more important than luck."

Or, Brant mused, as he finally closed his eyes, were they the same?